THE TROUBLE WITH MIRACLES

The Cannastar Factor

*A Miracle Cure for Viruses
That Big Pharma Will Kill to Stop*

Stephen Steele

SPEAKING VOLUMES, LLC
NAPLES, FLORIDA
2021

The Cannastar Factor

ISBN 978-1-64540-425-5

THE TROUBLE WITH MIRACLES

The Cannastar Factor

A Miracle Cure for Viruses
That Big Pharma Will Kill to Stop

Books by Stephen Steele

The Trouble with Miracles *series*
Book One: *The Cannastar Factor*
Book Two: *The Organ Grinder Factor*
Book Three: *The Fusion Factor*

For Beverly

Chapter One

A Winter's Tale

Like any date with destiny, this one was blind. The letter was an invitation, if you could call it that, from a friend he had not heard from in almost twenty years. Mainly it was a list of reasons why he shouldn't come—which made it all the more compelling. The timing couldn't have been better. Alex Farmer had lost his way and desperately needed to get his life back.

The commuter jet was less than a mile out when the airfield finally appeared through the overcast. The plane screamed out of the sky and touched down on the frozen runway. A December wind moaned softly and blowing snow swirled across the tarmac as the passengers deplaned. It was one of those winter days in Montana when even the cows can't stand it.

Alex headed for the terminal with the other passengers, clutching his jacket to his throat. He was a tall, slender man with thinning sandy hair who for the past year had walked slightly bent and with a small limp from the pain in his back—a pain that had returned with a vengeance now that he was off the prescription drugs. Sleepless nights had taken their toll on his handsome features and given him a haunted, haggard look. Thirty-eight years old, he looked less like a young doctor now and more like a sailor too long at sea.

The hospital director in Los Angeles had given him a choice: he could resign his position in the ER or lose his license. That's what sent him into rehab. He was clean and sober for the first time since the accident. He didn't know how long it would last.

Alex stood looking for his ride, shivering at the airport curb with his only luggage, a backpack, slung over his shoulder. All he saw was the snow that blew across the icy asphalt. He didn't think it was possible to lose the feeling in his fingers this fast.

Then out of the colorless day came the grinding sound of an ancient engine and a wreck of an old truck pulled up under the airport canopy. The driver reached across and pushed open a passenger door that creaked on rusted hinges.

"Alex Farmer?"

He nodded, too cold to speak. Whatever his old friend might look like now, this wasn't him. In fact, as near as Alex could tell, it wasn't a *him* at all. It was a *her* who was muffled under so many layers of scarves, sweaters and long johns that the only thing visible under her hat was a glossy mane of raven-black hair that fell long and dark around the shoulders of a coat that was almost as worn out as the truck.

He hesitated, his breath coming in small clouds, and for a moment was captivated by the lush mystery of light, like sun on ice, that reflected off her shining hair.

From within the shapeless mound of clothing, the muffled voice spoke again. "It's not any warmer in here than it is out there. Probably better if you changed your mind anyway." She leaned back across to close the door.

Alex caught the handle and, with a grunt of irritation, swung himself and his pack inside. "I must be out of my mind."

"No argument there."

"I see he sent the limo." She looked at him sharply and he saw in her pale blue eyes that she had been crying. "Sorry . . ." Her unabashed sadness had somehow touched him deeply. She saw him looking at her and her eyes lost all expression. "So where is he," Alex went on quickly, "Maury Bernstein I mean?"

She motioned with her head to indicate the bed in the back of the truck. "I had to bring him into town anyway."

He followed her gaze, rubbed the fog from the rear window with his sleeve, then rubbed frantically again and stared. In the bed of the truck was a body wrapped in a dirty tarp and hastily tied with ropes.

"What . . . what is this?" His words stuck in his throat. "Who is that back there?"

Her reply was lost in a terrible grinding of gears as the truck lurched forward. Smoke belched from the exhaust pipe and was quickly lost in the flat light as the truck followed the empty road out of the airport.

Badly shaken, Alex asked how his friend had died.

"Hunting accident." Her voice was flat, almost a monotone. "I'm not the one that found him."

"Maury doesn't hunt. He hated guns."

"I didn't say he was the one hunting." There was a pause each time before she spoke, as if she were waiting for distant voices to tell her what to say next.

"What about the police?"

"Police?"

"Are you saying you haven't called them?"

"This is Montana."

"What the hell is that supposed to mean?"

She was concentrating intently on the icy road ahead and didn't answer.

"How do you know Maury?" he asked impatiently.

"I worked for him at the university when I was there." The truck lost traction, started to slide, and she deftly corrected the skid. "Also, I'm his landlord. Now stop bothering me so I can drive."

Ten minutes later, the beat-up truck with the bound roll of canvas in back containing the body of Maury Bernstein pulled into a driveway and stopped. The sign in the front yard, half buried in snow, read "Appleseed Funeral Home".

Alex stared. The mortuary was in a huge, gracious, somewhat dilapidated three-story brick Victorian house with a wraparound front porch, a witch's hat turret and blacked out windows on the third floor. It was painted a hideous red color with green and black trim—a color pallet that made it look like a mansion haunted by colorblind ghosts. Attached to one side of the house, in front of where they were parked, was a modern structure that didn't go with the rest of the house at all—a flat-roofed garage-type building that Alex assumed was where they kept the bodies and parked the hearse.

The girl beeped the truck horn, the garage door opened, and she abruptly opened the driver's door and got out. A robust and extremely overweight undertaker stepped out into the cold wearing a short-sleeved shirt that fit snugly around his gigantic biceps. His professionally somber mask gave way to something far sadder as he came forward to hug the girl. With all the clothes she was wearing, he was unable to get his big arms all the way around her. Alex cautiously pushed open the creaking truck door on his side and stepped down. As he did, the faint smell of marijuana in the fresh air made him gag. He wrinkled his nose. The smell was mixed with something else he couldn't identify—a sweeter odor almost like chocolate.

The undertaker, struggling with his emotions, hugged the girl again before self-consciously breaking away. "I couldn't believe it when you called. I still can't."

"No tears, Otis. If this ever happened, we said no tears, remember?" She took his hand, squeezing it tightly.

"You loved him too," he whispered. "I know you did."

When the girl made no reply, Alex broke in. "I'm going to need to examine the body."

Otis, shivering now in his short-sleeved shirt, looked at Alex suspiciously. "What would you want to examine a dead body for, man?"

"Hobby of mine," Alex replied evenly.

"He's some kind of doctor," the girl explained.

Alex helped the undertaker load the bulky, ice-covered tarp in the back of the truck onto a gurney. The three of them wheeled it through the garage past a long white hearse and into the mortuary's preparation room where Otis heaved the deceased onto a stainless steel table equipped with metal gutters, trays, pans, instruments and tubes. The room was cold as death. Alex tried to lift a corner of the canvas that covered the body, but it was frozen solid and wouldn't budge.

The beefy mortician went to a thermostat on the wall and turned it up. "Why don't we go inside and warm up a bit while we let him thaw out." He led the way into the house without looking back. "You two look like you could use something hot to drink anyway."

Alex had never been a big fan of funeral homes, but this one was so bizarre he couldn't help but be fascinated. Hot, humid air enveloped him as soon as he stepped through the door. It felt like he had walked out of a refrigerator into a sauna. The pungent, earthy smell of a rainforest filled his nostrils. Potted plants were everywhere, large and small, some with vibrant colors, others with enormous leaves, none of which had he ever seen before. He heard the sound of water rushing over rocks and had an image of himself paddling upstream in a dugout canoe. He could almost hear the screech and cry of birds and monkeys. It was more of a premonition than he could ever imagine.

Otis continued on through the lush foliage, leading the way past a display room full of coffins cheap and plain next to caskets made of the most expensive materials and lined in velvet. Further on he stopped at a kitchen door.

"Cyd, why don't you take our guest into the parlor while I put the kettle on." He returned her anxious look with a reassuring smile. "Nothing like a nice hot cup of Lipton on a cold winter day, that's what I say."

The humid air was making it hard for Alex to breathe. He looked and saw Cyd shedding her layers of outer garments. He was stunned at how slender and shapely she was in her jeans and t-shirt, at how young and radiant she looked. He guessed her to be in her late twenties, and for a moment his grief seemed far away. Then, like the pain in his back that was always there, his despair and confusion returned.

Otis entered the room balancing a tray that held a steaming pot and three mugs. He bent to pour, and he and Cyd exchanged another private glance. "It's just Lipton," he reassured her.

Alex blew on his tea and set it back down without tasting it. He has so many questions he didn't know where to start. "What kind of research was Maury doing when he died?"

"Why do you want to know?" Cyd demanded. "What did he say to you?"

Otis touched her arm patiently. "Let's hear him out, why don't we."

Alex searched his pockets, pulled out a crumpled envelope, removed a letter and cleared his throat. The rotund undertaker and the attractive girl were staring at him intently.

"Dearest Alex," he began with a wistful smile. "If I sound desperate, it's because I am. This thing is so big, and I am in so much trouble. I only have two, maybe three people I can trust. It isn't enough. I can't tell you to come, a friend wouldn't ask that. Too late anyway, I should think. It's getting worse by the day, and I badly need your help."

Cyd and Otis listened with pained expressions.

"I hate to burden you at a time like this," Alex went on. "A former colleague of mine in Los Angeles told me of your troubles, and I am so sorry. Such a schmuck, I am. Brought it on myself. Thought they'd want it, welcome it with open arms. How could I have been so naïve? How do you save a world that doesn't want to be saved? It's all about greed, you know, about not rocking the financial boat. And this is a boat-rocker, my friend, let me tell you. Can you imagine? Revolutionize modern medicine—is that such a bad thing?

"Ignore this letter, Alex. Don't get involved. I didn't know where else to turn. Please forgive me." Alex looked up. "It's signed Maury Bernstein, and it came with a plane ticket. You want to tell me what this is all about?"

Otis studied the bottom of his teacup.

Cyd was typically silent before answering. "All I know is he'd been upset for weeks. Not sleeping or eating well. Keeping to himself. I was getting like really worried about him . . ."

Alex came abruptly to his feet and headed out of the room, wincing from the pain in his back as he stood.

Cyd called after him. "Where are you going?"

"I need to spend some time alone with my friend."

"There's a down parka by the door," Otis offered. "Put it on if you want."

A cold wind whistled around the old house.

Alex entered the preparation room hugging Otis's gigantic parka around him. He went over to the canvas-wrapped body on the table and stood looking down. The room was getting warmer, but he didn't notice. Tears ran down his cheeks.

Otis and Cyd came in an hour later and found him still crying. Alex angrily wiped at his eyes and gave the frozen tarp another tug. The canvas came away stiffly and made cracking sounds as he forced it back. He was so intent on removing the covering that it was a minute or two before he looked at the colorless face of the corpse. It was Maury all right. Same single bushy eyebrow, same kinky black hair and beard—except that now they were flecked with gray and dotted with bits of ice.

Otis put a sympathetic hand on Alex's shoulder. "Sorry, man."

Alex set about examining the body. He found two bullet wounds in a relatively tight pattern, both in the back. One had gone through the shoulder; the other had punctured a lung. This was something he knew a lot about. The bullets came from a high-powered rifle, fired at a distance, with a great deal of accuracy. One might be an accident; two this close together was murder. His face flushed red and he drew himself up. "I'm calling the police. Where's your phone?"

Otis looked nervous. "Better you let me do it."

"And why's that?"

"Might look better," he answered mildly, "me being the county coroner and all."

A cadre of police and detectives arrived at the funeral home and stayed for hours. They made careful notes of everything they saw and everything Cyd told them. It was Betty Little Horn who had found Maury up on the mountain and brought him back down to Cyd's ranch on horseback. "You get to Betty's place through mine," Cyd explained in breaking voice. "She's been riding her horses over my dad's property since before I was born. She knew Maury was staying with me."

One of the detectives turned to Otis. "We're gonna need a complete autopsy."

Otis nodded. The detective was used to the part-time coroner's somber demeanor and thought nothing of it. Morticians were supposed to act remotely sad and sympathetic. He had no idea how personal this case was to Otis or how much the undertaker had at stake.

Chapter Two

Fire and Ice

The drive north to Wolf Creek from Helena took nearly an hour in Cyd's old truck. The canyon walls got steeper as the interstate climbed the pass. Then they were off on a winding two-lane road that continued northwest, rising steadily as it left the river and the trees behind. The ancient truck wheezed in relief as the asphalt leveled out across rolling wheat fields turned white and clean with snow. It was after dark by the time they arrived at Cyd's ranch. The lack of heat in the truck had caused Alex to lose the feeling in his toes.

He stomped his feet on the ancient floorboards. "You can afford a ranch like this, but you can't afford a decent truck?"

Silence as the night winds swirled around them. "It runs," she replied. "And who says I can afford the ranch?" Another long pause. "His lab is in the barn. You want to see it tonight?"

"Morning will be fine," he shivered.

The truck rattled past a cluster of weather-beaten ranch buildings and corrals that Alex could barely see. Inside a windbreak in one of the corrals stood two shaggy horses pulling hay from a round bale with their teeth and munching it lazily. One was a black gelding that belonged to Cyd and the other, a gray-backed dun mare, had been her father's horse. Cyd stopped in front of an old two-story log house that was dark and silent. Snow crunched underfoot as they got out.

"All we need now is howling wolves," Alex remarked under his breath. Just then a wolf howled at the stars. "Great," he muttered, "just great."

"Why are you limping?" Cyd asked indifferently as they entered the house.

"Was I limping?"

It was colder inside the house than out. Cyd knelt by the stone hearth to light the fire. It flared quickly and the flickering light cast long shadows over a tall ceiling of rustic log rafters that stretched from the living room to the dining room to the kitchen in one long rectangle. A log staircase ran up one wall and led to the second floor.

Cyd pushed herself to her feet and headed up the stairs. "The couch pulls out into a hide-a-bed."

He called after her quietly. "Cyd, what the hell was Maury doing all the way out here?"

"Research."

"What kind of research?"

She stopped halfway up the steps. "It had to do with transgenics. With the human immune system."

"In his letter he said he was in trouble. Do you know what kind, exactly?"

She disappeared down the hall at the top of the stairs, and he heard a bedroom door close softly behind her.

Alex sat on the sofa staring at a crackling fire that seemed to offer solace and security from the immense stillness that seeped through the windows from the remote land outside.

Heads of dead animals stared down at him from the log walls, eyes glinting in the firelight, unconcerned with what the rifles in the glass gun cabinet next to the front door had done—or could do. He laid back on the sofa exhausted, pulled a quilt up over him and was asleep the minute he closed his eyes.

Loud bangs and crashes startled Alex awake out of a restless, freezing sleep. The fire had gone out, but yellow shadows flickered wildly across the floor and walls. Cyd bolted out of her bedroom and down the stairs pulling her coat on over her nightgown as she went.

They ran outside only to find the barn on fire. Flames shot from the roof and smoke bellowed from the doors and loft. The horses screamed from the relative safety of their corral. Cyd ran straight into the flames. Alex hesitated before he could bring himself to follow.

Inside the barn, the timbers were burning and falling around them. He was blinded by smoke. Burning hay was floating in the air. There were no animals in the barn, only a large metal-sided room built in the center of the floor under the hayloft. He saw Cyd dart inside the metal chamber through the metal door and he ran after her. Inside, he could hear glass crashing and breaking.

Looking around wildly, he saw he was in a laboratory. The room wasn't on fire yet, but it was so hot it was melting the computers. The chemical stench was awful. Gagging and covering his mouth, he searched and couldn't find the girl. Then through the smoke he saw her on her hands and knees under a lab table, frantically pulling up the floor-boards. He lunged forward and hauled her to her feet just as she pulled a briefcase out from between the floor joists. A barn timber crashed onto the roof of the lab and the overhead lights exploded in a sparking shower of glass. They clawed and fumbled their way toward the door with Alex clutching her to him. Another timber crashed as they came back out into the burning barn. She fell, and the briefcase slipped from her hand and skidded across the dirt floor. She groped for it blindly, her fingers clos-ing on the handle just as he grabbed her up and lifted her into his arms.

Alex burst through the smoking barn door and out into the open air where he fell choking to the ground, spilling Cyd into a snowbank. Pain from his back shot through his butt and down the backs of his legs. There was a horrible burning in his eyes and his lungs were on fire. In the distance he could hear the sound of engines. The sound grew louder until a caravan of pickup trucks appeared, barreling down the drive, bouncing over the frozen potholes, headlights flashing at crazy angles in the dark.

"Don't let them see this," Cyd gasped, holding the briefcase out to him.

Alex took it from her and flung it into the bushes just as the trucks skidded to a halt in front of the barn and dozens of men piled out with pickaxes and shovels. A big yellow water truck was just behind. The heavy construction vehicle tipped dangerously as it wheeled to a stop in front of the barn spilling water. Men swarmed the truck and almost instantly had it pumping water on the fire.

Half an hour later, Cyd sat on the tailgate of a truck, huddled under a blanket, staring at the smoldering remains of her barn. Alex checked her pulse and helped her wash out her eyes, cursing the fact that he didn't have any oxygen to give her.

A soot-covered rancher, not as tall as Cyd but about her age and barrel-chested as his water truck, came over and put a comforting arm around her shoulders. "It didn't get to any of the other buildings, Cyd. I think you're going to be okay."

She jerked away and glared at him. "How did you know my place was on fire?"

The tiny mouth in his round head smiled patiently. "Whole damn sky was lit up. Good thing one of my men spotted it."

"A fire is easy to spot if you're the one that started it," she flared. "Why didn't you just let my whole damn place burn down?"

The smile stayed frozen on his face. "Come on, Cyd, don't be like that."

She looked like she was going to take a swing at him. "Get the fuck off my property, Ty."

The short, round man shrugged and walked away. "Suit yourself."

12

"Who was that?" Alex asked, watching him go.

"My asshole cousin."

"He lives around here, I take it?"

"He lives everywhere *but* here, and he's not going to live here," she answered angrily. "Not if I can help it."

The sun was just coming up as the trucks were leaving the ranch. The moment the last truck was gone, Cyd threw off her blanket and ran for the bushes. Alex was puzzled until he remembered the briefcase. Moments later, she reappeared holding the old-fashioned leather satchel to her chest with both hands and heading straight for the house.

He ran to catch up.

"I'll just be a minute," Cyd told him, backing through the front door in a lame attempt at secrecy while holding the briefcase behind her.

"You want to tell me what that is?"

"It's nothing. Don't worry about it."

"My best friend is suddenly dead," Alex cried furiously, "your barn burns down in the middle of the night, you almost get us killed over a briefcase you dig out from under the floorboards of some kind of high-tech lab in a horse stall, and you say it's nothing? That I shouldn't worry? What the hell is going on here?"

She backed farther away. "Who are you, Alex Farmer? I don't even know who you are."

His voice was cold and full of frost as the morning air. "I'm a friend of Maury's."

Chapter Three

The Three

Alex Farmer, Maury Bernstein and a third friend, Joe Volkova, had grown up together, but it was Joe alone who adopted the aggressive, streetwise, in-your-face attitude it took to survive a New Jersey childhood. Alex and Maury didn't need it. What bound the three unlikely companions together was a mutual intelligence that surpassed everyone they knew in school, including most of their teachers.

They came together naturally through the logistical coincidence of growing up on the same block of identical working-class row houses in the town of Mt. Ephraim, New Jersey, just south and east of Philadelphia. And because few bonds are ever forged as quickly, easily, or more deeply—and with so little judgment or discretion—as those formed in childhood, they were best friends. Later, after their lives diverged, it would be a bond that would stretch but never break. If they had never known each other as kids and had met in later life, they probably would not have been friends at all. But because of that universal common denominator—youth—they would always be.

Alex, with his crooked, easy smile, was always somewhat amused and rather amazed by what went on around him. He was good at sports but didn't take them seriously. He had a crooked smile that was so natural he didn't even know he had it, a smile that inspired in girls the urge to either kiss him or slap him—sometimes both at the same time. He had the zero-body-fat metabolism of a runner, a hairline that was already receding and, even then, a doctor's healing hands.

Maury cared only about science, loved chemistry and tried too hard at everything. He was always ebullient, always overly excited about his latest scientific discovery—the typical nerdy Jewish kid with black kinky hair and one bushy eyebrow that ran all the way across his forehead. He had no concern for his physical appearance and went about his disheveled life with the boundless energy of a scientific cheerleader. As far as he was concerned, his body was just something to work in like the mismatched clothes he wore. Alex was so used to Maury's odd combinations of stripes, plaids and clashing colors that he hardly noticed. What he saw was the beauty of his friend's mind. Early in grade school, Alex and Joe took on the job of protecting Maury, and as a result Maury didn't have to endure the childhood taunts and torments that normally would have been his fate. Maury thought that everyone loved him, not just his two friends, and never suspected why the other kids showed him so much respect.

As for Joe, he stole things. He didn't even have to think about it—he had already found his profession. Joe was a crook. He shadowed the lives of his two friends like a ghost; a small, wiry, chain-smoking son of Ukrainian immigrants who spoke New Jersey English in a rasping voice, but was fluent in Ukrainian. Joe had a head of soft, wavy brown curls that most any girl would die for, and a hook nose you could use for a letter opener.

While Alex and Maury were getting straight A's, Joe was cutting classes and making other types of friends—the kind they would one day make wise-guy movies and TV shows about. He was every bit as smart as Alex and Maury, smarter than either of them when it came to math. He was so good at handicapping sports that by the time he was seventeen, the local bookies wouldn't take his bets anymore because he had won so much money off them. Out of necessity, he had to keep going farther away from home to place his wagers. Finally, the word was out for thirty miles around: if a pint-sized kid with a hook nose shows up and wants to make a bet, don't take his money.

The edict forced Joe to perfect his other talent—stealing and not getting caught. He didn't care what it was, he loved to steal. Things would disappear from trucks, stores, houses, parking lots and boat docks, and it was as if a phantom had stolen them. No one saw him come, no one saw him go; he didn't exist. The liquidation of his stolen merchandise required that he get to know certain other men whose professional lives were lived in the same shadows that Joe would come to know so well. His fame as a master thief soon surpassed his reputation as a gambler. The old hoods and thugs who hung out in the social clubs in New Jersey were most impressed.

Alex admired Joe's talents, his expertise, his enterprise; he admired his balls. In Maury he found true scientific genius. In himself he saw little to appreciate. He felt he was a fake—not a fake in the sense that he wasn't smart, but a fake in the sense that he was certain he lacked the creative talent of his friends. He had no idea what he wanted to do with his life. He was good at sports, but so what? Professional athletes had a short shelf life. Amongst the three, Alex thought if greatness was reserved for any of them, it wasn't him. What was most amazing was that he didn't resent his friends for their abilities. On the contrary, Maury and Joe were probably the only two people his age that Alex truly admired.

After high school, Joe got the inspiration that there was a lot more money to be stolen legitimately than illegitimately and got a job as a runner on the floor of the New York Stock Exchange. It didn't matter that it didn't pay much to start. He had another source of income— the New York bookies who didn't know him yet. Alex and Maury were offered full academic scholarships to the prestigious University of Pennsylvania and went off to college together. Maury would never see Joe again. Alex would keep in touch, but many years would pass before they reunited, and by that time they would be in desperate trouble and asking each other for the impossible.

In college, Maury grew the bushy black beard that was to become his lifelong trademark. And Alex found something he could finally get serious about—after undergraduate school, he was going to go to medical school and become a doctor. The idea suddenly appealed to him: he might be able to help ease some of the suffering he saw everywhere.

They made a strange pair huddled together in the coffee houses off campus—the tall, slim athlete and the short, dumpy scientist—intent on endless discussions that revolved around science, chemistry and physics. Had Maury stopped to think, he would have realized he loved Alex as much as Alex loved him, but it wasn't something he thought about; he had more important things on his mind. Mainly what he appreciated about Alex was that he was one of the few people intelligent enough to keep up with him during his endless disjointed technical ramblings and diatribes.

So, Alex smiled and laughed and coasted his way through undergraduate school while Maury went about proving his genius as a research scientist. When they graduated, they went their separate ways. Maury went on to Harvard and eventually earned a PhD in molecular biology. Alex accepted a scholarship to UCLA because he had always wanted to live out west. When he finished medical school, he joined the Army where he did his internship and served two tours of duty in Iraq.

After he got out of the service, Alex moved back to Southern California and applied for work in the emergency room at Martin Luther King Hospital. On his employment application, under *List any special skills or specialties*, he scrawled, "If it isn't an IED or a bullet wound, I don't know how to treat it." The irony in his personal evaluation escaped the hospital administrators, but this was East Los Angeles and the bullet wound part appealed to them greatly, so he got the job and bought himself a condo in Santa Monica. It wasn't until later, after his life had blown up in his face, that he bought the boat.

On his first day at work, he met the horny-flighty-beautiful Alicia Mills, a stunning blond nurse with high cheek bones, a quick wit, a sleepy smile and a body that made him weak in the knees. Three months later they were married.

The accident that injured his back and left him in pain happened four years after that. It ruined his marriage and destroyed his life. The fires and explosions in the wake of his growing pill addiction kept getting bigger and louder until, a year later, he was the one that blew up.

By the time he was asked to resign, Alex had worked in the emergency room at MLK for almost five years. During that time, the city had puked drugs and violence into his ER until he felt like he had lived his entire life in a war zone. Leaving the hospital was a harder adjustment than leaving the military. He figured he had two choices, rehab or suicide, and if one didn't work out, he thought he might try the other. Maury's letter reached him the day before he was scheduled to get out of rehab. A trip to Montana to visit an old friend sounded like just the thing he needed.

Chapter Four

Betty Little Horn

Cyd snatched a bottle of bourbon off the table, poured herself a drink into a dirty glass, knocked it back and quickly poured another.

"Well . . . I don't trust you." Angrily picking up the glass, she banged it back down without drinking it. "I don't trust anybody."

Alex took a deep breath. "I know how frightening this all must be for you."

She gestured with the bottle. Did he want a drink?

He dismissed the offer with a flick of his hand.

A long pause. "I thought Maury was going to have a heart attack waiting for you to come, he was so anxious. I don't know . . . maybe you're right, maybe I'm just being paranoid. You would be too after all that's happened. The last thing he said to me yesterday when he left the ranch was if he didn't make it back in time, I was supposed to pick you up at the airport no matter what."

"Who would want to kill him?"

She shook her head. "Nobody, everybody, who knows? All I know is what Betty said. Somebody shot him."

"Open the briefcase."

She didn't move.

"I said open it!"

Cyd slammed the briefcase on the table and petulantly unfastened the buckles. Opening the flap, she looked in and stared . . . then began frantically digging around inside. "They're not here," she cried. "Where the hell are they?"

"What are you talking about?"

She turned the bag upside down and shook it. It was empty.

"What was supposed to be in there?"

"His research papers! The documentation for everything he's done!"

"So, is this why he was murdered?"

She sat down, put her hands flat on the table, blew out her cheeks and bowed her head. Then looking up, "You know Rxon (*Rex-on*), the big drug company?"

He sat down cautiously across from her. "The one that's been buying up all the other drug companies?"

Another maddening pause. "Maury had a research grant from them. His lab was in Missoula at the University there. I worked for him part-time for two years while I was finishing up my master's in plant genetics. Maury was one of my faculty advisors, my favorite. He was close, so close to a breakthrough. Then one day I come in and he's acting all crazy, running around like a madman, stuffing things in boxes and shredding papers."

"What happened?"

"He said he'd heard from somebody at Rxon. A friend of his. He had a lot of friends, you know. He was a genius."

Alex nodded. He'd known long before anyone else what Maury was.

"Whoever it was told him they were going to shut down his project. The rumor was that they were going to bury his research, not bring it to market, not even go through the testing to try and get FDA approval. Basically, they were pulling the plug."

"Why?"

"I don't know. All I know is he was scared. We had about a week to phony up some fake research documents before they came to padlock the lab. When they showed up, we acted all surprised and angry and indignant and then we quietly left town with the real research. It was a pretty good performance on both our parts if I do say so myself. That was a little over a year ago."

"And that's when you came up here?"

"Maury needed a place to work where no one could find him or bother him. It was like he was obsessed. I'd just inherited the ranch. I promised my father before he died that I'd keep it no matter what. I grew up here, you know." She looked wistfully out the window at the snow-covered front yard where she had played as a little girl. "Anyway, I couldn't even pay the taxes on the place. Maury offered me a full-time job, plus he rented my barn from me. It was enough to keep me afloat. He built the lab with his own money." A stricken look came over her. "What am I going to do? The research—it's gone!"

"Research for what?" he demanded. "What was Maury researching?"

No response.

"Are you saying you didn't know? He made his breakthrough here, didn't he? His research was a success!"

Close to tears, she turned away.

"Whatever he was looking for, he must have found it. That's why they killed him, isn't it? Speak to me!"

She turned back to confront him. "How do I know you're not working for Rxon yourself? How can I know you're not one of *them*?"

He studied her a moment with a doctor's patient compassion. She'd been through a lot. She was horribly upset. She wasn't thinking clearly. "You're all alone," he acknowledged. "You're scared. Who wouldn't be? I understand, I do."

Some of the tension seemed to go out of her body.

He got to his feet with a grimace of pain, went to the door and pulled on the parka Otis had lent him. "Let's go."

"Go?"

21

"I want to talk to this Betty woman who found Maury's body . . ."

***

The trip to Betty's place was a thirty-minute ride over frozen, bumpy roads. Alex sat in silence, buried inside a parka that fit him like a sleeping bag. Cyd turned to study him as she drove, cocking her head to one side. It made her angry to think she was actually attracted to this man.

"What?" he said.

"I never thanked you for saving my life back there."

"I'm used to saving the lives of people who are trying to kill themselves—it's what I do for a living." He couldn't help noticing the splay of freckles that ran across the bridge of her nose and scattered out along her cheeks, couldn't help admiring her pale skin and the brilliant black of her hair. She was beautiful in the way a glacier is beautiful, he thought, then reminded himself that glaciers are best admired from a distance.

"I mean it. Thank you."

He smiled his easy smile. "I can see why Maury believed in you. Why he would have wanted you for a partner."

Was he mocking her? His smile made her angrier still.

***

Betty Little Horn was a little hard of hearing, her concentration was on the horse's hoof she was filing, and the blower on her gas forge was going, so she didn't hear Cyd and Alex come in. She was a small, compact woman with a handsome head of short gray hair that looked like she cut it, or rather hacked the long ends off herself. A ring of keys jangled on the outside of her belt. Betty had no tolerance for fools and even less for the trappings of femininity like wearing makeup. She made her living shoeing and training horses.

Betty looked up, saw she had visitors and promptly ignored them. She finished off the hoof she was working on, went over to her anvil and pounded on a horseshoe with a hammer, sighting down it to make sure it was true. Going back to the horse she was working on, she lifted its leg again to see if the shoe fit the hoof. "With you in a minute," she mumbled, her mouth full of nails.

Cyd brightened. "No worries."

A couple more whacks of the hammer, and she was satisfied with the fit. She nailed the shoe on, clenched the nails and finished off the hoof with a file. Then with one hand on the small of her back, she straightened up, unhooked the horse from the cross ties and put him in a stall. Then rejoining her guests, she took off her leather apron. "How you holding up, Cyd?"

"They burned down my barn."

"I seen the smoke. Anybody hurt?"

"Not physically. Betty, this is Alex Farmer."

"So, you finally made it." The lady farrier crushed Alex's hand in hers. He had never felt a hand so calloused. "Let's go inside," she continued. "I got coffee made."

Betty led the way out of the shed, past a round pen that was half fallen down, past a rusted creaking hot-walker that was leading a string of horses around in a circle, and toward a house with peeling paint and a roof with several missing shingles. Without slowing her pace, she spoke over her shoulder. "I still got six horses left to ride, so we gotta make this quick."

Alex stood letting his eyes get used to the dark interior. The inside of the house was a crowded museum of battered cowboy boots, saddles, horse blankets, ropes, chaps, tack and antique spurs and bits, none of which had been dusted since the beginning of time. Betty poured out three cups of steaming black coffee, set them on the kitchen countertop and leaned back against the counter on her elbows.

"You're him then," she observed, looking Alex up and down. Betty saw things in black and white, right and wrong, and once she made up her mind about somebody, that was it. "Maury thought a lot of you. Thought you were alright."

"He never was a very good judge of character," Alex smiled.

Betty gave him a final going over. "You'll do," she concluded. "How's your coffee? I cook it with the grains in the pot. Some people don't like it that way."

"It's good," Alex lied.

"I taught him to ride, you know. If it wasn't for me, maybe Maury wouldn't . . ." She looked off into the distance at things too hard to forget.

"Can you tell me how he died?" His voice was gentle, kind. A doctor's voice, consoling a patient.

"I didn't see him actually get shot and I never seen who done it, I was too busy running. We was up on the Dearborn . . ."

Chapter Five

Counting the Stars

On a beautiful Fall afternoon three and a half years earlier, Sam Seeley was preparing to celebrate his seventieth birthday at his sprawling 180-acre Virginia estate located less than an hour's drive outside the Washington Beltway. The invitations read, "Come one, come all and join us for Senator Seeley's 70th birthday!!!" Tickets were $10,000 for organizations, $3,000 per individual. To accommodate the some twelve-hundred people who were expected to attend, great white party tents, a band shell and an outdoor dance floor were being set up on the expansive lawn behind the twenty-seven-thousand-square-foot Georgian mansion that overlooked the lawn, the manicured gardens and the dome of a brand new glass greenhouse that gleamed on the bank of a private lake just beyond.

Like a shark is the perfect eating machine, Senator Sam Seeley was the perfect political machine. He was a short, dumpy man who made up for any limitation in size by being enormously cruel. He had a big mouth, brass balls, no integrity or morality of any kind and was not burdened by anything resembling a sense of right and wrong. His decades of service to the American people had been devoted almost exclusively to the pursuit of making himself even wealthier than he already was. He'd worn his game face for so long, it *was* his face—a permanently frozen smile that was not so much a smile as a warning along the lines of *Trespassers Will Be Shot.* His legendary public charm was only slightly less legendary than his reputation for being cold-hearted, mean-spirited and bull-headed stubborn. While some might suspect him of sociopathic tendencies, he viewed himself merely as a good businessman.

The Senator stood in his boxer shorts staring out the balcony window of his upstairs bedroom at the army of people scurrying about down on his lawn making final preparations for his party and felt a familiar sense of boredom. He sighed, brushed back his fatherly mane of white hair, took a sip of his cocktail and walked into a closet the size of a bedroom. From his rack of fifty expensive, big-shouldered suits, he chose a lighter-colored one for today's occasion. From a Gatsby-size collection of shirts, he selected a soft pink dress shirt with white collar, then found a festive red and white striped tie to go with it. From his eighty-odd pairs of custom-made shoes, he selected a pair of tasseled loafers. Once dressed, he adjusted his tie, inspected himself in the mirror and smiled with satisfaction. More than rich, he concluded, he looked powerful.

Before the party started, he had to go outside and deal with his wife's contractor. The man—he couldn't remember his name exactly—had just completed the colossal new greenhouse down by the lake and wanted his final payment. His wife's passion was growing flowers, but that was not why he had let her build her Titanic glass shit-house. He would have let her build it twice as big as long as it kept her off his back. Personally, he hated the damn thing; he didn't want to have anything to do with it and had no intention of ever setting foot inside it.

The contractor was waiting for the Senator down by the lake next to the greenhouse. A decent, competent family man, Jim Toomey had a redneck crew cut, thick hands and the beefy build of a barroom brawler. He prided himself on his integrity and in always bringing his projects in on time and on budget. Unfortunately, this one was neither. He was personally on the hook for over half a million dollars and needed to get paid immediately or the bank was going to take his house. Annie Seeley, the Senator's gracious wife, was a nice lady and he wanted to please her, but all her nervous fussing and constant changes had run the job way over in both time and money.

He rubbed his hands together nervously and the calluses on his big palms made a dry sandpaper sound. He looked up at the sun glinting off the enormous, gracefully curved structure of double-pane glass he had built and, in his mind, examined it for problems. Try as he might, he found none; it was perfect, not a flaw. The greenhouse itself was divided into separate climate-controlled rooms to create different growing environments. He had personally installed the plumbing, heating and air conditioning in each of the separate locations to make sure it was just right. It was going to be a big feather in his cap, this unique project. After getting the Senator's stamp of approval, the greenhouse would get him a lot more work among what he called "the psycho-rich." What was important at the moment, however, was getting his money so he could get the hell off this particular job; the Senator's mercurial reputation made him nervous.

He had waited two weeks for this appointment and when Sam Seeley finally appeared beside the greenhouse, impeccably dressed in a pink shirt and red and white tie, he was greatly relieved. The contractor stepped forward, extending his hand in anticipation of getting his check and getting his life back to normal.

The Senator snorted an inaudible greeting and shook hands, grabbing Toomey's hand by the fingers and squeezing until it hurt. "Let's have a look around, shall we?" Sam commanded. "Got a goddamn birthday party to go to." For a short old guy, the senator was quick. He managed to make it around the corner of the greenhouse before Jim could catch up.

"What's this?" the Senator demanded. He had dropped to his haunches and was sighting down one of the eight enormous walls of hexagon-shaped glass panels set in the complicated curve of the metal frame that made the eight-sided structure look like a small domed foot-ball field. "This wall isn't straight."

Jim squatted behind the Senator to sight down the wall. Because of the reflections in the glass, it looked like it wavered in places—and in fact it did move in and out a bit as it went. "That's just the nature of glass and metal frame structures," he explained.

"It doesn't line up," Sam Seeley insisted. "I'm not paying for a building that isn't straight. No fucking way." He stood abruptly and started back toward the house.

"What about my check?" Jim called desperately.

"Do it right and you'll get paid!"

Toomey watched helplessly, a horrible sinking feeling in his stom-ach, as the Senator walked away.

***

That evening the sky was dressed in its finest stars. Music, laughter and the drone of party conversation punctuated by squeals of laughter drifted out over a lake that reflected the nighttime sky and danced in a confusion of party lights from the lawn. A thirty-piece orchestra was whirling and churning the small outdoor dance floor in a blur of designer gowns. Throngs of Washington's elite ate and drank under the tents, peering at each other's name tags and shaking hands like they were pumping for oil. Drug companies, insurers, hospitals, medical supply firms, health-service companies, associations of health professionals—their representatives were all here to celebrate the birthday of the man best suited to represent their interests, a man who chaired the commit-tees that could fulfill their wildest dreams of avarice by getting them everything they wanted.

Long before he was the object of all this unmitigated affection, Sam Seeley was the heir to a vast Montana ranching, timber and mining fortune. Moreover, he was one of those rare individuals who held both a MD and a JD, meaning he was both a doctor and a lawyer. He had never practiced medicine, but as a lawyer he had amassed a separate fortune winning massive settlements in medical malpractice suits. Thirty years ago, when he decided to enter politics, the insurance companies were more than relieved to welcome him over to their side.

The galaxy of partygoers swirled around the powerful Senator like planets around a black hole, inexorably drawn by the gravity of greed. Sam himself had the annoying habit of losing interest in a conversation once he got the gist of it and walking off before the other person was finished talking, and the drunker he got the worse it got. His other limitation as a host was that if the number on a donor's last contribution check was not followed by at least four zeros, he could not remember the contributor's name. Neither shortcoming in any way impugned his popularity among those seeking his favor.

A Middle Eastern man with an unpronounceable company name on his nametag approached with an eager smile. "Happy Birthday, Senator!" he exclaimed in perfect English, extending his hand. "My name is Ahmad Hamad al Tayyib. I was hoping at some point we could sit down and I could tell you a little about the energy-independent profile of our Wyoming project. My clients will be seeking some regulatory relief from . . ."

"Yeah, yeah. Talk to one of my aides," the Senator replied with a limp handshake before quickly moving on to be immediately swallowed by a crowd of suits from a large health insurer.

A big scratch-golfer with a military haircut and an ingratiating University-of-Texas, fraternity-boy smile was politely moving people aside with his broad shoulders as he made his way toward the Senator.

"Riley Gray!" Sam Seeley cried, a smile lighting up his flushed face at the sight of Rxon's chief lobbyist. "Thank heavens!" He slipped his arm through Riley's and moved him away from the crowd. "Let's go get us a drink, shall we?"

They made their way to the bar, where they ordered drinks and stood overlooking the formal circus of partygoers swarming the lawn below.

Riley didn't waste any time getting to the point. "Sam, I need to talk to ya 'bout somethin'," he drawled. "Need a favor."

"Now what?" The reply was gruff and noncommittal, but both men knew the favor would be granted, no matter what it was. Senator Seeley didn't have any problem at all remembering the number of zeros on Rxon's contribution checks—it was like counting the stars.

Annie Seeley, the Senator's wife, backed into the shadows and snuck quietly away from the party. Her tiny feet followed the darkened cobblestone path by memory toward one of her musty-smelling old greenhouses that would soon be replaced by the big glass-domed new one down by the lake. The moon reflected off the silver of her tomboy haircut and swam in the startling violet of her eyes—eyes that made her elderly face look young.

A dark form waited for her in the starlit greenhouse. Annie switched on the lights and the two women cried with delight when they saw each other. They embraced amid an explosion of chrysanthemums that filled the old shed with oranges, reds, blues, yellows, pinks and whites that rioted around them like a fireworks display.

"Annie, your flowers are gorgeous," the young girl exclaimed. "I can't even believe it."

"They're not as pretty as you, darling." A southern breeze, soft and gentle and warm, blew through her speech. "I used to be that pretty, but not anymore."

"I could never be as beautiful as you." The girl's hair was as black as Annie's was white.

"I'm so proud of you, Cydney. Imagine! A bachelor's degree in botany from Cornell." Annie was Cyd's aunt by marriage, but she could not have loved her more if she had been her own daughter. They had a special relationship and a special bond that was grounded not only in mutual affection, but in a mutual love of all things that grew from the ground. "And you got through school all on your own. I had to do that too, you know."

Cyd paused. "I did it on a partial scholarship and by waiting tables until I thought my feet were going to fall off."

"Well, now we have to get you on to graduate school, don't we?"

"If only. I can't afford graduate school, Annie. I could barely afford the gas to stop by here. I'm on my way home to Montana."

"We'll ask Sam," Annie stated firmly. "I swear, when you were a little girl, I'd never seen anyone who could grow things like you could."

"You know he hates my father," Cyd lamented. "Sam Seeley's side of the family hasn't spoken to my mother's side of the family since my mother married my father. I mean, look at the two of us. We're still meeting in secret because he hates my Dad, his only brother, so much."

"You let me worry about that," Annie insisted. Her parents were tobacco farmers from North Carolina, and she knew all about family feuds and what it was like to grow up as a poor relation. "He's just covering up for the fact that he married someone from the wrong side of the tracks too. Now you go in the house and wait for me in the library."

It wasn't hard for Annie Seeley to get her husband away from the party. As a politician's wife she knew something about politics. She merely told him that someone important with a lot to contribute wanted to see him in the library and that he needed to come immediately. Sam had already talked with everyone at the party that mattered and was bored to death anyway, so he welcomed the diversion.

When he entered the library with Annie on his heels and saw the attractive young woman standing there, he almost had a heart attack. For a horrible moment, he thought that one of his girlfriends from town had shown up uninvited. He would never divorce his wife—she was the mother of his son and besides, it wouldn't look good come reelection time—but that didn't mean he didn't have his own "friends". "Who says money doesn't buy happiness," he often said in regard to the ladies of Washington, D.C. whose living expenses he subsidized. "And you can take that to the bank."

Moments later he realized he had never seen this particular girl before and sighed in relief.

"Sam, you remember your niece, Cydney Seeley. Cyd, this is your uncle Sam."

The Senator turned red in the face. "Charley's kid? The one with the mother from that lowlife family of welfare cases?"

"That's the one," Cyd flared. "I'm outta here."

"Wait," Annie pleaded. "Sam, please. Look at her. Does she look like anybody you could hate?"

Sam looked. His wife was right, the girl was a knockout. He put his hands on her shoulders, held her at arm's length and examined her like he was buying a horse. "Last time I saw you, you weren't four feet tall and had a black eye from fighting."

"How flattering." Cyd had the creepy feeling she was being scrutinized by some kind of pervert.

"I only meant that you are very pretty, young lady. You should get to know my son, Ty."

"I know my cousin Ty," Cyd replied evenly. "I think he prefers sheep to girls."

Sam laughed. "You could be right. Have seat." She hesitated and he added, "Please."

Cyd sat tentatively on the arm of a leather wingback chair.

"She just graduated with her bachelor's degree," Annie told her husband excitedly. "Isn't that wonderful? She's a botanist."

"My wife's into flowers too," he remarked with a sharp look in Annie's direction. "Spends a small fortune, but I've never seen her make a dime off it. What good is a degree in flowers, anyway?"

The blossoms that grew in Annie's gardens and greenhouses filled her enormous house year-round. In fall, the bedrooms, breakfast room, library and French drawing room were adorned with chrysanthemums. In winter, amaryllis, poinsettias, narcissus, camellias and azaleas graced the halls, and in early spring flushes of sweetly scented freesias, lilies, snapdragons, Bells of Ireland and forced tulips were placed around everywhere. Potted plants filled all the nooks. Long-stemmed flowers were arranged in magnificent centerpieces for the dining room table and in lavish sprays for the drawing room and pavilion.

Undeterred, Annie rushed on. "Cyd plans on going on to graduate school. She wants to study plant genetics. I thought maybe we could help her out."

"That's what she has a father for," Sam sneered.

Cyd came rapidly to her feet. "Thank you, but I really have to be going."

Sam touched her arm in restraint. "Easy now. Sit on back down. Tell me where you want to go to school?"

"University of Montana."

He couldn't believe his ears. "That a fact. In Missoula?"

"Last time I checked."

"Interesting, very interesting. Maybe we can work something out after all." He was amazed that the solution to his lobbyist friend Riley

Gray's problem would fall in his lap so easily and quickly. "If I did help you, paid your tuition and all . . ." He paused to think. "I'd expect you to get a job to help pay your way."

"I've always paid my way," Cyd declared. "And I don't need any help from you or . . ."

Sam raised his hand to stop her. "I might even know of a position that's open. Something in your field, how about that?"

Cyd was suspicious. "How about what?"

"I just heard of a guy over at the University of Montana that's doing some pretty amazing stuff in plant biotechnology. One of the big drug companies, Rxon, is funding his research. What if I could get you a job working for him?"

She hesitated. "Go on."

Sam saw the growing excitement in her eyes and smiled to himself. "I'll put you in touch with the point man from Rxon. He'll want you to report back to him. Keep him posted on the research, what kind of progress is being made, that sort of thing. They're putting a lot of money into this guy and he has this psychotic obsession with secrecy . . ."

"You want me to be a spy, is that it?" The very thought of it angered her.

"They have a right to know where their money is going, wouldn't you agree? Be kept up to speed so to speak. Is that so horrible?"

Cyd hesitated. "I suppose not."

"Good, it's settled then. His name is Bernstein, I think, this scientist that's doing the research."

"Maury Bernstein?" Cyd cried. "He's the best in his field. He's the reason I want to go to Missoula in the first place!"

"Yeah, that's him. Well, anyway . . ." The Senator was done with the conversation and already headed for the door. "See my secretary for anything you need. I'll tell her you'll be in touch." He looked back over his shoulder with a humorless smile. "You keep us in the loop now, you hear?"

When he had gone, Annie spun around with a triumphant grin and gave Cyd two thumbs up.

Chapter Six

The Dearborn

The Dearborn River emerges from a mountain in the Scapegoat Wilderness, flows through the canyons and scenic valleys of the Rocky Mountain Front and out onto the Montana prairie. It was along this river, Betty explained, high up in the trees near the headwaters of the Dearborn, that Maury Bernstein died.

After hours of bouncing in the saddle, Maury's butt was raw, but he was too anxious and nervous to care. They had been following a trail that more or less paralleled the winding river and were at a place where the path veered uphill sharply to the right. He watched as Betty left the trail and urged her horse into the stream, crossing at a shallow ford and continuing on up a secondary trail on the other side that wound between the trees—a path that would have been invisible under the snow had his guide not been coming up here most of her life. He followed gingerly behind, leaning forward in the saddle to try and take the pressure off his aching rear end. Under any other circumstances, even though he was a terrible rider, Maury would have been thrilled to be on horseback in the Montana back country in winter. But not today.

The steep trail came out in a clearing and they reined in their horses. Betty Little Horn took off a battered cowboy hat, wiped her brow with her sleeve, turned in her saddle to check on the miserable-looking scientist behind her and called back. "Remote enough for you?"

"This will do fine. I need to go on alone from here." Maury kicked at his horse, flailing his arms to make him go. "The rapids you said are just up ahead, correct? If I'm not back in an hour, call the rabbi."

"As your friend, Maury, I gotta tell you I don't like it. Whatever you're planning, let me come with you and help."

"I'll be fine, don't worry about me. The less you know, the better."

"Amen to that," Betty muttered under her breath, watching in dismay as the bearded, kinky-haired scientist disappeared over the hill. Taking a round tin of chew out of her shirt pocket, she put a pinch between her cheek and gum and settled in to wait, spitting occasionally to one side.

Thirty minutes passed in silence.

When she heard the shots, she sat up straight in the saddle, gathered her reins and spit out her wad of tobacco. She was spurring her horse to the top of the hill when she saw Maury's horse come racing back toward her with its rider slumped over in the saddle. Her eyes grew huge and she kicked her horse into the path of the runaway animal, grabbing its reins and yanking hard. The horse cried out and reared and Maury fell off backwards.

Betty jumped to the ground and bent over his body. Blood was spilling freely onto the rocks, turning them dark red. She tore open his coat, saw the extent of his wounds and was suddenly weak with fear. Maury gagged as blood and foam trickled from his mouth. He grabbed her by the coat, pulled her down to him, pressed a note pad into her hand and began whispering urgently in her ear. "Understand?" he gasped when he was done giving instructions.

Too frightened to speak, she could only nod.

"So, get out of here already. Go . . ." His words were gargled in blood.

"No way am I leaving you behind." Betty started to lift him, then gasped as he shuddered and went limp. She frantically yanked off her glove, pressed two fingers to his jugular and dropped her ear to his nose to listen for breathing. He was dead. Behind her, from the direction of the river they had crossed, came the faint sound of horses thundering up the trail.

Betty swung onto her horse and with a reluctant, desperate glance back at her dead friend, took off in the opposite direction. She cut left and right in a slalom course through the trees, flying over unmarked terrain she had ridden a thousand times before. Moments later, three riders came pounding up the hill and reined in hard over Maury's body. They jumped off, stripped him of his clothes and searched him from head to toe. When they found nothing, one of them, a Native American cowboy with sunken cheeks and a pockmarked face, looked around and saw Betty's tracks leading off into the forest. He pointed in the direction she had gone with a hand that was piously tattooed on the back with a large religious cross. In an instant the three riders were back in their saddles, following her tracks.

Betty had a good head start and she knew exactly where she was going. Again she veered, this time uphill, spurring her horse over loose rock so she wouldn't leave tracks, climbing toward stone cliffs that towered overhead.

Under one of the cliffs was a narrow slit in the rock, invisible from below, just wide enough for a horse and rider. She Ducked down and urged her horse inside. The interior of the cave was cold and damp and frozen. Her sweating horse gave off steam and danced nervously over the charred remains of an old campfire. Betty had discovered the cave as a little girl riding her ponies up here and it was a place of grand adventure for her, a secret hideout where she'd camped many times.

She dismounted, breathing hard, and snuck back to the cave entrance to peer out. Far below she saw three cowboys ride by and continue on down the mountain with their rifles across their saddles looking like frustrated hunters returning home without a kill.

Betty waited until dark before coming out, then led her horse gingerly down over the loose shale to the trail. From there she turned and headed back up to where she had left Maury. She found him lying stripped half naked, white and bloody in the moonlight. His horse nuzzled at the frozen ground nearby, cold, tired and hungry. The temperature was dropping by the minute.

Betty struggled, finally managing to slide Maury up and over his saddle and get him tied to the stirrups. It was a long trip down off the mountain. She rode in silence, turning occasionally in the saddle to make sure the load on her pack horse hadn't shifted.

It was after midnight when Cyd heard Betty calling from outside the house. "Where the hell have you been?" she insisted, throwing open the door. "I've been worried sick . . ." And then she screamed.

Cyd helped Betty wrap the body in a tarp, bind it with rope and lay it safely on a bed of hay in the barn where the cold would preserve it and the wolves couldn't get at it. It was the best they could do for the night. Despondent and miserable, they went back to the house.

Betty stood with her back to the fire, warming her hands behind her. Her clothes were stained with blood and she was angry with Cyd. "I don't know what the two of you were up to, but it got him killed. I hope you know that."

Cyd blinked rapidly, covered her face with her hands and burst into tears.

***

Betty tried pouring Cyd and Alex more coffee, but her hand was shaking and she ended up spilling it and had to set the pot back down. This was the first time since Maury's death she had spoken of the tragedy and relating the details to Alex had clearly upset her.

"Maury wasn't much of a cowboy and he talked funny," she remembered with a forced smile, "but he sure had great tips on how to grow my tomatoes. Showed me how to change the pH in the water. Talk about improving the taste. I'll get you some to take home with you if you want."

Alex shook his head 'no'. He had the feeling she was holding something back.

Betty wiped impatiently at her eyes. "There's not so many of us Jews in town that we can afford to lose one, you know?"

"Is there anything else you want to tell us?" Alex asked evenly.

"I almost forgot. There is something." Betty began rapidly opening and closing kitchen drawers, fishing around in the back of them until she found what she was looking for. Taking it out, she pressed it into Alex's palm. "Knew it was here somewhere."

He looked down, staring at an orange key with a number on it. "What's this?"

"A key to one of the lockers out at the airport. I don't know what's in it and I don't want to know, so don't tell me. All I know is Maury said it wasn't safe anymore out at your place, Cyd, and if something happened to his lab, I was to give this to you. I expect it has something to do with why he was killed."

Cyd took the key from Alex, closing her fist around it excitedly.

"You're a good friend," Alex told Betty, giving her a kiss on the cheek that startled her greatly. "I can see why Maury trusted you."

"Lot of damn good it did him," she replied.

"What are we waiting for?" Cyd was already heading for the door. "Let's go!"

"I'm right behind you." Alex rose and was following her out when he noticed something on Betty's mantel that caught his eye. Nestled in among her collection of dusty horse show ribbons and trophy buckles was a large pickle jar. Peering closely, he stared at a pale, curved piece of fleshy sausage, severed at one end and pointed at the other, that was floating in a jar of formaldehyde. "What in God's name . . .?"

"Pickled penis," Betty replied indifferently.

Alex's voice caught in his throat, all medical objectivity gone. "Whose?"

"Mine."

"Yours?" Alex took a step back and almost fell over the sofa.

"Don't believe her," Cyd told him. "She got it in a pawn shop."

Betty shrugged. "That's because I had to hock it one time when I was short of cash."

Chapter Seven

Property of Dr. Maury Bernstein

By the time Alex and Cyd got to the airport in Cyd's old truck, it was early afternoon. Helena being a small town, the terminal was practically deserted at this time of day.

The bank of airport lockers was against a far wall near the bathrooms. Alex inserted the key Betty had given him into a locker door with a matching number on it, and the door opened easily. Inside was Maury's lost research.

Cyd let out a squeal of delight, looking around quickly so see if anyone had heard. Alex removed a huge manila envelope that was stuffed with papers, then reached back in and withdrew a CD wallet. The small soft case was packed with compact discs, each in a plastic sleeve. Across the face of both the manila envelope and the CD wallet Maury had scrawled in marker pen:

Property of Dr. Maury Bernstein

Alex turned abruptly to Cyd. "The lab computers in your barn are toast. Where can I look at these CDs?"

"The library has computers," she remembered.

"I'll follow you there. Then we're going to open these files together, and you're going to explain to me exactly what it is I'm looking at."

"What do you mean, you'll follow me?"

"I'm renting a car. I'm done freezing my ass off in that thing you call a truck."

"Fine." She held out her hand. "Give me the papers and the CDs then."

He drew back. "You tend to lose things. I'll hold on to them. Meet me in the rental car parking lot."

Cyd walked away muttering under her breath. "Asshole."

Alex rented a red four-wheel-drive Jeep Grand Cherokee. Walking toward it in the rental car parking lot shivering from the cold, he tried to imagine what the warmth of the car heater was going to feel like. Sliding into the driver's seat of the jeep, he smiled gratefully when he pushed the ignition and the engine fired immediately.

Waiting for the car to warm up and for Cyd to appear and lead him to the library, he pulled some of Maury's papers out of the tightly packed envelope and began thumbing through them. Most of what he saw were mathematical calculations and early lab test results. A chill went through him because the heater wasn't putting out any heat yet. He pulled more papers from the envelope. These had more recent dates on them and the tests were headed, "Weeds in the Attic." What the hell is that supposed to mean, he wondered?

The temperature gauge moved off its peg and the heater began to fill the car with warmth. Alex looked skyward, thanked a god he no longer believed in, and hastily stuffed the papers back in the envelope. Just then there was a terrible screeching of brakes as Cyd pulled up behind him. He put the Jeep in reverse and waited for her to move, but she just sat there staring straight ahead. The rear window of the Jeep was still defrosting. He couldn't see that well, so he beeped his horn. When she still didn't move, he got out of the car . . . and that's when the lights went out. Something struck him on the head from behind, and he went down hard in the snow.

When he opened his eyes, the snow around him was red with blood from the gash in the back of his head. His vision was cloudy. A blur of boots were running away, he couldn't tell how many. The sound of an engine roaring off. Someone shaking him. He rolled over and Cyd's face came partially into focus. She had a black eye and a bloody mouth, and she was crying angry tears.

"They took the papers and the CDs! They're gone!"

"Who . . .?" He couldn't focus and his head was swimming.

"Two men. They were waiting for me by my truck when I came out. They were wearing ski masks, and I thought they were shoveling the walks or something. They wanted Maury's research. When they found out I didn't have it, they started hitting me and hitting me until . . . Oh Alex, I'm sorry!"

He struggled to sit up, reached out and gently touched her battered face. "You're hurt . . ." His voice sounded far away even in his own ears.

"Those papers were the only documented evidence we had of the discovery," she wailed. "The only way to replicate . . ."

"Who are you again?" he asked vaguely, fighting to clear his head. "What . . .?"

"I think I'm going to need stitches. How are you with a needle and thread?"

She struggled to get him to his feet. "We need to get you to a hospital."

"Emergency rooms are good. I used to work in one, did I tell you?"

She tried loading him in her truck, but he kept turning back toward the Jeep. "Let's take the pretty red one," he repeated over and over. "I like red." Finally, she gave up and tumbled him into the passenger seat of his rental car.

Cyd had read somewhere that short-term memory loss could sometimes accompany a concussion. On the way to the hospital, his memory started coming back but in reverse, beginning with his earliest memories.

". . . and then I took my little brother up on the garage roof and tied a towel around his neck and told him he could fly. He believed me and jumped off and broke his arm, and that was when I started wishing I was a doctor so I could fix it . . ."

"Where is he now, your brother?" Cyd was driving as fast as she could while trying to keep him talking so he wouldn't fall asleep.

"Gone. Eaten up with cancer," he mumbled. "Wish now I'd been nicer to him."

The cut on Alex's head took seven stitches. It was almost dark by the time they left the hospital. Alex had a clean white bandage taped to the back of his skull and a splitting headache, but at least his memory was back. They got into the Jeep, Cyd started the engine and then just sat there, fighting back tears.

"It's all my fault," she cried.

"How is it your fault?" He leaned over to look more closely at her eye that was almost swollen shut.

"I blew it, it's over! We got the research back, and now we lost it again!"

"Did you get a look at the men who robbed us?"

"They had on ski masks, I already told you. One of them, I think, had a cross on his hand."

"A cross?"

***

Back in the airport parking lot, a fist was coming at Cyd's face. She turned and it struck her in the mouth, and blood spurted from her lip. She tried to focus, and in a terrified blur of pain and confusion saw a black religious cross tattooed on the back of the hand that was drawing back to hit her again.

"If you don't have it," a rough voice demanded, "then where is it?"

***

Alex sat beside Cyd in the passenger seat of the Jeep in the hospital parking lot with his head feeling like it had been crushed under the wheel of the car. It hurt to speak, it hurt to think. "I need you to start from the beginning and tell me what the hell this is all about. I want it all, every detail, right now!"

"I've already told you . . ."

"What does 'Weeds in the Attic' mean?"

A shocked pause. "How do you know about that?"

"I know, that's all." A jolt of pain shot through his head. "Now spit it out, damn it!"

She hesitated, jammed the Jeep in gear, spun the tires and drove off without a word.

Chapter Eight

Weeds in The Attic

Minutes later they pulled up in front of Otis's funeral home. Cyd jumped out and marched toward the front door. Alex started to follow but fell back in the seat with another shooting pain in his head. He tried again and this time made it out of the car.

They found Otis in his kitchen warming up a pizza. He heard them come in, turned and smiled broadly. "You're just in time. I got plenty . . ." His voice trailed off in alarm when he saw Cyd's bruises. "My God, what happened to your face?"

"He knows," Cyd told the funeral director.

Otis craned his neck to peek at the bandage on the back of Alex's head. "We should have told him yesterday. Were you two in some kind of car wreck or something?"

"We got mugged," Cyd fumed. "They got Maury's research papers."

Otis let out a long breath and sat down slowly. "Everything?"

"Everything."

"This just keeps on getting worse," Otis sighed.

Alex glared at the dejected mortician. "Let's cut the bullshit. What's your part in all this?"

Otis came to his feet with amazing agility for a man his size. "You're going to want to follow me upstairs."

They climbed an ornate Victorian staircase in single file order. On the second-floor landing, Otis opened a small door to a much smaller staircase, glanced back over his shoulder to make sure they were still behind him and continued to climb. His broad shoulders brushed the narrow walls. At the top of the stairs was another door that opened onto a huge, high-ceilinged attic.

Alex stepped into the room and stopped, staring in amazement. A massive array of bright lights hung down from the exposed rafters. Under the lights were at least a hundred plants over eight feet tall, their jagged-edged leaves reaching for the lights like grateful hands. The plants sat in plastic buckets with their roots suspended in nutrient-rich, oxygenated water—a happily crowded hydroponic jungle reaching up toward what looked like the landing lights of a hovering spaceship. Narrow pathways wound between the buckets under a canopy of green foliage.

Alex recognized the plants immediately, and it made him furious. "You brought me up here to admire your pot garden?"

Otis drew himself up with wounded pride. "Not marijuana. More like transgenic creations of a most unusual nature."

"You think I don't know weed when I see it . . .?" He broke off, staring at a small table in the center of the room spotlighted by a narrow cone of light that shown down on a strange-looking plant that in turn sat in a bed of sand, boxed in on all four sides by a clear plastic box. At its base, the plant looked like a miniature bowling ball, albeit a bright red and pockmarked one bristling with long hairy spines. From its center grew a tall, thin stalk that erupted in a hypnotic swirl of dazzling colors that climbed upward to wash over its leaves and onto a delicate flower at the end of the stem. It was the most amazing thing Alex had ever seen, and he reached to touch it.

"Stop!" Otis cried. "Don't get any closer!"

Alex quickly pulled back his hand. "What is that thing?"

"It's called a Death Star," Otis explained in relief. "Indigenous to a single remote region of the Gobi Desert. One of the most poisonous plants on earth. Touch it and it'll make you sick, get pricked by one of its spines, and it will likely kill you faster than a coral snake."

Alex was aghast. "What's it doing here?"

"Saving the world," Cyd replied casually.

"Oh, that," Alex exclaimed. "I thought it might be something important."

"It's the key to all of Maury's research," Otis suggested. "It's how he made his discovery."

"What discovery?" Alex smiled cynically. "How to grow better pot?"

"You want to hear this, or you want to keep making stupid remarks?" Cyd mocked.

Alex turned to Otis. "How do you even know Maury?"

"Cyd introduced us."

"Why?"

"I've known Otis all my life." Cyd was rapidly losing what little patience she had. "Otis can make anything grow. Not only does he have a green thumb, his whole body is practically green."

Otis smiled modestly "I'm the tree that everybody wants to hug. Maury, he was like into secrecy big time. He needed to keep a low profile and he needed somebody who could plant what he was trying to invent and make it thrive. He tried doing it himself, and his early versions all shriveled and died."

Cyd turned her anger on Otis. "So now that Maury's dead, we tell the first person that comes along the whole program? What if he's police?"

"She has a point," Alex agreed.

Otis went on patiently. "There's a reason why Maury used cannabis as the basis of his genome research. The healing properties of the marijuana plant are amazing. It's been proven that it treats glaucoma, AIDS wasting, neuropathic pain, the spasticity associated with multiple sclerosis. It relieves chemotherapy-induced nausea, helps anorexia sufferers, improves movement disorders, asthma, allergies, inflammation, infection, epilepsy, clinical depression, bipolar disorders, anxiety disorder and it helps people dealing with dependency and withdrawal issues. It's a treatment for autoimmune disease, neuroprotection, fever and blood pressure disorders. It can relieve tics in people with obsessive compulsive disorder and Tourette syndrome. It's been shown to help prevent Alzheimer's disease, reduce arterial blockages, and even help prevent certain types of epileptic seizures. In other words, if you're trying to genetically engineer a new drug, it's not a bad place to start."

"You're supposed to be a doctor," Cyd challenged. "What do you know about gene splicing?"

"I'm an ER doc. I know trauma. All I remember about DNA is that it's an acid, and the parts of the DNA that carry the genetic information are called genes. They're like little computer chips with blueprints or recipes on them that tell a living organism what it is and how it's going to be built. I know you can take a gene with a desirable characteristic from one DNA molecule and splice it into the DNA strand of another molecule, and come up with something that's theoretically better than the sum of its parts. Don't ask me any questions because that's all I know."

"You're oversimplifying it . . ." Cyd began.

"Which brings us to the Death Star," Otis continued. "It's resistant to everything. Nothing short of a forest fire can kill it, and there aren't any forests where it comes from. Anything that attacks it only makes it stronger. The plant has a million defenses. It has the most astounding capacity to reinvent itself on the spot, to identify an invader and mutate a portion of itself into the thing that will kill it. It's a hostile plant, a killing plant, with the most seductive flower on earth. It wants you to touch it so it can kill you."

Alex was appalled. "So, if you combined weed and your fatal-attraction flower here, wouldn't you just end up with pot plants that are poisonous? A trail of dead stoners from here to Mongolia?"

Cyd ignored the cynicism. "That's the beauty of genetic engineering. You transfer whatever parts you want and leave behind the parts you don't want. Maury was able to manipulate the genomes of the plant cell, isolate the curative gene in the Death Star and transfer it to the marijuana plant, all without transferring the poison to the hybrid. The linkage maps of the two plants are surprisingly similar, so it was easier than you might think—they practically have the same genetic makeup."

"Cannastar!" Otis proclaimed with a grand sweep of his hand that encompassed the whole attic. "Glorious, genetically altered weed. Boil it into a tea and drink it, and it turns the human immune system into a lean, mean, fighting machine. An army of soldiers are turned loose in the blood stream that can kill anything that attacks it from cancer to the common cold. What you see before you is the end of illness, the end of viruses and disease, the end of suffering as we know it. Instead of making you high, it makes you well, Alex! You are looking at a whole new world here, a whole new era where people aren't sick all the time, where everyone is mostly healthy, where most illnesses are a thing of the past. That's what Maury died for and that's why we have to be so careful about who we tell and how we proceed from here."

In his growing amazement, Alex forgot about his pounding head. "So, in a way it's like a vaccination?"

"Only better," Otis replied with boundless enthusiasm. "An outright cure."

Alex was overwhelmed and asked for water. Otis handed him a bottle of spring water, and he downed half of it in one gulp. "Let me guess," he went on. "Rxon was a little upset when they realized they'd paid to develop a drug that could put them out of business."

"What they thought they were paying for was for Maury to develop a cure for the common cold," Cyd replied. "That was what he was supposed to be working on. The rest just evolved from there. Rxon was fine with a cure for the cold; colds come back. What they weren't fine with was a permanent cure for practically everything else, especially cancer. Two hundred billion dollars a year is spent on cancer research, treatment and drugs.

"Losing all that money in annual revenue didn't exactly fit their business model," Alex mused. "Is that what you're saying?"

Cyd nodded bitterly.

"And to keep it quiet, they murder the guy that invents it and then steal his research." Alex saw them watching him closely and smiled ironically. "I'm guessing the rest of the medical community would have helped Rxon pull the trigger if they knew how much revenue they were going to lose if this Cannastar plant of yours hit the market."

"Well, now they don't have anything to worry about, do they?" Cyd seethed. "Once they destroy or bury the research they stole, it's game over. They win."

"Not necessarily." Otis was beaming with a sudden revelation. "We still have the progeny! As long as we have the plants, we have the seeds." He went over to one of the bushes and lovingly cupped a flowering seed pod in his hand. The tiny seeds in the pod were striped in the same kaleidoscope of colors as the Death Star. "See these?" he announced delightedly. "These are all we need! Seeds contain the genetic information so a plant can replicate itself—forever. You plant it and it grows, and then it makes more seeds! On top of that, the Cannastar plant is a true hermaphrodite, meaning it can fertilize itself." He paused and frowned. "Of course, you wouldn't want to swallow one of these seeds or let one get in the tea you're drinking. In and of themselves they're . . . a little poisonous."

Alex was appalled. "A *little* poisonous? What's a *little*?"

Otis shrugged.

As a doctor, Alex was a scientist, and as a scientist he remained skeptical. "How do you know it works?" he insisted. "I need proof. How much testing have you done?"

"There was all the usual testing on lab rats," Cyd offered. "That was before Otis was diagnosed with pancreatic cancer."

"What . . .?" Alex was incredulous.

"Pretty much a death sentence if it hadn't been for Maury," Otis confessed. There was a profound sense of love and affection in his voice every time he mentioned Maury's name.

Alex was having a hard time processing what he had just heard. "You've taken the drug yourself?"

"Every day," Otis admitted. "I'm cancer free. Complete remission. There's only one catch."

"You're slowly poisoning yourself to death?"

"Nope. You have to keep taking it. Once the herb has hyped your immune system and turned it into an army of little ninja warriors, you gotta keep taking it or the effect wears off and you go back to dying of whatever you were dying of before you started taking it." Otis smiled proudly. "Tell him about your cancer, Cyd."

"He doesn't need to know about that," she snapped.

"Cyd had breast cancer," Otis went on indifferently. "Show the doctor your breasts, Cyd. The lumps are completely gone."

Cyd hesitated, then in frustration started to remove her sweater.

He struggled to hide his embarrassment. "Uhh . . . that's okay, really. So . . . so you take it too?"

"Twice a day," Cyd admitted. "Apart from getting a little buzzed, it's like drinking decaf."

Alex had goose bumps, he was so excited. "This is a miracle. We have to tell everyone, get all the approvals, get it out so people can start . . ."

"Well, you know, that's the thing," Otis began. "They killed Maury to stop it, so what's to keep them from killing us?"

Just then there was a great pounding and splintering of wood downstairs and the sound of heavy boots on the stairs. The attic door burst open and a squad of drug enforcement agents wearing black DEA vests surged into the room, all yelling at once and waving automatic weapons.

"Everybody down! On the floor! Hands behind your heads!"

Alex was slammed to the floorboards and his arms were wrenched behind him. Military-style boots stomped past close to his head. The confusion of soldiers all barking commands at once sounded like a pack of baying hounds. Cyd screamed and kept on screaming until someone slapped a gloved hand over her mouth to muffle the sound. Otis was thrown down with a loud grunt. Alex turned his head, cheek to the floor, watching in horror as the agents started ripping up the Cannastar bushes and stuffing them in plastic bags.

"Nooooo!" Otis wailed. "Not the plants!"

It took two men to hold Alex still while a third put handcuffs on him. "You have the right to remain silent. Anything you say can and will . . ."

Alex felt his arms being nearly ripped from their sockets as he was cuffed and hauled to his feet.

Across the room, the officers were going through the attic like locusts, hacking down the forest of plants, destroying and bagging the Cannastar as fast as they could.

"Stop, please stop!" Cyd screamed frantically above the din. "Listen to me! You don't know what you're doing!"

Alex turned to see that she was not in handcuffs and was being carefully helped to her feet by the squadron commander.

"Let us do our job, Ms. Seeley," the commander urged.

"Then put me under arrest too," she insisted. "Why aren't you taking me in?"

"You're not part of the investigation."

"What do you mean . . .?"

"I'm just following orders, ma'am. Please step out of the way now."

Alex overheard the interchange, and it made him sick to his stomach. "What the hell's going on?" he yelled, bobbing his head left and right to get a view of Cyd through the swarm of agents. "How do you know who she is?"

"Answer his question!" Cyd screamed.

The commander remained politely calm. "You can stop pretending, Ms. Seeley. We have all the evidence we need now."

Alex saw the shock and sadness on Otis's face as they were hauling him up from his knees.

The officer closest to Alex spoke in his ear. "We only want to question you, sir. Promise to behave yourself and I'll take the cuffs off."

Alex stood fuming as his handcuffs were unfastened. Rubbing his wrists, his eyes widened with full realization that Cyd had betrayed them, betrayed Maury, betrayed everything his lifetime friend had worked and died for. All he could think was that he wanted to strangle her and lunged for her throat. "Lying twisted BITCH!" he bellowed.

A burly officer grabbed him, pulled him off her and struggled to re-cuff him. "Don't move. Don't fucking move! Gimme your arm!"

Alex was fixated on Cyd. "What have you done? What have you done?"

"I can explain," she begged. "It's not what you think . . ."

Otis was hauled off in cuffs and pushed roughly down the staircase. Alex was shoved in the same direction. He looked back from the top of the stairs and caught a final glimpse of Cyd. The commander was talking to her, trying to calm her. She was crying and waving her hands helplessly at the devastation. One of the officers reached a hand inside the clear plastic box and started to pull up the Death Star.

"Don't touch that," she screamed. "You'll die if you do!"

Chapter Nine

Eloise

Otis pled not guilty, put up his mortuary as collateral and made bail the next morning. The judge cautioned him not to leave town.

On their way out of court, Otis's lawyer told him not to worry, it was just a routine pot bust and a first offense at that. "The courts don't take illegal marijuana cases that seriously anymore, particularly here in Montana," he advised. They would sit down with the prosecutor and cut a deal. "You'll change your plea to guilty and probably the worst that'll happen is you'll get probation and a fine."

The attorney's assurances that all of this would go away fairly quickly did not have a calming effect on Otis. If anything, he grew more agitated.

"You'll probably lose your coroner's job," the lawyer went on, "but I thought you might at least be happy to hear that you're not going to jail."

Otis looked around anxiously. "An illegal grow is still an illegal grow, man—even in Montana. This is about a lot more than a simple pot bust, trust me."

The attorney either didn't hear him or didn't want to hear him. "If you're looking for your friend Alex, they're probably done questioning him by now."

"That's not who I'm looking for . . ."

After grilling Alex for hours about his possible involvement in Otis's pot farm, he was finally able to convince them he didn't know anything, and they released him. He was headed for the exit when he passed Otis at the property window picking up his belongings. They walked out together, shaken and shattered.

Alex looked over miserably at the big man striding beside him. "It feels like they murdered Maury all over again."

"They did," the terse reply.

"So, what do we do now?"

"We're screwed. End of story." Otis pushed the exit door open with a violent shove and a blast of cold air hit them hard. Looking up, they saw Cyd waiting at the curb with the motor running in the red rental Jeep.

Cyd watched them come out of the courthouse, got out of the car and rushed up to them anxiously. Alex grimaced going down the concrete steps, his back killing him from being manhandled by the police.

"I didn't tell them anything," Cyd pleaded, "you have to believe me." Cold as it was, their stares made her shiver. "All I did was I gave them updates on Maury's research while I was in school."

"Gave who updates?" Otis wanted no more to do with her than Alex did.

"The people at Rxon."

Alex made a move toward her with clenched fists, and Otis restrained him.

She rushed on breathlessly. "It's how I paid my tuition. I know it sounds horrible, but it didn't seem all that horrible at the time. I was broke and my Uncle said . . . Okay, so I was wrong. But the more they pressed me for information, the less I gave them—so help me. I admit I'm the reason they knew about the discovery, but by the time they closed Maury down, I'd stopped giving them information completely. I feel so guilty, I'm so ashamed, only I swear I'm not the one who told them about what Otis was doing, or what he had in his attic."

Her pleas were met with stony silence. She stumbled after them as they continued on toward the Jeep. "Listen to me, you two!"

"Get away from the car," Alex growled as he got behind the wheel.

She turned desperately to her old friend. "Otis . . .!"

Otis squeezed himself into the passenger seat and slammed the door. "You heard him."

"I'm not like that," she yelled after them as they drove off. "You know I'm not . . ."

The Jeep disappeared up the street, and she broke down sobbing.

***

It was a short drive back to the mortuary.

Alex pulled into the driveway and switched off the engine, staring straight ahead in frustration. "We can't just give up. I can't do that to Maury."

"We almost saved the world," Otis sighed, "and then we didn't. We're lucky to be alive is what I think. You come up with a plan, you let me know, all right?"

Alex was still staring into space. "Think. Who else could have known about your grow? Did you tell anyone, anyone at all?"

Otis opened the car door, dejectedly heaved himself to his feet and headed for the house. "Later, man." He couldn't imagine it was Eloise, not his Eloise, so he didn't even bother to mention her name. He just hoped and prayed she would be at the house waiting for him when he got inside.

Three months before Alex Farmer's frigid arrival in Helena, when Montana was still warm and fine and the trees were still bright with fall colors, the local chapter of the Montana Garden Society was holding its monthly meeting.

The featured guest this evening was Otis Appleseed, who stood addressing an enthralled audience of some thirty ladies and two gentlemen on the subject of hydroponic winter gardening. An entertaining and knowledgeable speaker, Otis was enjoying the audience as much as they were enjoying him. He had covered the various types of media available for this type of gardening, gone on to irrigation techniques, the different nutrient solutions that were available, and was just going over the cost and relative effectiveness of various types of grow lights when he was distracted by the adoring stare of a woman in the audience he had never seen before. His gaze kept returning to her as he spoke. In the middle of his big close where he was recounting the statistics on the amazing crop yields that could be achieved with hydroponics over conventional farming, the lady that had been staring at him with such adoration caught his eye and held it. He lost his train of thought and stood staring at her in silence.

"Sorry." The rotund speaker quickly roused himself. "All this talk about growing food makes me so hungry I can hardly think."

Everyone laughed and Otis finished to a big round of applause. Afterward, people crowded around asking him all manner of questions about gardening without soil. When he had dutifully answered them as best he could and the crowd had moved on, he saw that the woman who had been staring at him all this time was still sitting in her chair with the same soft, sensual look in her eyes.

"Did you have a question?" he asked politely.

"Yes," she replied. "Can I buy you a cup of coffee?"

The café and bar were in one of the many antique stone buildings on Last Chance Gulch in downtown Helena. The woman introduced herself as Eloise Small, and they sat at a table talking for what seemed to Otis like minutes but was actually hours. He was grateful for her endless, earnest questions about gardening and flower growing because it gave him something to talk about. His lively and passionate answers seemed to delight her.

There was nothing especially pretty about Eloise. She was a big woman with unremarkable features, glasses, dyed red hair cut in a perky style and a spider web tattoo on her neck. The spider in the center of the web was a black widow with a single red dot on its back. But taken all together, she was gorgeous in a way only sensual women can be: warm, soft, vulnerable and inviting; a living, breathing, open invitation to get lost in the soft warm folds of her ample flesh. Otis fell immediately, hopelessly, utterly and completely in love.

For Eloise the attraction was simple: she had a thing for gardening and a thing for heavy men—they turned her on. Besides that, she was obviously a bit of a Goth, and a date with a mortician was more than a little appealing.

Country music was playing over the bar's sound system and it re-minded her of Texas and home. "I want to dance," she said, extending a chubby hand. "Come dance with me."

Otis loved to dance but hadn't had the opportunity in years. He rose on nimble feet and followed her gracefully out onto the dance floor. She pressed herself against him and his mind went blank.

"You're really quite good," she remarked. "Where did you learn to dance like this?"

"You wouldn't know from looking at me, but my nickname in high school was 'Lightfoot.' "

She laughed gaily and intoned, "I believe it," before pressing closer. He felt a surprising warmth coming from her body, almost as if she had on an electric blanket and was slowly turning up the heat. He tried to ignore it by making conversation.

She was in town on business, an accountant from Houston. Her boss was thinking of buying a company in town—one that would be a nice complement to his existing organization—and had gotten her a job in the accounting department. She was supposed to keep her eyes open, spot any weaknesses or irregularities, report back on the efficiency and effectiveness of the company's operation and on the relevancy of its key personnel. In that way her employer could evaluate his final decision on making an offer.

"Kind of like a spy," Otis questioned and felt the rheostat on the electric blanket go up a notch.

"Something like that," she admitted with a smile that had nothing to do with what they were talking about.

It turned out to be the best night of Otis's life. He awoke in her hotel room the next morning and thought he was dreaming until he rolled over and pressed his face to her neck tattoo. She smelled like . . . lilacs.

Eloise opened her eyes to find him smiling at her. "So, when do I get to see where you live?" she asked sleepily.

"Right after breakfast." He kissed her and she responded, and he felt the now familiar sensation of her body temperature beginning to rise. "You hungry?"

"Starved . . . but first things first."

Eloise couldn't get over Otis's enormous Victorian mortuary, couldn't stop admiring the overgrown rain forest that crowded his rooms. They were on the second floor when she spotted the door to the attic.

"What's up here?" she asked enthusiastically, opening the door. "I bet you're saving the best for last."

Otis was not subtle in pushing the door closed. "Just a lot of stuff you wouldn't be interested in." He could tell she was an honest person and hiding something from her felt like a breach of trust, but he had another trust that was more important that he couldn't violate, a secret that absolutely could not be told.

She looked disappointed, then brightened. "Can I see a dead body then?"

Eloise kept her hotel room since her company was paying for it and she didn't want them to think she wasn't focused on her job, but she spent every night from then on with Otis at his mortuary. For the rest of the fall and into early winter they were inseparable. Then one day she surprised him by walking in on him in the attic while he was tending the Cannastar plants.

"Far out!" she cried. "Why didn't you tell me? This is so cool!"

"I thought I told you not to come up here."

"Oh, don't be such an old grouch," she chided, giving him a brief hug and a kiss and running up the now-familiar rheostat on her body warmer. "When can we smoke some?"

"It's not ready to be harvested yet," Otis explained mildly. During the time he'd know her he couldn't eat or sleep from thinking about her. As a consequence, he couldn't stay mad at her for that long either. He wished he didn't have to lie, wished with all his heart he could share his proudest achievement with the woman he loved. He would, he vowed, once they were married. He had bought a wedding ring and was planning on proposing over a special dinner that very evening.

***

Having dropped Otis off at his mortuary, Alex drove away with the foul taste of Cyd's betrayal still in his mouth. Conflicting images of her clashed in his mind. He wanted to believe it was somehow Rxon and not Cyd who was behind Otis's growing operation being raided. Yet it was certain that she was working for Rxon and had been all along. He remembered the deferential way the cops had treated her during the bust at the mortuary. She had to be in on it, who else could have known that Otis was growing Maury's Cannastar up in his attic?

At the same time, Otis rushed into his funeral home to find his beloved. He was glad she hadn't been there last night when the police came—he didn't know where she'd gone—but after the terrible loss of the Cannastar, he needed her now more than ever.

"Eloise!" he called as he came through the door.

No answer. He went from room to room calling her name. She wasn't there. He tried dialing her cell phone and got a message that said it had been disconnected. He called the company where she worked. They had never heard of her. His hearse was parked behind his car, and rather than taking the time to move it, he jumped in the long white Cadillac and drove as fast as he could, fishtailing around corners on the slick roads, arriving at her motel and skidding sideways into the parking spaces in front of a two-story row of rooms.

***

Hurt and alone, Cyd wandered away from the courthouse. Her eye and lip still hurt like crazy from the attack, but she hardly noticed. Down the block she saw a Starbucks. If ever she needed a cup of coffee, it was now.

A cowboy named Jesse Long Bow, his greasy black hair hanging down below his hat, was just coming out of a mailbox store next door that advertised drop off services for express delivery companies. He cut in front of Cyd at the coffee shop door and did not wait to hold it open for her. Perfect, she thought, tugging the door back open and following him inside. She stood behind the cowboy in line. He paid for his coffee and picked up his cup. As she stepped up to the counter, she noticed his pockmarked face and cold, dead eyes.

"Can I help you?" the barista at the register said.

Cyd was suddenly staring at the cowboy's hand and backing away in horror. On the back of his hand was a tattoo of a large black cross.

"Can I help you?" repeated the coffee clerk, eyeing the growing line of customers behind Cyd.

Long Bow turned and headed for the door as Cyd started shaking. Fear and anger ran through her as she ran after him and saw him get into his truck.

Casually lighting a cigarette, the cowboy started the engine. On the side of the truck door was a familiar logo—the double-S brand of her uncle Sam Seeley's ranch, the ranch run by her cousin Ty, the Senator's son.

Cyd was too stunned to move. Her first thought was to call the police, then realized if she did, she would have to tell them what this monster had stolen from her. Stomping her foot in helpless frustration, she let out a furious scream as she watched him drive off.

***

Wheezing Loudly, Otis ran up the motel stairs to the second floor and down the hall to Eloise's room. A housekeeping cart was outside the door, and he almost turned it over pushing it aside. A startled housekeeper looked up from the bed where she was changing the sheets.

"Where is she?" Otis demanded. "The woman who's staying here, have you seen her?"

"Lady she check out late yesterday, *señor*."

Frantic for some trace of her, Otis started tearing the room apart, opening all the empty drawers, throwing open the doors to the empty closet, looking under the bed, searching under the bathroom sink.

The housekeeper stood by afraid for her life. "*Señor*, maybe I help you find. What you looking for?"

"I don't know!" Otis cried. "Where's the stuff that was in the waste baskets?"

The terrified housekeeper pointed to a large plastic bag that was tied at the top and stuffed with papers. Otis tore it open and dumped the contents all over the floor. The housekeeper saw it as her chance to escape and fled the room in a panic.

Otis fell to his knees, desperately digging through the pile, opening wadded sheets of paper before throwing them aside. He found nothing. Still on his knees, he buried his face in his hands and closed his eyes. When he opened them again, he caught a glimpse of a large tan envelope that must have fallen behind the dresser. He reached underneath the chest of drawers with a groan, fished the envelope out and tore it open. Inside was a pile of paid bills and old credit card receipts, all with the name Eloise Funk on them and a Houston address. Funk? he thought in a panic. Funk? Her name is Small!

He pulled out his phone, referred again to one of the bills he'd found in the envelope and did a quick MapQuest search for her address in Houston. Three hours later, out of control and out of his mind, he was on a plane to Houston. And because there was so much of Otis to love, he had to buy two seats.

Chapter Ten

To Your Health

Love in a man is a great wave that washes all logic and reason out to sea.

It was after midnight on December 19th, six days before Christmas, when Otis landed at the Houston airport. He rented a minivan and made his way onto the freeway. The traffic was light at this time of night, and there were no real delays.

Following the directions from the kindly female voice hidden somewhere deep inside his vehicle's navigation system, Otis sped past an endless sprawl of shopping centers and business complexes until at last he reached a remote suburb. He got off the freeway and wound through a maze of darkened streets, religiously following the turn instructions voiced over the car speakers by the patient lady, hoping to hell the lady knew what she was talking about, until at last, with great relief, he arrived at the street and then the house number he was looking for.

Otis looked around and found himself in a run-down, blue-collar neighborhood, once proud, decorated now in graffiti with old cars and trash piled up on weed-choked lawns. He was parked across the street from a modest duplex that had the only well-tended yard on the block. The house was dark and silent. A late-model, four-door blue Honda in good condition sat in the driveway.

He watched and waited.

The sound of someone grinding on the starter of a car that didn't want to start jolted him out of a deep slumber. The first light of day was just filtering through the smog. He sat up with a snort, rubbing at his eyes, in time to see a shiny black Town Car driven by a man in a white shirt and tie pull up to the curb in front of the duplex. Otis tried to scrunch down in the seat to make himself less visible, but it was like trying to hide an elephant in a cookie jar. The door to the duplex opened and Eloise came out wearing a business suit over a blouse with a high collar that hid the tattoo on her neck. Otis started to get out of his car, then stopped when he saw someone else coming out of the house behind her.

The driver of the Town Car came around to open the rear door as a young boy of nine or ten followed Eloise down the walk to the car carrying a school backpack. Otis was taken aback by the sight of him. The boy was completely bald in the milky-white way of someone who is going through chemotherapy. Eloise helped the boy into the lush leather interior of the Town Car and got in after him.

Otis watched them drive off as he fumbled to start his engine. In his haste he pulled away from the curb without looking and had to slam on his brakes to avoid plowing into the side of a lowrider car that was backing out of a neighboring driveway. A car stereo was shaking the earth with vibrations. The young bald-headed driver—a different kind of bald this time—shot Otis the finger. For his winter ensemble, the hairless youth had chosen a no-frills white undershirt accented by thick ropes of gold chain from Tiffany's and diamond stud earrings by Cartier. Otis gunned his rental van around the angry driver with a pounding heart and sped after the Town Car.

The chauffer-driven limo was easy to follow in the early morning freeway traffic that was slowly starting to coagulate, but still flowing smoothly. After half an hour, they turned off the freeway and drove at a faster pace down a broad industrial boulevard that ended at the entrance to an industrial park. Otis followed at a safe distance as they continued on past a dazzling array of tall glass high-rise office buildings. At the rear of the park, in the center of a sprawling one-hundred-acre campus, towered the tallest building of all.

The entrance to this private campus was marked by a low, modest sign on a knoll that was colorfully planted in flowers. Leaping over the sign, seemingly suspended in midair, was Santa and his sleigh drawn by a team of nine flying reindeer. Behind the knoll rose three proud flag poles, the taller one in the center flying the American flag, the one on the left flying the flag of Texas and the one on the right flying a company flag with a logo on it. The logo was spectacular: a globe of the earth with the top cut off, the center scooped out and a stem added at the bottom to make the world look like a giant goblet. Overflowing the goblet, erupting from this decapitated world, was a cornucopia of prescription pills of all sizes and shapes that poured down the sides of the earth in candy-coated colors. Across the globe was written the word RXON with the right leg of the R extending down and a small line crossing the leg at the bottom to form an x like on a prescription pad. Under the graphic were the words "To Your Health!"—the company's message and wish for the world.

Otis hung back, following the limo as it wound through the beautifully landscaped grounds, continued on past a building the size of an airplane hangar with a sign out front that read Pharmaceutical Manufacturing, past a small fortress of a building with a sign that said Security, and stopped in front of a school with a playground full of squealing children. These low-rise structures, and others like them, all worshiped at the base of the gleaming glass and steel tower that rose from their midst like a moon rocket, dwarfing everything around it.

The curbside sign in front of the school read Wellness Center. As he drew closer, Otis was surprised to see that many of the kids in the schoolyard were wearing caps and scarves on their heads, and that the ones that were bare-headed had bone-white skulls like the boy who was riding with Eloise.

The boy got out of the black car, tolerated a goodbye kiss from his mother, then ran off to be with his friends. The car moved on with only one passenger now in the back. They passed a gymnasium with a running track, tennis courts, pools, basketball courts, climbing wall, weight, cardio and aerobics rooms, and a separate spa. The sign in front said Employee Health Center and the company motto—"To Your Health!"—was scripted in big letters on the outside wall of the gym.

Further on, the limo finally stopped, and Eloise got out. Walking briskly, she passed a sculptured Roman fountain, then disappeared through the gigantic front doors that framed the entrance to the main tower. Otis parked in guest parking where he could see the entrance, got out and tried to follow her inside—only to be stopped at the front door by heavy security. When he couldn't produce a pass, they asked his name so they could check to see if he was on any of their lists. Otis said he had forgotten something, and that he would be right back. He went out to his car to sit and wait. He was starving, but dared not leave or look away from the busy front doors for fear of missing her.

He waited all day, finally bribing one of the groundskeepers to go and get him some hamburgers. At five o'clock, people started to leave the building, and he saw Eloise come out just as the limo pulled up to the curb. The driver let her into the rear of the car, and they drove back to the campus Wellness Center where she picked up her boy. Otis followed them out of the industrial park and back onto the freeway.

It was a long drive home, the freeway moving in starts and stops now like a single car with a faltering engine. Finally, they pulled off and were back in the seedy neighborhood they had left earlier that morning. The driver dropped off his passengers and waited until they were safely inside the house before driving away.

Otis got out of his car, marched across the street, up the walk and rang the bell.

When Eloise answered, she gasped and tried to close the door on him.

Otis angrily pushed his way inside. "It's Funk, isn't it? Eloise Funk? Help me out here because I have a hard time with last names."

"Get out of my house! How did you find me?"

"Never mind about that. Why did you leave? Why didn't you tell me?" Despite his anger, Otis couldn't help noticing how much she looked like a frightened hen protecting her nest—a nest that was neat and clean and furnished inside with delicate antiques that clashed horribly with the macabre posters of Goth rock bands and vampire movies on the walls.

She backed away. "You're scaring me!"

"How much did Rxon pay you? Do you know what you've done? Do you have any idea the damage you've caused?"

She staggered backward in horror, fell onto the sofa and buried her face sobbing into a pillow. "I can't lie anymore. I can't. I hate to lie."

Otis towered over her. "I'm not going to hurt you, Eloise. Just tell me what happened."

A flood gate opened and her heartbeak poured out. "My boss made me do it. I didn't have any choice. He said if I refused, he was going to fire me, and I was going to lose my health benefits and . . . oh God!"

"So, it was all just some kind of game you were playing to get information out of me? To make me look like a fool?"

"No. Never. Don't think that. Maybe in the beginning yes, but . . ."

Otis saw her staring at something behind him and turned to follow her gaze. The boy with the bald head had come out of his room and was standing there looking at them, his eyes wide with fear. Up close he was thinner and sicklier than he appeared at a distance, his chalky skin traced in blood vessels that looked like red thread.

Eloise hastily dried her tears with the backs of her hands. "Otis, I want you to meet my son. Elton, this is Mr. Appleseed."

Otis felt his anger melting away. "Nice to meet you." He reached out a meaty hand to grasp the child's tiny fingers in his. The boy had to transfer the action figure he was holding into his other hand in order to shake. "Did you get your good looks from your mom?"

"I look better with hair," the boy asserted sadly.

"Nonsense. Bald guys rock. How old are you?"

"Nine and a half." His bloodshot eyes were bright—too bright. Elton glanced down at the toy figure in his hand, then looked back up at Otis with dawning recognition "You look like the Hulk."

"I know. The Hulk is cool, right?"

"The coolest. You want to hold him?"

"Thanks." Otis reached out and the boy reverently placed the green monster in his palm. "Your mom and I are just talking. Is it okay if I talk to your mom?"

"Sure. She's always saying she wishes she had somebody to talk to. Besides me, I mean."

"Why don't you go to your room and do your homework," Eloise urged. "We'll call you when we're finished."

"Mind if I hold on to the Hulk until then?" Otis asked.

Elton headed happily back toward his room. "You can keep him. I've got two other ones. You can see the rest of my collection after if you want."

"Cool."

When the child was gone, Otis turned back to Eloise who was looking at him with a mixture of gratitude and alarm.

"That's some boy," Otis allowed.

"Yes, he is. And he's dying of leukemia."

Otis put his hand over his heart in a gesture of devastation and sat sympathetically beside her.

"I don't expect you to understand," she went on, "but I did it for my son. To keep him alive—that was my only reason. Not for the raise, not for the car and driver, not for the new house they promised me. If it wasn't for Elton, I wouldn't even have considered it. I know seducing you was a lie, and I don't blame you for hating me. But you and me, Otis, that wasn't a lie; that was real. And now I've lost you, and I only have myself to blame."

Otis sat thoughtfully watching her. "Something my size is hard to lose."

"I'm so ashamed that I spied on you. I've never done anything like that before. It's not like me. I'm a whore is what I am. I'm a terrible person . . ."

"We all make mistakes. What did you tell them? What is it you think you saw in my attic?"

"I didn't know what you were doing up there, I still don't. I was supposed to find you, find out everything I could and report back every detail, no matter how small. I think they had someone following that Cyd Seeley woman around is how they knew about you. I told them I'm not suited for this sort of thing. They said I was perfect. I told them I wouldn't do it and that's when the threats started. What was I going to do? I have my son to think about. I couldn't pay for one week of his treatments if I had to do it on my own. I can't just stand by and watch him die without . . ." Her eyes grew large and rivers of dark eyeliner began to run down her cheeks.

"You say you have no idea what it is you saw at my place?"

"You grow pot, right? I'm guessing it's a special hybrid kind that's like super powerful? I figured they wanted it so they could be ready when the Feds finally legalized it—and the Federal government will eventually legalize it, you know. Sooner than you think. Then, as usual, Rxon will have the rights to the best drug on the market, and they can sell pot at a really high prescription price like they do everything else."

Otis sat considering what he had just heard. "Good thinking. Wrong, but good."

"I'm sorry, I'm sorry, I'm sorry," Eloise wailed. "I never meant to hurt you. I couldn't stand the thought of never seeing you again, but they told me they'd gotten everything they needed and that I had to be on the next plane to Houston, no questions asked. I was afraid if I didn't do what they said, I'd be out on the street."

Otis believed her because he wanted to believe her. Nodding absently, he sat lost in thought, trying to make a decision. He only had so much of the dried Cannastar leaves left and no way to grow any more. His stash was hidden in one of the few places the DEA agents hadn't looked when they raided his funeral home. It was a few months' supply at best. Cyd would get sick again, but maybe she wouldn't die. He would. As an undertaker, he didn't think his own death would be all that traumatic to contemplate, but now that it was real, now that he was faced with the reality of it, it was.

Coming out of his reverie, he smiled. "Ask Elton to come back in here."

Eloise hesitated, then went to get her son. Otis pushed himself off the sofa and went into the kitchen where he took down a sauce pan, filled it with water from the tap, put it on the stove and turned on the gas. When the water was boiling, he took a packet of crushed green leaves from his pocket and dropped some in the water, stirring them slowly. Then he took down two mugs.

"What are you doing?" Elton asked, appearing in the doorway.

"Making tea," Otis declared. "Want some?"

"I don't like tea."

"You might like this kind." Otis poured out two steaming mugs through a strainer, blowing on his and taking a tentative sip. "Mmmmm," he mimed. "Tastes just like chocolate mint. You like chocolate mint?"

Elton allowed as how chocolate mint was his favorite—even though he'd never tried it.

Otis handed him a mug and the boy blew on it the way he had just seen his large friend do. Then tentatively, he took a sip.

Eloise looked on anxiously. "Is that medical marijuana? I've heard it can help."

"It's a special tea."

"I don't believe in homeopathic remedies myself."

"Here's the rest of the packet. When I get back home, I'll send you some more."

"I don't see how a tea is going to help him," the boy's mother complained. "I'm just saying, you know? I mean, what does it do?"

"It cures leukemia."

Eloise's mouth worked open and closed, but nothing came out.

"It's good, really good," Elton allowed, taking another sip. "Do I get to drink this all the time?"

"As long as it lasts," Otis sighed. Then to Eloise, "Give him all he can hold for a week. After that, two cups a day, morning and evening."

"How . . . how is it possible?" she gasped. "If it's true, why would Rxon want to stop it?"

"Your employer, Big pharma, they don't want to permanently cure cancer. Big pharma doesn't want to permanently cure anything. There isn't any money in making people well and then keeping them that way."

"I have a hard time believing they'd be that mercenary."

"They murdered the man who invented this tea, stole his research and turned you into something you're not. They got me busted and had my plants destroyed. What does that tell you?"

Her incredulity turned to wonder. "That my boy is going to live? That he's really going to get better?"

"Temporarily."

"I don't understand."

"I don't have that much of it left. Unless I can grow some more . . ."

"You'll find a way. I know you will." Eloise was beside herself with happiness. "Oh, my God!"

"You can't tell anyone about this. If anybody finds out, I won't be able to help you any longer, and he won't get well." He turned to Elton. "That goes for you too, son. Not a word, okay?"

Eloise looked at her boy, playfully pinched her thumb and index finger together, drew it across her lips, turned an imaginary key at the corner of her mouth to secure her lips and threw the key away. Elton nodded enthusiastically and the pact was sealed.

"To your health, then!" Otis said, raising his tea mug in a toast and clinking rims with Elton.

The boy raised his mug with both hands and buried his face in it, smiling at Otis over the rim. The smile won the funeral director's heart forever.

After Elton was in bed asleep, Otis and Eloise sat on the sofa holding hands and talking like teenagers in love, mindful of what they had almost lost, treasuring it all the more for having regained it.

She wanted to know more about the research that was stolen. He explained it was the complete records, the only records, of the Cannastar project his murdered friend Dr. Maury Bernstein had been working on and that without it there was no way to replicate the discovery. He went on to explain more about the healing powers of the drug, about getting arrested, about how the only existing plants had been summarily torn up and hauled off by the police. He left out the part about how he would die without it.

Eloise was not overly surprised to learn the truth about the company she worked for. "I never had a good feeling about them," she confessed. "That goes double for my boss."

"What's his name?"

"Dick Tremble."

"What does he do? His title, I mean."

"CEO. It's his company."

Now that Otis's obsession over Eloise had somewhat subsided, his obsession with the Cannastar came back with a vengeance and he smiled grimly. "I want to meet this Dick Tremble character. I want to meet the man that had Maury Bernstein killed and had me arrested. I want to know what kind of person would keep a thing like this from the world."

"You can't be serious."

"I need to get inside that building where you work, Eloise."

She looked flustered, then quickly brightened. "I think I may know a way."

"You do?" He wanted to kiss every square inch of her ample body.

"The company is hosting a Christmas party tomorrow night. It's for top management and their key assistants—which includes me. We can bring our 'significant others.' Do you want to be my significant other?"

Otis's grin widened. "I do."

"I can leave a pass for you with security, no problem. Just to be safe, though, we should come up with different name for you. Who do you want to be?"

"How about Charles Darwin?"

"How about Sergio Lancelot?"

Otis laughed, then saw that she was beginning to have second thoughts.

"I . . . I hope I'm doing the right thing," she worried. "You won't get me fired, will you?"

"Nobody ever got fired for bringing a date to a Christmas party." Later, when it was too late, he would remember these words and cringe at the thought.

Her mood lightened. "All right then, be there about six. I guess you know where to find us."

Otis raised one hip and fished in his pocket for his cell phone. "I have to call Cyd and Alex and tell them everything you just told me. Poor Cyd, she probably hates us for not trusting her. This changes everything."

Eloise stood with a sensual smile, reached out her hand and motioned with her head toward the bedroom. "That can wait. First things first."

Chapter Eleven

Fear and Greed

Early the next morning, Alex turned off I-15 at Wolf Creek and drove his rental Jeep up the narrow, freshly plowed road that led to Cyd's ranch. All around the car, snow crystals sparkled like fireflies in the mountain air. The road flattened out when he reached the rolling plane, and he leaned forward to look up through the windshield at the vast expanse of blue overhead. The sky really is bigger up here, he thought. They weren't just kidding.

Otis had called him with the exciting news—Cyd didn't turn them in after all, it was his girlfriend Eloise. But it wasn't her fault either; she was threatened and coerced. "All she did was tell her boss—who happens to be the CEO of Rxon. Do you know what this means? She's on our side, Alex. In fact, she's taking me to a Christmas party tonight—at Rxon's corporate headquarters, if you can believe that!"

Alex was worried; he didn't like the idea. "Call me after the party and tell me you're alright. And don't do anything stupid while you're in there."

***

Cyd, fresh out of the shower, answered the door in a loosely tied bathrobe that fell partially open as she bent to wrap a towel around her wet hair. Alex forced himself to avert his eyes.

"Otis already called me and told me everything," she informed him. "What do you want?"

Alex leaned in close to examine her discolored eye and puffy lip. "I came to apologize."

"Apology accepted. Now go away."

"I don't blame you for being mad." He searched for something more to say. When nothing came, he realized he'd made a mistake in coming and turned dejectedly to leave. "I'm sorry, Cyd. Sorry I doubted you."

She watched him go, hesitated and called after him. "Alex wait. I was about to have my tea. I can make some coffee."

He smiled his boyish grin. "Coffee would be good."

A huge, noisy fire was making Cyd's log cabin so warm that Alex had to shed his jacket and sweater. Cyd went upstairs, came back down wearing baggy sweats, disappeared once more into the kitchen and returned carrying two hot mugs that she sat down in front of them on the coffee table between the sofa and the fire. Alex watched over the top of his mug as she began angrily brushing out her damp hair. The heady fragrance of her shampoo filled his senses and made it hard to think.

"How could I let them use me like that?" she lamented. "How could I have been so naïve and stupid?"

"They took advantage of you," he admitted. "It could happen to anyone."

"The Cannastar is gone, Alex! Otis will die, millions of people will die, I . . ." Her voice trailed off.

It saddened him to think of her perfect breasts being laid waste by cancer. "How much do you have left for yourself?"

"Some. A little."

A thought occurred to him. "What if we went to the press and made it all public?"

"Without the research or the plants, what proof do we have?"

"There's always options."

"Like what?"

"I don't know. Crooks and thieves are never as smart as they think they are. There's got to be a way."

"What way? How?"

"We'll figure it out. We can't let Rxon steal and exploit Maury's discovery, it's too important. And we can't let them bury it just so they can keep on giving people false hope with overpriced cancer drugs that don't work in the first place."

She stopped brushing her hair, laid down her brush and looked up in anguish. "They had Maury killed. Rxon murdered him, I know they did."

"And all we have to do now is prove it."

A new light came into Cyd's eyes. "They arranged for the pot bust that got Otis arrested. They arranged to have us mugged and robbed. Rxon's behind the whole thing and you know what? This is bullshit. We're obviously in over our heads but fuck the bastards. They haven't beaten us yet, and they're not going to beat us."

He laughed admiringly. "That's the spirit."

It astonished her that he had restored her courage and made her brave again. She tried to smile, but the effort hurt her lip and she flinched. "Let's hope Otis turns up something."

"He could get in a lot of trouble doing what he's doing. He's a brave man."

"I just pray he's careful."

They fell silent staring into the fire. It felt like a great weight was descending on them, something neither of them could control. Cyd brightened and turned to Alex. "Tell me about L.A., doctor. It's the one place I never wanted to go."

He avoided her eyes.

"Did I say something wrong?"

"The sailing is nice, if you like that sort of thing."

"You sail?"

"I live on a boat down there."

"I've always wanted to try sailing." She paused. "Why did you quit the ER? Didn't you like being a doctor?"

"I didn't quit, I was asked to resign."

She raised her eyebrows in question.

"Long story," he sighed. "And yes, I love being a doctor. It was the kind of medicine I was practicing that I didn't like."

"How so?"

"I wasn't relieving suffering; I was just postponing it, prolonging it. For me, the ER stopped being about medicine and became more about watching people doing everything they could to destroy themselves with both hands." She was clearly interested, so he went on. "I got tired of trying to save people who were going out of their way to die. I want to help people who want to live, not ones that keep coming up with new and better ways of committing suicide—not that I'm any different, as it turns out." He ignored her questioning look. "It got to the point where it felt like I was just making it safer and easier for the bangers to bang, the junkies to shoot, the drunks to drink. I know that doctors are sworn to help everybody, but I didn't become a doctor to help people who refuse to help themselves. Some people insist on being victims. It's all they want. I'm sorry, but spending your life trying to fix it for everybody else is what gives you cancer. That and keeping your anger bottled up inside. That'll kill you just as certain as a head-on with a semi."

"So, why did they ask you to resign? Because you stopped wanting to help everybody who came through the door?"

His silence told her she was trespassing on private property.

"I'm curious," he said at last, "how did you come to be working in Maury's lab in the first place?"

He just changed the subject on me, she thought. It gave her an uneasy feeling. "My uncle is Senator Seeley," she answered. "*The* Senator Seeley. He got me the job. It was the first time in my life he was ever nice to me."

"Interesting."

"Isn't it though."

The sun streaming through the window was reflecting off her freshly washed hair and making little mirrored flashes in it. She was incredibly beautiful, he thought, even with a swollen eye and a fat lip.

He roused himself and went on. "Getting myself fired was a good thing. If I hadn't gotten out of L.A. when I did, there's a good chance somebody would be looking at my toe tag right now, trying to figure out where to ship the body."

"You got yourself out of a bad situation," she suggested. "Good for you."

"Jury's still out on that one. What's it like living on a ranch out in the middle of nowhere? Don't you get lonely?"

She smiled happily. "It's Montana. I like the solitude. And I love to sleep, and I sleep really good out here. At least I used to. What I miss is Maury, having an exciting research project to work on, helping to grow something truly miraculous. I don't know . . . maybe I'll try farming next." Her smile faded. "Like your last name—it's Farmer, right?"

"Don't let it fool you. I once had a fake tree that died."

"So," she laughed, "what do you *like* about being a doctor, Dr. Farmer?"

He thought a moment. "Getting a patient stabilized and out of danger. It's a good feeling, knowing I was able to help save a life."

Suddenly, there was a loud banging at the front door.

***

While Cy and Alex were inside the cabin talking by the fire, the tiny silhouette of a lone horse and rider appeared on a rocky ridge overlooking the ranch. The rider squinted into the sun that was reflecting off a snow bank to watch a black one-ton Ford pickup with big tires come up the road, turn in at the ranch entrance, proceed down the dirt drive and stop in front of Cyd's house.

The driver stepped down off a chrome rail in butterscotch colored ostrich skin cowboy boots, closed the door behind him and headed for the house. On the truck door was the distinctive double-S brand of the enormous Seeley ranch that surrounded Cyd's small spread.

The rider on the ridge pressed a spur into the side of the horse and laid a rein against its neck. The horse wheeled on its haunches and disappeared out of sight back over the ridge.

**

The banging came again as Cyd crossed the room, opened the door and flared. "What the hell . . .?"

The uninvited visitor brushed past her and entered the house like he lived there. Looking around, he saw Alex and extended his hand.

"We met at the fire," he declared. "I'm Cyd's cousin, Ty Seeley."

Alex ignored the outstretched hand. "Cyd told me who you are."

"What are you doing here, Ty?" Cyd demanded, hands on her hips.

Ty tried to imitate his father's dangerous smile, but, with his undersized mouth, he looked less like an intimidating bully and more like a butterball with lips.

"The family is concerned about you, Cyd. Everybody knows you can't afford this place now and that you're about to lose it. I'm here to solve your problem, but before I do, let me ask you a question. Would you rather be a wealthy botanist or a homeless rancher? I suggest wealthy botanist."

"I suggest you wipe that silly smirk off your face before I wipe it off for you," Cyd fumed. "Your family has been trying to steal this land from us for generations, and I'm not going to be the one to lose it, especially to you."

"I can buy it now or buy it at auction from the bank," Ty shrugged. "Your choice."

"I got a question for you," Cyd replied. "That Indian that works for you with the cross on the back of his hand—what's his name and how much did you pay him to mug me?"

Ty made little snorting sounds that Alex assumed was laughter. "You know, Cydney, I didn't want to have to do this, our being cousins and all, but you leave me no choice. Now I'm just going to have to marry you."

Chapter Twelve

Office Party

It was almost dark by the time Otis drove his rented minivan back onto the Rxon campus, passing the entry sign with the flying sleigh where the nose of the lead reindeer was glowing red now, lighting Santa's way. The trees lining the road through the campus twinkled in a fairyland of white lights. Otis continued on and parked in the shadow of Rxon's corporate headquarters. The futuristic tower loomed overhead, casting a pall over the holiday cheer below. He got out and walked toward it.

Otis had been too upset to notice any of the detail the first time he was inside the tower, but now he stopped and stared. The lobby was a vast crystal cathedral with soaring bundles of pointed glass spears that looked like clusters of stalagmites reaching up from the floor at bundles of stalactites reaching down from the ceiling. High overhead revolved a hollowed-out world with the word Rxon scrawled across it, pouring forth an endless flood of tasty colored pills. The armed guards at the front desk had the look of a grim army of mercenaries. Otis approached and identified himself to one of the uniformed officers, a man even bigger than himself. The officer ran his finger down a list until he found the name that Eloise had given him, wrote Sergio Lancelot on a badge, and solemnly handed it over to the guest.

Otis walked toward the elevators pinning on his badge while craning his neck to look up at the gleaming glass spikes that were pointing down at his head. He entered one of the express elevators and pushed the top button that said Executive Dining Room. The doors closed silently, there was a giant sucking sound, and the elevator launched like a rocket to the stars. The ride was over in seconds, but it felt like he had left his stomach on the ground floor. With a whoosh, the doors opened onto a loud, drunken Christmas party crowded with revelers.

Otis stepped out into a high-ceilinged room with tall windows draped in red ribbon and hung in red and green holly. Even before he saw the serving tables laden with enough food to feed half of Houston, he could smell the mouth-watering flavors. A mountain of shrimp and another mountain of king crab legs overflowed a separate table. There were fruits and salads and a desert bar that exploded with colored and frosted delights. Bowls of spiked eggnog were being replenished by bartenders in bow ties and Santa Claus hats. Shouts and whistles went up, making the rotund mortician jump until he saw gurneys piled with Texas barbequed ribs being wheeled from the kitchen. Live carolers in Dickensian costume strolled through the throngs of partygoers, circling the sumptuous buffet and singing holiday songs, somehow staying on-key despite the noise and confusion.

"Sergio, Sergio," cried a voice, which Otis immediately ignored since Sergio wasn't his name. The voice came again, this time in a stage whisper. "Otis!"

He turned and Eloise was standing before him, a forced smile on her face, two cups of eggnog in her hands, looking absolutely beautiful in a high-necked black gown with a corsage of holly pinned over her heart.

"Darling!" she swooned, rising on tiptoe to kiss him, forcing a cup of eggnog into his hand and hissing in his ear. "Follow me out onto the terrace. I have something exciting to tell you."

The view from the terrace was like standing on the wing of an airplane looking down at the city. The distant sounds of the party and the carolers inside were carried away by the wind. In her distraction, Eloise put her cup of eggnog down on the railing too close to the edge, and it fell off, tumbling into the darkness, spilling Christmas cheer as it went.

"Oh, silly me," she said loudly for the benefit of anyone who might be listening. Looking around and finding no one within earshot, she rushed on. "Listen . . . my boss got a Federal Express package today. I opened it like I do all the mail and guess what?"

***

The connecting door between Eloise's small office and her boss's larger office was open when the Federal Express delivery arrived that afternoon. Eloise was busy with other correspondence and only glanced at the packages before one of them caught her eye. It was addressed, as they all were, to Mr. Dick Tremble, CEO, Rxon Pharmaceuticals, but this one was from Helena, Montana. She snatched it up, tore it open and was pulling out the contents just as her boss came striding into her office through the common door.

"I'll take that," Dick Tremble ordered.

Eloise glance down just as he took the large stuffed manila envelope and CD wallet from her hands. Across both, in bold handwriting, was scrawled the words 'Property of Dr. Maury Bernstein'.

***

"What did he do with them?" Otis whispered tensely in Eloise's ear. He was so excited he knocked his own drink off the balcony rail. "Are they still in his office?"

Eloise nodded and grinned.

"Can we get to them? How do we get in there?"

"Easy," she whispered back.

***

Eloise leaned forward and across her desk to watch as her boss verified the contents of the envelope and CD holder, then walked quickly to a Flemish painting on his wall—an original oil that was worth a fortune. Grasping the edge of the frame, he swung it out to reveal a safe. His fingers spun the dial and pulled on the handle. The vault opened, and he put the two items inside, closing and relocking the safe before swinging the painting back in place.

***

Otis closed his eyes and heaved a sigh. "So, we're screwed."

"Nope," Eloise grinned. "I'm not supposed to know the combination, but I do. He's always having me hold things for him while he opens the safe, and I've looked over his shoulder a thousand times. You may not know this about me, but I'm naturally kind of a snoop."

"Actually, I did know that." Her devilish smile made him love her more in that moment than he ever thought possible.

They went back inside, hurrying toward the elevators, and in their haste bumped straight into Dick Tremble himself who was talking with his good friend and old fraternity buddy, Riley Gray. The affable crewcut lobbyist was home from Washington for the holidays to play a little golf and tag up with his boss—which among other things meant attending his boss's Christmas party.

"Eloise!" Tremble boomed in a slightly intoxicated baritone, bending to kiss his executive assistant on the cheek. He wore a gaudy Christmas tie that showed a grinning Santa riding in a sleigh full of pill bottles. "Merry Christmas, darlin'. Did you get your bonus check?"

Dick Tremble was a street fighter with a mean streak; a man who had no qualms about doing what needed to be done. His father had owned low-income apartment buildings, and one of Dick's favorite things growing up was going out to one of his housing projects and slapping people around who didn't pay their rent. Young Dick made his wealthy father very proud. Tremble still had a full head of blond wavy hair, a pugilistic face to go with his personality and a permanently broken nose that was pushed slightly to one side—a trophy from his days as a middleweight boxer in college and in the Army. A narrow mustache barely masked a permanent sneer that almost looked like a permanent smile. He had married the plain-faced, big-breasted, not-very-bright but oversexed granddaughter of Rxon's founder, and that's how he got to be CEO of the company.

"Yes, sir, thank you very much," Eloise responded in a supreme effort to compose herself. "Mr. Tremble, I want you to meet my boyfriend. Sergio, this is Mr. Tremble, my boss."

Tremble vigorously shook Otis's hand. "What do you say, big guy? What do you do for a livin'?"

"I bury people," Otis replied evenly.

"Me too," Tremble smiled. "Fun, isn't it?" He turned back and resumed his conversation with the lobbyist before Otis could reply.

"Merry Christmas," Eloise called as she took Otis's arm and led him away. Her words fell on deaf ears.

Tremble gave Otis the chills. He looked back over his shoulder at the two men talking, oblivious to the crowds of people that eddied around them. Beyond them were the heavily laden food tables. It was one of the few times in Otis's life when he didn't feel hungry.

"What about Elton?" Otis inquired as they waited for the elevator.

Eloise smiled grimly. "I had my mother pick him up. She's going to keep him overnight and bring him back to school in the morning."

They went down one floor and stepped out of the elevator onto a hushed and darkened floor of opulent, high-ceilinged executive offices. Eloise led Otis down a dimly lit hallway paneled in exotic Hawaiian koa wood and hung with expensive art and continued on through the door to her office. She crossed quickly to the door that connected her office with her boss's and eased it open. Otis followed her into an enormous suite that was more of a throne room with a view than an office. They walked soundlessly over priceless carpets past a shadowed wall filled with humanitarian awards, all with Dick Tremble's name on them, and on to the Flemish painting on the far wall. Eloise swung it carefully aside, fumbled with the dial, and seconds later the safe door swung open.

Otis shivered in the dark as Eloise reached inside the safe and pulled out the manila envelope and CD wallet. She handed them to him, and they did a little victory dance together. Then carefully closing the safe, she eased the painting back over it, and they snuck back out the way they had come.

Eloise fidgeted nervously in the foyer as they waited for the elevator, her heart pounding in her chest. The bell dinged, the doors slid open . . . and four snarling security guards stepped out and grabbed them by the arms. Eloise screamed and struggled, Otis tried to throw them off, but it was no use. They were handcuffed and taken into custody.

***

After the opulence of the executive suites, the inside of the campus security building looked more like a prison—cold, hard and hopeless. Otis and Eloise were shoved stumbling into one of the holding cells and an iron-barred door was banged closed behind them.

"What are they doing with jail cells in a place like this?" Eloise asked, thinking out loud as she looked around in terror at the windowless walls, the two thin mattresses on the two narrow bunks, the stainless-steel toilet with no lid.

"Let us out of here!" Otis yelled. A loud bell sounded, and the lights went out, plunging the cell into total darkness.

Sometime the next morning—it was impossible to tell when exactly because their watches, along with their other belongings, had been confiscated—the lights came back on with another clanging of the bell, and a mute guard brought them two bowls of watery oatmeal for breakfast. An hour later, they were taken out of the cell and ushered into the harsh glare of a concrete interrogation room lit from above by bare light bulbs. The guards shoved them down into two cane chairs in front of a bare metal table.

Minutes later, the door opened, and Dick Tremble entered carrying Maury's research files and looking fresh as the morning. He dropped the manila envelope and CD wallet on the table and sat on one corner, dangling his leg over the side.

Otis struggled to get up but was pushed back down in his chair.

"Let me tell you 'bout mah daddy," Tremble began, adjusting an already perfectly knotted tie—not the one with the Santa on it—over a freshly laundered shirt. "He used to buy old buildings and turn them into apartments, and while he was refurbishing them, he'd put up signs that read *Trespassers Will Be Hung*. What he was sayin' was that the common side effects of breaking and entering in Texas can be . . . unpleasant." His smile morphed into a sneer. "We aren't near as tolerant of criminals down here in Texas as some of your liberal states up north."

Otis's face turned red. "That research doesn't belong to you!"

"Ah paid for it, and it's in mah possession, so under the law that pretty much makes it mine, wouldn't you say?"

"Not when you commit murder and robbery to get it."

"You're a long way from home, Mr. Appleseed. Does the judge know you're gone?"

"What do you want from us?"

Dick Tremble drew the manila folder toward him with one hand and snapped his fingers with the other. One of the guards left the room and returned moments later with a shredder in his arms which he plopped down on top of the table and plugged into a wall socket.

"Y'all need to understand somethin'," Tremble grinned. "You're fightin' a losin' battle here. It's over and you lost, and if ah can't convince you of that, well, all ah can say is, this is gonna get ugly."

Eloise's eyes grew big as dinner plates. "You're evil, pure evil."

Tremble shook his head in disappointment at her betrayal, switched on the shredder and pulled a handful of research papers out of the envelope. "Eloise darlin' . . . ah'm gonna miss you, ah truly am."

She was close to tears. "I used to think you were human at least."

"People often make that mistake."

"You're looking at maybe the most important discovery since penicillin," Otis cried. "This thing is going to change modern medicine. It's going to change the world . . ."

"Ah had a chance to look over some of these papers, and you're wrong about that." Tremble began feeding the first of the documents into the shredder. "There's nothin' here of any real value."

The teeth of the shredder chewed contentedly as Otis came howling out of his chair, and the guards wrestled him back down.

Tremble drew more papers from the envelope and fed them into the machine. "You grew a plant that never existed, Mr. Appleseed. I strongly suggest you go home and forget you ever heard of it."

"How can you want people to be sick?" Eloise pleaded. "How can you not want them to be well?"

"Capitalism is money and money is war," Tremble drawled. "Sometimes there's casualties."

"You call this capitalism?" Otis flared. "Way I see it, capitalism thrives on just enough government interference to keep everybody honest, not on using the government to crush the competition and bleed the country dry of its resources. A true capitalist relies on his own integrity to make his fortune, on his willingness to be responsible for his own actions, not on making money by manipulating the government bureaucracy. Big Pharma today is a creation of the lobbyists, for the lobbyists, by the lobbyists. It thrives on successful politics, not successful commerce. What you call capitalism, sir, is theft—theft of the American dream, theft of every principle of moral decency that America ever stood for."

Tremble laughed. "Words are turds, boy. You can spread 'em, but you can't spend 'em."

Otis looked away as a great sadness came over him. "Politicians promise universal healthcare. We vote them into office and that's the last we ever hear of it. People at the highest level of government gave Big Pharma and the health insurers a license to steal—and America got screwed quicker than a coke whore on a street corner. Thanks to politicians from both parties, any controls on drugs or insurance costs disappeared and the price of prescription drugs and insurance premiums has been skyrocketing ever since. The government solution to all this? None!"

"You know," Tremble smiled, "Rxon just came out with a new pill for obesity. I can get you some free samples if you like."

Eloise, taking her courage from Otis, lost her temper. "The pharmaceutical industry isn't in the business of health and healing. I know because I work here—or at least I did. Big Pharma is in the business of disease maintenance, symptoms management and chemical castration. They're not in the business of curing anything . . ." Her voice trailed off in horror as Tremble picked up one of the CD files that contained Maury's findings, showed it to them like he was tempting a dog with a treat, and fed it gingerly into the shredder.

Otis exploded. "Murderer! You'd put the health of the whole world through the shredder for the sake of a dollar."

Tremble continued casually shoving CDs into the metal jaws until he had ground the last of Maury's disks to shreds. "Well, that's that," he announced, brushing his hands in satisfaction. "Eloise, you need to pick up your brat from school and remember . . . we know where you live." He turned his back and walked to the door. "And if ah ever hear that either one of you so much as mentions the word *Cannastar* again . . . well . . . let's just say that murder is messy and complicated, which is why the two of you aren't dead already." He paused and smiled back at them over his shoulder. "Y'all have a nice day now, hear?"

***

Otis and Eloise picked Elton up from the Wellness Center and, in a daze, drove away from the Rxon campus for the last time. The boy sensed something was wrong and sat sullen and brooding in the back seat.

"Dear God," Eloise said in utter devastation. "Dear God." There wasn't anything else to say.

When they got home, Elton went straight to his room.

Eloise turned to Otis. "What about his medications, his treatments? How am I going to pay for even a small part of what he . . .?"

"Don't worry." Otis took her in his arms and stroked her hair. "It'll be all right. He won't be needing any doctors or anything like that . . . at least not for now."

"But what am I going to do? I don't have a job and . . ."

"You and Elton are coming home to Helena with me."

She looked up at him and tried to smile. The nightmare of the last twenty-four hours felt unreal, other-worldly, almost as if it hadn't happened. Her house was the same, her son and Otis, they were the same, she was the same—and yet everything was different.

"I'll fix us something to eat," she said absently.

He wasn't hungry, but he let her do it because it gave her something to do. While she was in the kitchen, he called Cyd.

"Where have you been?" Cyd cried with relief. "We've been worried sick."

Otis could hear Alex in the background asking if he was all right.

"Not really," Otis replied, then proceeded to tell Cyd everything that had happened.

Alex listened with his ear close to the phone. When Otis was done, Cyd was dizzy. She passed the phone to Alex and sat down.

"At least you're not hurt," Alex suggested.

"Put Cyd back on. I need her to do something for me."

When she came back on the line, Otis tried and failed to take the urgency out of his voice. "I want you to go over to my place, go in the coffin display room and look in the bottom of one of my coffins, the rosewood one . . ."

Otis finished giving her instructions, then told Cyd that when he was done helping Eloise pack up and put her things in storage, he would be driving back to Helena with her and her son. "I'll be home in about two weeks," he added.

Cyd hung up and headed for the door.

Alex hurried after her. "Wait up, I'll drive you."

***

Cyd tiptoed into Otis's coffin room while Alex wandered around the big house watering Otis's plants for him.

The stifling silence, the open coffins with their lace trimmed pillows and white satin liners, gave Cyd an eerie feeling. She found the rosewood coffin, gingerly fished around inside it and pulled out the liner as Otis had instructed. Underneath the liner was a false bottom. She opened it up and inside found a row of neatly tied clear plastic kilo bags of dried Cannastar leaves.

Grinning with joy, an idea suddenly occurred to her. She snatched up one of the bags, shook it excitedly and held it up to the light. Nothing. She grabbed another and then another, repeating the process with each one. If there were any seeds left in the bottoms of theses bags, just a few, it might solve their whole problem. She shook and inspected the last bag. Otis had done a good job of cleaning his stash and ridding the leaves of any of the colorful, poisonous little Cannastar seeds. She couldn't find a single one.

"Take two of the bags," Otis had said. "Overnight one of them down to me and keep the other one for yourself. And Cydney . . . try to make it last because that's all there is."

With a sigh, she did as instructed, closed the false bottom and put the liner back in place. Three bags of Cannastar leaves remained hidden in the bottom of the coffin.

Alex drove Cyd to the Federal Express office and afterward they went next door for coffee. Cyd couldn't help remembering what had happened the last time she was in the coffee shop, took one look around, and had to leave. Driving back to the ranch, she called Betty Little Horn to tell her they had retrieved the contents of the locker, but that they had gotten mugged, and Maury's papers had been stolen.

"Shit," Betty said. "Shit, shit, shit."

***

In January, Otis pled guilty to the possession for distribution of a schedule I drug and was given a heavy fine and fourteen years' probation. The DEA was then free to destroy the evidence.

Agents in surgical masks and gloves built a bonfire in a three-sided cinderblock enclosure out behind their office. The heat was intense. Shielding their faces with their arms, they threw the bags of "pot" confiscated in the raid on Otis's funeral home onto the fire. The inferno roared to new heights as it embraced the dried greenery. It made a pleasant smell as the smoke rose in the still air and drifted into the winter sky. Blazing brightly in the center of the flames was a red spiny ball. When the ball got hot enough, it exploded and, like a dying star, went out in a violent burst of color and light. The agents jumped back, startled at the sound and staring at the light show.

Chapter Thirteen

Seed for The Pot

The day broke clear and cold on the morning after Cyd shipped the bag of Cannastar down to Otis in Houston. The lone horse and rider again appeared on the ridge above her ranch and this time, with no unwanted visitors in sight, began a slow descent down the slope toward the house. Cyd's two horses trotted along inside the fence in greeting as the horse and rider passed close by their corral. A rifle was tucked into a leather scabbard under the rider's leg.

The visitor dismounted and knocked on the front door, stomping her boots even though there was no snow on them. Cyd opened the door and to her delight found Betty Little Horn standing on her front porch.

"Nice shiner," Betty observed, taking off her coat as she came inside.

Alex, watching from the kitchen, knew by now that no matter the occasion in cowboy country, you offered the visitor coffee. Betty took a sip from her cup and hesitated, searching for the right words.

"What is it?" Cyd asked.

"This isn't a social call," Betty began. "I don't know how to tell you this, but Maury left you something else."

"Something else?" Alex asked suspiciously.

"I wasn't supposed to give it to you unless everything got completely screwed up. I'd say this pretty much qualifies."

"Pretty much," Alex agreed.

Betty withdrew a small notepad from her pocket and handed it to Cyd. The corners were stained in blood. Cyd opened the cover and squinted at the barely legible handwriting as Alex leaned over her shoulder.

Cyd looked up helplessly. "I give up."

The notebook read:

N47 18 32

W12 46 18

Rock/Trees—Log

Alex blinked rapidly as an uninvited flashback made sparks behind his eyes. A filthy hut. American combat soldiers with flashlights huddled around a topographical map on a dirt floor, plotting their next movements . . . Iraqi advisors with automatic weapons sitting on their haunches, muttering inscrutably among themselves and pointing at the map. Dr. Alex Farmer close by in one corner . . . trying to save some poor kid's leg after he stepped on an IED.

"What does it mean?" Betty asked, shattering Alex's reverie. On Maury's instructions, and out of a sense of self-preservation, she had not opened the notebook. Now she couldn't contain herself.

"These are coordinates," Alex declared excitedly. "Latitude and longitude. A specific location." Then quickly to Betty, "Why the hell didn't you give us this before?"

"Because if I had, you two fools would have lost it just like you did everything else he left you. Maury died giving me this notebook and he told me to protect it. He said to hold it back, keep it as a fail-safe. He said, 'If this gets lost, everything is lost.' Those were his exact words. I was following orders and keeping it out of harm's way until you really needed it."

Cyd drew her into her arms. "You did good, girl, real good. He hid something up there for us, that's the important thing." She paused and brightened. "Can you guide us? Can you take us to the place where Maury was killed?"

Betty smiled. "Guiding I can do. Guiding is something I'm good at."

"Maybe we should wait and let things cool down a bit before we go rushing off," Alex cautioned.

Betty shook her head adamantly. "Whoever's out there isn't going away. Now or later isn't going to make any difference, not if this is as important as you say it is."

"Stay if you want," Cyd told Alex. "If I don't do this, I'll never feel safe again."

They're right, Alex thought. He was as anxious as they were to find what Maury had left them. His medical-and-military-trained mind was already making a list of the things they were going to need if they were going to come out of this alive. "I'm going into town," he announced abruptly.

Cyd frowned.

"Hunting and fishing is like a religion in Montana, right? I need a good hunting and fishing store."

Cyd looked at him like he was crazy. "You think this is some kind of vacation or something?"

"Just don't leave before I get back."

***

Alex walked rapidly up Last Chance Gulch toward a building with a tall, Romanesque façade of hand-hewn stone. The name 'Atlas' was chiseled into the building's round stone parapet five stories above the cobbled street—a street lined with tall, narrow stone buildings built on postage-stamp-size lots that began as mining claims; a street that wandered like an old man's memory through Helena's past; a river of dreams where men once panned for gold in the gutters and the mud of the wagon ruts.

Alex entered the Atlas Building, passing under a colorful wooden sign that hung from a granite arch and read:

MONTANA OUTFITTER
Camping, Hunting & Fishing Supplies

Minutes later, he came back out with his purchase: a digital, hand-held Global Positioning System device preloaded with one hundred thousand topographical maps. With this new GPS in hand, he could, in an instant, pinpoint his exact location anywhere in the U.S. no matter how remote. He had also bought the warmest jacket they had in the store—one that actually fit him. When he got back to his car, he flicked on the GPS and entered the coordinates from Maury's notepad. Tightly spaced elevation lines appeared instantly indicating steep terrain squiggled around barren peaks and along deep mountain valleys in dizzying swirls. He was staring at a vast, uninhabited wilderness and swallowed hard at the realization that he was headed straight into the heart of it.

Before leaving town, he needed to make one more stop—a pharmacy.

***

Betty helped Cyd tack up her two horses and load the saddlebags with supplies. Cyd jammed a rifle into the scabbards on both saddles. She didn't know how long it would take to find whatever it was they were looking for, or what would happen once they found it; so just to be on the safe side, she tied bed rolls behind the cantles on both their saddles. By the time she saw the red Jeep coming back down the drive, she and Betty had been ready to go for almost an hour.

Alex parked by the corral, got out, and walked toward them. This was the part he'd been dreading. He didn't know what to expect, but he knew it was going to hurt. Cyd handed him the reins to his horse. He hesitated before making his confession. "I don't know how to ride."

Cyd caught Betty's eye and rolled her eyes. "It's easy," she chided, gracefully swinging a leg over her horse. "Just hold on and don't fall off."

"Your little horse has been climbing these hills all her life," Betty assured him. "All you got to do is stay out of her way, and she'll take good care of you."

Alex groaned. There was a well-worn hat and a pair of chaps hanging off his saddle horn. Assuming they were for him, he awkwardly buckled on the chaps and tried on the hat. To his surprise it almost fit. He checked to make sure the GPS was safely tucked inside his parka and with an awkward effort managed to get on his horse.

They started off to the northwest, Betty in the lead on her spotted appaloosa with Alex following behind on the gray dun. Cyd brought up the rear on her solid black gelding, her hair hanging long and dark from underneath a black cowboy hat, a red bandanna tied around her neck. Turning in his saddle, Alex was so taken by the sight of her on her horse that for a moment he forgot about the beating his butt was taking bouncing along on the back of an animal that weighed over a thousand pounds.

***

The three men who had ambushed and murdered Maury felt no need to hurry or follow too closely. Resupplied and freshly mounted, they had a pretty good idea of where their three victims were headed, and they weren't going to make the same mistake twice. This time they would wait and watch and let their prey do the work for them before they made their move.

***

It seemed to Alex that they had been riding for days instead of hours. His back was killing him, and he was already exhausted. The sky was still clear, the sun was out, no fresh snow had fallen and what was left on the ground was soft and wet. They were on a gradual trail that rose and fell and twisted, climbing steadily alongside the Dearborn. High above them, the trees climbed ever steeper terrain until they were lost in the sky.

Betty led them to the place where she had left the trail with Maury to cross the river. She negotiated the busily flowing water and went up the bank on the other side. Alex hesitated, then urged his horse into the stream with Cyd watching to make sure he didn't fall off. He shivered as he looked down at his mare's feet dancing through the frozen water on shallow rocks. His horse bounded up the far bank, and knives of pain shot up his back. By the time they topped the trail and reached the clearing, Betty was waiting for them at the spot where Maury had died. Cyd got off her horse and squatted on her haunches. Reaching out, she tentatively touched the black bloodstains on the rocks and bowed her head.

Alex saw Betty getting down to stretch her legs and gratefully did the same, barely able to walk at first. He looked at his GPS and saw they were about two miles north of the Continental Divide where it runs along the spiny ridge of Scapegoat Mountain.

"The police helicoptered me up here so they could investigate the scene," Betty explained. "I only took them to here. Said this was where we were shot at. I don't know what happened when Maury went on up the trail, but I don't think he would have wanted me to take them there."

"No shit," Cyd agreed, grabbing a fist full of mane and making a little hop to catch the stirrup with her foot before swinging her other leg over the saddle.

Betty led them in the direction Maury had gone when he left her in the clearing. Alex kept his GPS out, checking their location as they went. Up ahead they could hear the river again. They came to the edge of a bluff, and he told them to hold up. A hundred yards below, the Dearborn was cascading furiously over big rocks that were hung in giant icicles.

Alex looked down again at his GPS, and with the flat edge of his hand, pointed at a small meadow at the bottom of the hill where a rock the size of a house stood beside the river. Behind the rock was a stand of aspen.

"Down there," he indicated, wagging his hand at the rock. "Betty, I want you to stay up here and keep watch."

Betty nodded and took up a position in the rocks where she could watch both the meadow below and the trail they had just come up at the same time.

Alex urged his horse over the cliff, then grabbed the saddle horn with both hands and held on for dear life as his horse slipped and slid down the slope on its hocks, skidding over the loosely frozen earth.

***

Maury had somehow managed to make it to the bottom of the same hill in one piece. He rode across the meadow and dismounted between the rock and the trees. Standing on tiptoe, he untied the leather thongs that held the collapsible camping shovel to the back of his saddle and unbuckled his saddlebags. Between the boulder and the aspen trees, he dug a hole. When it was deep enough to cover the saddlebags, he threw them in and stood back studying his work. It was the best he could do. He quickly filled the hole, patting the mound of fresh earth down with the back of his shovel when he was done. Then he spied a dead log and drug it over the top of the make-shift grave for good measure. From his parka pocket, he took out a GPS similar to the one Alex would later buy, got a reading on the location, and hurriedly scribbled the coordinates down in his notepad. Brushing the dirt and snow off his pants, he looked around for anything he might have missed. Satisfied, he struggled back onto his horse and started back up the hill.

His horse was climbing in mighty leaps and breathing hard. He was almost back to the top when three riders appeared out of the trees, reigning in on the trail on the far side of the river. One of them raised a high-powered hunting rifle to his shoulder and took careful aim. The target bounced around in his sites . . . his finger closed on the trigger . . . and the gun recoiled. The shot echoed up and down the river and the shooter's hand, tattooed on the back with a large black cross, levered another shell into the chamber.

The first bullet struck Maury in the shoulder and threw him forward in the saddle. His horse made one final leap to clear the top of the hill as another shot rang out and slammed into his back. The horse broke into a gallop with its barely conscious rider hanging off the saddle to one side.

The three riders realized they were trapped on the other side of the boulder-strewn river and couldn't make it across. They angrily wheeled their horses and spurred them back downstream to find another way across.

***

Cyd followed Alex's precarious descent down the hill, leaning back in the saddle and calmly sitting her horse as it picked and slid its way down the slippery slope.

Alex dismounted by the huge boulder, took out his GPS and read the screen as he turned slowly in a circle. The river was rushing loudly over the icy rocks, drowning out all sound. A few paces behind the big rock, he took another reading: 47° 18' 32" North, 112° 46' 18" West— it matched exactly. He was practically standing on the log Maury had drug over his hole. Reaching down, he pulled the deadfall aside. Underneath was a fresh mound of earth. He fell to his knees and began digging with his gloved hands. Cyd dropped down beside him and they dug furiously together. A foot down, they found the top of the hidden saddlebags.

"Eureka," Cyd cried.

Alex grinned. "Help me get it out."

They tugged hard, the saddlebags came free, and Cyd quickly brushed away the dirt with her hands. Together, like triumphant treasure hunters, they lifted the saddlebags in the air for Betty to see.

Betty, peeking out from behind her rocks, gave them a thumbs-up.

Alex opened one flap on the saddlebags, and Cyd tore at the buckles on the other. Almost simultaneously, they each pulled out two heavy leather pouches that were tied at the top with rawhide strings. They fumbled with the knots, and Cyd got hers untied first. Holding the big leather pouch under her arm like a beanbag, she poured out part of its contents into her hand, then stared in wonder at the mound of tiny rainbow-colored seeds that filled her palm.

A cry of excitement escaped her throat. "It's the Cannastar! It's the seeds. We've found them."

Alex opened his bag, peered inside and raised his eyes to the heaven in soft-spoken gratitude. "Thank you, Maury."

"Alex, this is the answer! We don't need the research; we have the seeds. These little puppies can reproduce themselves without any help from anyone. Maury's miracle isn't lost after all."

A look of anxiety crossed Alex's face. "I'll feel a lot better once we're off this mountain." Retying the pouches, he hurriedly stuffed them back in the saddlebags and threw them over his shoulder. "Come on, let's go."

Cyd was too thrilled to be scared. They mounted their horses and Alex led the way back up hill, his little mare climbing the slope like a tree squirrel. Cyd's black gelding bounded up behind him. When they reached the top, riders and horses were out of breath. Betty came out of hiding to join them.

"We found treasure!" Cyd beamed.

Betty turned away with a forlorn smile.

Cyd saw her sadness, reached down from her horse and put her hand on the normally-stoic woman's shoulder. "Maury didn't die for nothing, Betty. He did a brave thing. What he hid for us down there is beyond important."

Betty impatiently swiped at her eyes with her sleeve. "Good to know. We should get out of here."

Alex nodded in agreement and adjusted the weight of the saddlebags on his shoulder. Betty mounted her horse and together they rode back down the hill to the clearing. When they got there, Betty kept on going without looking back, immediately guiding her horse down the trail they had climbed earlier.

Alex called after her to hold up a minute.

Betty turned and saw that he and Cyd had stopped their horses in the place where Maury had bled out. She could see they were talking urgently, but she couldn't hear what they were saying.

"I've got a bad feeling about this," Alex was telling Cyd. "We shouldn't go back down the way we came up." His eyes were making little flashes of anxiety behind his eyelids and for a moment he was back in Iraq.

***

Alex's squad had just left the hut with two men carrying the wounded soldier he was tending. The plan was to backtrack the way they had come and go around the village by wading through a field flooded with sewage. It was the only safe way to get through a section reported to be heavily mined with IEDs. Laden down with medical supplies along with his field gear, Alex walked ahead, retracing his steps exactly . . . or so he thought. He didn't usually go on patrol. Most of his time he was needed in the hospitals, but it was a bloody surge and three medics had recently been killed in separate explosions. They were desperately shorthanded, and he had volunteered. Now he was very much regretting his decision.

Everything was mud brown, the houses were all bombed out, the neighborhood destroyed. It looked like the end of the world—only he didn't think the end of the world would look this bad. He was about to take a step when he stopped, staring down at a slight indentation in the dirt under his boot. Reeling backward, he raised his fist and shouted for a halt. His team froze.

The probing took an hour once the ordnance squad arrived. They set off a terrible explosion— right in the spot where, earlier, Alex was about to step. He watched from the distance, badly shaken. From that time on, he was known as Dr. Bigfoot. Alex didn't mind the nickname, it reminded him that maybe someone or something was watching over him and that maybe death wasn't as random as it seemed, that perhaps it wasn't arbitrary; that it might be a choice after all. The feeling of impending doom when he was about to put his foot down on the hidden bomb was one of the worst feelings he had ever had.

***

And the feeling he was having at the moment was the same. He shouted again to Betty to stop. Cyd didn't know what to make of it, but Alex's repeated warnings that they shouldn't go down the trail they had come up had her convinced that he might be right.

Betty spit tobacco juice from the corner of her mouth thinking she didn't believe in any of this candy-ass, touchy-feely, new-age psychic bullshit. "You two can catch up when you get cold and hungry enough," she called. "I'll be up ahead."

They watched her ride off.

Cyd frowned. "How long are we going to wait?"

Alex shook his head and shrugged.

The minutes crept by. Cyd squirmed impatiently in her saddle. Alex was still staring in the direction Betty had gone when they heard the crack of a rifle shot from below. Their horses shied and Alex grabbed at his reins.

Moments later, Betty came bursting out of the trees at a dead run, a bloody rip in her jacket sleeve, her arm hanging limp at her side. She reined in beside them breathing hard. "Maybe we should try another way down," she panted.

"What happened?" Alex demanded.

Cyd had her rifle out of the scabbard. "Anybody behind you?"

"Not exactly," Betty grinned, still trying to catch her breath. "They got, what you might say, delayed."

Alex was still trying to calm his horse. "By what?"

"Grizzly."

***

Back down the trail the armed men had been lying in wait.

Betty came around the bend, and one of them got overly excited and fired too soon. The bullet went through her arm, and she cried out in pain. The shot startled a giant grizzly bear that had been foraging upwind with her two cubs close behind where the three men were hiding. The cubs ran screaming for safety, and the sow rose up on her hind legs, howling like a banshee. The would-be assassins turned to see Mother Nature herself in all her fury towering over them in an avalanche of teeth and fur.

Holding her arm and looking back over her shoulder, Betty saw the three men climbing trees faster than she had thought men could climb. They looked like monkeys on a string being yanked into the branches by an invisible hand, scraping their hide off on the bark as they went. One of them, a lanky cowboy with half his teeth, wasn't fast enough. The bear caught his foot and hauled him back down, slashing him to death with her oversized claws. Blood from his wounds sprayed the ground like water from a garden hose.

"I like bears," Betty muttered to herself, spurring her horse back up the trail toward the clearing. "Always have, always will."

***

Betty led Cyd and Alex away from the clearing in the same direction she took to evade the attackers when Maury was killed. "Bear should keep the other two busy for a while," she remarked. The bullet wound in her shoulder was starting to throb and pain shot up her arm every time her horse jostled her in the saddle.

"Let me take a look at that arm," Alex called to her from behind.

"It's broke, what more do you want to know?"

They rode swiftly and before long were at the place where Betty had turned off the trail onto the rocks to ride up to her cave. Alex made her get down so he could tend to her injury and this time she didn't resist.

The bullet had gone through without hitting any major arteries. He cleaned and disinfected the wound as best he could, wrapping it in gauze from a small first aid kit that Cyd had brought along. Then he tore up his shirt and fitted her arm in a makeshift sling. His instructions were that the arm needed to be set and that she was to get herself to a hospital for x-rays as soon as possible.

The patient didn't argue. Instead, she quickly explained to them how to find the cave, pointing out landmarks under the sheer rock cliff above. "You won't be able to see the entrance until you're right on top of it," she added. "I'll head back down the mountain and leave a trail for them to follow. Those old boys are gonna be mighty pissed once that bear gets bored enough to wander off and they can come back down out of them trees. You two get on up there and hide. Protect what Maury left you, that's your job." She winced painfully as she got back on her horse. "Me, I'll just mosey on along home."

"What if they catch up to you?" Cyd asked anxiously.

"They won't catch me. They won't even see me. My grandfather was Crow Indian, you know, even if my mother was a Jew."

Cyd put her hand over her heart in sympathy as she watched her friend ride off. Further on up the trail, still holding her arm close to her side, she raised one cheek out of the saddle, and they heard her fart.

"That's just in case they can't follow my tracks," she remarked from a distance as she disappeared into the trees. "They can follow my scent."

Chapter Fourteen

Somewhere Safe

Smoke was being drawn back into the darkness of the cave toward an unseen vent far inside the mountain. Near the back of the dank cavern, the gelding was munching grain that Cyd had brought along and the mare was drinking from a small pool fed by a trickle of water that came out of the rock and made icicles as it ran down the stone. The horses seemed to know they needed to be quiet.

Alex watched Cyd turn sideways to get through the cave opening with a wide armload of deadfall, then drop the wood beside the fire he had built. She stood brushing loose bark from her arms, her lightly freckled cheeks flushed from the cold. Her beauty in that moment stunned him.

A sound like ragged breathing was coming out of the dark, and he nervously cocked his head to listen. "What are the chances there's a bear sleeping back there somewhere?" he asked.

"What are the chances you're afraid of the wind?" she laughed.

"I'm afraid of bears."

She sobered and quickly looked about. "This is more the kind of place where you would find mountain lions."

"You mean like the one behind you?"

Her eyes grew wide and she froze, then heard him laugh.

"Jerk," she retorted.

"What's for dinner?" he asked, rummaging through her saddlebags while trying to keep the pain off his face. The agony in his back after all the horseback riding was almost unbearable.

The freeze-dried beef and vegetable stew turned out to be delicious. Cyd brewed her Cannastar tea over the fire in their only pot and they sat together on top of their bed rolls talking with their saddles as backrests. The two pouches of Cannastar seeds lay safely between them. Cyd kept touching them as if to reassure herself they were real. Each time she did, they renewed her hope. Beyond the fire, like a banner of light in the dark, the mouth of the cave revealed a narrow vertical strip of brilliant stars.

Alex adjusted his sitting position, grimacing in pain in an effort to get comfortable.

"You all right?" she asked.

"Never better." He didn't know when or how it had happened, but as a doctor, he had become as passionate about the seeds as she was. He stared openly at her, marveling at her tenacity and courage.

Fascinated, she met his gaze and stared back until she remembered the urgency of their situation and looked away. "Alex, I'm frightened. How do we keep the seeds a secret? How are we going to keep them safe?"

"I don't know. You got any more friends around here you can trust?"

A long pause. He loved that it took her forever to say anything; it gave him more time to admire her.

She sat up suddenly and brightened. "I do, actually. Not here, but . . . on the other side of here. Can I see your GPS a minute?"

Alex handed her the global positioning device he had used to locate Maury's hiding place. She bounded to her feet, stepped outside the cave entrance for better reception and began scrolling through the topographical maps on the screen. Finding and enlarging the one she was looking for, she brought the brightly lit screen back inside for Alex to see.

"This is how we go," she told him, tracing a route west with her finger and scrolling north as she went. "We follow this valley, see? That connects with this other valley here. We cross the river . . . about here, I think, and that leads us eventually to Pablo."

"Who's Pablo?"

"Pablo is a town. The seat of government for the Flathead Nation."

"You know someone there?"

"You might say that." She touched his hand in excitement and a current of electricity went up his arm. "We need a place where nobody can find us, right? Somewhere safe where we can get these seeds in the ground and make them grow?"

"You saying we just show up on an Indian reservation in the middle of winter and start a farm?"

"The Flathead Reservation is covered in beautiful grassland and the Salish Indians are gracious people. They'll hide us until we can figure out what to do."

"I hope so, because I have a feeling this cave might have plumbing and heating problems."

A slow grin lit her face. "The seeds, Alex! We actually have the seeds!"

He smiled at the irony of his own newfound passion over the seeds. "I'm already starting to regret this." He saw her mood darken and asked softly, "What is it?"

Tears began running down her cheeks in long wet lines. "I'm sorry. It's just . . . Maury. Everything that's happened. How cruel and selfish people can be. It's all . . . it's just so sad, you know?"

He gathered her in his arms, rocking her gently. "I know, I know. It shouldn't be like this, but it is . . . it is."

She fell asleep in his arms and he held her a long time, afraid to move for fear of disturbing her. His tortured back was so inflamed that he had to bite his lip to keep from crying out. When he was certain she was sound asleep, he eased her down gently onto her bedroll and stood to build up the fire. Staring into the flames, he took from his pocket the bottle of OxyContin he had bought at the pharmacy in town and began rolling it around in his hand.

There were a lot of reasons why he shouldn't take the narcotic pain-killer, all of them good. Unfortunately, his back and his addiction had even better ones. Long hard day tomorrow, he thought. Got to sleep, have to sleep . . . this is what they're for . . . one can't hurt . . . not like I'm starting up again. Then berating himself he argued, one hour at a time, one hour at a time. And later, when he could stand it no longer: just one . . . one can't hurt. Then, no-no-no . . . I can't, I can't do it . . .

He carried on this way for what seemed like hours before lying down beside Cyd for warmth and carefully pulling the blanket back over them both. She snuggled close in her sleep and smiled.

The pain was jamming daggers in his back. It felt like it was being barbequed over hot coals. He reached for his pills, eased off the cap, shook two out and quickly tossed them down his throat. Soon after, a warm stillness came over him, and, in the calm of the immense relief, he felt his eyes grow heavy.

Out of the darkness something silky soft was nuzzling at his cheek, and hot breath was blowing on his face. He came out of a sound sleep with a start, staring up at the enormous muzzle of his horse who was nudging him with her nose. A fresh pain shot up his back.

Cyd couldn't help laughing. "Your horse is trying to tell you you're burnin' daylight."

"Easy for her to say."

Rubbing at his eyes, he saw Cyd bent over a blazing fire blissfully brewing her tea and cooking powdered eggs and Canadian bacon. Every joint in his long lanky body ached from sleeping on the cold stone floor.

"Coffee?" she offered.

He managed a smile as she handed him a steaming cup. His mind was still repeating the mantra from last night that he was never going to take the pain pills again, not after all that had happened. Just let me get through today, he thought. Then I'll go back to not taking them.

Seeing his discomfort, Cy grew concerned. "If you're thinking about getting your pants on and getting out of here, be my guest."

He looked around at the water dripping from the stone walls. "After all you've done to decorate the place? I'm staying. This is home."

"So, you don't mind that I went out and bought curtains?"

"I knew I shouldn't have left my credit card with you."

Relieved that he wasn't going to abandon her, she began rapidly packing up their things. "Credit card or no credit card, if you're not ready to go in ten minutes, I'm leaving without you."

"How long you figure it will take us to get there?"

"Two days, if the weather holds."

Inwardly, he withered at the thought of what two more days in the saddle would do to his back. He waited until Cyd was busy saddling the horses and took another pill. Just until this is over, he promised himself. Just until then.

***

It was a long hard ride over rugged terrain. The wind blew cold, but the sky stayed clear. Crossing the Continental Divide, the trail was so steep and narrow Alex was afraid to look down. Cyd rode ahead on her coal black horse, steadfast and silent, her red bandana a beacon light leading the way. According to his GPS, they were making less than three miles an hour.

The vastness of the land overwhelmed him. It was as if man had never existed—and in this place, perhaps he never had. An eagle circled overhead, motionless on an updraft, rising almost a thousand feet in what seemed like seconds. Once he saw a bull elk moving off in the distance, the width of its horns wider than the span of his rifle. Down valley, wolf pups were yipping in their den, hungry for the kill. The wind conducted an orchestra in the trees on a keyboard made of ragged mountains. And the sky—always the sky—its pregnant belly swollen blue with light over a wilderness where life and death were all the same to something larger than a man could know.

They rode northwest along the southern boundary of the Bob Marshall Wilderness and, after a long descent to the valley below, crossed the South Fork of the Flathead River an hour before sundown. Alex had the feeling they were being watched and for the thousandth time that day turned in his saddle to look over his shoulder and saw nothing.

They made camp at Big Salmon Lake next to a meadow where there was enough brown grass still poking up between patches of snow that the horses could feed. It was as safe a place as any to spend the night. They had been traveling almost twelve hours and had come a little over thirty miles. In hospitals in the Middle East and stateside where he had worked, Alex was used to pushing himself beyond exhaustion. This was harder than that.

Dark storm clouds were building to the north as Cyd unpacked their things and spread out their bedrolls in the failing light. Alex had taken another pill along the trail, but the effects of it had worn off and the pain was getting worse by the minute. He saw Cyd on her knees digging a coiled fishing line and a tiny can of corn out of her saddlebag, then watched as she slumped forward in fatigue. He took the fishing gear out of her hand and helped her to lie down on the blanket.

"I have to catch us a fish for supper," she protested.

"Why don't you let me give it a try. You stay here and rest."

"Just bait the hook with the corn and . . ." Her smile faded, her eyelids fluttered, and she was sound asleep.

Alex covered her with the blanket, laid her rifle next to her and picked up his own rifle before heading down to the lake. He went no further than the edge of the water where he could keep an eye on her sleeping form.

To his utter astonishment, he caught a two-pound trout on his first cast. Hauling it in over the shallow rocks flopping and thrashing, he noticed its sides were almost as colorful as the Cannastar seeds in the leather pouches.

Cyd awoke an hour later to a warm fire and the smell of fish cooking on a stick propped over the flames. Suddenly, she was famished. Alex cut up a potato and fried it in their pan and they feasted on greasy potatoes and trout, gingerly pulling the hot meat away from the stick with their fingers and drinking from a flask of whiskey that she had thought to stick in her pack at the last minute.

Cyd smiled with grease running down her chin. "Thanks for dinner."

"If you like my trout, wait until you taste my pheasant."

She laughed and he reached over with their dishtowel and wiped at the corners of her mouth. It was a fine party.

Afterward, they sat contentedly watching the campfire with their bellies warm with food. The pain in Alex's back was relentless, but watching Cyd's lively emotions play out across her face and her dark hair spill over her shoulders took his mind off it.

The wind picked up and the flames bent sideways, sending sparks up into the air. Alex scanned the darkness, unable to shake the feeling that they were being watched. Beyond the fire the forest moved with darkened sounds and restless ripples marred the lake.

"We should take turns standing guard," he cautioned, checking to make sure his rifle was close at hand and loaded. "I'll take the first watch."

"Merry Christmas," she murmured, lying back and closing her eyes. It was Christmas Eve.

He came to his feet stifling a groan. His back felt like someone was trying to cut it in half with a rusty hacksaw. He took the bottle of Oxy-Contin out of his pocket, opened it and in one swift movement popped a pill in his mouth—just as Cyd's eyes fluttered open.

Suddenly she was staring in wide-eyed concern. "What are you doing?" she demanded. "What is that?"

"Just something for my back."

"Your back?"

"Pain pills. Why, what's wrong?"

She stood and snatched the bottle out of his hand, reading the prescription label in horror. "My mother died from an overdose of this poison, that's what's wrong."

"I . . . I didn't know. I'm sorry."

The pill bottle fell from her hand as she walked off in despair. Beyond the firelight she stopped, staring in desolation at something only she could see.

He moved to her side. "Cyd?"

"Leave me alone!" Terrible memories flashed through her mind. Nine-year-old Cyd padding softly into her parent's bedroom to wake her mother because it's late and she's going to miss the school bus. Her mother lying in bed on her back, cold and still and deathly white. Her father beside her on his back. Motionless. Staring up at the ceiling and hyperventilating. Cyd shaking her mother by the arm and calling her name. Screaming "Motherrrrrr!" with her father just lying there breathing fast. Shouting through her tears for him to do something. Pounding on her mother with her tiny fists, then running to the bathroom to get some water to wake her up. Seeing the empty pill bottle rolling around on the tile floor. Fumbling with the phone to call 911 and sobbing into the receiver. Paramedics, firemen, police—huge men in uniform crowding her parent's tiny bedroom, trying to revive her dead mother. The sound of their awful voices: ". . . must of swallowed the whole bottle and then slipped into bed so's not to wake him . . . just laid down beside the poor bastard and died without making a sound . . . damn." A blur of bodies blocking her view. Rough hands pushing her, pulling her, restraining her. "Looks like the wife got the last word in after all." Hearing their terrible laughter. Another voice adding, "Women usually do." Then more laughter.

Standing motionless in the forest beyond the flickering fire, Cyd remembered how her father never showed any emotion after that. How he never spoke of the suicide again. She was that little girl again, with all the same emotions.

Alex's voice brought her back. "I was in a car accident," he was saying. "All this jarring on the horse, it's killing my back."

She nodded absently.

He took her gently by the arm. "Come back to the fire and let me explain. Please."

Cyd let him lead her to a log beside their campfire and ease her down on it. Her face was a blank.

"Before I came to Montana, I was in rehab," he began. "To get over taking pain pills."

"And you're right back on them again." Her voice was a distant monotone.

"Cyd, it's not a problem, believe me."

She looked up with sad eyes. "I don't . . . I can't."

In halting sentences, he told her about the car wreck. It hurt as much to tell it as it did to live it, but he made himself recount it anyway. How it was one of those torrential downpours in LA. How the other car crossed over the line and hit him almost head on. How it was lying laid up in the hospital for days with the pain in his back at an eleven on a scale of one to ten. "Doctors make the worst patients," he confessed. "If I was ever going to get out of there and get back to work, I was going to have to take the narcotics they were offering me. Innocent enough decision. One that thousands of people make every day." He drew a breath and went on. "The addiction, it wasn't like I planned it. I didn't set out to become a drug addict, Cyd. Pain pills sneak up on you that way."

She nodded like she understood but couldn't shake the feeling there was something he wasn't telling her.

He avoided her eyes. If omission was a lie, then he was lying. He hadn't told her the worst of it—the part about his wife being in the car with him when they wrecked.

"Why do men have to be so macho?" It was like she was asking herself.

"I wasn't being macho," he argued. "Well . . . a little, maybe."

"You could have told me you were in pain, at least."

"Would that have changed anything?"

She looked exasperated, got up, went to the fire and poured out a boiling cup of Cannastar. "Try this," she instructed, shoving the cup in his hands.

He looked down and then back up. "I don't want to take your tea."

"Just drink it, all right?"

He obediently took a sip. It tasted sweet, like licorice. "You think this might help?"

"The marijuana you get in stores and the kind street dealers sell helps with neuropathic and neuromuscular pain. Cannastar should amp that a thousand times over, especially if your injury is to your central nervous system. It was one of Maury's theories that he never got to test. That makes you the guinea pig, I guess."

He smiled and took another drink, a big one this time. It scalded his throat going down. Then bending, he picked up the bottle of pain pills from where she had dropped it and held it out to her. "Here, take these. Do with them what you want."

She recoiled. "Get away from me with those things."

Impulsively, he threw the bottle in the fire, then watched as the flames licked around the plastic and it began to melt. "I was quit before. I'm twice as quit now."

Chapter Fifteen

Big Foot

In the morning they awoke to thunder. To the north the pale morning sky was under attack by jagged lightning strikes that were electrocuting the air. The horses, tied to stakes in the meadow, pulled against their halters. They hurriedly packed their things to try and get on the trail and stay ahead of the storm. Cyd's tea was brewing on the fire. When it was ready, she poured out a cup for him.

He blew on the hot, sweet-smelling liquid. "I'm sorry about your mother. It must have been rough."

She didn't respond.

The storm broke at noon. Thunder exploded so close overhead that Alex Ducked. They hurried off the mountain under a boiling sky, skirting the little town of Condon and crossing Highway 83 just as the sky opened up and started to pour. Their horse's hooves made a hollow clicking sound on the slick, two-lane blacktop. A trailer-tractor rig screamed by, throwing sheets of water at their startled horses. Rain ran down off the brims of their hats and pattered on their leather chaps. They reined in under a tree to let the squall pass.

Alex remembered the hellish nightmare of trying to get off the pain killers the first time. How he had fought the people who were trying to help him, and how he wasn't willing to admit he even had a problem. And later, deep in the throes of withdrawal, swearing if he ever survived, he would kill himself before going through this again. He realized if Cyd hadn't stopped him, he would have been right back in rehab—or more likely laid out on Otis's stainless steel table. He'd been kidding himself that he could handle it, that taking a few pills wouldn't make a difference and the minute he got to wherever the hell they were going he would stop.

"Amazing what suckers we are for our own bullshit, " he muttered aloud.

"What?" Cyd asked over the sound of the rain.

A feeling of gratitude welled up in him for what she had done—followed by a stab of fear for what he might now be facing without the pills. Then suddenly he realized today wasn't like yesterday. He wasn't about to pass out from the pain, and it was actually tolerable at the moment. He tested his back by cautiously shifting his weight in the saddle and miraculously it no longer felt like he was being tortured with hot tongs.

"Cyd," he cried. "Guess what?"

She was struggling with her own emotions and didn't hear. Was she starting to have feelings for this man? "I don't know," she answered vaguely. "I just don't know."

"Well, it's amazing is all I can say!"

"Is it?"

They were both shivering.

"How long before we're there?" he asked. When she didn't answer he added, "Hope your friends, the Indians, at least know how to build a fire."

"So now you're a racist, is that it?"

"Wanting to be warm and dry is not racist!"

***

Late in the afternoon, they reached the outskirts of the reservation. A light snow had begun to fall that was dusting the flat terrain and turning it white. They rode numb and silent past depressing hovels with old tires and garbage strewn in the yards, past worn-out single-wide trailers sitting bleached and broken on cinderblock foundations. Cyd rode steadily on, shoulders slumped, head down. Alex urged his horse up alongside her, but she did not look over.

The rutted road turned into a smoothly graded gravel lane, and before long they were riding through a sprawling subdivision of five-acre lots. The farther they went, the more prosperous the homes became. Wooden structures turned into brick residences with swing sets, soccer nets, and abandoned toys in the yards. Most of the houses had a large RV and/or an expensive boat on a trailer parked beside the garage. The pastures were fenced in neat rectangles and many had little barns where horses were grazing or standing motionless with half-closed eyes. Cyd's relentless pace had Alex thinking she might have fallen asleep in the saddle.

And then they came to it.

Up ahead was a house of colossal proportions. It sat in the center of twenty acres on a grassy knoll that rose sharply from the land around it and was a wonder to behold. Fashioned from large, white, flat-roofed cubes jumbled together at startling angles, it formed a modern mosaic of glass and steel that might have gone well in Los Angeles or the Hamptons, but here in Montana on an Indian reservation, it looked about as much at home as a whale in a goldfish bowl.

The chaotic structure grew larger as they rode up a long drive that was bordered on either side by a clean white fencing. Dogs began to bark as they approached. A garage with a dozen overhead doors flanked the near side of the house. On the far side was a separate cubical attached to the house by a long glass passageway. Mirrored walls could be seen through tall glass windows that reflected a hardwood dance floor. Ballet bars ran around the inside of the cube and ropes of pine boughs decorated with brightly colored Christmas balls hung down in graceful loops from the ceiling.

The barking stopped as a robust man in shorts, sandals, and a Hawaiian shirt opened the front door and stepped out into the falling show. He was about sixty, six feet two inches tall, two hundred and twenty pounds, and had a ponytail nearly as long and black as the one on Cyd's horse. With his dark skin, high cheek bones and Hawaiian shirt he looked more Polynesian than anything else. When he saw Cyd, he beamed broadly, spread his arms and let out what sounded to Alex like a war whoop. She jumped from her horse and ran into his arms where he scooped her up and tossed her in the air like she was a rag doll.

"Cydney! You stay away too long!" he shouted. "Skinny as ever, I see. My wife, she'll fix that. You brought a friend. What did you do to him? He looks terrible."

"Clarence, this is Alex Farmer. Alex, meet Clarence Big Foot."

"Pleasure," he said, stiffly dismounting his horse.

Clarence extended the arm that was currently holding up Cyd's bottom—he had to adjust her weight to keep from dropping her—and vigorously shook Alex's hand. For a gregarious man in a loud shirt, he had a surprisingly gentle handshake. Alex reached to help him with his burden. "You need a hand with that?"

"I got it," Clarence boomed, playfully carrying Cyd through the front door and depositing her inside. "Come in, come in, the both of you . . . Mary!" he called. "Guess who's come to visit?" Then in a stage whisper to Cyd, "Watch this. She'll have a heart attack."

There was a scream of delight as a tall, willowy white woman in her mid-fifties swept down the hall to give their guest a big hug. She was wearing dance clothes and had her graying hair pulled back severely into a bun. She kissed Cyd's face and cheek and head, then held her at arm's length to admire her as the two of them started chattering excitedly.

Alex glanced back through the open front door in time to see a sullen, wrinkle-faced old man dressed in insulated bib overalls appear to take away their horses. It was a point of honor with the old man that he administrate all things concerning the livestock on the estate. Alex went back out for the saddlebags containing the seeds, and he and the old man had a small tug of war before the ancient guardian grudgingly gave them up.

He came back in with the saddlebags over his shoulder in time to hear Mary say excitedly, "We're having a Christmas party tonight. And Cyd, dear, Robert is invited. I hope that's all right?"

Cyd hesitated. "Sure, I guess."

The entry hall was decorated with a Christmas tree large enough to accommodate the full-size toys hanging from its branches. To make room for the tree, a modern sculpture of a human torso, its appendages contorted in positions more suited to a body that had fallen off a roof, had been pushed to one side. Alex looked back trying to make sense of the statue as they were ushered into a high-ceilinged living room where colorful oil and acrylic canvases of incomprehensible shapes and swirls rioted along the walls. Floor-to-ceiling windows looked out on a vast, fertile valley dotted with cattle ranches. A gas log fire burned brightly behind a piece of fireproof glass mounted on a solid wall of cold hard marble. Alex stood with his back to it but could feel no heat. "Quite a house," he remarked to Clarence.

Big Foot grinned proudly. "Like it? My wife just got done redecorating it for the third time."

"It's . . . really something," Alex agreed.

"How far have you come?" the Indian asked, eyeing their bedraggled, stressed, exhausted condition now with some concern.

"From Helena," Cyd replied.

Mary was appalled. "At this time of year? In this weather?"

"It wasn't like we had a choice," Cyd replied bitterly.

"Whatever kind of trouble you're in, you can tell me about it later," Clarence told her, encircling them both with his fatherly arms and guiding them toward a clear plastic staircase that hung suspended from the ceiling by steel cables. "Right now, you're going to have a hot bath and a good meal, and tonight you're going to sleep in a real bed."

Alex smiled gratefully. "If I'm not up in a week, come and get me."

Clarence took them upstairs to a bedroom where they could clean up and rest before dinner. Cyd pushed a button and a drape descended like a theater curtain over a glass wall of windows, coming to rest above a window seat of gray concrete decorated with colorful throw pillows. Alex went into the marble bathroom and turned the water on in the whirlpool bath, then came back out while the tub was filling. Cyd was shedding her damp clothes and throwing them on the chair where Alex had hung the saddlebags.

"How do you know these people?" Alex asked her, gratefully pulling off his wet socks.

The only sound was the running bath water. Then, "I used to be engaged to their son."

"You broke up with their boy, and they still treat you like their daughter?"

"He broke up with me. Clarence and Mary are family." She paused. "Just like Maury was family." Steam was coming out of the bathroom. She went in and locked the door behind her.

"Take as long as you want," Alex said through the door . . . wishing it was him and not her in there—or better yet that they were enjoying the bath together.

When she came back out, he was asleep on the bed. She shook him awake and watched as he got up and went into the bathroom. He was clearly in pain.

"I'll fix you some more tea when we go downstairs," she offered.

He wanted to kiss her.

While he was letting the hot water jets massage his back, she came blithely into the bathroom. He scrambled to cover himself with his washcloth as she entered the little room that enclosed the toilet and closed the door behind her. Through the door he asked her where Clarence had gotten his money.

"Software engineer," she answered, her voice somewhat muffled. "He worked in Silicon Valley during the early '80s and ended up founding his own company. In the late '80s he sold the company for something like eighty million. Since then he's built a hospital and a school for his people, and in his spare time started a new software business that does something, I'm not sure what, for the defense department. It employs most of the people in the subdivision that we rode through on our way to the house."

***

Big Foot's festively decorated dining hall echoed like a sports arena. Cyd and Alex walked in after three days of camping out, and the smell of hot cooked food nearly overwhelmed their senses. Friends and relatives milled about an organically shaped metal table that stretched thirty feet or more, its burnished surface piled with holiday fare. High-backed chairs made of metal rods and fitted with small, black, hard-leather seats ran down either side of the tabletop looking like they needed seatbelts for the rigid business of sitting—which may have explained why the guests were still standing.

Alex was introduced around to the guests. Most were baptized Roman Catholic with Christian names, but, at family gatherings, used their traditional names. There was cousin *Hethonton* (Towering Antlers) and his two sons, *Hebazhu* (Little Antlers) and *Heshabe* (Dark Antlers), known respectively as Doug, Tom. Bill Medicine Horse was the local vet. Uncle *Demonthin* (Talks As He Walks) looked like a tottering bowling pin and his wife, aunt *Watewin* (Victory Woman) was short and round and looked like a formidable bowling ball. Cousin *Shonge* (Wolf), his wife, *Zitkala* (Bird), their son, *Shongesabbe* (Black Wolf) and daughter, *Zitkalatu* (Blue Bird) were a close-knit family that hung together and talked softly only among themselves. The names all ran together in Alex's head and more were arriving by the minute. He smiled and shook hands until he finally gave up trying to keep them all straight. Clarence Big Foot was known on these festive occasions as *Wekushton* (One Who Gives Feast Frequently) and Mary was called *Donama* (The Sun Visible to All).

Alex thought his hosts made the perfect couple. Mary was dressed in a Santa Fe-style skirt with a silver Concho belt, colorful blouse, and turquoise jewelry. Apart from the obligatory ponytail that most of the men wore, she was the only person in the room who had made an effort to adorn herself with anything even remotely ethnic. She and her husband were clearly devoted to one another—with the tacit understanding that she was the boss. Perhaps, as Cyd explained later, her tendency to take charge was because she had been a prima ballerina with the San Francisco Ballet. "Or maybe it's just because she was brought up to believe that no man is her master," she added with a sanctimonious sniff. In any case, the understanding was clear, and Clarence was fine with it. He doted on his family and preferred spending his time thinking about his software business and his community work rather than thinking up new ways to order his wife around. His egalitarian view of women rankled the other members of his clan who held their tongues out of respect for the fact that he was "the richest son of a bitch in the valley," but privately disagreed with his policy of never disciplining his wife.

While Alex was meeting everyone, Cyd went into the kitchen and brewed some of her tea for him. He drank it down and felt an immediate relief wash over him. It was like being granted early release from the dentist's chair.

He noticed that someone had been staring at Cyd ever since they walked in, and now that someone was walking toward them. Alex didn't usually give much thought one way or the other to another man's looks, but even he could see that this fellow was spectacularly handsome. He was about Cyd's age with the same hair color down to the same length, high cheekbones, six feet tall and gifted with brilliant teeth with which he smiled brilliantly at all the guests. Cyd introduced him as Clarence's son, Robert. He shook Alex's hand without taking his eyes off Cyd.

Alex took an immediate dislike to him. "You a Flathead too?" he asked.

"We call ourselves Salish," Robert smiled, ignoring Alex while continuing to stare into Cyd's eyes. "It means 'The People.' My dad said you've been on the trail for days, Cyd. How can you still look so beautiful?"

"Robert is a geologist," she explained uncomfortably. "We used to go together, but that was ages ago. He works for the different tribes now, helping them develop the natural resources on their lands. Oil and gas, that sort of thing." She seemed captivated by his stare. "We haven't seen each other in—how long is it, Robert?"

"Two years, thirteen months."

That really is some smile, Alex thought. I'd like to break his teeth for him.

At the dinner table, Alex sat on one side of Cyd, Robert on the other. Every time her former boyfriend made her laugh, Alex wanted to strangle him. Down at the other end of the table, sitting next to Mary, was an emaciated girl about five years younger than Cyd who kept coughing into her napkin. She was a long-legged, bird-like creature with tiny bones that looked like they might snap in a high wind. Her hair lay dull and lifeless against her skull. She had once been a striking beauty with flowing raven-black hair, prettier even than her mother at her age when Mary was an aspiring ballerina. Now she was pale and sickly and far too thin. Alex noted her condition, but mostly what he saw was her sadness. He asked Cyd about her.

"That's Robert's sister Tiffany. Her real name is *Washudse* which means Wild Rose, but she hates everything Indian." She looked off and looked back. "Tiffany has HIV."

After dinner, Clarence offered Alex a cigar and they went out onto the terrace to smoke them. Alex was surprised after their long trip over the mountains that the cool air could feel this good. His host, dressed in different shorts and a different Hawaiian shirt from earlier in the day, seemed invigorated by the cold as well.

"Bigfoot was my nickname in the military," Alex told his host, by way of making conversation.

Clarence nodded thoughtfully. "What did it mean, exactly?"

"That I'm careful where I step."

Clarence studied his guest while puffing on his cigar. Alex wasn't sure that he hadn't said something to offend him. Finally, the playful man in the Hawaiian shirt said solemnly, "Careful Where He Steps. It is a good name. I think you wear it well."

"How do you say it in Salish?"

"I don't know, I only speak English."

For some reason they both found this funny and they laughed, and in that moment they became fast friends.

Chapter Sixteen

Ghosts of Lovers Past

It was late morning by the time Alex and Cyd made their way back downstairs to the kitchen. When they came in, Lupe, the cook, was setting out large pots of water on the black granite countertop and pouring different kinds of beans into them to soak in preparation for making her famous seven-bean soup. Lupe was a good-natured, hard-working woman who, despite being Hispanic and not Salish, was considered a member of the family. She stopped what she was doing and cordially made them breakfast, informing them that Mary was in her studio teaching a dance lesson, and that Mr. Big Foot would like to see them in his office when they were done eating.

Cyd made them both tea. Alex accepted his eagerly, took a sip and smiled in genuine gratitude. "I don't know how to thank you for this."

She smiled sadly. "Thank Maury."

They walked together down a glassed-in hallway. Alex had the saddlebags containing the seeds over his shoulder. The hallway led to another of the seemingly endless cubes that made up the house. They came to a door that was slightly ajar and Cyd knocked softly.

Clarence, talking on the phone in his office, waved them in and motioned them into a pair of ergonomic chairs in front of his desk. He wore yet another Hawaiian shirt, this one adorned with hibiscus blossoms. While they waited for him to finish his conversation, they looked out his high wall of office windows at the vertical rise of daunting mountains east of the reservation that they had crossed the day before.

The office itself was a wonder of technological gadgetry. An array of computer monitors hung above a massive circular desk that was piled with jumbled papers. Bookshelves overflowed with technical manuals carelessly propped up by pictures of Clarence Big Foot shaking hands, standing and smiling with various politicians, presidents and celebrities. Against one wall, between the door to the bathroom and a remarkably life-like, life-size bronze of an attacking bear, was a tall black gun safe with gold pinstriping and a digital combination lock.

Clarence laughed at something the caller said. "Thanks for your help, Sam. See you at the fundraiser." He chuckled again and hung up. "That was your uncle in Washington. The Senator is helping me with government financing for a new hydroelectric plant over in Missoula that's going to provide income and electricity for the tribe forever. It's amazing what a hundred-thousand-dollar campaign contribution will buy you. I told him you arrived here safe and sound, and that I was taking good care of you."

"Fuck," Cyd swore under her breath.

Clarence looked puzzled. "Excuse me?"

"I really wish you hadn't said that."

"He was worried about you," Clarence insisted. "He said you disappeared four days ago without a trace. People at his ranch were afraid you might have gotten lost in the mountains or something. His son apparently sent men out looking for you. Sam was delighted when I told him you were all right." He saw that Cyd was still alarmed. "What is it, dear heart? You can tell me."

"Sam Seeley isn't who you think he is."

"He's your uncle, Cyd. He's only looking out for your best interest . . ."

Alex shook his head. "I'm afraid that's not all he's looking for."

Clarence was rapidly losing patience "All right, out with it. What are you two being so secretive about?"

Cyd picked up their saddlebags from the floor between their chairs and held them out for their host to see. "We need a place to hide this."

Clarence stood and came around his desk, relieved that there was something he could do. "That's easy." He crossed the room to his gun safe, punched in the combination and swung open the door. Inside was his collection of frontier firearms, all in good working order. "Good enough?" he asked proudly. "The man who sold me this safe said it was guaranteed burglarproof *and* fireproof."

Cyd kissed him on the cheek before placing the saddlebags in the safe, doubling them over so they would fit inside.

Clarence closed and locked the door and gave them the combination in case they needed to get into it when he wasn't around. Then going back to his desk, he sat down and ceremoniously folded his arms over his chest. "I'm waiting."

Alex shook his head. "Better that you don't know."

"The seeds in those saddlebags can give your daughter her life back," Cyd blurted suddenly.

Clarence searched her face, trying to divine her meaning. "That would be . . . a miracle. Have you brought us a miracle, Cydney?"

They spent the next hour telling their host how Maury had bioengineered a cure for cancer and been killed for his efforts, how they themselves had been arrested, chased, attacked and almost killed trying to protect it, how and why they ended up on his doorstep in the condition they were in looking for help.

Clarence listened intently. When they were done, he sat digesting what he had just heard. "Seeds," he mused. "I get it. You don't need the blueprint if you've got the building."

"It's probably best if you let me tell Tiffany about the Cannastar," Cyd advised. "She needs to know there's a possibility it might not work for her."

"But it will," Clarence insisted excitedly. "I know it will."

"We'll see," Cyd smiled. "I certainly hope so."

Clarence sobered. The more he thought about their story, the more upset he became. "If your suspicions are true . . . I mean, I knew Sam Seeley worked for the drug industry. Hell, he works for anybody that pays him, but never in a million years did I suspect . . . My God, what have I done?"

"You didn't know," Alex consoled. "Any more than you knew that we were probably followed here."

Cyd looked at him sharply. "Why do you say that?"

"Just a hunch."

"I believe Careful Where He Steps has good hunches," Clarence observed admiringly. "What can I do? How can I help?"

"We need someplace to go where we can't be found," Cyd agonized. "Somewhere nobody would think to look. The only way these seeds are going to be of any good to anyone is if we can get them in the ground and grow them without getting killed or caught. I was hoping maybe . . ."

Big Foot put his foot down. "Try and grow your Cannastar here on the reservation and you might as well cultivate the land around the police station. This place is practically Times Square it's so heavily traveled in the summer. You'd get busted in a heartbeat."

"I was afraid of that," Alex sighed. "At least we're safe for now."

Cyd look out window in desolation at the winter landscape. "What does it feel like, to be safe I mean? Frankly, I forget."

That afternoon, Alex found himself still tired from his ordeal on horseback and went upstairs to take a nap. Two hours later he awoke with a start, got up and went to the bedroom window rubbing at his eyes. Looking out through the fading light, he saw it had begun to snow again. Then something down by the swimming pool caught his attention.

Cyd was just coming out of the pool house—a white cabana with double French doors at either end. Robert came out of the pool house behind her and they stopped to talk.

Steam rose from the heated water, enveloping them in a mist, as impossibly large snowflakes drifted down and stuck in Cyd's dark hair. The snowflakes gave her the devout look of wearing a white veil in a snowy church. They stood close together, too close as far as Alex was concerned, and there was an urgency to the way Robert was speaking to her. As he watched, Cyd nodded solemnly, stood on tiptoe and kissed her companion. Then fondly caressing the side of his face with the back of her hand, she walked away.

Alex heard the door to the main house open and close. He hurried out of the bedroom and intercepted her at the bottom of the stairs just as she was starting up.

"What's new?" he asked, trying to sound casual.

"Nothing," she sighed. "Just old business."

"I saw you and Robert out by the pool. He looked pretty intense."

"He wanted us to get back together. He said he'd made a big mistake breaking up with me."

"That so? And what did you say?"

She paused to study him. "Alex Farmer, I do believe you're jealous."

"I'm not jealous, I'm a doctor!"

She turned and danced up the stairs like a delightfully precocious child, mocking him in a sing-song voice. "Jealous Doc-tor Far-mer. Liked a girl and couldn't tell her."

Chapter Seventeen

Tagged and Bagged

It took a lot of convincing the next morning, but Tiffany finally agreed to go along with Mary and Cyd on a trip to Missoula to do some after-Christmas shopping. The trip was Mary's idea, and she was determined that the two girls she loved most in the world should come with her. Cyd thought it might be the perfect opportunity to break the news to them about the Cannastar as a possible treatment, if not cure, for Tiffany's debilitating virus.

Mary loaded Cyd and Tiffany into her new green Range Rover with the cream-colored leather upholstery—a Christmas present from her adoring husband—and waved goodbye to Clarence and Alex who stood on the front porch watching as they drove off.

Nervous about driving her new car to begin with, Mary was so excited to have her two girls with her that she didn't stop talking. As a result, the fifty-mile drive into town took an hour. Cyd was ambivalent about being back in Missoula. So much had happened there that was over, done, finished. The streets, the stores, the clubs and restaurants that were once so familiar now seemed like they belonged to someone else. The town was no longer hers. She was a stranger in a familiar place.

Once they got there, Tiffany came to life. Cyd wanted to try and reconnect with her before revealing her wonderful news, so she helped her buy some new jeans and a couple of tops and actually got her talking and laughing. For the first time in a long time, Tiffany felt like one of the girls and not like someone on the outside of her life looking in. She was still coughing her dry cough, but, with the drugs she was taking, the fever and the night sweats hadn't been so bad lately, the diarrhea had subsided, her headache was gone and, for once, she had a little energy. I'm so lucky I didn't get HIV before they found a way to turn it into a chronic illness instead of a fatal disease, she thought.

She had once loved the ballet and tried very hard to live up to her mother's expectations. Mary was encouraged by her enthusiasm, her natural grace, her long, strong body, and for a time thought her daughter might actually have the talent for the professional stage. That seemed like a lifetime ago. Permanently depressed over her illness, Tiffany no longer danced or even thought about dancing. Much of her time was spent hating the boyfriend who had infected her—the cute football player she intended to marry before he slept with a hooker at a victory party to prove to his teammates that he wasn't gay. But she wasn't thinking about any of that today; today was a good day. She was out with her mother and Cyd, and for a little while she could forget about who she was, what she had become and what her fate as a spinster might be.

Seafaring memorabilia decorated the barnwood walls of the bistro where they ate. Their seafood salad lunch was served with a carafe of wine, and when that was gone, Mary ordered another. Cyd was biding her time and not drinking. She knew that what she had to tell them would rock their world, and she did not want to do it in a crowded restaurant. It was 2:00 pm by the time they left the cafe to head home.

Drunk and happy, Mary said she didn't feel like getting a DUI and asked Cyd if she would mind driving. Cyd was only too glad to oblige, since Mary's sober driving on the trip down had frightened her. The statuesque dancer with the swept-back, graying hair tossed Cyd the car keys—which went flying over Cyd's head and landed on the sidewalk.

"Oops," Mary giggled.

***

Coyotes travel in packs and are deadly hunters with lethal stalking skills. Typically, one will jump out and startle its prey, spooking it so that it turns and runs straight into the waiting jaws of the rest of the pack. And that is how it happened.

Cyd followed Highway 93 north from Missoula through the 1.3-million-acre Flathead Reservation and turned west onto Route 211 at the town of Ronan. She crossed a bridge over a river and the deserted asphalt road turned to gravel. A mile farther on, with nothing to see for miles around, she pulled over to the side of the road. Mary asked in confusion why she had stopped and Cyd began telling them about the Cannastar.

Mary's screams of joy could be heard up and down the rural road. Then mother and daughter were peppering Cyd with questions, beside themselves with joy at the answers they were getting.

Cyd kept trying to tell them that Cannastar was still experimental and that there was a chance it wouldn't work, but Mary and Tiffany were having none of it, especially after learning about Cyd and Otis's success with curing their own cancer. Cyd didn't tell them about the seeds or their dilemma over where and how to grow them. Her problems were her own and she felt a strong need to keep them secret.

While they were talking, a police car came up behind them and stopped. The occupants of the Rover were so engrossed in conversation that they didn't notice, so the cruiser crawled around in front, its tires crunching gravel, and rolled to a second stop blocking their way. A startling burst from its siren got their attention.

The officer got out of his car, and the three occupants of the other vehicle giggled like schoolgirls. He walked toward them, hand on the butt of his holstered revolver, cigarette dangling from his lips, and their smiles faded. Cyd noticed that the officer's uniform didn't quite fit him—the shirt was too big at the neck, the sleeves and pants too short. Then she saw the dead eyes in the pockmarked face, and she froze.

Back down the road a few miles, an esteemed officer of the chronically understaffed Flathead Tribal Police Department lay dead behind some rocks wearing only his shorts and an undershirt, his limbs twisted and contorted in ways unnatural to a living body.

The uniformed policeman rapped on the driver side window of the Rover with his knuckles and Cyd jumped, letting out a squeal. He rapped again, harder this time. On the back of his hand she saw the tattoo of a black cross.

"Ma'am, would you step out of the vehicle, please."

Cyd jammed the Rover into reverse and floored it, throwing gravel as she rocketed backward down the road. When she thought she was clear she slammed the car in drive, cranked the wheel and spun around, fishtailing back the way they had come. The officer drew his gun and took careful aim . . . before jerking the barrel up into the air without firing. His orders were to kidnap, not to kill. He turned and ran for his car.

Cyd drove like a madwoman in an effort to reach the main road where there might be some traffic and some help. Mary and Tiffany were screaming, but Cyd ignored them. All she felt was raging anger. She rounded a curve going nearly eighty, wheels clawing for traction, almost going in a ditch before pulling it out at the last second. Up ahead was the bridge where the asphalt started. Two cars were parked across the road, blocking her way, and she had to slam on her brakes. The heavy four-wheel-drive vehicle skidded wildly on the gravel, looking like it was going to broadside the roadblock before coming to a halt at an odd angle inches from the other cars. Men wearing ski masks and waving weapons swarmed the Range Rover and the panicked women inside.

***

It was a little after 6:00 pm by the time Clarence and Alex realized something was wrong. Clarence had been trying to reach Mary and Tiffany on their cell phones for the last two hours, but there was no answer. He tried one more time, then pulled out his laptop computer, turned it on and brought up a program that he helped develop for the military to track and record the movements and locations of their vast fleets of mobile weapon systems as well as their combat, utility and assault vehicles—a program that had since been adapted for wide commercial use.

Alex watched anxiously. "What is that?"

"Permanent GPS log," Big Foot replied absently while punching keys and concentrating on the screen. "Works anywhere in the world, no matter how remote the location. All my vehicles have it." Hitting the last key, he pointed to a red dot on a digital map. "Gotcha! They're in Polson. The car isn't moving."

"Where's Polson?"

"North of here about thirty miles."

"I thought they were going to Missoula. Isn't that south?"

"Maybe they changed their minds. Maybe they got a flat or the car broke down or something . . ."

Minutes later they were barreling down Clarence's driveway in his white Bentley. A few minutes after that they were crossing the river and speeding past the place where the kidnapper's cars had blocked the road. There was no sign of the struggle that had taken place there earlier.

It took them half an hour to reach the south shore of Flathead Lake. They entered the town of Polson with Clarence repeatedly glancing at the laptop that sat on the console between them and showed the exact route his wife's car had taken. They pulled into the Safeway parking lot and saw Mary's Range Rover sitting off by itself in a distant corner. Clarence rocketed across the empty, darkened lot, screeching to a halt beside the green Rover and jumping out.

A single dog bark echoed in the night.

Clarence jerked open the Rover's driver-side door and stuck his head in as the pungent smell of new leather filled his nostrils. The car was empty. He slid behind the wheel and found the keys in the ignition. Alex got in the other side to look around. There were scuff marks all over the seats and dash suggesting the women had been hauled kicking and screaming from the car.

Clarence's cell phone rang, startling them both. The caller ID said it was Mary.

"Hello-hello? Mary, thank God! Where are you?"

A zombie voice: "Give us what they dug up in the mountains that the scientist hid out there, and you get the women back. Wild Horse Island. Skeeko Bay. Seven o'clock tomorrow morning."

"Who is this?" Clarence shouted. "Let me speak to my wife!"

"Any tricks or police and the bitches are history."

There was a click and the phone went dead.

Clarence turned to Alex with a terrified look.

***

Earlier that afternoon, Jesse Long Bow had made another call on Mary's cell. "Tagged and bagged," the cowboy with the tattooed hand told the person who answered. "We got three altogether. What do you want us to do with the other two?" Silence as he listened. "It was the whole package or nothin'. We even got their car; a nice one, too." The angry yelling on the other end forced him to take the phone away from his ear. "Sorry, boss. I didn't think . . ." He listened contritely as further instructions were given. "Yes, sir. Whatever you say, sir." He looked at the phone. The line had gone dead.

***

Alex sat with Clarence in the abandoned Range Rover as wave after wave of fear went through him. With the fear came terrible words, echoing in his brain, telling him Cyd was going to die, and he would never see her again. He knew it was his fear talking, but he let it have its say. When it was done, when it had worn itself out flailing its arms and yelling in his face, he spoke back. "Fuck off," he said.

"What?" Clarence asked.

"Where's this Wild Horse Island?" he replied. An urgent calm had settled over him, the same calm he felt in the emergency room when someone's life was in his hands and he was the only one who could save them.

Clarence pointed north up the lake. "A few miles that way."

"How do we get there?"

"The tribe keeps a couple of boats in the water year-round down at the marina." His voice trembled as he spoke. "We can use one of them."

A brief discussion about calling the police followed, but they had both heard the caller say, "Any tricks or police and the bitches is history."

Clarence roused himself decisively. "We need to go back to the house, get the saddlebags, and tomorrow morning make the exchange."

"Cyd would sooner die than lose those seeds," Alex lamented.

"My wife and daughter are going to die if we don't cooperate."

"We'll cooperate," Alex agreed grimly. "Then we'll see."

***

146

The 24-foot pontoon boat was basically a floating platform with a canvas awning, plush seats and eighteen cupholders. Alex untied the dock lines and Clarence backed out of the slip, jamming the throttles forward the moment he was clear of the dock. A pair of large outboard motors screamed to life. It was 6:30 am.

After receiving the phone call in the Safeway parking lot in Polson, they had rushed back to Clarence's house, retrieved the saddlebags from the safe and returned to the marina on the south shore of Flathead Lake just before dawn. Now, as they sped across the lake, the faint shape of Wild Horse Island loomed darkly before them, its two thousand acres teeming with bighorn sheep, mule deer, songbirds, waterfowl, bald eagles, falcons and yes, three wild horses. The high whine of the outboards shattered the stillness of the freezing mist that lay on the water and the pontoon boat's twin aluminum hulls left a wide, flat, foaming wake on the mirrored surface.

Clarence guided the boat into Skeeko Bay as Alex scanned the dim dawn, straining to make out any shapes ashore.

"The irony," Clarence commented nervously in an effort to stay calm, "is that the Salish people used to pasture their horses out here to keep them from being stolen by other tribes. Now we come to this place to get back what was stolen from us."

"You got that right," Alex replied.

They had been on the water maybe twenty minutes when Clarence slid the twin pontoons up onto the sand and killed the motors. They looked up and down the shoreline in the meager light. The beach was cold and deserted. They shivered impatiently. Clarence poured coffee from a thermos Lupe had made for them before they left the house, offering some to Alex who shook his head and drank instead from a thermos of Cannastar he had brought to keep his back pain at bay. Clarence looked down distastefully at his coffee, tossed it out with a hasty flick of his wrist and screwed the cup back on the thermos. Nothing had any taste to it this morning.

Alex checked his watch. It was 7:05 am. They aren't coming, he thought. It was all a diversion. Then the faint sound of an inboard engine, closing fast, could be heard, and he cocked his head to listen. The sound grew to a thunder as a fast speedboat rounded the point and headed straight toward them. "Lock n' load," he ordered.

Clarence picked up the saddlebags that lay on the seat between them. Alex checked the rifles he had taken off their saddles and hidden under the boat seat cushions. Under another cushion were two antique revolvers, fully loaded, that Clarence was hoping he wouldn't have to use.

The speedboat landed fifty yards up the beach. There were six people on board—three armed men wearing cowboy hats and ski masks and three women who were bound and gagged with plastic garbage bags draped loosely over their heads and their wrists taped with duct tape. The prisoners were hauled roughly out of the boat and made to kneel in the sand. Faint moans and cries could be heard coming from inside the stifling bags.

Alex and Clarence jumped from the pontoon boat into the shallow water and started up the beach. Jesse Long Bow had the bottom of his ski mask pulled up over his nose so he could smoke. He took the cigarette out of his mouth, casually flicked it away and shouted for them to stay where they were. Clarence raised the saddlebags over his head as if he were making an offering to the gods.

Long Bow left one of his men to guard the women kneeling on the beach and brought the other one with him as he approached. Striding up, he snatched the saddlebags out of Clarence's hands, fumbled to unfasten the buckles, opened a flap and yanked out one of the heavy leather pouches.

"You have the seeds, now give us the women," Alex demanded.

"Please," Clarence pleaded. "We've done as you asked."

Long Bow was busily untying the knot in the string that bound the top of the leather pouch, and Alex recognized the tattoo on the back of his hand that Cyd had described. He thought of that hand blackening her eye and splitting her lip and the urge to lunge at the man and rip his throat out nearly overwhelmed him.

Long Bow got the pouch open and poured out a handful of seeds in his hand.

Alex's eyes widened and his mouth went dry.

The seeds were not the tiny rainbow-colored ones from the Cannastar plant, they were ordinary beans—black beans, red beans, pinto beans, white beans, Anasazi beans and lentils! Long Bow put a few in his mouth, bit down and spat them out in disgust. "Soup beans!" he snarled, drawing a hunting knife and slitting open the other pouch. Alex and Clarence watched in horror as more soup beans spilled out. Long Bow looked up with a merciless smile. "This all they mean to you, your women?"

Alex's mind was racing. "That's it, that's all we found out there," he hurried to say. "They might look like soup beans to you, but they're not . . . they have special qualities, special properties . . . believe me, I know." He knew it was a lame explanation, but it was all he could think of to say at the time.

"Here's what I believe." Long Bow's voice was barely above a whisper. "I believe you two just made the biggest mistake of your lives." He abruptly jumped to his feet and started back up the beach with the other man following on his heels.

The third masked cowboy, the one guarding the women on the beach, raised his gun and pointed it at Alex and Clarence to cover his two companions as they made their retreat to the speedboat. Once they were safely aboard, he hauled the kneeling women to their feet and began pushing them toward the boat.

Long Bow held up his hand, ordering his man to stop. "Leave them on the beach," he yelled.

For a fleeting moment Alex had the wild hope that they were in fact going to leave the women behind. The next instant Long Bow picked up an automatic weapon and opened fire. The bullets cut the three women in half. Their hooded bodies fell dead in the sand with blood oozing from the holes in the plastic bags.

"Let that be a warning," Long Bow shouted as the third man dove in the boat and they backed off the beach. The engine roared, the craft went flying across the water and in an instant disappeared around the point.

It was the longest fifty yards Alex ever ran. Stunned, horrified, sickened with grief, he fell to his knees in the sand beside the bloody corpses, crying out as he tore frantically at the garbage sacks.

"Oh no . . . oh no . . . oh no," Clarence wailed as he dropped down beside him, clawing at the tape on their wrists.

Unable to believe their eyes, they stared. The lifeless faces of three dead women looked up at them from the sand—the faces of three Mexican women they had never seen before. Alex's mouth worked open and closed, but nothing came out. Clarence lowered his head, sobbing into his hands. Alex began automatically checking the bodies for pulses, moving in what seemed a slow-motion nightmare, gently closing their eyes as he went. When it was done, he fell back on his heels gasping for air and began to retch—but nothing came up.

"They're dead," Clarence grieved. "Mary, Tiffany, Cyd, that's what it means. They're gone. If they were alive, those men wouldn't have tried to fool us with these poor women."

Alex had seen a lot of death in war and in the ER; seen how people often went into denial claiming their buddy or their loved one was somehow still alive when he had just told them they were gone. He wasn't in denial; he knew that Cyd was still breathing. He couldn't explain it, but he could feel it. She was alive.

"Clarence, listen to me. If Cyd was dead, I'd know it."

"You just don't want to admit it. Neither do I. Oh, God . . ."

"It's a fear tactic," Alex explained evenly. "I saw it in the military, and I saw gang bangers do it in L.A. It's what terrorists like to do to break your spirit and get you to spill your guts. They tell you lies. If the exchange didn't work out, and they didn't get what they came for, their plan was to scare us to death so the next time we'd be sure to hand over what we found. This was a warning, I'm certain of it. They're holding the women hostage somewhere."

"If only it were true."

"Tattoo Hand even said it, remember? He said, 'Let that be a warning!' They plan on killing them, you can bet on it, but not before they get the seeds. I mean, what would be the point?"

"So where are the seeds?" Clarence moaned. "We still need to find them and hand them over to these creeps if we hope to ever get our girls back."

Alex shook his head. He didn't have a clue where the seeds were, and that's what really scared him.

Chapter Eighteen

In the Outhouse

The three kidnappers traveled a long distance up the lake, their speedboat slicing the mirrored surface of the water and making rows of tiny waves as it went until finally idling into the tiny, tree-choked cove it had departed from earlier that morning. Tying up to a small dock, the men scrambled out of the boat and started up a narrow path that led into the woods.

***

Alex and Clarence took the pontoon boat back to the marina, jumped out and headed for the car. Clarence jerked open the passenger door, sat down heavily and told Alex to drive. Not knowing where to go or what to do next, Alex got behind the wheel, but didn't start the engine. His stomach was in knots. Clarence opened his laptop and began working the keyboard.

"Grasping at straws, probably," the tech millionaire muttered, "but I want to see all the places the bastards went yesterday in my wife's car and exactly what stops they made." He turned the computer screen so Alex could see. "Even if they only stopped to take a piss, this will tell us what tree they pissed on."

A roadmap of the area took up most of the screen. On it was a moving red line that tracked the Range Rover's progress along its route. The cursor could be moved up or down to move the location of the Rover forward or back, but not to anywhere they hadn't gone. Running down the left of the screen was a log that indicated the exact speed, time and location of the car at any point of its trip along the red line.

Clarence adjusted his reading glasses and pointed. "Here they are leaving Missoula at 2:04 pm. Here they turn onto Route 211 off Highway 93. Here they cross the river. Right after they go over the bridge they stop, see here? That was at 2:40. They're stationary for six minutes, then turn around and go back to the bridge. At this point they're being chased because the Rover is doing over eighty miles an hour. See that?"

Alex nodded with growing interest.

"They stop again at the bridge and they're there for twelve minutes. Then they're moving again. Going back to 93. Heading north. At 3:10 they go through Pablo and ten minutes later they're in Polson, but they don't stop there. They continue on, look here . . ." The red line went through Polson and continued around the lake, following the narrow twisting road. "They go another eighteen miles until they come to this spot where they turn off the main road and go cross-country and finally stop . . . right here!" The map indicated a remote location in the trees on a large tract of private land along the east side of the lake. "The Rover stays there for 16 minutes and then they drive it back to Polson. They abandoned it at 4:27pm in the place where we found it last night."

"That's it then," Alex cried, pointing excitedly at the isolated location in the woods by the lake. "That's where they are. They dropped the women off, probably left somebody there to guard them, and brought the Range Rover back to Polson. A second car must have picked them up from there."

Clarence motioned for Alex to drive. "Go, go, go! I'll call the police and tell them to meet us."

Alex quickly started the engine and careened out of the marina parking lot.

A green four-door Chevy sedan driven by Jesse Long Bow passed through Polson heading south just as the Bentley left the marina to head north. Alex and Clarence missed seeing Cyd riding in the front seat of the Chevy by less than a minute.

When Clarence called the tribal police on his cell phone to tell them about the abduction, he told them where they were going and why. He also told him about the three dead bodies they had carefully covered with beach towels from the pontoon boat and left out on the island. The officer said he would see to the dead and report the kidnapping to the FBI in Missoula, but that his own men were at least an hour away, maybe more, and not to do anything until they got there. He informed Clarence that the reason they were so busy this morning was that one of their officers had just been found murdered out on Route 93.

* * *

Returning empty-handed from Wild Horse Island, the trio of kidnappers followed the path through the woods until it came to a rundown summer cabin. The walls of the cabin were sheeted in delaminating plywood and insulated with wadded up newspaper from seventy years ago. It sat at the end of a rutted dirt road, buried in the trees, its rusted metal roof covered in snow and pine needles. In front of the house were the two Chevys, one green and one tan, used to barricade the road when the women were kidnapped. An outhouse sat behind the cabin on the edge of a cliff overlooking the lake.

Inside the cabin, in a freezing bedroom with peeling, yellowed wallpaper and bad smells, Cyd, Mary and Tiffany lay bound together on a sagging bed. Tiffany could not stop coughing. Her lips were cracked and blistered, her nose was running and she was burning up with fever. Mary was more frightened for her daughter than she was for herself.

The fourth kidnapper, the one left behind to guard the women, was named Tad. He was the smallest of the four and wore an enormous trophy buckle for bull riding that he didn't win. He opened the bedroom door to check on his prisoners, then closed it again just as his three companions came storming in from outside. One look at their faces told him things had not gone that well.

The four cowboys stood crowded together in the small outer room of the cabin, a room that served as kitchen, dining room and living room all in one. The furniture consisted of a chrome-legged Formica table with two plastic-covered chairs to match, plus a sofa and armchair with the stuffing coming out of the arms. Bookshelves laden with rows of dog-eared copies of Reader's Digest, carefully arranged by date, lined the walls, and dozens of beat-up VHS tapes of old movies were piled up on a dusty video player that was hooked to a TV with aluminum foil rabbit ears. A small fire burned in a wood stove, the smoke from the fire seeping into the room through rusted pinholes in a chimney pipe that ran through the ceiling.

Jesse Long Bow flicked his cigarette into the kitchen sink, drew his hunting knife from the sheath on his belt and went straight for the bedroom.

The three women screamed in unison as the door burst open.

Long Bow bent over the bed and cut Cyd free with a single swipe of his knife, pulled her out of bed and hauled her into the living room by the hair where he flung her onto the sofa.

Cyd sat up defiantly rubbing her wrists. "You're home early, darling. How was the trip?"

Long Bow smiled the way any coldblooded mammal would smile— with hungry teeth. "Who put the beans in them sacks?" he asked. "Was it you?" Cyd returned his chilly stare in kind. "You don't seem all that surprised," he concluded. "It was you, all right."

She realized Alex and Clarence must have offered the saddlebags up as ransom. A chill went through her and suddenly she was terrified that she might have gotten them killed.

"What happened?" she demanded. "What have you done to them?"

"Taught them a lesson," Long Bow laughed. "One I'm guessing they won't soon forget."

Cyd lunged, lashing at him with her nails and gouging his cheeks. "Fucking psycho!"

Tad stepped up, stood on tiptoe, and backhanded her across the face. The blow drove her back onto the sofa. Tad giggled as Cyd rubbed her jaw.

Long Bow went on as if he hadn't noticed the blood trickling from the scratches on his face. "Listen to me carefully because I'm only going to say this once. Whatever was supposed to be in them bags, you know where it is. You can tell me now or I start killing your friends."

Cyd spat at him.

"Bring me out one of them bitches," he ordered, turning to the two men who had been with him in the boat. The cowboy with the bald head and shaggy red beard was named Homer and the other, Louie, had a bulbous pitted nose, puffy eyes and two fingers missing from his left hand. "Move!" Long Bow shouted.

Startled, the two men scurried into the bedroom, reemerging moments later dragging Tiffany by the arm. Slender and frail, she squirmed and struggled with the last of her strength. Mary screamed from the bedroom and they slammed the door on her, but she went on screaming, the sound muffled by the door.

"Leave her alone," Cyd cried. "She's sick. She needs a doctor, or she might die!"

Long Bow grabbed Tiffany's hair, jerked her head back and laid the blade of his knife across her throat, pressing it into her sallow skin. "Then why don't I just put her out of her misery right now?"

"No, wait! Stop!" He looked like he was going to do it. "I hid the seeds. I can't tell you where, I have to show you. You'll never find them on your own."

"Not good enough."

Blood began to trickle down Tiffany's neck from a thin red line across her throat.

Cyd was frantic. "I mean it. I'll show you. Otherwise, you'll never find them."

Long Bow shoved Tiffany aside and sent her sprawling across the floor. She landed huddled and whimpering in a corner. "All right then," he growled. "Your friends stay here. If you're lying, they're dead. You got that? Tad, you're coming with me." Turning to Homer and Louie, he added, "If we're not back by dark, you two can have your fun with them before you kill them."

They looked at each other and beamed, revealing enough tooth decay between them to put a dentist's kids through college. They didn't know what the rest of this was all about, but rape was something that had been on their minds ever since they grabbed the women up at the river.

The pint-sized cowboy put his face close to Cyd's. "I'm a trick rider by profession," Tad giggled. "How about on the way if I mount your back and show you some tricks?"

Cyd flared. "You men lay one hand on any of us and I'm telling you nothing!"

"Fair enough," Long Bow agreed, glaring at Homer and Louie and drawing his finger along the edge of his knife until a thin line of blood appeared on his skin. "Either of these lowlifes rapes your ladies before we get back, I'll cut off his balls and stuff them down his throat myself." He smiled humorlessly and licked the blood off his finger. "Think the two of you can remember that, or should I carve it in your foreheads?"

Wide-eyed and fearful, Homer and Louis bobbed their heads up and down like bobble-head dolls.

Cyd was shoved out the front door and made to sit in the passenger seat of the green Chevy. Tad got in the rear, Long Bow slid behind the wheel, and the sedan took off up the dirt road bouncing over the ruts. Tad sat in back pointing a large-caliber revolver at the back of Cyd's seat, giggling every time the car hit a pothole and bounced him in air. The gun looked enormous in his child-sized hand.

***

Clarence looked down at his computer and motioned for Alex to turn left off Route 35 onto a gravel road. The Bentley's tires vibrated over a cattle guard while passing a faded sign nailed to a broken-down fence that read:

SEELEY LAND & CATTLE CO.
PRIVATE
NO HUNTING

Recent tire tracks leading to and from the paved road made dark muddy lines in the snow that covered the ranch road. Alex followed the lines, the road growing progressively worse the farther they went. Eventually, they came to a dirt road leading off to the right that was nothing more than a pair of wheel ruts. The tire tracks they were following had turned right here, and Clarence motioned for Alex to follow. The elegant Bentley bottomed out several times going down the same slippery road that Long Bow, Tad and Cyd had bounced up in the Chevy sedan less than half an hour earlier.

They reached the bottom of the hill, and a cabin came into view through the trees with a thin line of smoke coming from its chimney. A tan sedan, the second car used in the kidnapping, was parked in front of the cabin. Alex coasted silently to a stop as Clarence pointed at the flashing target on his computer screen that indicated they had arrived at their destination.

Alex backed up the road to a flat spot and nosed the Bentley into the trees where it was all but invisible among the snow-covered branches. They got out and softly closed the doors behind them. Clarence had his revolvers stuck in his waistband; Alex carried a rifle. They crept closer, their hearts racing. Alex looked over at Clarence and hardly recognized him. The Salish Indian with the long black ponytail had gone into a stealth crouch and was moving soundlessly through the trees. He raised his fist and Alex froze. Peering through a screen of branches, they saw one of the kidnappers come out of the cabin and go around back to the outhouse. He had a shaggy beard, carried a rifle in one hand and a Reader's Digest in the other.

Clarence motioned for Alex to go down to the house. "Stand at the corner and watch the door," he whispered in a harsh rasp. "Wait for me to make the first move. If anyone comes out, kill him. Think you can manage that, doctor?"

Alex angrily levered a shell into the chamber of his rifle. "Not a problem."

They snuck down to the house, and Alex pressed himself against the outside wall. An image flashed in his mind of watching a soldier in Fallujah approach a mud hut, step on an IED and seeing it nearly blew his leg off. Faint sounds of women crying from inside the cabin brought him back to his senses and he softly flicked the safety on his rifle to 'off.'

Clarence slipped past him and continued on in a crouch until he reached the outhouse. From there he carefully placed his hands firmly on the rotting, weathered wood, planted his feet and gathered his considerable strength under him. A moment later Alex heard him make a sound he had never heard in his life and hoped he would never hear again. It wasn't Indian, it wasn't animal and it certainly wasn't human. It was, perhaps, the way the legendary Big Foot might sound if the poor foot-challenged creature were to find himself in a similar situation. In any case, the blubbering bellow was so terrifying Alex had to cover his ears.

Inside the outhouse, Homer was tearing pages out of the Reader's Digest and wadding them up in readiness. Hearing the inhuman howl coming from the other side of the wall, his bowels let go all at once and he lurched forward, grabbing at his pants in an effort to flee. At the same time, Clarence gave a mighty heave, lifted the outhouse off its crumbling foundation and sent it rolling down the hill.

Louie, the kidnapper inside the cabin guarding the women, heard the sound Clarence made, and, for a horrifying moment, thought it was the bear that had chased him and Jesse up the tree. Then came Homer's God-awful screams as the outhouse rolled down the hill, and Louie thought for sure the bear had gotten him. Hearing it crash onto the rocks below and splinter into a thousand pieces sent him running for the door.

At the bottom of the cliff, Homer lay wedged between the rocks, impaled on a splintered piece of wood that was sticking through his chest and drowning him in his own blood.

Alex stood waiting beside the house, the butt of his gun pressed against his cheek, as Louie came bolting out the door frantically pointing his rifle this way and that. Alex sighted carefully down the barrel and squeezed the trigger. The bullet went in one side of the kidnapper's head leaving a fairly small entry hole. When it came out the other side, the hole was rather larger leaving Louie dead before he hit the ground.

Hysterical screams were coming from the cabin as Clarence appeared, running with both pistols drawn. Together, they burst into the living room. The sounds were coming from the bedroom. They rushed the door and banged it open, and the next second Clarence was holding his sobbing family in his arms, trying to comfort them, freeing them from their bonds.

Alex fearfully searched the cabin. Cyd wasn't there. He put an urgent hand on Mary's shoulder and tried gently to ask her where she was.

Mary Big Foot, her graying hair in tangles around her face, turned from Clarence and flung her arms around Alex's neck. "Oh, thank you. You saved my daughter's life! Thank you, thank you, thank you."

"Mary," Alex insisted, "where's Cyd? What have they done with her?"

Sobbing softly, Mary told him the other kidnappers had taken her. "She was going to show them something, I don't know what. She said they couldn't find it without her. I think she was buying us time is all, trying to keep them from killing us. It had to do with beans or seeds or something. Does that make any sense?"

Alex remembered seeing Cyd coming out of a white cabana beside a swimming pool with steam rising all around her and snowflakes falling in her hair. Robert was with her beside the pool, standing too close, speaking urgently, but there was something about the pool house . . .

Tiffany made a small cry beside him and her knees buckled. Alex caught her in time, eased her back down on the bed and gave her a quick field exam—a procedure he had done many times before that required one-part medical knowledge and one-part intuition—the kind of intuition he had just used to remember the scene of Cyd at the pool house.

He took the girl's pulse, looked into her red-rimmed eyes, had her stick out her spotted tongue, felt her forehead and put his ear to her chest so he could listen to her ragged breathing. Then he kissed her sweaty brow and straightened.

"She has pneumonia," he announced, handing Tiffany off to her mother. "You need to get her to a hospital immediately." Then to Clarence, "I know where they've taken Cyd. You stay with your family. I'm going to borrow that other car out front, if I can find the keys."

"And do what?" Clarence asked.

"Get to your place as quickly as I can."

"That's where they've taken her? How can you be sure?"

"I am, that's all. She hid the seeds in the pool house."

Clarence thought a moment, then said urgently, "I'll make a call and see if I can't get you some help."

Alex looked back at him on his way out the door. "Out of curiosity, that sound you made back there. What did it do to the guy in the outhouse?"

"It made him fall off the cliff."

"While he was still inside that thing?"

Clarence nodded gravely.

"Shitty way to go."

Chapter Nineteen

War Party

Long Bow looked down at the Chevy's gas gauge and saw that he was almost out of fuel. He pulled into Joe's Jiffy Stop on the south end of Pablo just across the street from the Salish Kootenai College campus, lit a fresh cigarette and got out of the car leaving the engine still running. Tad stayed in the back seat still pointing his gun at the seat in front of him. Cyd sat searching the gas station frantically with her eyes for any sign of help.

An older Ford pickup pulled into the Jiffy Stop and stopped facing the opposite direction on the other side of the gas island where Long Bow's Chevy was parked. Tachini Pete got out of the truck, unscrewed his gas cap, swiped his card, inserted the nozzle and put the handle on automatic. He was good looking enough to be Robert Big Foot's younger brother—a big, athletic engineering student with an engaging smile, shoulder length black hair and an academic scholarship to the college across the street. He'd been offered a football scholarship to play for the University of Montana Grizzlies, but had to turn it down because of a bad knee. He smiled politely at the good-looking girl who was leaning forward in the front seat of the Chevy across from him, staring intently. He averted his eyes when he saw that she looked a little crazed, then noticed that the Chevy engine was running and that the guy pumping gas was smoking. He politely cleared his throat. "Dude," Tachini said amiably, "how about putting the cigarette out and switching off your engine?"

Long Bow ignored him and continued to pump his gas, the lighted cigarette dangling loosely from his lips.

Tachini grew agitated. "Read the sign, okay? It says 'Turn off your engine' and 'No smoking.' You trying to get us killed?"

Long Bow looked up and slowly smiled. A long ash fell off his cigarette.

Tachini turned up his palms and raised his eyebrows in a gesture of impatience and disgust.

Long Bow's smile widened sadistically.

Tachini turned away, angrily returning his nozzle to the pump with the intention of getting the hell out of there before he did something stupid. "Asshole."

"Hey?" Long Bow called.

Tachini turned.

Long Bow took the cigarette out of his mouth, fingered it, and flicked it in Tachini's face. The sparks burnt the boy's skin and he yelped in pain.

"Happy now?" Long Bow inquired.

Tachini lost his temper, bunched his fists and leapt across the island. Long Bow took a wild swing at him, but the young football player ducked and buried a fist in the smoker's stomach. Long Bow gasped and fell to his knees, unable to breathe.

Cyd screamed from inside the Chevy, jerked open the door and ran around the car. Tad made a grab for her from the back seat but didn't come close.

"I'm being kidnapped!" she yelled. "Help me!"

It took Tachini a second to realize what was happening. He got to his truck door just in time to open it so Cyd could dive inside. "Hurry up," he exhorted, glancing over his shoulder.

Cyd scrambled across the console and into the passenger seat. "They've got guns!" she shouted.

Tachini jumped in and fumbled with the ignition. Tad was running around the front of the Chevy to get a clear shot. Tachini's truck roared to life and rocketed away from the pump with smoking tires.

Tad leveled his gun at the back of the retreating truck and was about to fire when Long Bow, still doubled over and gasping for air, batted his hand down.

"Moron!" he wheezed, lurching himself into the driver's seat of the Chevy. "We need her alive!" He jammed the car in gear and took out after the truck. Tad had to run and jump through the window to keep from being left behind.

"You all right?" Tachini yelled, almost losing control of the truck as he hung a left onto Division Street and accelerated down the empty, narrow two-lane road.

"Better than I was," Cyd smiled.

Tachini looked over at her and grinned excitedly, thinking she looked better up close than she did at a distance. "Better put your seat belt on," he advised, glancing in his rearview mirror. "This could get a little hairy."

She fumbled with her belt. "Appreciate the lift."

"Anytime, ma'am. Where would you like me to drop you?"

"How about that police station up there?"

They were coming up on the Tribal Law & Order station house doing about ninety with Long Bow's Chevy closing fast. No squad cars were in the small police station lot at the time; everyone was out dealing with the murder and the kidnapping. Tachini desperately slammed on his brakes to turn in and the truck began fishtailing all over the road. The Chevy caught the truck's rear bumper, rammed it and sent it into a slide. The pickup skidded off the road, hit the embankment and rolled, flipping end over end twice before coming to rest on its roof with gas spilling from its tank.

Cyd hung upside down inside the battered truck. She opened her eyes and through the broken window saw Long Bow's black cowboy boots walking toward her. Tachini hung unconscious from his seatbelt on the other side of the cab.

Cyd was covered in small red cuts. She shook her head to try and clear it. Long Bow bent down, reached inside with his knife and unceremoniously sliced her seatbelt in half. She dropped hard onto the roof of the truck and he hauled her out through the window, but not before lighting a fresh cigarette.

Tad rushed up to take her off his hands, twisting Cyd's arm behind her and frog-marching her back to the Chevy where he stuffed her into the front seat kicking and screaming. Long Bow, his face a blank, took a long drag off his cigarette as he studied the wreckage where Tachini was still trapped. Then taking his cigarette between his thumb and middle finger, he flicked it into the spilling gas. The fuel exploded with a whoosh, engulfing the truck in flames.

Cyd could hear Tachini's screams coming from inside the truck as the Chevy sped away. She looked back in horror crying desperate tears as the pickup was consumed by a giant fireball and a thick plume of black smoke rose into the sky.

***

Behind the upscale subdivision of brick homes that Alex and Cyd had ridden their horses through when they first arrived at Clarence's house was a dirt fire road that ran between the houses and the ranchland beyond. Long Bow's green Chevy bounced along this same dirt road, circling the subdivision until it came to a stop in back of the grassy knoll where the jumbled cubes of Big Foot's modern home stood out against a gray winter sky.

Tad prodded Cyd out of the car and she led her two kidnappers at gunpoint up the backside of the knoll. Her mind was racing with ways to avoid having to give up the seeds, but she kept coming back to the same conclusion—it was either this or get Mary and Tiffany killed. She was furious with herself for having put them in this situation.

Behind the main house was the swimming pool and behind that was the cabana with the glass French doors at either end, which was the first structure they came to coming up the back of the hill. Cyd led the way around to the front of the pool house, casting a desperate glance in the direction of the main house in the hope of seeing someone inside. Not even Lupe was around; the place was dead quiet.

Long Bow and Tad followed Cyd into the cabana. The heat was turned down to 50 and the place was crammed to the ceiling with summer things stored there for the winter. A poker table and a pool table had plastic covers over them and dozens of seat cushions for the outdoor furniture were stacked on top of them in teetering rows. Dusty liquor bottles lined the glass shelves behind the bar. Round glass tables with holes in the center for umbrellas were pushed against one wall with a row of poolside loungers lined up in front of them. Balls and nets and blowup pool toys, mostly deflated from loss of air, were piled on top of the loungers and tables. Along another wall, rows of nested pool chairs were stacked in front of the showers and a steam room.

Cyd hesitated and looked around, still trying to figure a way out of this.

"Quit stalling," Long Bow growled menacingly.

Tad giggled, motioning with his gun for her to hurry it up.

She sighed and went over to the piles of outdoor seat cushions on the pool table, looking them up and down. Even she couldn't remember which stacks she'd used. Two days ago, Cyd had stood in this same place surveying the same cushions . . .

***

Clarence had been gracious enough to let them put the saddlebags in his gun safe, but Cyd couldn't shake the gnawing feeling that it wasn't a secure hiding place. Something told her, if she left the seeds in there, they would lose them. Maybe it was just the paranoia she had lived with for so long while protecting Maury's discovery, but at the moment she didn't trust anyone. And if she was wrong and moved the seeds and nothing bad happened, so what? No harm done. The nagging feeling wouldn't go away, so that afternoon, while Alex was taking a nap and Clarence and Mary were out with Tiffany somewhere, Cyd wandered through the empty house looking for a better hiding place. Eventually, she ended up in the pool house.

She stood inside the lovely white cabana amid the piled and crowded furniture, wondering where she could safely hide the seeds. The showers and boiler room were out. There weren't a lot of good possibilities. Then she saw the rows of stacked pool chairs and her eyes moved to the waterproof seat cushions with the colorful floral print covers that were stacked in uneven rows on top of the pool table. She took one of the cushions down and studied it, turning it over in her hands. A zipper ran along the back of the cushion and around two of the corners. She opened the zipper all the way, reached inside and pulled out the foam rubber pad. Perfect!

She walked briskly back to the house, entered Clarence's office, went directly to the gun safe and punched in the combination he had given them. Removing the heavy saddlebags, she started back to the pool house and, on the way, stopped outside the kitchen, peering around the corner to see if anyone was inside.

The darkened designer kitchen was cool and still and spotless with everything in its place. Lupe was the only live-in help; the rest of the staff lived elsewhere on the reservation. Cyd guessed that Mary had given the woman the day off after all the work she had done preparing and supervising Christmas day dinner yesterday.

Opening the door to the big walk-in pantry, Cyd went inside and closed the door behind her before switching on the light. The room contained enough stockpiled food supplies to feed half the reservation. She searched the stacks of built-in drawers until she found the one that contained the boxes of plastic bags, taking out one that held gallon-size Ziploc bags.

Opening the saddlebags, she removed one of the four large leather pouches and untied the rawhide string. Holding a plastic bag open, she began nervously pouring the precious rainbow-colored seeds into it. It felt like she was pouring gold dust. The bag held about half of what was in the pouch and she took another from the box, filling it full as well, then repeated the process with the other three pouches until she had eight one-gallon plastic bags bulging with Cannastar seed and four empty leather pouches.

She realized she still needed to refill the pouches with something and looked around for an appropriate substitute. On one of the upper shelves she saw a neat row of glass canisters containing the soup beans that Lupe used to make her famous seven-bean soup. One by one, she pulled them down and poured them into the leather pouches, tying off the tops when they were full and returning them to the saddlebags. The empty glass canisters she put back on the shelf.

Lupe's collection of reusable canvas shopping bags hung from a hook inside the door. Cyd took two of them down and filled them with the plastic bags of seed. She then left the shopping bags sitting on the pantry floor while she went back to the office to return the saddlebags with the beans in them to the safe. Returning minutes later to the pantry, she retrieved her two shopping bags, carried them out of the kitchen and out the back door. Struggling down the back steps with a heavy shopping bag in each hand, she went around the pool deck and waddled toward the cabana.

Once inside the pool house, she started unzipping the removable seat covers and pulling out the foam rubber pads. Into each cushion cover she inserted two plastic Ziploc bags of Cannastar seed, flattening the bags out as best she could to make them look like padding before zipping the seat cover closed. When she was finished, four cushions contained two bags of seeds each. She inserted the cushions back in the teetering stacks of cushions, slipping one each into the middle of four different stacks. When she was done, she tossed the four foam rubber seat pads and the two empty shopping bags into the boiler room and closed the door.

Coming out of the pool house, she ran into Robert. He had been over at a friend's house watching football but couldn't keep his mind off Cyd. All he could think about was getting her back. Seeing her yesterday at Christmas dinner with that tall, skinny doctor, seeing how beautiful and feisty she was, made him realize what a mistake he'd made in breaking up with her. He'd come back to his parent's house just now to find her and tell her he still loved her.

His declaration of devotion didn't go as planned. Cyd told him, as gently as possible because she was still very fond of him, that she wasn't interested, that she had moved on, that she had other, more important things to think about right now.

He hung his head. The news was devastating.

***

Tad had been eyeing the pool table in the cabana ever since they came in. Finally, he couldn't resist. He brushed past Cyd and threw off the piles of seat cushions that were stacked on top, scattering them all over the floor. "Always wanted one of these," he exclaimed. "How about a game of nine-ball, Jesse?"

"Moron," Long Bow snarled, smacking him upside the head.

"You didn't have to do that," Tad whined, rubbing his scalp.

"You guys are a couple of real geniuses," Cyd laughed, starting to search through the scattered seat cushions that were now all over the floor. "Just keep that idiot away from me if you want me to find what I'm looking for."

***

Alex pulled up in front of Clarence's house in the tan sedan, got out carrying his rifle and ran to the door. It was locked. He started around the back, following the jagged line of the jumbled cubes, eventually coming to the chain link gate to the pool area. To his relief it was unlocked. He opened the gate and went through. From there he could see the cabana on the far side of the swimming pool and the people moving around inside.

***

Cyd found one of the four seat cushions that contained the seeds and handed it to Long Bow. He looked confused.

"Unzip it and we can all go home," she said in exasperation.

The cowboy undid the zipper, jerked out one of the two plastic bags, opened it and plunged a tattooed hand inside. Beautifully colored seeds sifted through his dirty fingers.

"This is it?" he scoffed. "This is what all the bullshit is about?"

"Pretty much," Cyd replied. "What could a bunch of seeds be worth, right? Why don't you just give them back and we'll forget the whole thing."

He studied her while he lit a fresh cigarette off the stub of his old one. Suddenly, viciously, he drew his knife and started stabbing the cushions on the floor that Cyd hadn't searched yet.

"Stop that!" Cyd yelled.

Long Bow smiled with tobacco stained teeth. "You saying there's more?"

"I might have missed a couple," she admitted shakily. "Let me keep looking."

Alex was just outside the pool house doors now. He could hear them inside talking and thought if he could somehow get the kidnappers to come running out, he might be able to pick them off one by one like he had done with their buddy at the cabin. On impulse, he leaned his rifle against the building, picked up a big landscaping stone from one of the flower beds, held the rock over his head like a basketball . . . and heaved it through the French doors.

Glass shattered and Tad wheeled and fired. The bullet went wide and struck the wall beside the doors. Long Bow pulled his gun, and they both started firing wildly. In their distraction, they forgot about Cyd who was picking up a pool cue. She crept forward and broke the fat part of the stick over Tad's head. The tiny man crumpled in a heap. Shit, I killed him, she thought as she turned and ran for the French doors at the other end of the room. Long Bow saw her, aimed, then spun back around as a second rock came crashing through the other doors.

The last time the pool man was out to clean the pool, he had left a long-poled leaf skimmer leaning against the wall of the cabana. Alex grabbed it, stood to one side and started waving it frantically in front of the opening. Long Bow saw something moving outside the door and emptied his gun at it.

Alex snatched up his rifle and sighted down the barrel as the other set of French doors flew open . . . and Cyd came running out!

"Don't . . .!" she screamed, seeing him pointing the rifle at her.

Alex let out a shaky breath, lowered his rifle and motioned urgently for her to run behind the cabana. She bolted around the corner of the building, he went the other way and they met breathlessly in the back, falling into each other's arms.

Alex knew it would only be a matter of seconds before Long Bow was reloaded and running after them. He pointed two fingers at his eyes, then pointed left and right for her to help him watch the corners of the building. A second later, Long Bow appeared at the corner closest to him. Alex fired, the cowboy ducked back, and the bullet struck the corner of the building sending plaster flying.

Below them was the grassy hillside. They were exposed with no place to hide and no place to run if Long Bow came charging back around the corner and Alex couldn't drop him with a single shot.

Then, from the bottom of the hill, came the thunderous sound of roaring engines and blaring horns. Cyd and Alex turned in the direction of the noise, gaping at the shocking sight.

Stampeding up the knoll on all sides was an armada of pickup trucks overflowing with armed tribesmen. Over a hundred trucks were making the charge with men standing in the beds waving guns and firing them in the air. It was an army, an invasion, an attack of wild-ass, kick-ass, drunk-ass Indians, charging the knoll from all directions. Clarence's son Robert stood in the bed of the lead truck, leading the charge.

Alex grinned. "I was beginning to think we might have a problem here."

Cyd laughed nervously as Long Bow appeared again at the opposite corner and fired. The bullet sounded like a mosquito whizzing past her head. Alex fired back and he turned and ran, shooting wildly at the advancing enemy.

Trucks were coming up the hill from all directions— Fords, Chevys, Dodges, GMCs, Toyotas, Nissans, Hummers, Mazdas and Suzukis of every size, age, color and description, turbo chargers screaming, tires throwing mud and gravel. Clarance's entire house was suddenly surrounded by a circular wall of pickups. Four hundred guns dismounted, leaping from the trucks with whoops and shouts as they stormed the house. They wore boots and jeans, plaid shirts, cowboy shirts, sports jerseys and baseball caps, but the effect was no less fearsome had it been war paint and feathers; this was one scary bunch.

They ran Long Bow from one end of the compound to the other, flushing him out of first one place and then the next as they tightened the circle. Finally, they had him cornered by the swimming pool. He ran up and down the pool deck like a snarling animal, pointing his gun this way and that . . . then stopped in his tracks with nowhere to turn, breathing hard, the circle of men closing in.

Robert stepped forward and approached the fugitive. The cowboy backed up, then stopped when the crowd of men behind him took a step forward. He grinned slowly, opened his mouth, inserted the muzzle of his gun . . . and pulled the trigger. There was a *click*, but nothing happened. The pistol was empty.

Robert's arm shot out and he shoved him in the pool. A whooping, cheering touchdown roar rose up from the pickup cavalry as he hit the water. The men around the pool howled with laughter as the angry kidnapper flailed his arms, trying to stay afloat. Then Long Bow discovered that the pool was only four feet deep and was so embarrassed he looked like he was going to explode. The rescuers had to lean on each other for support they were laughing so hard.

Just then Tad stumbled out of the pool house half blind and with his head reeling from where Cyd had split his skull. The crowd ceremoniously parted to let him through, and he staggered drunkenly straight into the pool, wailing loudly and sputtering water as he surfaced. Watching him thrashing about, the war party broke out in fresh convulsions of laughter.

Cyd and Alex were in a state of shock. They looked at one another and fell desperately into each other's arms. Tears of relief were streaming down Cyd's cheeks. It was over, it was actually over. They were safe and the seeds were safe. Impulsively, she kissed him. Alex was both startled and delighted and passionately kissed her back. Cyd pulled away searching his eyes for answers—Who are you? Who are we? What are we doing and is this real?—until more urgent questions entered her mind. "How did you find me?" she asked. "How did all these men get here?"

"Ask Robert," Alex smiled. "I think he's trying to impress you."

Just then Robert walked up. "I'm impressed," she said, giving him a grateful hug.

Robert made a call on his cellphone to tell the police to come and get the two outlaws they had just captured. The dispatcher told him what he had told Clarence earlier in the day—it was going to be an hour or more before they could get there and not to do anything until they did.

"Wouldn't dream of making a move without you," Robert responded, smiling as he hung up.

Cyd suddenly remembered Mary and Tiffany. Alex assured her that they were safe, and Tiffany was on her way to the hospital. Cyd wanted to know what happened back at the cabin, but before she could ask, another fear washed over her.

"The seeds are still in the pool house," she rasped urgently. "We need to get them out of there before the police find them. Otherwise, they're going to get confiscated for evidence. Too many people know about this already."

Alex nodded and they quietly slipped away. The war party was too busy keeping an eye on the prisoners trapped in the swimming pool and celebrating a job well done—a rather large quantity of iced beer had mysteriously shown up in a galvanized washtub—to notice that Cyd and Alex were gone.

Chapter Twenty

Dances with Pickups

Cyd retrieved Lupe's shopping bags from the cabana boiler room and scurried about loading them up with the Ziplock bags of Cannastar seed she'd hidden in the cushion covers. Alex, meanwhile, called Clarence on the pool house telephone.

Clarence picked up immediately. They were at the hospital in Kalispell. They had just gotten there, and the doctors were still with Tiffany. All he knew was that she was alive and apparently stable.

"We kind of had a pool party at your house," Alex began, telling him about capturing the kidnappers, how Robert showed up last minute with the cavalry, assuring him that he and Cyd were okay. "I'm afraid the pool party is still going on."

Clarence laughed and was saying how relieved he was when Mary came on the line, asking to speak to Cyd.

The two women cried together happily as Mary told her what Alex and Clarence had done to rescue them. When Cyd hung up, she was staring at Alex in a curious way.

"What?" Alex asked.

"She said you saved their lives. And for the second time since I've known you, you saved mine." She saw the accusatory look on his face, and it confused her.

"Three women got killed because I didn't have the seeds," he said. "Why weren't they in the safe?"

"I moved them."

"What the hell for?"

"I had a bad feeling, okay? I was being cautious."

"Your feeling got three innocent Mexican women killed."

"And a fine young boy as well," she added sadly, remembering Tachini being burned alive in his pickup. "But," she went on with rising anger, "if I hadn't done what I did, three other women you know would probably be dead instead. Not to mention the countless thousands of people who might get a chance to live now because the seeds didn't get lost."

The crease between his eyebrows went away. "You're right," he admitted. "I'm sorry. War is messy."

"It is a war, isn't it?" she mused. It was something of a revelation.

He nodded slowly. "If we can do some good with those seeds though, if we can save some lives with them, then maybe, just maybe, it won't have been for nothing."

She smiled with satisfaction now that they had an understanding. "So, how's your back?"

"Never better."

"Don't lie to me."

"If you're offering, I could use a cup of tea." Pale-eyed, freckle-faced and scratched, her hair a mess, he thought she was still the most beautiful thing he had ever seen.

"That, I can do."

***

Next morning, Alex and Cyd brought a thermos of the Cannastar tea to Tiffany at the hospital in Kalispell in the hope she'd be well enough to drink it. Clarence and Mary, who had been there all night, greeted them when they arrived. The antibiotics were helping, but Tiffany was still alternating between fever and chills. Alex examined her chart. As he'd feared, it was pneumocystis pneumonia—the worst kind.

It broke Cyd's heart to hear Tiffany cough and listen to her troubled breathing. Clarence and Mary stood at the end of their daughter's bed, watching anxiously, and the painful looks on their faces broke Cyd's heart all over again. "I can't promise anything," she told them, unscrewing the top of the thermos and pouring out a cup of Cannastar, "but let's give this a try, shall we." She put her hand under the sick girl's head. "Tiffany, can you hear me?"

Tiffany opened her eyes and managed a weak smile.

Cyd raised her head and put the cup to her lips. "Drink this, Tiff, it's going to make you better." She fed the girl the tea in tiny sips until she fell back, exhausted, onto the pillows. The tea in the cup was only half gone.

Just then an officious nurse came in and demanded to know what was going on.

"Get out," Clarence boomed in his commanding voice.

"I'm calling the doctor is what I'm doing," the nurse muttered, retreating in a huff.

Clarence put a comforting arm around his wife. "Keep the faith, honey."

"Faith is all I've got," Mary scoffed. "How else could I stand here thinking a cold remedy is going to cure my daughter of AIDS?"

"It's like putting your immune system on steroids and throwing it into overdrive," Cyd assured her. "It cured me and cured my friend Otis, so I'm betting it can cure Tiffany. I'll leave you the thermos."

Mary hesitated. "How much of it do I give her?"

"As much as she can drink for now. I'll keep making you fresh batches. I don't have that much with me because I didn't think we were going to be gone that long, but I have more at home that I can send you when I get back."

Mary took the cup from Cyd's hand and was able to get Tiffany to take another sip.

Two days later, Tiffany's condition had improved to the extent that they could bring her home from the hospital. The doctors said she was making a remarkable recovery. Mary was beside herself with joy. It was New Year's Eve.

***

Clarence stood watching as Cyd and Alex returned the Cannastar seeds to his gun safe.

They were discussing what to do next—there weren't a lot of options—when Mary walked in demanding to know if the thing they were so busy hiding was what almost got them killed.

Cyd reached back inside the safe, took out one of the Ziploc bags and handed it to the tall dancer. "What this does is grow up and become the thing responsible for your daughter's rapid recovery."

Mary looked down in amazement at the colorful bag she was holding. "You just plant these in the ground and they grow like any other seeds? That's it?"

"No," Alex replied, "unfortunately, that's not it. We go into the farming business around here and we might as well take a stroll through a firefight with a target on our backs."

"We stopped the kidnappers," Cyd explained. "What we didn't do is stop the people who hired them to kill us."

Mary passed the bag of seeds back to Cyd like she was handling over a newborn.

"The other problem," Cyd went on as she placed the bag back in the safe, "is money. Even if we could find somewhere to farm, starting a

Cannastar grow of any size is going to cost a small fortune. I can't even afford the mortgage on my ranch, I'm so broke."

"What's worse," Alex added, "the longer we stay here, the more we put you all in danger. We need to leave. Now."

Mary flushed with anger. "You're my guests and you're not going anywhere. Nobody's going to intimidate me in my own home."

"Mary darling," Clarence cajoled, "let's not forget what they just did to you and our daughter and Cyd?"

"They?" she responded with growing fervor. "Who are *they*, exactly?"

Cyd took her hand and held it. "The drug companies, Mary. Rxon in particular."

"Why would . . ."

Alex assumed his accustomed demeanor of the doctor explaining a medical condition to a patient. "If an effective, low-cost cure for viruses and other diseases gets into the hands of the public, if people suddenly have easy access to an affordable cure for debilitating and even fatal illnesses, then a whole lot of expensive, profitable drugs become suddenly obsolete. The only reason the drugs exist in the first place is because of illness and disease. Take that away, the drugs go away and with them goes a major portion of the medical community. Kind of like what happened to buggy makers and livery stables when the automobile came along. It's hard to find a place to get a wagon wheel repaired these days. The drug companies are owned and operated by some of the richest, most powerful people on earth. Along with the insurance companies, they practically own the government. Big Pharma would start World War III before they let something like Cannastar put them out of business."

Mary was incredulous. "Can people really be that selfish and cruel? That . . . that's evil. Nothing but pure evil."

Alex nodded. "It's a crooked world, Mary."

"If all that's true," Mary challenged, "just what do the two of you think you can do about it?"

"I can't speak for Cyd," Alex responded, "but as for me, I'm just trying to get one thing right. For once."

Cyd gave him an admiring glance before turning back to Mary. "Imagine a world where tens of thousands of people don't die from a flu virus every year. If we can make Cannastar as available as aspirin, it might mean the end of the flu season forever."

Mary was astounded, but she still wasn't satisfied. "So, what now?"

"Now we make sure Tiffany gets well," Cyd assured her. "That's the important thing."

Mary thought a moment, then brightened as an idea occurred to her. "We'll pay for it!" she announced.

Clarence looked perplexed. "Pay for what?"

"Everything," Mary cried. "If it's going to make Tiffany well, then it can make a lot of other Tiffanys well too. We'll give you two all the money you need. Figure out what to do and how to do it, and we'll foot the bill."

Clarence made an uncomfortable sound deep in his throat and Mary replied without looking at him. "Isn't that right, dear?"

"Yes . . . yes, of course," said the soft-spoken man who could roar like a bear. "We have more than we need. More than we can ever spend, actually. It's not doing us any good sitting in the bank." The enormity of what might be accomplished with his help was just beginning to dawn on him. This could be the greatest public service of his life. He always wondered why he had gotten so rich. He thought it was so he could do good for his community, for his people, but maybe it was more than that—maybe it was a lot more. "This . . . this could be something," he said wistfully. "Really something . . ."

Mary gave Cyd a hug. "It's settled then."

Cyd hugged the statuesque dancer back with tears in her eyes, then flung her arms around Clarence's neck. The gesture startled him, and he reddened in embarrassment.

"You do realize we could spend an awful lot of your money and accomplish nothing," Alex cautioned.

Clarence smiled excitedly. "Let me worry about that."

"Attaboy, Pop." They turned to see Robert leaning casually against the door sill, listening to their conversation.

Clarence, the humblest of men at heart, quickly changed the subject. "I hear my son has a new name," he bragged.

"Clarence . . ." Mary warned. She had lived with her husband's cornball sense of humor too long not to know what was coming.

"Cyd, Alex, do you know what my son's new name is?"

They both shook their heads.

"Dances with Pickups!"

Alex laughed, Mary looked exasperated and Cyd grinned in approval.

Robert shook his head in disbelief. "Good one, Dad. Thanks a lot."

"It is a good name," Clarence claimed proudly. "He wears it well, my son, don't you think?"

***

Music is a language that almost everyone speaks.

It was 8:00 pm and the gravel parking lot outside the Snake Snot Saloon in Pablo was already jammed with many of the same pickup trucks that had taken part in the cavalry charge up Big Foot's hill three days ago. Robert, Cyd and Alex had to park out on the street, it was so crowded. Walking toward the bar, Alex glanced up at a marquee that read:

Happy New Year!
THE CUSTER BUSTERS BAND
Tonight Only

He turned to Cyd and frowned. "Custer Busters?"

"Little Big Horn?"

"You saying there's actually a country band with a trumpet in it?"

Cyd walked on with a look of exasperation.

The saloon was packed with more cowboys than a Fourth-of-July rodeo. Crowds of men in snap shirts were parading their ladies around the dance floor in time to a two-step. Tables jammed with revelers and cluttered with beer bottles surrounded the dizzying swirl of dancers. Boots with riding heels, work-worn boots with steel toes and everyday boots with holes in the soles were lined up at the bar three deep. Balloons hung from the ceiling, Happy New Year signs were plastered to the walls and confetti and feathers sparkled on a sea of cowboy hats.

Robert seemed to know everyone in the place, and after what had just happened out at Clarence's house, everyone seemed to know Cyd and Alex. Cheers and applause greeted their arrival, chairs were shuffled, and the couple was quickly wedged into the ongoing celebration. The men at their table, all members of the victorious pickup cavalry, introduced Cyd and Alex around to their giggling, hollering wives and girlfriends who eagerly embraced the pair of outsiders they had heard so much about.

For the benefit of the newly arrived guests, enthusiastic lies and exaggerated stories were told and retold about what had become known as "The Great Swimming Pool Massacre." Apparently, it was not just two armed cowboys that were captured in Big Foot's pool that day, but more like twenty—or was it thirty?—all of whom had to be subdued with nothing more than fists and knives. It was a brave band of warriors who had won honor and glory for the tribe that day at Big Foot's pool; the stuff of legend.

A cocktail waitress was making her way between the tables. She was sexy as a ripe pear with an ass that Betty Little Horn might have described, had she been there, as 'three axe handles and a snus box wide.' Watching her maneuver with her tray of drinks was like watching a farmer plow a field with a bulldozer; she cut a wide and formidable swath.

The waitress was known as Puffin, but it was a subject of some debate as to whether that was her first name or her last. She wore a midriff shirt and low-cut camouflage pants with lace and spangles on the rear pockets. Bending over a table with her back turned, Alex was awarded a view not only of her butt crack, but of her tattoo as well. The indelible proclamation stretched the full width of her backside in elaborate, two-inch tall letters that read: *TROUBLE.*

Hungry eyes followed the warning sign around. Most were of the opinion that the size of the tip should at least equal the size of the tattoo if there was any possibility the cowboy might go home alone tonight. Since having it done, Puffin was able to buy not only a new car, but a new house as well for herself, her mother and her young daughter.

Cyd could see that both Alex and Robert wanted to dance with her and thought she'd put a quick end to the nonsense. "I should warn you . . . I don't dance."

"The two-step is easy," Robert countered. "Quick-quick, slow—slow. That's all there is to it."

"No friggin' way am I getting me out on that dance floor. Get over it."

The Custer Busters Band had a real gift: they could cover almost any hit country song and make it sound just like the band that first recorded it. It was almost as if the members of the Country Music Hall of Fame were all on the stage at the same time. The band was playing a song at the moment that Alex knew well, and for the life of him he couldn't tell the difference between their version and the original.

Robert stood and tugged Cyd to her feet. She stretched back with one arm, managed to grasp a shot of whiskey and toss it down before allowing herself to be towed out onto the dance floor. Robert took her in his arms, and she stiffened.

"It's easy," he smiled. "Just relax and follow my lead. Quick-quick, slow—slow. Quick-quick, slow—slow."

She quickly stepped on his foot. "Sorry, sorry," she moaned. "Can I sit down now?"

"You're doing fine. Try not to watch your feet. See? Much better. You're a natural."

Cyd made an effort to relax, but it was like rigor mortis had set in. A couple glided by dancing really well, and it was a moment before she recognized Alex as half the duo. The other half was one of the girlfriends from their table who must have asked him to dance. Pretty little thing, Cyd thought bitterly. All that blond hair and mascara. Big eyes with false eyelashes. She looks like one of those beanpole bimbos on a TV dance show. Where did he learn to dance like that? Well, to hell with it. If he can do that, so can I.

"Cyd?"

She looked up and saw Robert smiling down at her. "Sorry," she apologized. "Did I step on your toes again?"

He laughed. "You're doing really well, actually. You might even be ready for one of my mother's ballet classes."

"Fat chance." She gave Alex and his partner the evil stare as they went gliding past again like a float in the Rose Parade. What could he possibly see in her?

Robert was watching her sadly. "You've fallen in love with him, haven't you?

"Who?"

"Alex. You're in love with him."

She dropped her head so he couldn't see her face.

He gently lifted her chin. "Cydney, I do believe you're blushing."

"I don't blush."

The song ended and they made their way back to their table. The ubiquitous Puffin brought more beers and, after another song, the band began a waltz. Another of the girlfriends at the table, apparently unaware how far her top was falling open, leaned over to ask Alex to dance. When did he become Mr. Popularity? Cyd wondered and then, to her surprise, heard him politely refuse.

"May I have this dance?" It was Alex, offering her his hand.

"Don't make me," she pleaded. "I'm terrible."

"You're beautiful, come on."

Cyd turned to the woman beside her, a jolly, middle-aged housewife who had befriended her when she first sat down. "He thinks I'm beautiful," she bragged.

"Go on now, honey," the mother of three encouraged.

Robert watched as Cyd rose and followed Alex out onto the dance floor. He put his arm around her waist, and they began moving slowly to the music.

"Alex," she worried, "what good is Clarence's money if we don't have a plan?"

He smiled like a forty's movie star with dentures. "Whatever happens, we'll always have Pablo."

She studied him with her head cocked to one side. "Alex Farmer, I do believe you're a romantic."

"You found me out. And you?"

"And me, what?"

"Are you a romantic?"

She snorted her disdain, but her eyes were smiling. She had never allowed herself this degree of vulnerability before. Not with any man. It felt like the time she tried to bungee jump—just before stepping off the ledge. She was falling through space now and without realizing it, she was waltzing perfectly.

"I thought you said you couldn't dance."

His voice was a breath of wind and sounded like love. "I can't," she murmured.

Robert stood at the bar watching them dance. If he didn't know better, he could have sworn her feet weren't touching the floor. Cyd had never looked at him the way she was looking at Alex. It made him sad in a way, sad for his loss. At the same time, he was glad for what they had found.

Chapter Twenty-One

The Lies That Bind

Senator Sam Seeley received a call from the Montana Attorney General that his son Ty had been arrested for murder and was being extradited to Polson. Sam called his pilot and told him to fuel the plane, and by late that afternoon the Citation was on its way back to Montana with Sam and his wife Annie as passengers.

Lake County District Attorney Lydia Stone was an aspiring Native American screen writer. She had entitled her latest screenplay, "The Great Swimming Pool Massacre: Based on a True Story". It was her belief that this was the script that was finally going to get her through the door and launch her Hollywood career . . . *if* she could win a conviction. It looked easy, but it was the easy ones that could fool you.

Jesse Long Bow knew he was going to get the death penalty. It didn't matter that there wasn't enough evidence to charge him in the murder of the scientist he had killed some time earlier in the mountains. There were witnesses to the three other murders out on the Wild Horse Island, a witness to the kid he had torched in his truck in Pablo, and forensics had matched the bullets in the dead cop they had found beside the road near Ronan to Long Bow's gun. He was a dead man walking.

Most of what the key witnesses told the police was true. Cyd said that she, Mary and Tiffany had been kidnapped for ransom. Alex and Clarence confirmed that Long Bow was not satisfied with the ransom they brought him out on Wild Horse Island. Cyd confirmed that as a result, Long Bow decided to rob Clarence's safe and that he took her with him as a hostage, to show him where the safe was and how to get into it. Cyd said if she hadn't cooperated, they would have killed Mary and Tiffany, which was absolutely true. The police assumed that when the witnesses referred to such things as ransom and safe robbery, they were talking about money. No one contradicted them.

As far as District Attorney Stone was concerned, however, something didn't add up. Why did this Long Bow character keep talking about seeds and strange little colored ones at that? Was he crazy? Delusional, maybe, but not crazy. The story was bizarre. The feeling she couldn't shake was that somebody was lying. In fact, now that she thought about it, it felt like everybody was lying. If Long Bow was after something other than money and killing all these people over a bunch of seeds made no sense at all, then he had to be working for somebody else. Find that somebody else, she told herself, and you've solved your case.

The detectives that got the D.A. her answer told her they wanted a royalty when she sold her screenplay. It wasn't that hard, really. They simply told Long Bow he had a choice: he could face certain execution, or he could maybe look forward to getting out of jail before he died of old age. Did he want to die in prison like the scumball he was, or take his chances of getting released in time to retire to Arizona?

Long Bow didn't even have to think about it; he could have won an Olympic medal with how fast he flipped. He worked for Ty Seeley, he told them. Ty Seeley was paying him and all he was doing was following the little runt's orders.

Bingo, thought District Attorney Lydia Stone after listening to the tape and reading Long Bow's handwritten confession. Hollywood, here I come.

***

Ty Seeley sat cuffed to a table in an interview room in the Helena jail, awaiting the Lake County van that would take him to Polson. He looked like a plump navel orange in his orange jail jumpsuit. Sitting across from him was his Attorney, Milos Flintlock.

Milos was one of the best criminal defense attorneys in the state. Sam called him the minute he heard his son had been arrested. In the early days, Milos had helped get Sam Seeley elected to the Senate for the first time and they had remained close associates ever since. A man of charisma and style, Flintlock was a retired Navy Seal with a skinhead haircut and a demonic goatee. More to the point, he was a real snake charmer when it came to hypnotizing a judge and jury. Things that troubled most people, things like right and wrong, never entered his mind. His view of morality was that it was for missionaries and morons. What he loved most in the world was the game, beating the game, taking the law in a chokehold, as it were, and not letting go until it blacked out. "Justice and the law are incompatible lovers," he liked to say. "Sooner or later, one of them is bound to kill the other."

The rewards for being the best at making certain the worst of the worst went free were remarkable; he was a rich man with a high-rise, Manhattan-style townhouse in downtown Helena near the courthouse and a lavish winter home on a golf course in Scottsdale. His specialty was defending wealthy drug dealers, but he was not above defending the occasional murderer, bless his heart, if the unjustly accused killer could afford it. Such was the case with Ty Seeley. His father, Senator Sam Seeley, could definitely afford it. "Uncle Sam," Milos liked to call him.

However, even Milos didn't know how easy this case was going to be. Nor could he have imagined saying to his friend the Senator, "I'm almost embarrassed to be taking your money." The Senator's response on this occasion was classic Sam Seeley: "Milos," he would drawl, "if your balls were any bigger, you'd have to buy an extra wheelbarrow to carry them in."

At his first meeting with his client, the more Ty talked, the more hyper and agitated he became. "This Long Bow, man, he's crazy. Ever hear of a disgruntled employee? That's what this guy is, man, a disgruntled employee, because I fired him off the place for stealing."

Milos made a pyramid of his fingers and put them under his chin. "Go on."

"That's right, I fired him. That's what I did. I don't know what he was doing out there kidnapping and murdering people. I mean, what the fuck, man. It's my word against the word of a goddamn murderer, right? Am I right or am I right?"

Milos smiled—if you can call the slightly upturned corners of a reptile's mouth a smile. "You should have been an attorney, Ty."

"Well, I'm not taking the fall for this is all I can say. You hearin' me? I'm innocent, man. I'm being fuckin' set up."

"Meaning what, exactly?"

"You know what. The police are askin' me who *I'm* working for and by God . . ." He buried his face with his hands with a sob. "Fuck me, man."

What charm there might have been in Milos' smile was gone. "As your attorney," he hissed, "I advise you to stop talking."

"I'm not talkin', man. You see me talkin'? All I'm sayin' is, as my father's fuckin' attorney, you better do something about this, because if you think I'm goin' to jail for something that wasn't even my idea, you and him are both fuckin' crazy."

***

The press descended on Polson like a school of piranha, gnashing their teeth and tearing off bits and pieces of scandalous fiction that would later be reported as absolute fact. A Senator's son had been arrested in a sensational murder and kidnapping case and the tabloids and TV talk shows were in a feeding frenzy over the lurid and shocking details.

Ty Seeley's arraignment at the Polson courthouse where he would enter a plea and bail would or would not be set was scheduled to begin in thirty minutes. The courtroom was already jammed.

Annie Seeley sat anxiously on the edge of one of the hard, wooden courtroom benches, staring straight ahead, her gentle smile twisted in anguish. Cyd was crammed in next to her, holding her hand. Without Cyd at her side, she probably would have fallen to pieces. Alex was wedged in next to Cyd on her other side. She was as glad for his presence as Annie was for hers.

"I don't understand any of this," Annie lamented in a small voice. The gracious, silver-haired southern lady with the bright, youthful eyes looked tired and fragile. "What earthly reason would Ty have to kidnap and murder people—especially you, Cydney. Oh, my darling girl, I am so sorry. Are you sure you're all right?"

Cyd squeezed her hand and gave her a reassuring smile.

"He wouldn't have any reason for doing this," she went on. "Not for money, at any rate. He's wealthy in his own right. Anything he wants, he just has to ask." She shook her head stubbornly. "I don't believe any of it, not for a minute. This is all a monumental mistake."

Cyd took a deep breath. "Annie, there's a lot you don't know. It's not about money."

"Whatever do you mean, dear?"

"I . . . I shouldn't tell you. Not here. Ask me later."

Down the marble hallway from the courtroom, two officers stood guard outside the closed door to a private conference room. Inside, Sam Seeley was meeting with his son. The stubby defendant, dressed in a suit, tie and ostrich skin cowboy boots, was shackled to a chair. It was a secure room, and he was with his father, a United States Senator, so the guards outside the door were not concerned. Nonetheless, the muffled shouting from inside the room grew so loud that one of the officers opened the door and stuck his head in to make sure everything was all right.

Both Ty and his father were red-faced with anger. Sam Seeley smoothed a blue and white silk tie over a powder blue shirt and tucked it back inside the jacket of his immaculate suit, thanking the guard politely for his concern and assuring him he was just explaining some things to his bone-head son. The guard nodded knowingly and withdrew from the room, closing the door softly behind him.

Back in the hallway, the muffled sounds from inside the room once again grew heated. The two officers exchanged glances and the one who had just looked into the room rolled his eyes.

Minutes later the door opened, and Sam Seeley stormed out. "Ever wonder why you ever had kids?" he asked the officers, pausing to compose himself.

The guards were in complete sympathy since they both had children of their own.

Ty Seeley could be heard shouting at his father from inside the room where he was still handcuffed to the chair. "Just fuckin' do it and do it fast, man, or you know what's goin' to happen!"

It took every bit of self-control Sam had not to go back in there and throttle him.

"I told you," he said through clenched teeth, "it's being handled."

The hearing began on schedule. The bailiff announced, "All rise," there was a noisy shuffling of feet, the judge entered and took her seat.

A fuckin' Indian broad for a judge, and me on trial for murderin' a bunch of fuckin' Indians, Ty thought. I am so screwed.

Milos Flintlock sat next to Ty at the defense table looking pleasantly dangerous. Sam Seeley was in the first row behind the defense. Several rows back his wife Annie sat up straight and clutched Cyd's hand. District Attorney Lydia Stone, flanked by her two best prosecutors, smiled from the prosecution table at her old friend, Judge Whitefish. The judge returned her greeting with the smallest of nods.

I am so screwed, Ty repeated nervously to himself.

Judge Whitefish quickly dispensed with the preliminaries, read the charges and asked the defendant, "How do you plea?"

Ty tried to speak, nothing came out of his dry throat, and he had to try again. "Not guilty . . . your honor."

Just then the courtroom door opened and another attorney from the prosecutor's office walked in, moved rapidly down the aisle to the prosecution's table and huddled with Stone and her staff. The judge glowered impatiently as they talked in hushed whispers.

The huddle broke up with District Attorney Stone hanging her head. She looked up, sighed heavily and addressed the court in a shaky voice. "Your honor, the prosecution is forced to drop all charges."

"Approach the bench!"

Both attorneys dutifully obeyed.

The Judge looked down sternly. "Now will someone please tell me what the hell is going on?"

Milos gave the limp D.A. his reptile smile. He seemed unusually pleased with himself.

Lydia Stone sighed again. "The witness for the prosecution has been murdered, your honor."

Judge Whitefish turned white. "He was your whole case, I take it?" Lydia nodded in misery.

The Judge motioned in disgust for the attorneys to return to their seats, then banged down her gavel. "Case is dismissed," she announced in a stentorian voice. "Mr. Seeley, you are free to go."

The courtroom erupted in noise, reporters ran for the exit, Ty turned and gave his father a big bear hug and his mother Annie collapsed weeping into Cyd's arms.

***

In the extraordinarily violent world of the *narcotraficantes* (drug traffickers), Angel Ramon Ayala was the *Jefe de Jefes* (Boss of Bosses). He fancied himself the king of Mexico, which wasn't too far from the truth given that he had probably killed more people than the bubonic plague. It didn't seem to matter much. The homicidal psychopath was known and loved throughout Mexico for both his charm and his work with sick children. A devoted family man who had slaughtered countless families, a devout Catholic who had tortured priests, a builder of hospitals and schools who had blown up entire villages for revenge, this almost mythical *Jefe de Jefes* was affectionately known as Don Bueno, a corruption of the name of the patron saint of sick children, Saint Beuno Gasulsych. Many *narcocorridos* (ballads of the drug traffic) had been written and sung about him.

Chalino Garza, better known as *El Cirujano* (The Surgeon), had a face that looked like it was molded out of lumpy clay and left half finished. He earned his nickname by being good with a knife—so good, in fact, that as far as he was concerned, murder was an art form. Like many artists, however, he had an ego problem: he was proud of his art and wanted people to know who had executed it. His pride was his downfall, and as a consequence, he got caught. Up until then, and for most of his distinguished career as a coldblooded killer, The Surgeon had worked as a valued associate of Don Bueno.

The Surgeon had been brought up to Polson from the Montana State Prison in Deer Lodge as a witness in a separate murder trial that was scheduled to start that same week. It was a case involving a rival drug dealer that Don Bueno wanted put behind bars. The Surgeon, who had nothing to lose, was only too happy to oblige his old *Jefe* by providing the necessary testimony that was to put him away for good.

To his bewilderment, The Surgeon was awakened in the middle of the night, taken from his Polson jail cell and ushered into a brightly lit interview room. Shielding his eyes from the glare of a bare lightbulb, he discovered that Milos Flintlock had come to call. They shook hands warmly. He liked his former attorney even though Milo had failed to get him off and his trial had ended in a sentence of three consecutive life terms. He didn't hold a grudge. Hell, there were so many witnesses to his "artwork" that the Pope himself couldn't have gotten him off. And it wasn't a total loss. He felt he had finally received the public acclaim he deserved for his artistic talent.

Milos nodded to the guard that everything was all right and the guard left them alone. The defense attorney got straight to the point, telling the prisoner he needed a small favor. In return he was willing to offer money, a lot of money. *El Cirujano* stared back impassively—he already had money. Milo offered him unlimited drugs to sell in prison. The stoic stare didn't change—he had drugs. Milo offered a cushy job in the prison infirmary where he could be around lots of scalpels and other sharp instruments. A slow grin spread across the assassin's face and he nodded in agreement.

Milos slid the flat of his hand across the table and *El Cirujano* covered it with his own. The attorney then withdrew his hand, and The

Surgeon was left holding a plastic boxcutter with a flat, retractable razor blade about the size of a sharp carpenter's pencil.

The next day, in the showers of the county jail, they found Jesse Long Bow dead. A Smiley Face had been drawn across his neck in a thin red line that ended at a severed carotid artery on either side. One eyeball had been popped from its socket, adroitly cut and scooped, and left to dangle. The thumb from his tattooed hand had been removed and unceremoniously stuffed into the empty eye socket. The exact order of these events, however, was impossible to determine. The box cutter itself had found its way down the shower drain. It happened so fast that no one saw the assailant, but no one could argue that the murder wasn't the work of a true artist.

Chapter Twenty-Two

Annie's Gambit

When Eloise arrived back in Helena with Otis and her son, a startling thing happened—she gave up Goth. As a mortician's wife, death wasn't a game anymore, it was a business, and businesses have a way of taking the fun out of the most passionate hobby. Goth was therefore, lovingly, laid to rest in the place where youthful dreams go.

They were married in Las Vegas. It was a little out of the way to swing that far west on their drive north from Houston to Helena, but Otis was in no hurry, and he wanted Elton to see some sights that he might never get a chance to see again. Wedged behind the wheel of Eloise's small blue Honda heading west on I-10 through Arizona with his new family, he looked like ten pounds of laundry in a five-pound sack.

They spent the night in Phoenix and the next morning took U.S. 60 north to Wickenburg, picked up U.S. 93 north from there, turned west on I-40 and traveled to Kingman before again picking up U.S. 93. It was late in the afternoon when they arrived at Hoover dam.

While the boy was ogling the massive gravity-arch dam in the Black Canyon of the Colorado River, Otis and Eloise stood in the warm winter sun looking down at the dizzying, concave curve of concrete. Otis had been putting this conversation off, dreading the thought of it, but the truth had to be told. Before they went any further with this relationship, he wanted Eloise to understand exactly what she was getting into. The Cannastar plants were gone and there was no way of getting them back. Once the remaining bags of dried tea leaves ran out, he and Elton would die . . . slowly and painfully as anyone else with their respective illnesses. If they had more Cannastar, they would likely live long and healthy lives, but that was not the case. What they had at best was a reprieve, a stay of execution, a long farewell. In the end, Eloise would be left alone with not one loss, but two.

It was the hardest thing he ever had to say. Eloise listened in silence, then turned to look over the edge of the dam. The sight of the water rushing out of its base some seven hundred feet below left her feeling lightheaded. "You want to jump?" she asked when he finally quit talking. "Is that what you're saying?"

He looked down nervously and backed away from the railing.

"No?" she went on. "Then we're not going to die today, are we? You, me or Elton."

He vigorously shook his head.

"Tomorrow never comes, Otis. At least not the way we imagine it. We make stuff up and spend the rest of our time being upset about it. And you want to know the irony? Having something to lose and being willing to lose it is what makes life worth living. We all die too soon. It's about being grateful for what we have right now that counts. And right now, what I have is you. And you have me. Happiness like this isn't some kind of accident. It's a choice. Me, I choose happiness. What about you?"

He looked at her standing there on the precipice of that staggering concrete monument, the sun on her seductive smile and neck tattoo, and he thought his heart would burst with joy. "Thank you," was all he could manage to say without crying.

Eloise pressed herself against him and the rheostat on her amazing internal heater went up. "You're welcome," she replied. "Now here's what you're going to do. You're going to marry me, and if you say no, I'm going to throw you off this dam myself."

Otis was speechless.

"Don't think for a minute I can't do it, either. I lift weights."

And that was how they got engaged.

The sun was just going down over the desert as they drove up Las Vegas Boulevard gawking at the lights of a circus that was always in town. The ring toss and the dart throw had been replaced by sophisticated electronic games, but the carnies still took your money on the midway, the clowns on their stilts still laughed down at the rubes and the oversized panda still stayed on the shelf, a prize too high for anyone to reach. Elton, who to his mother's delight was actually looking and feeling better thanks to the Cannastar tea Otis was feeding him, pointed excitedly at all the G-rated rides that wrapped around the X-rated hotels. When he was told he could ride every one of them if he wanted to, the boy grinned like he hadn't grinned in years. Eloise noticed he was even starting to get his hair back. His head looked like the fuzz on a brand-new tennis ball.

They checked into the Wynn Resort, made an appointment at the hotel wedding chapel and before the night was out Eloise Funk, alias Eloise Small, became Mrs. Eloise Appleseed.

***

Annie, there's a lot you don't know. That's what Cyd had said. Annie Seeley couldn't get the remark out of her mind.

Clarence Big Foot loaned Cyd and Alex a truck and horse trailer so they could haul their horses back to Helena. When Cyd walked into her house, the red message light on her phone recorder was blinking and the digital readout said she had two messages. The first was from Otis: "Hey, Cyd. Hope you weren't too bored while I was gone. Guess what? I got married! Call me so you and Alex can meet my new bride."

The other was from Annie: "Cydney, dear. We're staying over at the ranch for a few days. That thing you said to me in court before the hearing started is very troubling. Can you please call me and maybe we can get together and talk? You did say to ask you later. I hope this isn't a bad time." She left her number.

Cyd returned both calls. She congratulated Otis, told him she was looking forward to meeting his new wife and said she had good news of her own. No, she hadn't married Alex, why would he think that? She didn't want to talk about it on the phone, it was too much to explain, but boy, was he going to be excited. She said she'd meet him tomorrow morning at ten at his place.

Next, she dialed the Seeley ranch, praying Annie would pick up. And, she did. Annie was glad Cyd wanted to get together, happy that she was willing to answer her questions, but was baffled by why on earth she would want to meet at a funeral home of all places. Cyd said she would try and explain everything tomorrow morning, asked if Annie could be there around eleven and asked her to please trust her until then. They hung up and Cyd thought, I just hope I can trust *you*.

***

Cyd and Alex came through the front door of Otis's densely foliated mortuary with Cyd wheeling a carry-on suitcase behind her. A friend of Otis's who owned another funeral home in town, Crane Stevens, had come over while Otis was away and faithfully watered his plants for him. Without Otis around to keep things trimmed back, the place was starting to look like a jungle reclaiming an ancient pyramid.

Otis greeted them with enthusiastic hugs. He was still heartbroken over what had happened in his attic and had not been able to bring himself to go up there since he had been back.

A large woman with dyed black hair and a boy with peach fuzz for hair came down the stairs. There was something immediately erotic about the woman and something immediately likeable about the boy. Cyd and Alex met and immediately adored them both. Eloise, of course, knew all about them from what Otis had told her and couldn't stop gushing over the effects of the Cannastar on her son Elton.

Otis made tea and he and Eloise listened on the edge of their seats while the harrowing stories were told of finding and digging up the seeds, the ride over the mountains, meeting Big Foot and his family, the kidnapping, the murders, the rescue . . . and of the charges against Ty Seeley being dropped after Long Bow was murdered in jail. When they learned that eight one-gallon bags of the Cannastar seed had been recovered, they cheered like they had been part of the war party that captured the kidnappers.

Cyd wanted to know where so many Cannastar seeds had come from, and Otis explained he had harvested them for Maury, but had no idea what the scientist had done with them. He assumed he was using them in his lab for more research.

Otis was so excited over the idea of growing more Cannastar that he couldn't stop talking. "We'll grow it for ourselves, we'll grow it for everybody in the world!" he cried. They would begin again, and this time they'd do it right and not get caught. Idea after idea poured out of him about where and how to grow the seeds—none of which were practical or realistic. Every time he thought of something that might work, he found a reason to reject it. He would jump up with one inspiration after another, only to sit back down again when he realized it was too risky or wouldn't fly. Finally, he fell back in his chair frustrated and exhausted, no closer to a solution than when he started.

Eloise smiled quietly. Her son and husband were going to live, that was all she knew, and that was all that mattered. Somehow, the news about the seeds didn't surprise her. She was telling Otis that he would think of something, that a solution was out there, soothing him confidently, when the bell over the front door rang and a small figure walked in bundled in an elegant fur coat and hat so large that only her nose was showing.

"Annie!" Cyd cried.

The matriarch of the Seeley dynasty took off her outer garments, scanned the entry and parlor of the funeral home with a gardener's eye and gasped at its splendor. She had never seen exotic plants like these grown with such success, not in Montana. The magnificence of the indoor rain forest momentarily distracted her from her anxieties.

Otis introduced himself, and from that moment on they were great friends. It was thirty minutes before Annie stopped asking Otis enthusiastic questions about how he had achieved this or that with his unusual plants and reluctantly turned to the subject of why she had come.

They went into the kitchen and sat around the table. Annie accepted a cup of chamomile tea but left it untouched. She needed information. Her husband and son were lying to her, of that she was certain. The way she could tell was by the way she felt when they answered her persistent questions. Instead of making her feel better about what had happened, their replies made her angry. What really sent up a red flag was when she asked about these strange seeds she kept hearing about, the ones the murdered kidnapper insisted he'd been hired to steal. Even if her suspicions were wrong, and he hadn't been working for their son, the seeds would have intrigued her in any case; seeds were life, seeds were her life.

Sam told her she was crazy if she believed the seeds existed, even crazier if she believed Ty had anything to do with it. It made her so mad when he said it, that the top of her head almost exploded. She would never have been so rude to say so in polite company, but privately she called it her 'bullshit meter.' The gauge was infallible; it was how she knew, in this case, that something was terribly wrong.

She turned to Cyd, who she had always trusted. "So dear, tell me please. All this talk about seeds. Is it true? The man that was murdered in jail who wouldn't stop talking about them, was he crazy? If the seeds exist, what are they? What do they do?"

Annie sat motionless as Cyd and Otis told her everything, right from the beginning, starting with Maury's research. Otis and Eloise then told her what had happened down at Rxon headquarters in Houston. And why. Annie's first show of emotion was when the name Rxon was mentioned. She jumped as if touched by a cattle prod; her husband mentioned them often. Otis told her about the hydroponic garden in his attic, about being arrested, and his Cannastar plants getting torn up and confiscated. He explained how it all led back to the drug companies, to Rxon in particular, and their frantic efforts to destroy anybody and anything that might threaten their cash flow. "Never mind that Cannastar could change medical science," he added. "Never mind that it could change the way people live and die forever."

Cyd saw her growing enthusiasm and touched her hand. "This is a dangerous game, Annie. Your husband and the people he works for at Rxon are fully aware we have the seeds now. That means we can never meet or talk about this again. The last thing I want to do is put you in danger too."

Annie was overwhelmed. This was too much. She shook her head and refused to believe it. Her world and her whole belief system were being challenged.

Eloise drew her son to her side. "Mrs. Seeley . . ."

"Please, Eloise, call me Annie." Her voice was polite, but distant and vague.

"My son Elton here was dying of leukemia," Eloise persisted. "Look at him. Does he look all that sick to you?"

Annie absently stroked the boy's fuzzy head. "Is it true, honey? Are you really sick with leukemia?"

"Not anymore," the boy smiled happily. "Otis gives me this tea to drink every day and every day I get better." His smile widened when he saw he had her ear. "Have you ever been to Las Vegas, Mrs. Seeley, because you should go. It's really cool?"

"I know, darling. I was there once."

"I had pancreatic cancer," Otis interrupted. "Cyd had breast cancer."

Annie's heart-shaped mouth fell open.

"We're both in complete remission thanks to the Cannastar," Cyd added.

The wealthy, unpretentious matron turned to Alex, visibly shaken. "What about you, sir? What are you dying of?"

"Curiosity."

"Curiosity?"

"I'm curious how a woman, any woman, could have the courage to sit here and listen to all this, knowing it condemns her family, without getting up and walking out."

"I thought about it," Annie admitted. "Believe me."

Cyd took her aunt's hand compassionately in hers.

Annie roused herself, heartened by Cyd's touch. "What . . . what about these seeds? What do they look like? Can I see them?"

Cyd got up, retrieved her carry-on suitcase from the other room, brought it into the kitchen and unzipped it. Inside, neatly packed, were eight bulging plastic Ziploc bags of Cannastar seed. The reason she had brought them with her today was because she knew just where she wanted to hide them: the coffin that had kept Otis's bags of Cannastar leaves safe during the raid. She took one out and handed it to Annie.

Annie turned it over in her hands and opened it. "May I?" she asked. Cyd nodded for her to go ahead.

Annie dipped her hand in and ran it through the colorful seeds, letting them sift through her fingers. A look of wonder came over her face and her eyes filled with tears. "My God," she said. "My God!" She tried to reclose the bag, but her hands were shaking. Cyd obligingly closed it for her. Annie laid her head on her arms and began to sob.

"Annie, don't," Cyd pleaded, putting her arm around her.

"My husband, my son, they're not murderers . . ." She looked up with tortured eyes. "They couldn't be!"

"I'm sorry," Cyd sympathized.

"It's a lie, isn't it? My marriage, my life. All one big, fat lie!"

"The only thing that isn't a lie, Annie, is you," Cyd assured her. "You're one of the truest people I've ever known."

"And look where it's gotten me!" A growing fear overcame her. "What do I do now? Where do I go, what do I do?"

They talked on into the afternoon as Annie struggled with her dilemma.

Otis was still having his business calls forwarded to his friend Crane Stevens's mortuary and did not have any funerals scheduled for this week. Until yesterday, when he had to appear in court, he didn't even know if he was going to go to jail or not. To his immense relief, it had all worked out. All he had to do now was not get caught growing marijuana for the next fourteen years and he would remain a free man.

Cyd tried to get Annie to lie down, but she wouldn't hear of it. They tried to get her to eat something and she wouldn't do that either. Alex finally got her to take some fluids. Crushed and betrayed, the more she talked the angrier she got.

"My son isn't bright enough or ambitious enough to come up with anything like this. Not on his own, at any rate. His father was pulling the strings as always." Saying it out loud for the first time inflamed her. "Sam turned Ty into a murderer! My husband is a murderer!"

"I wish I could tell you different," Alex said gently.

"Well, he's not going to get away with it," Annie fumed. "Not if I can help it."

"Take it from me," Eloise counseled. "Divorce the bastard."

"Pshaw. We southern ladies don't get divorced. We get even. The question is how . . ."

The clouds suddenly lifted and the sun came out, lighting her face. "You people say your only problem is a safe place to grow the seeds? Maybe I can help with that."

"You can't be involved," Cyd insisted.

"That's for me to decide. I've never heard of anything so amazing in all my life as this Cannastar of yours, and I have the perfect place to grow it!"

They looked at her skeptically.

She hurried on. "Where, you might ask? I happen to have the most beautiful new greenhouse in the world. It's absolutely huge. State of the art. Otis, you're going to love it."

"Me? How am I going to love it?"

"Because you and your wife and son are going to move back east with me and together, we're going to grow some righteous weed. Right under the old fox's nose. What do you think of that?"

"I think you're crazy." Cyd was appalled. "I can't go back there. Your husband knows what I look like, what Alex looks like. He or Rxon or both are going to be sending other people after us, after the seeds. We can't be seen hanging anywhere near your place."

"Then you'll have to wait and visit me after dark, won't you?" Annie smiled. "Sam doesn't know what Otis looks like. If he sees him around, I'll tell him I hired him to help me grow my orchid hybrids. Oh, Otis, you'll be perfect. I've seen what you can do. You're the only one for this job, you know you are."

Eloise happily clapped her hands.

"Sam is never around anyway," Annie assured them. "He spends most of his nights in Washington with his whores." She pronounced it *whoors*. "When he is around, he doesn't pay me the least attention and couldn't care less what I do. He told me in no uncertain terms he wouldn't be seen dead setting foot in my greenhouse—any greenhouse. He wouldn't want anyone to think he was a farmer, you know. As a fifth-generation rancher, he hates farmers."

"I knew there was something I didn't like about him," said Alex Farmer.

Annie's internal world was shattered, and it hurt more than she could bear. She wanted revenge, and she wanted to set things right. If I can help to heal the world, she thought, then maybe I can make up for my pathetic, miserable, wasted life. "I want to do this," she maintained. "Oh, Otis, please? Won't you say yes?"

Otis had turned pale. "I guess . . . I guess if I'm going to do this . . ." He mopped at his brow with a handkerchief. "I should start looking for somebody to buy my business."

"Bravo!" Annie cried. "Hurray for us." Then turning to Cyd and Alex, "As for the two of you, I suggest you start working on distribution."

Alex blinked rapidly. "Distribution?"

"I don't know that much about dealing drugs, darlings, but I do know, if you're going to grow something illegal, you're going to need a way of selling it to the public."

Alex couldn't believe what he was hearing coming out of this demure little lady's mouth. But she had a point. Even if they could grow it, how were they going to distribute it?

***

When she left the ranch the next morning to go back to Virginia, Annie could not bring herself to say goodbye to her son. Ty didn't notice. On the flight home, enveloped in one of the plush leather seats aboard their private Citation, Annie was so disgusted with her husband that she couldn't bear to look at him. Sam didn't notice either.

Then somewhere over Iowa, Annie began smiling to herself and had to cover her mouth to keep from laughing out loud. Her bright blue eyes darted furtively left and right. She had a secret, a wonderful secret, and it was a pretty darn good pain pill, all things considered. Safely stowed in the cargo hold of the jet, buried among her other luggage, was an extra carry-on bag. She knew that her sadness would catch up with her sooner or later, but mad was easier than sad, and right now she damn well wanted to be mad.

After much discussion, Cyd, Alex and Otis had come up with a plan. They agreed that the most likely targets, if someone were to come after the seeds, would be Cyd and Alex. The last place Sam Seeley or anybody else would think to look for them was in Annie Seeley's luggage. So, they divided up the stash. Annie would take four bags of the Cannastar seed with her on the plane and Otis would take four bags with him when he drove back east with his family. This way, if either of them got busted, all would not be lost and they would still have a backup.

Annie was amazed at the feeling of anticipation and satisfaction it gave her knowing that Sam Seeley was being so helpful in the orchestration of his own downfall. To think! She was going to be a part of taking down that murdering bastard of a husband of hers and maybe, in the process, even Big Pharma. It was a guilty pleasure that gave her the chills—so much so that she had to remind herself that she was *also* doing it to help mankind. And she would be helping to grow a whole new species of plant. Now that was truly exciting.

And more dangerous than she could possibly imagine.

Chapter Twenty-Three

A Love Too Far

A hulking, lumbering motor home towing a blue Honda toad exited the interstate and pulled into a RV park in Madison, Wisconsin, with its windshield and front end covered in road bugs. In the luggage area under the motor home, safely hidden behind one of the bulkheads, were four bulging Ziploc bags of Cannastar seed.

Otis wheezed as he came up the step and reentered the RV after attaching the sewer and electric lines. Plopping down in the driver's seat, he hit a series of switches and the luxurious home-on-wheels leveled itself on the concrete pad while four slides whooshed out of the sides of the coach and expanded the interior. It was the end of their second day on the road. Two or three more days and they would be in Virginia. Eloise and Elton couldn't wait, they were so excited.

Otis figured that once he got set up at Annie's, it would take him another four months or so to grow a new crop of Cannastar. That should give Cyd and Alex plenty of time to solve their marketing and distribution problems. If not, all the Cannastar plants in the world weren't going to help them.

In preparation for the move, he telephoned his friend and competitor Crane Stevens to tell him the Appleseed Funeral Home was for sale. Crane jumped at the chance and the deal was consummated in a week. The ambitious undertaker had always wanted to expand his mortuary business, and this was the perfect opportunity. With a small part of the proceeds from the sale, Otis bought the motor home and found, to his delight, that for once he could fit behind the wheel of what he was driving without being cramped.

That evening at the Madison RV park, Otis got a call on his cell. He answered, and the more he listened, the more distressed he became.

Eloise looked on with concern. "Anything important?" she asked when he hung up.

"That was Cyd."

"And?"

"She called to say Alex has left for L.A. That he's gone."

"Gone?" Eloise gasped. "To Los Angeles? Why?"

The retired mortician sighed and collapsed heavily into a chair. "She wouldn't say why."

***

Otis and his family had been gone two days when Cyd and Alex drove out to check on Betty Little Horn in Cyd's old truck. Ever since Annie suggested they "start working on distribution," they had puzzled over the dilemma and were no closer to a solution now than when they started. How to publicize an illegal product that a mega-corporation wanted destroyed and get it into the hands of an entire nation without getting murdered or arrested for it seemed all but impossible.

Betty was thrilled to see them. She was still recovering "from where the bastards winged me," but her spirits were good, and she was healing nicely. Her guests were given one-armed hugs and invited in for coffee—on the condition they didn't ask her to take them anyplace else or hide anything else for them. "Not that we didn't kick their butts," she reminded them, spitting into a Styrofoam cup.

Her problem at the moment was that her injury was keeping her from making a living. "A one-armed farrier," she claimed, "is about as much good as a one-armed paperhanger."

Cyd and Alex spent the afternoon telling her everything that had happened since she dropped them at the cave up in the mountains. Betty listened with delight, howling with laughter at hearing how Big Foot rolled the kidnapper down the hill in the outhouse and crying out, "Second best use of a shitter I ever heard." Then laughing even harder at the story of Long Bow's capture and how the war party had showed up at the last minute to save them. She was none too happy to hear that "sniveling little greaseball Ty Seeley" got off Scott free, but regained her spirits when told how Long Bow met his untimely end.

"They catch the guy that done it?" she asked.

Cyd and Alex both shook their heads.

"If they ever do," Betty grinned, "give him a big wet one for me."

It grew late and it was time to go. Alex was helping Cyd on with her coat when he caught Betty looking at them closely.

"When did this happen?" she asked.

Cyd smiled at the question. "When did what happen?"

"When did the two of you fall in love?"

They both were speechless. For all the emotion that had passed between them since their trip over the mountains to Clarence's place, they had never once discussed their feelings for one another, never found a way to say the words out loud, and in fact were yet to share a lover's bed.

On the way back home to Cyd's ranch, they rode in silence. When they pulled up in front of her log house, they got out of the truck and Alex followed her inside. She was heading for the kitchen when he stopped her.

"Cyd, can we talk about what Betty said to us? The last thing?"

She turned, the corners of her mouth quivering in the knowledge that their lives were about to change forever. "That would be nice. I'd like that."

Just then the phone rang, startling her out her reverie. She went to answer it, listened, took the receiver from her ear and held it out to him indifferently. "It's for you."

Alex said hello, then paled as he listened. He made a few muffled remarks and carefully hung up.

The agony on his face scared her. "What?" she asked. "Did someone die?"

His whole body was trembling. "My wife . . . She woke up. She's awake."

Cyd looked like she was standing in the path of a runaway train. "You're . . . you're married?"

"I'm sorry you had to find out like this."

"Like this?"

"I never thought it would ever come up."

"You never thought . . ." She turned red with anger. "Why would you even say a thing like that?"

He didn't answer.

"Alex, talk to me!"

"That car wreck I was in?"

"What about it?"

"Alicia, my wife, she was in the car with me. She wasn't killed, but it would almost have been better if she had been."

Cyd slumped into a chair in a state of devastation. "How do you mean?"

"She ended up a vegetable. Doctors said she would never wake up again."

"What . . . what happened?" Her voice was barely above a whisper.

"You really want to hear the story?"

She nodded as tears came to her eyes. "Tell me."

***

After four years of marriage, Alicia Farmer was hardly speaking to her husband. She had not let Alex into her bed in over a year. He had tried repeatedly to get her to talk to him or go to couples counseling, but she would always refuse, flaring angrily at the slightest suggestion that they try to work out their problems. They worked different shifts on different floors at MLK, so he rarely saw her at the hospital. At home she was a distant stranger and his patience was wearing thin.

Tonight however, for some reason, Alicia was her old, smiling, sensual self, flitting around the house getting dressed for a party they had been invited to that was being given by one of the doctors she worked with. She was wearing a skintight dress that fit her like a latex glove, and he felt the familiar stirring in his loins for her. Could it be that the worst of whatever was wrong between them was over and they were finally getting back to being a couple again? He had his fingers crossed.

Alicia sat at her dressing table combing out her voluminous blond hair, admiring her cover-girl features and humming softly to herself. She asked him to help her with the clasp to the diamond necklace he had given her for her birthday. Bending to fasten it around her neck, smelling her perfume, he felt lightheaded from wanting her so badly. It had always been this way. She was more like a drug than a wife—a sex drug with highly addictive properties. Viagra on steroids, he called her.

Out loud he said, "What's come over you?"

"Some people just know how to please a girl is all," she answered gaily.

Alex smiled. If he'd known that expensive jewelry was going to make her this happy, he would have bought out the store a long time ago and given it to her.

The party was at the home of Anton Learner, a doctor at MLK that Alex barely knew. He had been surprised when the distinguished black man stopped him in the hospital corridor and was so friendly and cordial in inviting him and Alicia to the party that he and his wife were throwing this weekend. Dr. Learner looked more like a towering, NBA basketball player than the renowned orthopedic surgeon he was. Alex was so taken by his toothy smile and gregarious personality that he accepted the invitation without thinking.

Learner lived on the strand at Manhattan Beach in a house with seven balconies, all with sweeping views of the Pacific. A valet took Alex's black BMW at the front door, as there was practically no parking on the narrow, seaside street. He and Alicia entered the house and were greeted warmly by both Anton and his gracious wife, Natalie. Alex was taken aback. Alicia and Natalie looked so much alike with their flowing manes of blond hair and Sports-Illustrated bodies that he could have sworn they were fraternal twins. The house was overflowing with people from the medical field, many of whom Alex knew from the hospital, and before long he found himself having a good time with old friends.

Alex was off in a corner talking shop with his dumpy looking, kindhearted boss, Conner Creel, the head of the ER at MLK, when he realized he hadn't seen Alicia in over an hour. He excused himself and went wandering through the crowd looking for her. Poking his head outside to see if she was on one of the balconies, he realized he had to take a leak. The bathrooms on the first and second floors all seemed to be occupied so he kept climbing until he was on the top floor where he found a restroom door that wasn't locked. He opened it to find Alicia on the countertop with her legs spread wide and Anton Learner undulating between them.

Alicia came running out the front door of the house with her clothes in disarray just as the valet was bringing Alex's BMW around. It had begun to rain, and water was coming down in sheets. Alex got in the car and took off just as she tore open the passenger door and threw herself into the passenger seat. They both were soaking wet. Alicia's hair was plastered pathetically to her face and her mascara was running.

"You had no right to embarrass me like that!" she yelled.

Alex slid around a corner on the wet pavement and accelerated up the block. He was so mad he couldn't speak.

"I want a divorce!" she shouted. "You're boring and stupid and I hate you!"

Alex clenched his hands on the wheel. "How long have you been sleeping with him? Is this the first time, or is it an affair?"

"We're in love, you stupid ass. He's going to leave his wife and we're getting married!"

"How long, I asked you!"

"A goddamn year! Maybe more if it's any of your business! What do you care, anyway?"

The rain came down harder as they pulled onto the freeway. The weather report hadn't said anything about thunderstorms, but what else was new? She started flailing at him with her fists and he shoved her back in her seat. He could see almost nothing through the windshield. All that was visible was a blur of taillights in front of him and the white line flashing by on the wet concrete. He didn't know how fast he was going, and he didn't care. All he wanted was to get home and get away from this woman who was screaming in his ear, flashing her fingernails at him and breaking his heart.

"You're my wife!" He shouted as he swerved to avoid a car that cut him off and laid on his horn. "How could you do this to me?"

"I won't be your wife for long, Doctor I-don't-have-a-specialty. Anton and me, we got plans, and they don't include you!"

"God *damn* you!" Alex slammed the steering wheel with his fist and Alicia jumped and shrunk back. "God damn you both, you lying whore!"

He sped up, cutting in and out of traffic. Through the driving rain, he saw up ahead that the traffic was beginning to make wild moves, swerving from lane to lane and diving for the shoulder. He started to hit the brakes, and, for an instant, all he could see was a pair of headlights, going the wrong way on the freeway, coming straight at him . . .

A blinding light.

Then nothing.

Fortunately, the MRI showed only minor damage to his back. The doctors had no real explanation for the excruciating pain he was in. The pills they gave him helped, but he knew even then they were no solution.

While recuperating in the hospital, he would struggle every day into a wheelchair, wheel himself down the hall, into an elevator, down another hall and into the room where they had Alicia on life support. She looked so calm and peaceful lying there with her long blond hair combed out over the pillow. If it wasn't for the breathing tube down her throat, he could have easily imagined she was just resting.

A doctor with a stethoscope stuffed in the pocket of his white coat came in and put a compassionate hand on his shoulder. "She's in a persistent vegetative state, Alex. That means . . ."

He shook off the hand. "I know what it means!"

"The humanitarian thing to do, as you know, is to let us . . ."

"Pull the plug?" He was aghast. "Are you crazy?"

The doctor left quietly and never brought it up again. As far as Alex knew, Anton Learner never bothered to come and see her. Not in the hospital, not any time afterward.

***

Cyd sat staring into space as he finished, too heartbroken to speak.

Alex stood watching her in agony. "I was hoping this was all in the past, but I guess the past is never over."

She looked up. "Not when you can't tell the truth about it. Alex, finding another man with his wife the way you did; anyone would have reacted the same way. It was a terrible accident that happened, that's all."

The desolation in her voice only made him hate himself more. "So you say."

"The car that hit you was going the wrong way on the freeway. How is that your fault?"

"I was driving, okay? Nobody else. Me."

"Why didn't you tell me before now? I could have helped. You can't keep this kind of guilt and shame bottled up inside, it'll kill you."

"I didn't want to burden you with it." Heartbroken, he smiled. "I didn't come to Montana to fall in love, Cyd. Not like this."

"Like this?"

"I love you more than I ever thought I could love another person."

Taken aback, she searched his eyes. "So . . . so where does that leave us?"

"It leaves me with unfinished business. I have to go back to L.A. I don't know for how long. I'll call you."

"Please don't."

"What?"

"You think you're the only one that's been hurt?" she flared. "You think you're the only one that's in pain?"

"No, that's not what I think at all. I understand . . ."

She threw her arms around his neck sobbing. "Do you? Do you have any idea how much I love you? Do you know what this does to me?"

"I just need some time to work things out. I have to see her, talk to her, put an end to all this."

She pulled away and slowly dried her eyes. "Go. Do what you have to do."

He hesitated. "You'll be here when I get back?"

She fell into one of her long, dark silences. "I'll drive you to the airport."

Chapter Twenty-Four

Alicia

Alex flew from Helena to Salt Lake City, changed planes and landed back in Los Angeles where he took an Uber to the marina. After the accident that put Alicia in a coma and totaled his BMW, he had sold his condo in Santa Monica and bought a sailboat in Marina Del Rey. It was where he lived during the year his life spiraled out of control, and now that he was back, it was the only place he had to go. His back was killing him. He had forgotten to ask Cyd for some Cannastar to take with him. He didn't care. The pain was penance for his sins.

His Uber pulled into one of the marina parking lots next to a seawall where rows of docks crammed with power boats and sailboats jutted out into a wide channel. Alex got out with his backpack and walked to one of the cars parked in the lot—a battered lime green sedan with rusted fenders that he had bought for transportation after the wreck and affectionately nicknamed "Slime".

His intention was to drive straight to the nursing home and see Alicia. He got in, turned the key, and nothing. Not even a click. Slime's battery was dead. A jolt of pain went up his back and left him feeling exhausted. Alicia would have to wait. He shouldered his backpack and headed down one of the gangways.

It had been less than two months since he'd seen his sailboat and was shocked at the decks, rails and rigging that were filthy from the air pollution. A storm was blowing in from the northwest and the boats along his dock were heaving in their slips and straining at their dock lines. Halyards rattled against a thousand masts around the marina sounding like a thousand windchimes. He went aboard intending to go below, but instead sat down in the dirty cockpit and stared out at the choppy water as a feeling of dread came over him.

He had named his boat Pequod because, in the poetry of Whitman and the prose of Emerson and Thoreau, a ship at sea is sometimes a metaphor for the soul, because *Ships at a distance have every man's wish on board,* as Zora Neale Hurston said in her novel *Their Eyes Were Watching God,* and because, like Captain Ahab in his relentless search for Moby Dick aboard the Pequod, he too was obsessed. Not in a self-destructive search for revenge against a pissed-off white whale, but revenge against the madness that had destroyed his life. He thought he had survived the madness when he found Cyd Seeley. But it had found him again.

The Pequod was a forty-eight-foot, center cockpit cutter and as fine of a cruising boat as a man could own, in his opinion. While in medical school he had dreamed of sailing to remote islands of the South Pacific and bringing modern medicine to the indigenous people there, but the dream had gone the way of his other dreams after the accident.

He grew cold and hungry from sitting in the empty cockpit, went below and started to open a can of soup. Thinking better of it, he laid down on his messy bunk just for a moment and closed his eyes.

The storm howling in the rigging roused him from a deep sleep. He sat up, still in his rumpled street clothes, and realized it was morning. Pain shot down his back and down his leg. Edgy and depressed, he didn't want breakfast, he wanted pain pills. One more hour, he told himself. One more day.

Limping up the dock to the parking lot, he ran into another live-aboard sailor who had a pair of jumper cables, and together they managed to get Slime started.

The nursing home where Alicia was being cared for was just off Beverly Boulevard, near Cedars-Sinai Hospital. Driving to it through the storm-flooded Los Angeles streets brought back painful memories of the night of the wreck. He parked Slime in the nursing home parking lot and entered the facility with his stomach in knots. Alicia was sitting propped up in bed staring out the window when he came through her door. She looked like a gaunt skeleton of her former self, a refugee from a concentration camp for anorexia victims.

He forced a smile. "Alicia, it's me."

She turned slowly.

"You're awake! I can't believe it. How are you?"

She was looking past him, straining to see if there was anyone else out in the hall. "Where's Anton?" she asked in a thin, raspy voice. "Has he come yet? Did you see him in the lobby anywhere?"

"I don't think he's around." Alex made an effort to calm his voice. "Was he supposed to be here?"

"I haven't heard from him yet, but he'll come, I know he will. I have to get my hair done. Have you seen my makeup kit?" She struggled weakly to get out of bed, and he eased her back onto the pillows. A nurse bustled in, Alicia sat bolt upright, then fell back in disappointment when she saw who it was.

The nurse smiled at Alex. "You would be Dr. Farmer, I presume?"

He gave a small nod.

"We start physical therapy this afternoon. We're very excited about that, aren't we Mrs. Farmer?" Alicia gave her a blank stare. The nurse smiled again and went on. "I'll check back later after the two of you have had a chance to chat."

"Tell Anton which room I'm in!" Alicia called dismally as the nurse went out.

"Has anyone else been in to see you?" Alex asked, trying to make conversation.

"Just my stupid sister. Says I have to come and live with her. She doesn't believe me when I tell her I'm going to go live with Anton. He's divorcing his wife, you know. She's quite the bitch."

"Do you remember anything about the night of the accident?" he asked. "Anything at all?"

The blank stare returned.

Alex looked out the window at the rain. When he turned back, she had closed her eyes and she was fast asleep. He forced himself to speak. "It's good to see you, Alicia."

Her eyes fluttered opened and she regarded him with hostility. "What?" Oh, yeah . . . you too. You better go. You can't be here when Anton gets here."

***

Meanwhile, Otis was arriving in Arlington, Virginia where he drove to an RV park and parked on a concrete pad complete with utility hookups and outdoor barbeque under the shade of a tree overlooking a small lake. The next day, he unhooked Eloise's blue Honda, squeezed behind the wheel and went to go find Annie. Eloise stayed behind in the RV researching the internet and making phone calls. She wanted to find a good school for Elton as soon as possible.

Otis followed the directions Annie had given him, driving for miles past rolling hills dotted with baronial mansions. Eventually, he came to an ivy-covered stone gatehouse sitting discreetly just off the road in the shelter of some trees. He pulled in and identified himself to the guard who called the house. The massive iron gates across the drive swung open, and he drove through feeling like he was entering the grounds of Buckingham Palace. He followed a narrow winding lane lined with majestic American Elms until a Georgian mansion came into view through the forest. He was wrong, he decided. It wasn't Buckingham Palace after all, it was Balmoral Castle—a rural retreat for royalty, a country home befitting a king and queen.

Annie was waiting for him under the *porte-cochere* and couldn't have been happier to see him if he had stepped out of one of Shakespeare's plays as the fat, vain, comedically boastful Falstaff himself. She got into the passenger seat of his Honda and pointed to her new greenhouse down by the lake. He followed her direction, circling a lawn the size of a soccer field before pulling up in front of the gigantic glass-domed structure.

Once inside the conservatory, Otis was overwhelmed and had to sit, staring in awe at the state-of-the-art facility. "You could grow a national forest in here," he remarked.

Annie beamed. "It's all yours, dear, yours and mine. You ready to kick a little Cannastar butt, or what?"

***

A month after Alex arrived back in Los Angeles, Alicia moved out of the nursing home and in with her sister, Beth Gunn. Beth lived in Rancho Cucamonga with her Korean-born husband and their four beautiful, intelligent Eurasian children. She was a large woman with thunderous thighs, ears that stuck out like side mirrors on a car and eyes that didn't quite line up. Her sister Alicia had inherited all the looks in the family and Beth had gotten the leftovers—which in her case included remarkable insight and an even more remarkable intellect. The mother of four was a computer programmer who worked from home and home-schooled her offspring. She rarely smiled and was extremely stern, but her four students adored her. Her husband, Gi Gunn, was a hardworking gardener who was approximately half her size and spoke very poor English but doted on his family with the same passion as his wife.

Alicia had put on a little weight since coming out of her coma and was walking now with the help of a cane. Alex had helped move her from the medical facility to her sister's house and most days made the two-hour drive on crowded freeways from the marina to Rancho Cucamonga to visit her. Stuck in traffic and breathing smog and exhaust fumes, his back would sometimes flare. On these occasions, he would scream with anger until he was hoarse. The screaming made his throat dry and he would drink a bottle of water. The water made him want to pee. Stuck in four lanes of cars that weren't moving, he would have to pee in the bottle he just drank from. Raised up and contorted around the steering wheel, he reminded himself that a doctor who's served in Iraq and spent five years patching up gang-bangers in east L.A. is nothing if he isn't resourceful.

This went on for another month until late one morning he pulled up in front of Beth's house to find Alicia sitting in the driveway on her suitcase and wearing a heavy coat even though it was a hot and muggy day. His stomach tightened at the upsetting sight. She had on too much makeup and her dry, fizzy hair with two inches of black roots showing was done up in a way that made her look like she had been struck by lightning.

"Alicia, honey, what are you doing out here?" he asked, getting out of his car and approaching her carefully. "Aren't you a little warm in that coat?"

"I keep calling and he doesn't answer so he must be on his way," she cried nervously, peering up and down the street. "Probably he's late, you know, because of the freeways and all."

"Traffic is pretty bad," he agreed.

Just then Beth came out of the house calling back over her shoulder. "You kids keep studying your math. There'll be a test this afternoon." She was wearing a t-shirt with the wild-haired head of Albert Einstein on it.

Seeing Alicia sitting so expectantly on her suitcase with Alex hovering over her, she stopped and put her thick hands on her ample hips.

"She's looking better," Alex observed, "don't you think?"

Beth snorted. "She's not better and she's not going to get better, so stop kidding yourself."

Alex nodded miserably.

"Alicia's my sister and I love her," Beth went on, "but I can't do this anymore. I don't have time for it, and she's scaring the children with her talk about this Anton character."

"I understand."

"Do you? Then do something about it."

"Like what?"

"You're her husband. You figure it out."

"It's either this or the home."

"The home it is then. Now was that so hard?"

He turned to Alicia who sat clutching her purse like she was protecting it from muggers. "Honey, how would you like to move into a nice nursing home out this way so you can be close to your sister? I bet she'll come and visit you every chance she gets."

"Of course, I will," Beth promised.

Panic crept into Alicia's eyes. Despite her once-spectacular beauty, she had always been flighty and unstable. Now that her looks were gone, she was a helpless bird, flapping her emotions like injured wings.

"Maybe he doesn't know I'm getting a divorce and that's why he hasn't come," she moaned. "Maybe he doesn't have Beth's address. If I move, Alex, will you tell him where I've gone? When you see him at the hospital, you have to tell him, all right?"

He smiled sadly. "If I see him, I'll give him your address."

Beth turned and called into the house. "Kids! You ready? Time for your test." Then turning back, "Thank you, Alex. You'll work it out, I know you will."

The moment she was gone Alicia motioned for Alex to come closer. He bent down and she whispered in his ear. "Bitch never liked me because I'm the pretty one."

***

The nursing home where they moved Alicia was just off the freeway in Ontario, a few miles from Beth's house. Alicia had a sunny room that looked out on a peaceful courtyard of grass and flowers, but she spent her time staring hopefully at the door and growing more morose with each passing day. Sometimes when Alex came to visit, she would barely acknowledge him. She kept an array of mood-altering drugs and pain pills in her bathroom, and every time Alex entered her room, he had to resist the urge to raid her medicine cabinet.

One day as he sat with her watching a basketball game on her television and she sat, as usual, staring at her door, she suddenly turned to him and pulled at his arm.

"I wasn't such a bad wife, was I? Do you hate me for being so awful?"

Taken off guard, he hesitated. "Part of me will always love you, Ali."

"Then you understand how I feel about Anton. It's like we're kindred spirits, you and me. I'm glad you're not mad at me."

But he was, oh how he was.

He often thought of Cyd. It was like she was always with him, sitting or standing at his side. At night, lying in his bunk aboard the Pequod staring at the ceiling, her lightly freckled, pale-eyed face and dark-flowing hair would float above him, and he would angrily turn over and pound the pillow.

Weeks passed undistinguished by the defining boundaries of time and space until one evening, when he was in the galley of his boat making pasta with meat sauce, his cell phone rang.

Alicia had committed suicide.

The people at the nursing home told him that when they found her, the mirror in her bathroom was broken and most of her pill bottles were empty.

***

The funeral took place at Forest Lawn in Glendale. Alex sat through the graveside service with a blank face staring at Alicia's flower-draped coffin suspended over a terrible dark hole in the ground. Beth sat next to him with her husband Gi and their four children lined up on folding chairs beside her. A few of Alicia's co-workers from the hospital had come. At some point Alex realized that Anton Learner was not among them.

When the dreadful ritual was over and the minister had said his piece, Gi Gunn took his children on a tour of the gardens, pointing out and naming the various varieties of plants and trees in an effort to take the bitter taste of death out of their mouths. Beth guided Alex away from the grave and they strolled silently along the peaceful pathways of the cemetery. Nature in all her splendor burst from the somber ground around them. They came to a pond with a sparkling fountain and sat down on a bench overlooking the water to watch the graceful swans glide by. Marble angels looked on modestly from a distance.

"She's dead," Alex reflected bitterly.

"Nothing ever dies," Beth sighed.

"You can't know that."

"Life is love, and I know that love never dies."

If he had any pain pills, he would have taken one. His back was killing him, pressure was building behind his eyes and his head felt like it was about to explode.

"There is no beginning and there is no end," she went on wistfully.

He winced and shifted his position on the bench. "Tell that to Alicia."

"Her body is gone, it's true. Her spirit though, her essence, her soul—whatever you want to call it—I believe that goes on."

"To where, Cleveland? To some Fantasy Island in the sky?"

"Back to where we come from. To all that is. To being a part of the great, ecumenical whole of the universe. From there we get to come back in a new, different, healthy body to try and do a little better next time."

"A lot of bullshit, if you ask me."

"You want to know what's bullshit?" She captured his gaze and held it. "You."

"What?"

"Alex, you're so full of emotion right now, mostly anger, that you're about to explode."

"What do you know?"

"I know you're not being honest with yourself."

"Okay, how's this for honest? I made a horrible mistake marrying your sister, I don't miss her at all, and I'm glad she's dead."

"Then stop going around like somebody did this to you and there's nothing you can do about it. People change. We create these challenges, these realities, so we can learn and grow. We're not stuck with them. We can create a new reality for ourselves any time we want just by telling the truth about our feelings." He tried to resist, but she went on. "Or . . . you can spend the rest of your life blaming yourself for what happened, or better yet everybody else. It really is completely up to you."

Inexplicably, he had begun to cry. His dam of resistance had cracked, and tears of rage were streaming down his cheeks. Rationalizations and excuses he had been carrying around since the accident washed up and were carried away in a flood of emotion he didn't even know he had.

"I . . . I don't know what's come over me . . ." His efforts to control himself failed, the dam that had already cracked bust open, and he wept uncontrollably. "Forgive me . . ."

Beth took him in her motherly arms and rocked him gently. "The only person who can forgive you is you, Alex. It's a choice. Same as when you *chose* to marry my sister knowing the kind of woman she was. Same as the two of you *choosing* the kind of relationship you had. Same as the awful fact that she *chose* her own death."

He shook his head in denial.

"Listen to me," she continued. "It's not your fault. Nothing is 'your fault'. It's not your job to beat yourself up over other people's choices. Your only job is to *get responsible* for the choices *you* make. Be accountable to yourself, no one else. Be angry, be afraid, be sad until you're not angry, afraid or sad anymore. And in the meantime, don't believe a single lie your emotions are telling you because they don't know what the hell they're talking about.

"Then afterward, when you have emptied yourself of your feelings, when the well is dry and the words and emotions are all gone, say *adios* and get on with your life. Get it on up the road. If you're waiting for someone or something to forgive you, the forgiveness bus never shows up anywhere. Forgiveness is a one-man job."

He was laughing and crying at the same time. "Well, at least now I won't have to spend twenty years going to a therapist."

"Your call, chief. Keep looking back over your shoulder and you'll end up falling in your own grave just like Alicia."

He stared in wide-eyed revelation as his tears slowly dried and stopped. It had been wonderful somehow, the release of emotion—like clearing a plugged drain; like opening the valve on an overheated boiler and letting off the pressure before it blew itself apart. His only regret was that it was over because it had felt so good when it was happening. He went home that night to his boat with Beth's words ringing in his ears, fell into bed exhausted and slept twelve hours straight.

It was late morning when he finally opened his eyes and lay blinking up at the California sun that was flooding his cabin through the portholes. He stretched and sat up, swinging his feet to the cabin floor before remembering that this movement always sent shockwaves of pain down his back and into his legs.

Without Cyd's Cannastar tea, getting up had become the hardest part of the day. The pain bent him double until he was finally able to hobble up the dock to the showers and let the scalding hot water limber him up.

He stood slowly, carefully, girding himself for an inevitable agony that never came. He carefully swiveled his shoulders, then his hips. Nothing. He bent over and touched his toes, sat back down on his bunk and quickly stood again. It was gone! No pain! Where the hell did it go?

Alex bounded up the ladder to the cockpit, grabbed one of the shrouds that supported the mast, balanced himself on the rail and shouted out across the channel.

"Jesus, Buddha, Krishna and Mohammed! It's gone!"

And all it took was a good cry, he thought. Now why was that so hard?

Chapter Twenty-Five

Little Odessa

Alex had been back in Los Angeles nearly four months now. During that time, he had called Cyd a few times, but not knowing himself what was going on, how long he would have to be in L.A., or what the outcome would be, there was little to say. He wanted desperately to tell her how much he loved her, how much he missed her, but in the end their conversations always ended up on a stilted, stifled note.

But now it was over. Alicia was no longer a guilty burden and he could tell her everything. He couldn't wait. So much had happened and there was so much to tell. Suddenly, miraculously, he was a free man, free of his past, free of himself, free to love Cyd unconditionally with all his heart. His first thought was to just show up and surprise her but decided there was no point in giving her a heart attack. Excitedly, he dialed her cellphone only to learn that it had been disconnected. He quickly dialed her ranch phone and was shocked when he got a message that it too was no longer in service. Anxiously, he called the airline and made a reservation for Helena.

At the Salt Lake airport, waiting to change planes, he couldn't help noticing all the people engrossed in their phones and computers while waiting for their flights. It gave him an idea. He still had no clue how they were going to distribute the Cannastar, but he thought he might know how they could publicize it. Cyd would be thrilled. Something else he couldn't wait to tell her the minute he found her.

His plane landed in Helena and he rented a Jeep, a silver one this time, and arrived at Cyd's ranch about sunset. Driving past the corrals, he was puzzled to see so many new horses in the pens. He parked, got out and walked toward her log cabin. Smoke was coming from the chimney, so she must be home.

He knocked, his heart in his throat. The door opened . . . but it wasn't Cyd.

"Well, suck a man blue," Betty Little Horn exclaimed, looking Alex up and down. "If you ain't a sight for sore eyes."

Alex smiled and hugged her. "Cyd, where is she?"

"Gone back east. Come on in."

He sat at the kitchen table—the same table he had shared with Cyd so many times before—drinking Betty's God-awful coffee. "When did she leave?" he asked.

"Few days ago."

"When will she be back?"

Betty shrugged. "No time soon."

"Where, back east?"

"We both thought it best if I didn't know."

"I tried calling her and her cell's been disconnected. Any idea what that's about."

"Said she lost it out on the ranch somewhere. Said she'd get a new one when she got to wherever she was going."

Alex blew out his cheeks in frustration. "I assume you're taking care of the place now?"

"I live here now."

"Live here?"

"Had to sell my spread. Couldn't afford it anymore. Cyd said I could move my operation over here in exchange for tending to her ranch while she's gone."

"What about the mortgage? I thought she was about to be foreclosed on."

"Friend of hers over in Pablo paid it off. Told her not to give it another thought. Wish I had friends like that."

"Big Foot," Alex muttered under his breath.

"The Abominable Snowman is rich? Who knew?"

"Not that kind of Bigfoot. A Native American fellow Cyd introduced me to who turned out to be our guardian angel."

"Now don't that beat all," Betty grinned. "We Indians got all the loot."

Alex fished in his pocket, pulled out his cellphone and urgently checked for bars. Seeing he had no signal, he turned to Betty. "I need to borrow your landline."

"Had it disconnected. I use my cell now when I get in range. Cheaper that way."

He came abruptly to his feet and headed for the front door.

"Where you going? You just got here."

"Gotta go make a call."

"You find her," Betty called as he went out, "you give her my love."

***

Clarence Big Foot picked up his phone on the first ring and was pleased to hear it was Alex, who he hadn't heard from in over months. He was immediately asked if he knew where Cyd had gone.

"Sounds like Careful Where He Steps has stepped in it this time," Clarence surmised with a smile in his voice.

"Maybe. I don't know."

Clarence laughed. "Annie Seeley will know where to find her."

"Phone number? Address?"

"Hold on."

Alex heard papers rustling, then wrote rapidly on his palm when Big Foot came back on the line with the information. "Clarence," he went on, some of the tension leaving his voice now that he had a way of locating Cyd, "can I ask you something else? We need to get the word out about Cannastar. Seeing people at the airport with their heads stuck in their phones and computers reminded me of how much time everyone spends lost in cyberspace. I think what it's going to take to publicize this thing is for it to somehow go viral on the internet. Blogs, websites, search engines, Twitter, Facebook, YouTube—I don't even know all the places people go to these days. Can you help? The danger is that nobody can know where the information is coming from. If Rxon finds out who's doing this, they'll shut us down in a second."

Clarence sounded amused. "Don't give it another thought, my boy. Of course, I can work the Internet and get this out for you. I could probably get somebody elected president without anybody knowing. It would be an honor to be your Wonk."

"Wonk?"

"You really don't know anything about computers or the internet, do you?"

"Less than I know about Cyd at the moment."

"Are you actually that much in love with her?"

The question took Alex a little off guard, but he quickly recovered. "You have no idea."

"I can guess."

***

Three days earlier, Cyd was having coffee in a boutique coffee shop and bookstore in a quaint little village near Annie's Virginia estate when she happened to glance at a copy of the Washington Post someone had left on her table. The newspaper's headline story was about one of their investigative reporters who had been doing a piece on the Ukrainian mob. Apparently, he'd received death threats before going missing.

Sipping her latte, she skimmed the article. The newspaper claimed their reporter was about to publish proof that the Ukrainians operated a vast network of drug dealers that stretched from Boston to Washington D.C. Allegedly, apart from moving vast amounts of heroin, cocaine, meth and fentanyl, they were also predatory sex traffickers. Their headquarters were said to be in Little Odessa, a Russian neighborhood of Brooklyn, New York better known as Brighton Beach.

It all meant nothing to her until a name caught her eye and she almost spilled her coffee. The supposed head of the cartel was a Ukrainian named Andriy Shevchenko. His daughter, Anna Shevchenko, had been Cyd's roommate all through college.

***

A premium black Uber crossed over the East River on the Brooklyn Bridge and traveled south the full length of Brooklyn until it reached the little beach community south of the Belt Parkway that many called Little Odessa. A confusing array of clapboard sided houses on narrow lots, narrow red brick houses on narrow lots and low-rise apartment buildings all crammed together on narrow, congested streets slipped by on either side of the ride sharing vehicle as Cyd and Anna chatted happily in the back seat.

"I couldn't believe it when you called," Anna grinned. "It's been ages."

Cyd smiled back warmly at her old roommate. "Too long. Life happens."

"I know what you mean."

"You look beautiful."

And she did. Anna was a long-legged blond with big brown eyes and a deceptively sweet smile that masked a growing reputation as a smart, tough, rising young attorney at the Manhattan law firm where she worked. Cyd had taken the train up from Washington and met her at her Midtown office, so Anna was still wearing her tailored business suit.

"Are you as successful as you look?" Cyd asked.

"Anything I've achieved has been strictly without my father's help," Anna insisted. "I love my dad, I do. He's the sweetest man in the world and, as far as I'm concerned, the rumors about him are entirely false. That said, and you know this from our college days, I make it my business to stay out of his business. Plausible deniability, if you know what I mean."

"I understand totally." Cyd's hair was pulled back in a ponytail and she was dressed for business as well in a straight skirt and blouse that she had bought for the occasion.

"Cyd, what is it you want to talk to my father about? I don't like the sound of this."

"Plausible deniability, remember?"

"Got it. Afterward however, we are going for drinks. We've got a lot of catching up to do."

"Absolutely."

The Uber slowed and stopped in front of a large, three-story red brick home that sat on a corner lot and dwarfed the other three-story brick houses on the street. The home had bars over the windows, a high security wall around it and was the only house on the block with an iron security gate. Guards with German shepherds in leashes could be seen patrolling behind the gate.

Anna stopped Cyd as they got out of the car. "You ready for this?"

Cyd nervously straightened her skirt. "No."

***

A happy throng of relatives, children and grandchildren crowded around the Shevchenko dinner table all speaking at once in harsh, loud, angry voices while helping themselves to a colorful array of ethnic dishes. To Cyd's ear, the gargled Hs and rolled Rs of the Ukrainian language sounded like they were all choking to death.

Andriy Shevchenko sat at the head of the table pleased and proud of his sprawling family. With his broad shoulders, flattened nose and thick ears, Cyd thought he looked like a retired boxer. When he spoke, it sounded to her like he was commanding some sort of army from fifty miles away. Anna, clearly her father's favorite of all his children, sat on his right and Cyd sat next to her. On his left was his wife Marta, matriarch and de facto ruler of the family. Marta's thick waist, large breasts, stout legs and stern, motherly face made her look more like a Ukrainian farm worker than the steadfast wife of a feared crime boss.

"So, my big-shot New York lawyer daughter," Shevchenko boomed at Cyd with a loving sideways glance at Anna, "she not bring you around since that Christmas you spend with us when you two go to fancy university. Why that is?"

"Cyd's a botanist now, Papa," Anna quickly intervened. "She does research at the University of Montana."

"So *vhy* you here? You miss us that much?"

"Just visiting my Aunt in Virginia," Cyd smiled. "Helping her out with some experimental gardening she's doing. I couldn't wait to see Anna."

Marta turned to Cyd admiringly. "You all grown up now. Beautiful woman. How many children?"

"I'm afraid I'm married to my work," Cyd explained.

"No children?" The matriarch was heartbroken. "My Anna, no children either. I have only cloth diaper when I raise my children. With disposable diaper, I have seven *dity* (children) by now at your age."

"Mama," Anna protested. "I thought we agreed. No baby talk."

Cyd laughed. "Sounds like I have some catching up to do."

Over coffee and desert, Anna told her father there was something Cyd wanted to talk to him about.

Shevchenko wiped his mouth on his napkin and leaned back magnanimously in his chair. "Speak!"

Cyd cast Anna an anxious glance.

"Not here, Papa. She says it's private."

"Private," Shevchenko repeated. "Vhy private?" He looked from one to the other, received no answer and stood abruptly. "My office, then."

"Be nice to my friend or I'll tell Mama," Anna warned as they went out.

Shevchenko winked at Cyd. "Only voman in vorld who frightens me, her Mama."

Cyd followed Shevchenko down a hallway to the rear of the family home where he opened a door and entered ahead of her. She followed him in, and her mouth went dry. His office looked like the back room of Brooklyn bar with a pool table, card table and private bar. Boxes and crates were stacked everywhere, and a pair of grim-looking tattooed men in leather jackets stood at the window smoking and talking softly. Through the window she could see a long black limousine being washed in a brick courtyard behind the house and more guards milling about.

One of the tattooed men approached and began running his hands over Cyd's body in a search for weapons or a wire. Startled, she froze. The man found the one-ounce bag of marijuana-looking leaves she was carrying and tossed it on his boss's carved wood desk.

"Give us room," Shevchenko ordered, seating himself heavily behind his desk as the two men left the office by way of the rear entrance. A bank of security screens on one wall showed every angle of the home's exterior. On another wall was video surveillance of half a dozen strip clubs in the greater New York area. The other two walls were decorated with pictures of Kyiv and its beautiful green and gold domed cathedrals.

Andriy Shevchenko's expressive, passionate face tuned cold at the sight of the baggie on his desk. "Why you bring drugs into my house, Cydney?'

"It's not what you think," she answered in a rush. "I . . . we have a business proposition for you."

He made a pyramid of his hands and looked at her impassively over the top of his fingers. "We?"

"My partners and I. Anna knows nothing about it." He made no response and she hurried on. "What we propose will make you the best loved . . . Ukrainian in New York, bar none."

He exploded in laughter. "For record, Ms. Seeley, "Ve are legitimate organization. I run honest business for honest profit. God forbid your proposal, it should involve anything illegal."

She stiffened. "If what I have to offer you wasn't illegal, Mr. Shevchenko, I wouldn't be here. In fact, it's dangerous. Very dangerous. Which is what makes it so profitable."

He smiled suspiciously, ripped open the Ziplock full of green leaves, took a deep breath and sneezed into it. "Your marijuana, it smell like licorice!"

"It's neither, I assure you."

He raised his bushy eyebrows.

"It's a drug, I admit. Only instead of making you high, it makes you well."

"Vell? How you mean, vell?

"What you have in your hand cures cancer, among other viral diseases. It's called Cannastar."

"Cannastar?" he repeated. "What means this, 'Cannastar?'"

From Cyd's confident, self-assured look, it was impossible to tell she was scared to death. "Cannastar is a genetically engineered, organic herb invented by a scientist who was murdered for his efforts. What that means as far as you're concerned is that instead of being feared and vilified as some sort of bad guy, you could end up a hero of the American people."

Shevchenko blew out his cheeks and sat back in confusion. "I know about genetically modified organism. Some say good, some say bad, these GMOs. Who vould vant to kill over it?"

"Rxon Corporation. If Cannastar gets out and people start using it, nobody is going to want to buy their drugs. They won't need them anymore. Big Pharma would kill the Pope himself if he was going to put them out of business this way. Which is why there is so much money in it. Rxon will kill to stop it, and they'll sic the Feds on anyone who tries to sell it."

"Vhy come to me? Vhy you think Shevchenko can help?"

"We need underground distribution, and you have a distribution network second only to Walmart. This is potentially the most profitable illegal drug in history. My partners and I can grow it, but we have no way of getting it into the hands of the public. Once the world hears about Cannastar and sees what it can do, there's going to be demand the likes of which even God has never seen. You'll be the richest savior on earth."

He regarded her thoughtfully. "How much THC it have in it?"

"None. Very little. It's not for getting stoned . . ."

"So, it's like oregano or catnip? For cooking and for cat to scratch?"

"You don't understand . . ."

"I understand perfectly. You bring an honest businessman a criminal enterprise and expect him to join you in your crime."

She hesitated. "I ask only that you think about it, sir."

He shook his head in disappointment. "Anna, she make mistake in bringing you here. You good girl, Cydney, but this thing . . ." He stood sadly. "I care too much for my daughter's friend to let her get involved in something that is way over her head. Ve go back to dinner party now and forget ve ever have this conversation."

Cyd struggled to keep her disappointment off her face. Grabbing a pen and piece of paper off his desk, she hurriedly scribbled her new cell phone number and handed it to him.

"Call me if you change your mind."

He handed her back her bag of Cannastar. "Take pot with you, please."

She forced a smile. "Keep it in case somebody in your family gets the flu."

Chapter Twenty-Six

A Good Cup of Tea

Shevchenko's limo took Cyd and Anna back to Manhattan. Cyd sat despondently in the rear of the luxury vehicle staring straight ahead as they crossed back over the Brooklyn Bridge.

Anna turned to her friend. "You look like you could use that drink now."

"I could use several."

They spent the night at Anna's Greenwich Village apartment, and the next morning Cyd woke with a splitting headache. She quickly showered, dressed, hugged and thanked her girlfriend and left with the promise of getting together again soon.

On the train back to Washington D.C., she sat staring out the window more upset than the night before over her foolish notion that a notorious Russian drug dealer could solve her distribution problem. Her cell phone rang, and she didn't recognize the number. She was about to dismiss the call when she changed her mind and answered it.

The caller identified himself as Joe.

"Joe who?"

"Joe Volkova."

***

Cyd took an Uber from Washington back to Annie's Virginia estate. Arriving at dusk, she slipped into Annie's shadowed greenhouse. The grow lights had been turned off for the night and the stars were beginning to twinkle through the hexagon-shaped panels of glass in the overhead dome.

"Over here," a voice whispered.

Cyd followed the sound, shouldering her way through a forest of thousands of maturing Cannastar plants that were already a foot taller than she was with jagged-edged leaves the size of elephant ears. Thanks to Annie's high-tech facility, Otis had been able to experiment with light, humidity, temperature and nutrients to fine-tune the ideal hydroponic growing environment for his Cannastar. As a result, the plants were thriving in a way he never thought possible.

Cyd found Otis and Annie in the dappled darkness next to a potting bench that ran the full length of one of the eight glass walls. At the sight of her friends, she burst into tears. They tried to comfort her, but she resisted. "What was I even thinking to put myself in a position like that?"

Otis wiped his hands on his voluminous apron and took her in his arms. "That was a really reckless thing you did, I'll admit."

"Shevchenko's family was there. His daughter Anna was with me. I knew I was safe, at least." She looked up at him tearfully. "I'm out of ideas, Otis. What do I do now?"

Annie kissed her cheek. "We'll think of something, dear."

"I was even fool enough to leave him my phone number, if you can believe that. Now I'm getting phone calls from some guy named Joe Volkova who talks a mile a minute in this raspy voice like he's the Godfather or something, and claims he runs a hedge fund. Says Shevchenko gave him my number. Says if I'll come to New York and prove to him that Cannastar really works, he'll pay me a million dollars."

"Take him up on it," Alex suggested, stepping out of the shadows. "I know Joe. He might be able to help."

Cyd made a small cry, jumped back and collided with the potting bench.

"Sorry. I didn't mean to frighten you . . ."

Otis tried to intervene. "He arrived just before you did, Cyd. Said he had a lot of explaining to do."

She threw her arms wildly around Alex's neck and showered him in kisses. "I don't care, I don't care, I don't care! You're back, that's all that matters!"

Annie put her arm through Otis's. "Let's give them a little privacy, shall we? Do you feel like taking a look at the tulips and pansies I've started, or is it too late?"

Otis grinned. "It's never too late for tulips and pansies."

Alex and Cyd walked through the overgrown greenhouse, found a bench and sat down in the moonlight. Alex looked around at the towering Cannastar plants. "Amazing, what you guys have done here. How does Annie keep her husband out?"

Cyd, too distracted by his presence to make small talk, answered impatiently. "Claims Sam wouldn't set foot in her greenhouse if his life depended on it. Said sometimes she thinks he's more married to the Senate than he is to her." She paused and went on urgently. "Alex, I missed you so much. I've been wanting to call you with my new cell number. I started to several times, but I didn't want to bug you. I didn't want you to think I was chasing you or anything. I knew you had things you had to work out . . ."

"A lot happened in L.A., Cyd. I have a lot to tell you."

"Let's go up to my room in Annie's house. We can talk there."

They sat on her bed in one of Annie's many beautiful bedrooms talking long into the night. He told her everything down to the last detail. She laughed, she cried, and, in the end, she understood. Suddenly, they were making love. It was the best night of Alex's life so far.

In the morning he opened his eyes to find her watching him, her face inches from his. "You ever leave me again like that," she warned, "and I'm going to have to hurt you."

"I would expect nothing less," he grinned, propping himself up on the pillows. She sat up with, "Cyd, we need to talk about Joe Volkova. I grew up with him. He's one of the biggest mobsters on Wall Street."

"You're connected. I knew it."

"Not me, him."

"How do you know?"

"We stay in touch."

"So now the mob is after me? Terrific. Thanks for the heads-up."

"It could have something to do with your proposal to the Ukrainian. We need to go see him together."

"Together? Why?"

"He's a little dangerous."

"What's 'a little?' "

***

The Amtrak ride from Union Station in Washington, D.C. to New York's Penn Station took a little over three hours. Cyd looked out at the passing countryside and was silent a long time.

"You alright?" he asked.

She kissed him passionately. "Never better."

***

They took a yellow cab from Penn Station and arrived in the financial district in Lower Manhattan around noon. The cab pulled away from the curb and left them looking up at a sky full of skyscrapers.

"It's that one," Alex indicated, pointing at a building that was so tall they could barely see the top. He started toward it, but Cyd didn't move. After a few steps he realized she wasn't beside him and looked back. "You coming?"

Her head was cocked to one side, and she was studying him. "You're not limping. You haven't asked me for any Cannastar tea. You don't seem to be in any pain to speak of. That must have been some talk you had at the cemetery with your ex-wife's sister."

He came back and took her arm to move her along. "All I can say is, I don't think I got the pick of the litter." He saw the constrained look on her face and smiled. "Don't tell me you're jealous."

She stiffened and walked on. "Never."

They got out of the elevator on one of the top floors of Joe's building and walked down the corridor. The name on the elegant, ten-foot-tall double doors at the end of the hall read 'True North Partners.' Pushing open one of the doors, they went inside, and Cyd told the receptionist they were here to see Joe Volkova.

"Tell Joe it's Alex Farmer, and he has Cyd Seeley with him," Alex added.

"Of course. If you'll just have a seat . . ." She picked up a phone, buzzed the intercom, spoke into the receiver and glanced up quickly with a startled look. "You can go right in."

A stern, harried, gray-haired executive secretary came out of her glass cubicle at the back of the office pool and motioned to them toward her as they entered. They walked past a dozen or so clerical workers sitting at workstations in front of their computers. The secretary led them to her boss's office, opened the door and closed it behind them as they went in.

The huge corner suite had a jaw-dropping view of the One World Trade Center, the Hudson River and New Jersey beyond. There were no wall decorations and no furniture in the barren room except for a pair of chairs in front of a desk that was crowded with computer monitors. A stocked bar and mini kitchen with refrigerator and microwave ran along one wall. On the black granite countertop next to the sink was a coffeepot and a blender.

A pallid-faced man in an Armani suit with piles of wavy brown hair and a hook nose came bounding out from behind his desk and almost knocked Alex over with a bearhug.

"Alex freakin' Farmer," he cried. "I can't freakin' believe it!" Beads of sweat stood out on his forehead. He coughed, covered his mouth and turned to Cyd. "What's a gorgeous woman like this doin' with the likes of youz?"

"Joe, I'd like you to meet the girl of my dreams. Cyd Seeley, this is Joe Volkova."

Joe pumped her hand in admiration, all the while talking so fast she could barely follow. "I had a feeling. I get these freakin' feelings, you know? Voices in my head? They always tell me what's what. So, you're not crazy, I'm not crazy, nobody's crazy, am I right? Shevchenko says I should meet you and here you are." He stepped back to admire them as a couple. "Cyd Seeley and Alex freakin' Farmer. Who knew?"

Cyd was mildly amused. "Pleasure to meet you, Mr. Volkova."

"Call me Joe, please." Another coughing fit overtook him, and he went back behind his desk to sit down. "Shevchenko, he says youz came to him wanting to turn his dealers into pharmacists over something called Cannastar. Crazy freakin' Ukrainian, am I right?" He tried to laugh and coughed instead. "Sit down, sit down. Been thinking about you lately, Alex. Thinking about youz a lot, actually . . ." He started to cough, snatched open a desk drawer, grabbed a handful of tissues from a box and began coughing up blood.

Doctor Farmer rushed around the desk, held Joe's forehead in his hand and gently stroked his back. The coughing eased and he took his patient's pulse, then mopped his forehead with more tissues he took from the drawer. Next to the tissue box, he saw a handgun.

Joe followed his eyes, saw what Alex was staring at and quickly closed the drawer. His effort to say something dismissive about the gun produced a wheezing whistle sound instead.

"Easy," Alex advised. "Try to breath." He poured out a glass of water from a pitcher on the desk and gave it to Joe, then watched with growing concern as he drank it down along with a couple of pills he shook from a prescription bottle. "Joe, just how sick are you?" he asked.

"Cancer," Joe wheezed. "Lung. Plus COPD. Bronchial tubes. Inoperable."

Cyd's heart went out to him. "I'm so sorry."

"Forget about it," he coughed. "Am I right?"

Alex regarded his friend sadly. "More bad news, Joe. Don't know if you heard, or not. Maury is dead. He was murdered."

Joe looked like he'd just coughed up a lung. "Geeze, Alex."

"Geeze, Joe."

The hedge fund manager rose in a state of shock and turned to the window where he stood looking out with watery eyes. Alex went on to explain what had happened to their childhood friend and how Rxon was behind it. By the time he finished, Joe was boiling mad.

"This Cannastar stuff, that's the reason they killed him, am I right?" The magnitude of the tragedy washed over him again, and he sat back down. "Bastards must have been freakin' terrified of what he discovered."

Joes reaction affected Cyd deeply. "I . . . I loved him too, Joe. We all did. He was a good friend."

"Youz and Maury were the only real friends I ever had, Alex." Joe swiped at his eyes, took an inhaler from his pocket and drew on it deeply. "Forget about it, am I right? This weed Maury invented, it really works then? It cures cancer?"

"Among other things."

"And the two of youz are mixed up in it how . . .?"

Just then the intercom buzzed. Joe picked up the phone and covered the mouthpiece. "Gotta take this. One second."

Cyd listened to Joe's loud, harsh conversation with its gargled Hs and rolled Rs and recognized the Ukrainian language she'd heard at the Shevchenko dinner table.

Joe grinned sheepishly and hung up. "Another satisfied client." He coughed and spit into a tissue. "So, show it to me, this miracle of yours. You got it with you?"

Cyd carefully placed a baggie of green leaves on his desk.

"How do you take it?" he asked, staring skeptically.

"You boil it in a tea," she explained. "Would you like me to make you some?"

Joe nodded eagerly. "Is the Pope freakin' Catholic?"

Cyd got up, went over to the mini kitchen, dumped some of her dried Cannastar leaves into Joe's blender and hit the button. In an instant the leaves were ground to bits. She put a filter in the coffee maker, dumped in a generous portion of shredded leaves, filled the reservoir with water and turned it on.

"While she's doing that," Alex suggested, "why don't you tell us how you know Andriy Shevchenko."

Joe cast a quick glance in Cyd's direction. "Can I trust her?"

"Can she trust you, is more the question."

"Shevchenko is another one of my clients," he coughed.

"Your clients are all drug dealers." It wasn't a question.

"You look surprised."

"Not really."

Joe grinned proudly. "We Ukrainians, we stick together."

"How many dealers?" Cyd asked excitedly from across the room. "Over how big of a territory?"

"I can't talk to you about it, I'm sorry."

Cyd promptly unplugged the coffee pot. "I understand. We probably shouldn't be talking about Cannastar, either."

Joe saw what she'd done and nearly had a heart attack. "The whole freakin' East Coast, alright? Now, plug it back in!"

Alex smiled patiently. "Tell Cyd what you do, Joe. If we're going to help you, you're going to need to help us."

He paled. "You don't know what you're asking."

"And don't leave anything out. I need to hear it too."

Joe sighed miserably. "Youz repeat any of this and there'll be a dozen guys like Shevchenko out lookin' to bury you in the city dump. You still want to hear?"

Cyd smiled agreeably and plugged the coffee pot back in. "I'll run the tea through twice for you so it's nice and strong."

Anxious from the beginning to brag about his success, Joe let his pride show through. "This is a freakin' license to print money, Alex. The sweetest setup I ever had . . ."

***

Joe Volkova was a market trader whose money-making skills were legendary. If his peers on Wall Street were to find out the real source of his income, however, even the most hardened of traders would be appalled.

His hedge fund, True North Partners, didn't actually make any money, but paid out huge profits using its client's own funds. What distinguished its customers from those who periodically get bilked by other Ponzi schemes was that True North's investors knew exactly what was going on and heartily approved. The reason was that Joe's distinguished roster of wealthy Ukrainians had a common problem: as the main wholesalers of illegal drugs on the East Coast, they all needed to launder vast sums of money.

Hedge funds in general were loosely regulated, lived in the shadows and operated under the radar. True North was no exception. Joe had deliberately structured his organization to be as complicated and confusing as the law allowed. And because the laws prohibiting such things as monopolies and conflicts of interest had long since been abolished or ignored, they were able to own all the other related, interwoven companies that made this possible. In other words, Joe's bank—"People's Capital Bank," it was called—its trading desk and even the two trading companies through which they anonymously placed their trades were entities owned and operated by Joe himself. Anyone investigating his company would indeed need a sharp knife, plus a lot of elbow grease, to cut through the tightly woven multitude of corporations and get to True North's smelly inner core—and even then, they probably wouldn't know what they were looking at.

Each company had a different and unrelated name. "Wealth House," for example, handled his equity and currency trades and "PT Hastings" cleared his commodity trades. Both companies were completely legitimate, both were extremely profitable, and both were controlled by Joe. The only thing that wasn't legitimate was the money these companies made for True North Partners.

Millions rushed into True North's customer trading accounts from successful, electronically verifiable market trades in short selling, leveraged program trading, swaps, arbitrage and derivatives that never happened in the first place. The electronic profits from these trades were electronically transferred into the appropriate accounts in People's Capital Bank. The money was then shown to have been paid out to the clients who, in turn, dutifully paid their taxes which made the IRS happy. As a result, the actual cash, which was already in the hands of the clients to begin with, was immediately available to be legally spent or invested in legitimate enterprises. New businesses large and small, as well as new construction projects large and small, were continually springing up from Maine to Miami.

The bank's books balanced, the money was washed clean as a freshly laundered shirt, and Joe got rich. He had a penthouse overlooking Central Park, a house in the Hamptons, his own jet airplane and he owned half an island in the Bahamas. What he didn't have was his health.

Andriy Shevchenko had called Joe to discuss his immediate "investment needs"—code for the amount of money he needed to launder this month—and while they were talking happened to mention his daughter's friend who had come to his house wanting him to distribute some kind of weed she'd grown that supposedly cured cancer. He didn't know whether to believe her or not, but knowing Joe's condition, he thought Joe should know about it. Joe's excitement over the news surprised even him, as did Joe's insistence that Shevchenko put him in touch with her immediately. He found Cyd's phone number in his wastebasket where he'd thrown it, fished it out and read it off.

Joe immediately called Cyd. When she picked up, he tried to keep the panic out of his voice.

***

Cyd was stunned at hearing Joe's story.

Joe coughed and used his inhaler again. "Sorry if I've shocked you, Cyd. There's two worlds out there—the one everybody lives in and the one you don't see on television, the one that runs the world."

"Shocked?" she cried. "I'm thrilled! This means your "clients" can start selling our Cannastar."

Joe nodded thoughtfully. "You criminalize something people want and you're going to create a black market for it, that's for freakin' sure. The more illegal it is, the more they freakin' want it."

"Exactly," Cyd agreed. "Think of it as a new income stream. A whole new way for your clients to make a boat load of money."

"No question."

"You'll be getting in on the ground floor," Alex added. "You'll *be* the ground floor."

Joe said nothing and instead looked out the window again at the view.

"So, you'll do it then?" Cyd prompted. "You'll go into the Cannastar business with us?"

Joe sighed and turned back. "No can do. I want to honor Maury's memory, but I'm afraid it's out of the question."

Cyd was incredulous. "I thought . . . You don't believe us when we tell you Cannastar cures cancer?"

"Oh, I believe youz alright. Maury invented it and Alex says it's true, so absolutely I believe youz. I'm as excited over it as youz are. That's not the problem. The problem is this: I can't ask my people to get involved in something so controversial and high profile that it'll blow the lid off their existing business. Illegal drugs are one of the most lucrative enterprises on earth. Cannastar would be a game changer. I can't even imagine the trouble it would cause. My clients would end up getting more unwanted publicity than a politician tweeting out a selfie of his privates. Not good, not good. National, federal, local law enforcement—they're way too interested in us as it is. Upsetting the status quo would mean risking everything. I'd recommend it to my people and they'd go for it, no question, because they trust whatever I say when it comes to investing in the latest business trends, but my hands are tied. Too risky, too dangerous. I'm sorry, I wish I could help."

Cyd and Alex exchanged bleak looks.

Joe brightened. "That's not to say I won't pay you the million dollars I promised. Hand over the Cannastar and the money's yours."

"It's not for sale," Cyd replied flatly.

Alex nodded in agreement.

"Everything's for sale," Joe argued.

"Joe, listen," Cyd insisted. "What do you think is going to happen to all the people who are terminally ill if you don't help us help them?"

"They'll die," he shrugged. "Same as always."

"Same as you."

Joe began to panic. "Not if I take Cannastar, am I right?"

"You'd likely get your health back in no time."

"Then what's the problem? My money ain't good enough for you?"

"The problem," Cyd replied evenly, "is at the present time, Cannastar is not available to the general public."

Joe turned red in the face. "Do I look like the freakin' public to you? I'll pay whatever you want. One million, two million? Name it, it's yours!"

"Distribution."

Joe drew desperately on his inhaler. "Talk to her, Alex! Tell her! She'll listen to you!"

Alex gestured helplessly. "She's not the kind of woman who takes instruction well."

"Then *make* her!"

"Like she said, you help us, we'll help you."

"There's got to be a middle ground here," Joe pleaded. "What if I put a couple of my dealers on it and we see what happens?"

"All or nothing, Joe. The whole East Coast."

Cyd looked on sadly. "I wish you'd let us help you."

"I can't, I just can't . . ."

"Anything's possible," Alex suggested, "if you want it badly enough."

"Tea's ready," Cyd added brightly. "Hate to see it get cold."

"Alright, alright!" Joe cried. "Let me think."

"Cyd, pour it out."

She dutifully took the coffeepot by the handle and held it over the sink.

"Alright, alright. Deal! You happy now?"

"One thing," Alex warned. "For Cannastar to work, you have to keep taking it. Every day without fail for the rest of your life, or your cancer comes back. If, for any reason, the distribution should go away . . ."

"Yeah, yeah, I get it," Joe groaned. "A deal's a deal. You have my word."

"Tea time!" Cyd announced, happily pouring out two steaming hot cups from the pot in her hand, carrying them across the office and putting one down in front of Joe. "I just love a good cup of tea in the afternoon, don't you?"

***

Late that same day, a hurricane of smoke and noise screamed past on shining rails, hurtling toward Washington D.C. from New York City. Inside the train, Cyd and Alex sat facing one another in plush, first-class business seats. Sitting on the table between them on two damp napkins were two cold beers.

Cyd took a sip from her bottle, smiling with her eyes. "That was intense."

"That gave 'intense' a bad name."

They looked at one another and the next instant they were laughing.

"We did it, Alex! We actually did it!"

"And, hopefully, we saved Joe's life."

"I just hope he doesn't forget it when he's talking to his clients."

"You were brilliant."

She smiled happily. "I had a brilliant partner." A thought struck, and her face fell.

"What's wrong?"

"Publicity," she agonized. "Now that we have distribution, how are we ever going to let people know what Cannastar is and how to get their hands on it?"

"Handled."

"Handled?"

"I had a talk with our friend Clarence. You won't believe everything he can do for us on the internet. Man's a genius."

"Indeed?"

"Indeed."

Outside their window the world rushed past in a green and watery blur. From under their feet came the rhythmic clattering of the rails. They raised their bottles and clinked them together. It was a day to celebrate.

Chapter Twenty-Seven

A Growing Concern

It was spring and Annie Seeley's estate was greener than a St. Patrick's Day parade. The high walls of English Ivy were chartreuse with new growth, acacia trees mushroomed with shade, white flowering dogwood blossoms popped like popcorn balls and tulips and pansies rioted everywhere.

A convoy of three rented cargo trucks rolled through the entry gates of Annie's estate at midnight and followed the winding drive until they came to the greenhouse that sat dark and silent beside the shimmering lake. Men in dark clothes and skull caps got out and rolled up the rear doors of the trucks.

Otis and Annie stood excitedly to one side as a mountain of overstuffed black garbage bags were taken from the greenhouse and silently loaded onto the trucks. Growing and harvesting this much Cannastar had not been difficult. The time-consuming part was curing it and removing all the poisonous seeds before it could be bagged for transport. But it was a labor of love, so it wasn't really work—it was fun. The two farmers watched proudly as rear doors rattled down, engines started and the trucks moved back up the drive and disappeared in the night.

The first crop was now shipped, and a new industry was born.

***

The IP address for the Cannastar website, located somewhere in Ukraine at the moment, kept moving around Eastern Europe. It was getting more hits than a free porn site. Even Clarence was amazed. The promotional campaign, targeted exclusively at the East Coast for now, was succeeding beyond his wildest expectations. People were clamoring for the product, and everybody was talking about it.

The website's FAQ page gave very specific instructions on how Cannastar was to be administered and used, cautioning that it might not be appropriate for all people under all circumstances. Common side effects, the facts stated, included robust health and a disease-free life. Visitors to the site were urged to give this organically grown, transgenic miracle a try with colorful animation that read: "See Your Neighborhood Drug Dealer Today! "

And they did. By the thousands. With urgent hearts and soaring hopes, people flooded from their homes to the streets, from the suburbs to the ghettos, from their arm chairs and canes and sickbeds, from their cancer and disease and despair, in search of a local pusher. The demand was overwhelming. Otis and Annie were working day and night and still they couldn't keep up.

***

Leonard Shope had worn his hair in a greasy DA, or "duck's ass," since grade school and wasn't one to give up on a style just because it had long since gone out of fashion. Other things in his life, however, he couldn't control so easily and as a result his sleepless nights had only deepened the lines in his face. His wife was dying of lymphoma, and, to make matters worse, he had just lost his job as a diesel mechanic which he had held for over thirty years.

Shope left his home in Stroudsburg, Pennsylvania in urgent search of this Cannastar he'd heard so much about for his wife and an hour later arrived in Allentown. In his hand—a hand permanently stained with ground-in grease and oil—he clutched a piece of paper where he had hastily scrawled the address of a reliable drug dealer that his neighbor had given him. He didn't know whether all the hype around this stuff was true or not, but he was desperate and doing something—anything—was better than sitting around feeling so helpless and scared.

The drug dealer turned out to be a friendly enough fellow who told Shope he wished he could help him, but that he had sold his last bag of Cannastar two days ago. Shope asked where he could look for more and was directed to the dealer's cousin in Newark, some eighty miles east. As of this morning, the cousin supposedly still had a little left.

Shope arrived at the cousin's house around dark only to learn that the dealer had just sold his last bag. After that he drove from neighborhood to neighborhood, getting out and walking the streets, stopping everyone he met and asking if they knew where he could find a reliable drug dealer. When people learned that he was looking for Cannastar for his wife, they were more than helpful, but every dealer he talked to told him the same story—they were fresh out and didn't know when they'd be getting another shipment.

Late that night he found himself on a bus bench in a desolate section of town agonizing over what he was going to tell his wife. He buried his head in his hands and felt someone tap him on the shoulder. Looking up, he found himself eyeball to eyeball with a tough-acting white kid of about ten who was waving a fat baggie of dried green leaves in his face.

"Hey, yo, what up?" the kid asked. "Brothers say you lookin' to score."

"I'm looking for some Cannastar," Shope explained, "not marijuana."

"What it is, homes. Three hundred bucks."

"That's three times the going rate!"

The kid gave him a look that would offend a bronze statue and turned to go. "Whatever, yo. Last bag in town. Don't need no punk-ass bitch rippin' me off for it."

"No wait. Please. I'm sorry. Here you go . . ." Shope shoved three hundred dollars at the boy who grabbed the money, backed away grinning, tossed the baggie to him and ran off.

When he got home, Shope and his wife followed the directions on the website exactly, carefully boiling a measured amount of leaves into a tea. They were encouraged when the tea didn't make her high. She drank the brew morning and night, and a month later she was dead.

The bereaved husband showed what was left of the baggie to the neighbor who had told him about it in the first place, telling him bitterly how it hadn't worked. The neighbor smelled the bag. There was no chocolate odor to it, only the vague smell of hemp.

***

Meanwhile, police were being called in to handle the traffic jams on garbage-strewn streets where once only junkies lived. Some street corners got so busy that the hookers had to shoulder the visitors aside just to make a living. A rising tide of sick and dying were abandoning their doctors and pharmacies for the open-air markets of the ghettos.

The medical community saw the growing danger and descended on Washington like angry locusts. Clamoring voices rang out in protest from drug companies, insurers, hospitals, medical supply firms, health-service companies and health professionals until the halls of Congress sounded like feeding time at the zoo. This Cannastar was a plague, an epidemic, a danger to all who used it and it needed to be stopped.

Law enforcement agencies on the national, state and local level were called in to find and eradicate the source of this noxious weed that was showing up everywhere. Investigations were launched. Arguments broke out over whether it was being grown inside or outside the country, the general consensus being that it was coming from Columbia. One day no one had ever heard of it and the next everyone was trying to score some. An agonized DEA agent, frustrated over his lack of leads, said his best guess was that it was "arriving here on cargo ships from Mars." Search and destroy teams were put on alert, ready to move on a moment's notice once the source of the menace was discovered.

***

Senator Sam Seeley and his lobbyist friend Riley Gray were in the Senator's office in Washington D.C. on a conference call to Houston. Sam had been fielding angry calls all day from some of his biggest donors in the medical industry, but this one was by far the worst.

The speakerphone on his desk rattled with Dick Tremble's furious voice. "This thing is turning into one big cluster fuck, Sam! What the fuck am I paying you for, anyway? I want this Cannastar crap stopped! Do your fucking job, or I will personally put somebody in your seat who can kill this noxious weed!" And that was probably some of the kinder things he said.

Sam told Rxon's CEO in a slow, amiably drawl that he needn't worry. He just needed some time to figure this thing out. After all, he did have the full weight of the United States government behind him. Hell, he *was* the United States government. "Let me work on it and I'll be back to you soon."

The Senator hung up and decided to do something he hadn't done in the middle of the week his whole career. He had his secretary cancel all his appointments, called his driver and went home to Virginia to think.

***

Sam's black limo wound its way up the treelined drive of his estate. His house came into view and he sighed in relief. This was without a doubt the most peaceful place on earth. Here, the world's problems practically solved themselves. He got out of the back of his car and noticed all the activity around his wife's greenhouse down by the lake. More f'ing nonsense with her stupid plants, he thought as he went into the house. But it went on all day. Every time he looked out the damn window, he saw people and trucks coming and going.

That evening Annie came back up to the main house tired and dirty from a long day of hard work. Sam's first words were to ask her what the f'ing hell was going on that she needed so many people to help her grow petunias. His unexpected visit took her by surprise, but she had carefully rehearsed her response should anything like this ever come up. Stalling for time as she mentally prepared for battle, she removed her gardening hat and gloves and rinsed her face in the sink. "My greenhouse, you say?"

"No, that Epcot Center of yours that you had me move up from Orlando for you. Yes, your greenhouse. What are you doing, running a truck farm?"

"Exactly," she replied brightly. "My new business."

"What kind of business. Exactly?"

"Gardening, dear. What other kind would it be?"

"It needs to make money before you go calling it a business."

"Oh, I'm making money, all right. Scads and scads of it, in fact."

"I find that hard to believe."

"This wonderful gentleman I hired to help me; he's developed the most amazing hybrid plant. It's really caught on. Everybody everywhere seems to want it. The demand is huge."

Sam exercised his habit of emotionally pulling the plug on a conversation once he lost interest by picking up the mail on the hall table and starting to open it.

It felt to Annie like he had physically left the room.

"Caught on?" he asked vaguely, reading a utility bill. What he saw made his jaw dropped. "Since you're making so much money," he growled, "how about you start paying the power bill. An estate like this uses a lot of electricity, but you could light a city with what you're using."

Annie looked at the bill and swallowed hard. "My goodness . . . I had no idea. Of course, I'll pay for it. In fact, I'm doing so well, I'm thinking of adding a second greenhouse."

"Like hell you will. What do you think you are, an f'ing farmer?" He said *farmer* like it smelled of fertilizer.

"Why yes, that's exactly what I am dear. A very successful one at that."

"Interesting. If it's all that successful, this growing operation of yours, maybe I should have a look at it. Put some of my people on it."

Annie was at a loss for words. Then quickly finding her tongue, she stamped her foot. "You'll do nothing of the sort, if you know what's good for you. You have your world, and I have mine. Unless you want me to start paying unannounced visits to you and your Washington *whoors*, I'll thank you to keep your nose out of my affairs."

She had always been so passive. This new Annie frightened him, even though he wasn't willing to admit it. "You live in a little dream world," he challenged. "You play with flowers and dig in the dirt all day. What the hell do you know about what goes on in Washington?"

"I know enough to ruin your chances for reelection," she smiled. "You think I don't know about the women you've had to pay off because you couldn't keep your hands to yourself?" His stunned silence made her want to laugh. "And as for me building another greenhouse, I'll put it in the trees where you won't have to look at it. Other than that, I'll thank you to mind your own business."

"You think you know everything!" he railed. "If you're that smart, why don't you just go ahead and move out then?"

"I would," she replied sweetly, "but I live here, and you don't. Oh, and the next time you want to come for a visit, I'd appreciate a call first. I'm not one of your mistresses that you can drop in on any time the urge strikes you."

Sam stormed out, slamming the door behind him.

***

With her husband out of the picture, at least for now, Annie was able to concentrate on getting her second greenhouse built. "Cannacot II," she called it. Her contractor, Jim Toomey, had been paid in full for the first one he built for her thanks to Annie writing him a check out of her own account. He agreed to build the second one, but only on the condition that he never had to deal with Senator Sam again.

With a little time on her hands, Cyd decided on a whim to cut her hair. She came happily bouncing out of the beauty salon with a short, feisty, stylish cut that made her feel like a new person. When she got back to Annie's, everyone was busy working in the greenhouse. It was a beautiful day and she didn't feel like being indoors so she put on her bathing suit and went down to the lake for a swim.

The glassy surface of the lake mirrored perfectly the dense growth of trees that surrounded it as she walked along the dock and dove in. The water was freezing, she cried out and quickly scrambled to shore with the mud from the bank squishing between her toes.

Alex found her sitting on a bench vigorously drying her new haircut in a towel. He sat down beside her and did a doubletake as she removed the towel and shook out her hair.

"I almost didn't recognize you."

Her face fell. "You don't like it?"

He stared.

"Say something, for heaven's sake!"

There were no words. "What did I do to deserve such a beautiful woman?"

She sighed and quickly kissed him. They parted and she searched his face. "You really like it?"

"It's the cutest haircut I ever saw. Really."

Reassured, her arms went around his neck and she kissed him passionately. They parted a second time and her look of satisfaction turned to concern. "Alex, we need to talk."

"Okay." He wanted her so badly he could think of nothing else and started to kiss her again, but she gently pulled away.

"We have to expand. The East Coast is a good beginning, but we need the whole country."

"That would take a greenhouse approximately the size of Virginia. Otis and Annie can't grow enough as it is to even service the territory we've got."

"There must be a way. There just has to be."

"We've got a more pressing problem at the moment."

"More pressing?"

"Joe Volkova called. He wants to see us."

"About what?"

"Wouldn't say. Sounded urgent. Said it couldn't wait."

She smiled ironically. "A life of crime with an emergency room doctor. Lucky me."

"It could be worse."

Cyd's raised her eyebrows and waited.

"I could be a proctologist."

She rolled her eyes.

***

Back in Washington, Riley Gray was assigned the task of finding someone who could orchestrate a campaign to poison the hearts and minds of Americans against Cannastar. Resourceful lobbyist that he was, he hired Griffin Gant. The infamous political strategist and dirty trickster had a narrow head, no chin, a pencil neck and sloping shoulders. Combined, his features made him look like an arrow with a crudely chiseled head. It was said that he couldn't be killed with a stake through his heart, but that was just a rumor since no one had ever had the guts to try it.

"Cancer is big business," Riley reminded him the first time they met. "Big as war."

"Don't worry," Gant responded in his dry and grating voice. "War is here to stay. And so is cancer."

***

Cyd and Alex took the highspeed train back up to New York and arrived at Joe's office midday. They found Joe at his desk wolfing down a hero sandwich and looking like he'd never been sick a day in his life. He mumbled an excited greeting while chewing rapidly and motioned them into his two chairs. The renowned hedge fund manager wore a sweatshirt with perspiration rings under the arms that gave the impression he had just been working out.

"You training for the New York Marathon now, or what?" Alex asked.

Joe took a big drink of his power shake. "How'd you guess? This freakin' Cannastar, man, it's freakin' amazing."

"So I hear," Cyd remarked.

Joe grinned. "Guess who wants to see youz?"

"The state's attorney general?" Alex asked. "The Department of Justice?"

"Angel Ramon Ayala! Don Bueno himself! Head of the biggest drug cartel in Mexico, youz know what I'm saying?"

"No, I don't know what you're saying." Cyd was appalled. "I hope you told him we'd left the country and left no forwarding address."

Joe laughed his staccato laugh. "I told him you'd be thrilled. He's sending his plane for you. Youz need to be at Washington Dulles at 7:00 am tomorrow morning."

Alex was alarmed. "And if we refuse?"

"Wouldn't suggest it. Be like turning down a freakin' summons from God."

"Probably more like from the devil himself," Cyd speculated.

Joe waved a cautionary finger. "Don't be stupid and blow this. You'll die of old age before Big Pharma legitimizes Cannastar. This man can get youz distribution for all of North and South America." He saw the skepticism in their faces and his façade of affability faded. "Keep in mind, the last person to tell him "no," their body parts were found from one end of Mexico to the other."

***

Rxon launched a massive propaganda campaign of lies and misinformation to discredit Cannastar, and thanks to Griffin Gant, the media became their bitch.

An army of scientific and academic "experts" were called to appear on the various talk shows and voice their concerns about Cannastar. Prominent politicians spoke of their fears of drinking Cannastar tea in phrases that began with, "I heard . . .", "It's been reported . . ." , "Those in the know are saying . . .", "Reliable sources claim . . .". Their remarks were then repeated *ad infinitum* as absolute fact on the 24-hour news cycle until a cacophony of voices were screaming from the rooftops: "Cannastar is poisonous!", "Cannastar is addictive!", "Cannastar is deadly!" It was implied, and later reported as gospel, that early testing in mice showed signs of Cannastar actually *causing* cancer rather than curing it. Doctors coast to coast were in agreement: common side effects from this new drug might possibly include nausea, vomiting and heart failure. "The medical community agrees," cable news outlets reported in breathless soundbites hours later. "Cannastar causes nausea, vomiting and heart failure!"

Kenton Krill, a long-haired geneticist from one of the Ivy League universities, drew cries of indignation from the audience on a popular afternoon talk show when he said, "To turn an untested, unproven GMO loose on the world without the research to show that it does not result in mass extinctions of both plants and humans is the height of irresponsibility."

The interviewer was shocked. "Are you saying Cannastar could start an epidemic?"

"What I'm saying," the geneticist postulated, "is that we don't know what it is or what it might do. And therein lies not only the danger, but possibly even an existential threat to all humanity and life on earth."

On another cable outlet the same day, Ashit Patel, a representative from a Middle Eastern pharmaceutical company, told an appalled panel of women hosts in a sing-song voice, "In the drug industry, when the technology advances too rapidly relative to the science, that is a sure sign we need to stop, slow down and take a closer look. Before a new drug is released into the marketplace, we are obligated to work closely with the FDA to accumulate hard evidence that the risks and hazards do not outweigh the benefits. These checks and balances are in place for a reason. Protocols absolutely must be followed."

Bud Sweet was the pugnacious deputy director of Plant Diagnostics for the Department of Agriculture. Before going to work for the government, the crew-cut, mid-west native was on the board of directors of Farmacopia, the international producer and marketer of food, agricultural, financial and industrial products. Bud went on a network morning show and made some disturbing remarks:

"Once you insert a gene into another plant, you have to ask yourself: will it escape and pollinate other plants? The unintended consequences can be potentially devastating. From the perspective of the Department of Agriculture, there is a criminal lack of any caution going on here."

He was asked if he could be a little more specific.

"Plants like Cannastar cross-pollinate actively and aggressively," he said. "It's surprising how quickly something like this can spread. Someone has put a rogue gene into a Marijuana plant—a gene that can't be stopped and can't be killed. Once it gets going, your guess is as good as mine as to what might happen."

On another morning show an expert in transgenics, Ira Lundski, decried, "This could be a potentially deadly event with worldwide consequences. By any reasonable assessment, we are going too fast and need to slow down. No one, to my knowledge, has run any clinical trials on Cannastar. So far as I can tell, any risk assessment is being done by the very people peddling it. This is nothing short of criminal, in my opinion. An invitation to disaster and even mass extinction."

To repeat here the soundbites the media gleaned from Mr. Lundski's remarks would only be redundant.

A farmer from Oklahoma named Dave Grow was interviewed on yet another network opinion show. "A 'volunteer' is a farmer's nightmare," Grow explained. "It's something that is seeded on the wind after growing in one field and landing in another. Cannastar volunteers are cross-pollinating other crops as we speak." He lowered his voice for effect. "This means that poison is getting into our food supply. The result could be that we are looking at the beginnings of a famine of biblical proportions."

His neighbor thirty miles away, dressed in bib overalls and a Sooners baseball cap, echoed Grow's concern. "If God had wanted us to have Cannastar, He would of growed it Hisself."

To bolster the non-stop media coverage extolling the horrors of Cannastar, a massive social media campaign was launched. Computer experts using software developed by the Department of Defense to combat cyber terrorism took information warfare to a new height by employing AI and network analysis to map the flood of positive discussions and personal success stories about Cannastar that were popping up everywhere on the internet. A network of some 3.5 million social media influencers were employed to boost counter narratives that argued against the positive publicity Cannastar was getting. Those with large social media followings were paid good money to set people straight: Cannastar was a hoax, plain and simple.

The campaign produced an exponential avalanche of negativity about the so-called cancer cure on every smartphone, tablet and computer in the country. Anyone praising the virtues of Cannastar, or sharing the miraculous results they may have experienced using it, would receive dozens of profane comments insisting their post was false and that it was part of a conspiracy to murder minorities and persons of color.

It was crazymaking behavior, bought and paid for by Rxon. Most saw it as brainwashing and were angered by the destructive nature of the manipulation and deceit. Others swallowed the propaganda whole and were terrified to think that Cannastar even existed. "Wouldn't touch it if my life depended on it," many claimed. Unfortunately, for some, it did.

Chapter Twenty-Eight

Children of The Devil

A private jet streaked south from the U.S. to Mexico at an altitude of forty thousand feet and a speed of Mach .80.

Cyd and Alex sat cocooned in the elegance of soft leather seats, listening to the muffled rush of air outside their window and dining on a sumptuous meal served on bone china. They had just finished their desert and coffee when an attractive flight attendant appeared, cleared away their dishes and politely asked that they fasten their seatbelts. Minutes later, the jet swooped out of the sky and landed on a short, high-altitude runway that had been built by scraping the steaming jungle off the top of a ragged mountain.

A helicopter was waiting to take them the rest of the way. The $18 million aircraft skimmed the canopy of a dense rain forest in a dizzying ten-minute ride that ended at the base of a roaring waterfall called *Cola de Diablo* (Devil Tail Falls). It hovered there a moment in the mist, then rose two thousand feet straight in the air, scaling the face of the cascading water in seconds. Clearing the rim at the top of the falls, it hovered again. Cyd and Alex looked out and found themselves staring into the eyes of a giant statue of Saint Beuno Gasulsych, the legendary grandnephew of King Arthur himself. The hundred-foot-tall marble carving depicted Saint Beuno benevolently replacing Saint Winifred's severed head. The charitable act of reattaching the poor woman's ragged neck to her shoulders was said to have miraculously brought her back to life.

Beyond the statue lay a broad, denuded mesa surrounded by jungle and beyond that, at the back of the mesa, rose jagged cliffs where another waterfall thundered down. At the base of this waterfall was a great pool that split into two natural rivers that, in turn, curved around either side of the plateau in a pair of three-mile waterways. At the end of their journey, the two streams quietly rejoined under the base of St. Beuno's statue and once again became a roaring torrent emanating from the statue's feet and falling off the cliff to form *Cola de Diablo*.

The two rivers surrounding the mesa on either side formed a natural moat that enclosed the compound of the drug lord known as Don Bueno. Along the banks of these rivers, strategically placed and manned by heavily armed militia, were mobile ground-to-air missile launchers. But that was not the amazing part.

Within the moat, dwarfing a massive Spanish-style hacienda in the center of the compound, was an amusement park somewhat smaller than Disneyland, but no less elaborate or fanciful. Children from all over Mexico could be seen swarming the park and grounds from morning to dark. It was a Neverland; a place where no one ever grew old. Tragically, there was a reason for this. The kids that lived at Don Bueno's amusement park were all terminal.

Apart from the obvious charitable aspects of the venture, *los niños y las niñas del diablo* (the boys and girls of the devil) served another, more nefarious purpose. So long as hundreds of sick kids lived at Don Bueno's Mexican Wonderland, no army of *Federales* or enemies of any other kind were going to come charging in there bombing and shooting up the place in an attempt to take down the infamous drug king. The children of the devil provided a dome of protection more bullet proof than any bulletproof glass.

Don Bueno's helicopter with Cyd and Alex aboard landed on the great stone slab of the tomb of Saint Beuno. The slab was only a replica, but in far off Wales, to this very day, people still brought their youngsters to lay on the actual tomb of the patron saint of sick children in the hope of healing their infirmities and diseases.

Spanish guitars and Peruvian flutes haunted the air as security guards with guns bulging under their coats came forward to escort Cyd and Alex to the hacienda. Following along in stunned silence, Cyd looked around in awe at the looping, death-defying amusement park rides clattering through the park.

Alex was no less shocked. "What the hell is this place?"

"Maybe we're dead and don't know it," Cyd speculated. "Do you remember the helicopter crashing?"

"Not that I recall, but now that you mention it . . . ."

They entered the magnificent *hacienda* of Angel Ramon Ayala, aka Don Bueno, aka *El Diablo* and were ushered into a living room the size of a hotel lobby. Glancing around, they saw that every wall was hung with pictures of smiling children. Under each picture was a small brass plate with a child's name and below that a pair of dates. The two dates were never that far apart.

Don Bueno himself was across the room dressed in a silly pirate hat and eye patch, actively engaged in a mock sword fight with a dozen screaming kids. For a man built like a bow-legged muscle car and reputed to have a nuclear temper with the firing pin filed down, he didn't look all that intimidating.

Cyd and Alex watched in amazement as the attacking horde easily overpowered the one-eyed buccaneer and ran him through again and again. The feared drug czar went sprawling to floor to the delighted squeals of the children as his mock blood spilled out all over his expensive rug. Seeing that he had visitors, Don Bueno suddenly rose from the dead and with a mighty roar shooed the kids from the room.

He took off his pirate hat as he approached, and they saw that the eye patch was not part of the costume. A ragged scar ran down from the top of his bald head, disappeared behind his eye patch and emerged beneath it. The effect was disturbing to the point that they wished he had left his hat on. One little girl had not left with the others and was still clinging to the pirate's pant leg while staring up at the visitors with enormous eyes.

Don Bueno smiled at Cyd. "You have children, *Señora?*"

"*Señorita,*" Cyd corrected. "And no, not yet."

"You are not Catholic then?" He looked saddened by the news.

She shook her head.

"*No importa!*" His heavily accented English sounded like cannon fire, big and loud. "Does it work?"

"Does what work?"

"What you think?"

"If you're asking about Cannastar, the answer is yes. It works just fine in most cases."

"Most cases? How about in children?"

"Too early to tell," Alex interjected. "I personally know of only one successful case. A nine-year-old boy named Elton who had leukemia."

Don Bueno petted the head of the little girl who still hung to his leg. "Winifred here was born with Down syndrome. It will cure that, no?"

"No," Alex replied. "I'm afraid we can't offer any hope in that regard. Perhaps if I were to examine her . . ."

"You would be Dr. Farmer, would you not?"

Alex nodded.

"Well then *Doctor Agricultor*, what *does* it cure?"

"Primarily viral and infectious diseases. And in most cases, the uncontrolled growth of malignant cells in the body."

"So, cancer. *Correcto?*"

"Correct," Alex answered.

"Show me!" Don Bueno reached out so quickly with his hand in expectation of being handed something that a small cry escaped Cyd's throat. Reaching in her pocket, she timidly passed him the only bag of Cannastar she had brought with her.

The drug dealer turned the Ziploc full of green-spiked leaves and colorful seeds over and over in his hand, held it up to the light, opened it and sniffed it, then took a bit out and tasted it. "This is a good thing," he announced loudly. "A good thing!" Hoisting Winifred by the waist, he handed her off to a nanny who appeared out of nowhere, kissed the little girl on the head and charged out of the room. "Follow me! Come!"

Cyd and Alex trailed behind in confusion as Don Bueno led the way down a flowered garden path and through the rugged wooden doors of an adjoining building that looked like the bow of an old ship.

"Noah's Ark!" their host proclaimed with a magnanimous sweep of his hand, marching ahead like he was leading a pair of giraffes aboard. The interior of the building was braced with wooden ship's timbers and looked as real as any vessel ever built. At the end of the hall they went through a set of double doors and found themselves in an immaculate hospital ward. Painted animals cavorted along the walls, grinning down at dozens of boys and girls who sat talking and playing games on two long rows of beds. Gentle nurses moved among the children tending to their needs.

"What do you think, Doctor? A beautiful infirmary for you to work in, no?"

Alex was aghast. "I'm no pediatrician. What's wrong with these children?"

"They are all dying. Sooner rather than later, I'm afraid, unless you can help them."

"Help them?" Cyd gasped.

"Cannastar!" Don Bueno boomed in his explosive voice. "You prove it now that this miracle of yours works. I give you one month."

"One what . . .?" Cyd asked, backing away appalled.

279

Alex stiffened. "We can't treat all of these kids with one bag of Cannastar."

"Then you shall have more!" the drug lord cried. "Tell me where my men, they should go. I send the plane!"

***

Eloise's little blue Honda looked out of place on the tarmac at Washington Dulles next to the Don Bueno's state-of-the-art Jet. She opened the trunk of her car and a uniformed pilot politely helped her remove a pair of overstuffed plastic garbage bags. Stepping back, she watched in fascination as the bags were loaded onto the plane and the doors were quickly closed. The engines wound to a high-pitched scream, the aircraft taxied away, and minutes later hurtled down the runway, lifted off and disappeared into the southern sky. Eloise got back in her Honda and quietly drove away.

It was the beginning of a new international threat that was to change the game of drug trafficking forever. Drug enforcement agencies were set up to handle drugs being smuggled *into* the country. Nobody stopped to think what might happen if drugs started being smuggled *out* of the country.

***

Armed guards made certain Cyd and Alex were comfortably settled in a thatch-roofed, tile-floored, open air bungalow.

Cyd turned to Alex the moment they were alone. "One month? Seriously? What are we going to do?"

He was as incredulous as she was. "I feel like we just won an all-expense-paid vacation to Devil's Island."

"The devil is supposed to be, I don't know—the devil!" Cyd fumed. "I had no idea he ran a children's hospital. This guy's a one-man Make-A-Wish foundation."

Alex looked out at the jungle that surrounded their bungalow. "I have a wish. I wish we'd never left Montana."

***

Two nerve-racking weeks passed during which Cyd and Alex ministered to the dying Mexican children by putting them on a diet of fresh, whole food and gallons of Cannastar tea. At the end of that time, some of the kids were beginning to show encouraging results while others were enjoying miraculous improvement.

Another long day in the hospital ward drew to a close as Cyd helped Alex take the vitals of a long line of waiting children. She marveled at the special connection he seemed to have with them. The kids appeared to absolutely adore their new doctor—almost as much as they adored their *patrón*, the pirate.

Their rounds complete, the kidnapped couple left Don Bueno's air-conditioned hospital and stepped out into the hot, sticky night, heading for their bungalow. Mopping at his brow, Alex noticed Cyd giving him a peculiar look.

"What?" he asked.

"You're something, *Doctor Agricultor, y*ou really are."

He waited for her to go on.

"I couldn't have done any of this alone, Alex. A lot of these kids would be dead by now if it wasn't for you."

Her smile of admiration made him forget how tired he was. "How about I take you on a boat ride this evening?"

She clapped her hands in delight. "I'll ask the cook to make us a picnic dinner!"

A short while later they walked through the amusement park's central plaza heading for the riverboat ride. Cyd carried a wicker picnic basket on her arm lined in a red and white checked tablecloth. The plaza itself was a spaghetti western replica of a colorful Mexican village complete with a flowing fountain in the center and an old adobe church at one end. During the day, *banditos* were shot from the rooftops here and in the afternoons joyous *fiestas* were celebrated to the frenetic strains of mariachi music. But now, it was night and the *piñatas* had all been burst and the push carts had all been covered until morning when once again they would be overflowing with candies and fruits of all descriptions, free for the asking.

Cyd and Alex continued on in their walk until they reached a dock at the edge of the park where a khaki-clad *asistente* (attendant) in a pith helmet was waiting. He helped them into one of the electric, fringe-topped riverboats that were used to take the kids on rides around the mesa-top mote. Casting off the dock line, the *asistente* gave the boat a shove with his foot that sent them out into the slowly moving current.

If the jungle ride at Disneyland was the real thing, Don Bueno's mote was what it would look like—a real jungle with real jungle sounds complete with eyes poking up out of the water that were reptilian and not mechanical. The firefly lanterns on the dock grew smaller until they disappeared entirely in the dark as the boat drifted away and the jungle engulfed them in humid, fragrant air.

Alex manned the tiller while trailing his hand in the water and marveling at the intoxicating site of the white orchid Cyd had plucked and put in her dark hair.

She noticed his hand in the water and her smile changed to alarm. "Unless you want to lose your fingers, I suggest you keep them in the boat."

He jerked his hand out of the water and cradled it to his chest. "Alligators? I don't see any alligators. Where?"

Her laugh was muffled by the moist, heavy air. They drifted along in silence listening to the noisy night and breathing the pungent smells of the jungle. Water lapped against the hull in a hollow rhythm. They rounded a bend and the sound of rushing water came from up ahead.

"Ever think about getting married?" he asked.

"I was once. Almost."

"Almost?"

"He was killed a week before our wedding. Bull riding accident."

"I didn't know. I'm sorry."

"We were both young. He was a good man. Like you in some ways. I think we would have been happy." She saw him watching her closely. "Sounds corny, I know."

"No. It's not. It's nice."

He negotiated a small white-water rapid, then let the boat glide through a calm pool below. She lay quietly looking up at the moon that filtered through the trees and dappled her face in light. "If I wasn't the only girl around," she asked, "would you still want me?"

An animal howled in the jungle, another answered, the first one howled back and it set off a cacophony of howls and screams that seemed to be coming from everywhere.

"I'd want you if there were a thousand girls around. Ten thousand, even."

"Pull over."

"Say what?"

"Stop the boat."

"Here?"

"Unless you're afraid of whatever the hell it is that won't stop howling out there."

He nosed the bow into a bank where the trees came down low to the water, moved next to her and suddenly they were kissing and tearing at each other's clothes with months of pent-up longing. He threw the cushions off on the floor and they slid down onto them just as a creature close by in the undergrowth let out a piercing cry. Alex sat up startled and looked around. She pulled him back down and the touch of her glistening body made the night sounds fade away. They made love in the stifling heat while the monkeys called the news across the treetops until all the creatures in the jungle knew that every now and then even humans got it right.

The next two weeks were an erotic blur of daytime tea parties at the infirmary and nighttime sex in their bungalow. They made love on every sheeted, carpeted, tiled and padded surface in their guest house. If sex was an Olympic sport, they would have medaled in gymnastics and marathon. The monkeys heard the jungle sounds coming from the human habitat and thought a tribe of primates were having a mating ritual.

The lovers lay spent and naked on a lounge chair on their outdoor patio looking like they had been making love underwater they were so drenched.

"Sauna sex," Cyd panted. "My new diet and exercise program."

"I'd give it a five-star review," Alex proclaimed and flopped exhausted onto his back. Cuddling was sticky business in this heat. He rolled on his side and kissed her instead. "I love you, Cyd."

"Call and raise."

"Come again?"

"I thought I told you. I made my spending money in college playing poker."

"You still haven't told me what it means."

"It means I love you more."

"Prove it," he challenged.

"I already proved it twice tonight."

"Who's counting?"

"You're right. What was I thinking?"

They embraced and nearly slipped off the lounger their bodies were so wet. Afterward he was gently drying her with a towel when he remembered something important. "Almost forgot. One of his goons told me that Don Bueno wants to see us at his *hacienda* first thing in the morning."

Her smile faded to a frown. "He say what for?"

"Either he wants to thank us or kill us, it could go either way. If *El Diablo*'s holding a pitchfork when we get there, run."

***

Don Bueno came charging across his living room and gave Cyd and Alex a robust group hug that they suffered in silence.

"*Mis personas que hacen milagros!* (My miracle workers!) So now we make a deal, no?"

"Deal?" Alex was confused. "What kind of deal?"

"The children are much better. They are all getting well! This Cannastar, it works!" He gave the St. Beuno medal he wore around his neck an emphatic kiss. "I want exclusive distribution. I am the only one who sells it, agreed?"

Cyd and Alex exchanged worried looks.

Don Bueno had wanted for some time to legitimize his vast business holdings and thought Cannastar might just be the way to do it, the way to show the world he wasn't the devil incarnate after all. As an orphan who had risen from impossible, unspeakable poverty to be loved and feared by his followers, he often wondered how God had gotten His start.

"Western hemisphere, eastern hemisphere!" the drug lord thundered. "I help children around the world, and I get richer than God! We grow it all right here in Mexico!"

"That's a dealbreaker," Cyd replied.

Don Bueno's one good eye bulged with anger.

Cyd stared back firmly resolved. We turn production over to him, she thought, and what does he need us for? We might as well sign our own death warrants.

Alex was looking at her like she was crazy.

"It isn't that easy to grow," she lied. "This isn't like marijuana that grows everywhere. One thing for certain, it doesn't like hot climates. Took us a long time to figure out what it does like and get the growing conditions just right."

The jagged scar that ran down over his head and under his eye patch pulsed red. "If you are worried about quality control, *señorita*, I can assure you . . ."

"I'm worried, if the wrong person gets complete control of this, they could blackmail the world with it. I won't let Cannastar become another illegal drug that people are killing each other over."

"Then you tell me," he suggested impatiently. He looked ready to explode.

Cyd took a deep breath. "You can have exclusive distribution. That's easiest for us anyway. But we grow it. *Hecho en* America, for a change."

"Such an operation, it is expensive, no? Don Bueno, he will pay."

"No," Cyd replied, a little too quickly. "I don't think I want to owe you money."

Don Bueno laughed his booming laugh. "Bueno! I wouldn't want to owe me money either, *señorita*. If only I had one bull as brave as you." He abruptly sobered. "You can do this alone? Without my money? Without my protection? *Es muy peligroso* (It is very dangerous)."

"What isn't?" she smiled. From the look on her face, no one would know she was terrified.

"Cyd," Alex said, no longer able to contain himself, "maybe we should listen to the man."

Her gaze remained fixed on his one good eye. "I think we understand each other perfectly well."

Again, the booming laugh.

"Don Bueno, look," she added reassuringly. "We're on the same side here. We're in this together. It's as important to us as it is to you that everybody in the world be able to buy Cannastar."

The drug dealer was suddenly all business. "How many tons a month that you can provide?"

Cyd thought a moment. "However many you want. Give us up to a year to get set up and we'll supply you with all the weight you can sell."

He nodded thoughtfully. "This is a promise then? Without fail you will deliver?"

"Without fail," she vowed.

Alex was inwardly horrified.

Don Bueno turned away and then spun back. "*Bueno!*" His mask of good humor fell away revealing a vicious will. "Sadly, many of my friends who did not keep their promises, they are *muerto* (dead)." His head went back in a savage laugh. "*Pero, no importa.* First, we take New York, then we take L.A . . . No?"

***

An hour later Don Bueno's helicopter dropped them off at his jungle-top airstrip where they boarded his jet for the trip home.

"Have you completely lost your mind?" Alex cried the minute they were airborne. "Are you trying to get us both killed? What were you thinking telling him we can grow that much Cannastar?"

Cyd leaned back and smiled contentedly. "We'll figure it out. We always do."

"Just how many greenhouses do you think Annie can build?"

"I suppose two is the limit."

"Jesus, Buddha, Krishna and Mohammed!"

Chapter Twenty-Nine

A Matter of Disagreement

Clarence's clandestine internet campaign about Cannastar as a cure for viral diseases like cancer had generated so much word of mouth that everyone was talking about it—which meant the smear campaign against it had to be stepped up. Big Pharma pulled out all the stops. Their approach wasn't smart or clever, it was vicious, mean and full of lies—which was why it was so effective.

On one of the business channels, Wall Street experts were forecasting a new bull market in pharmaceuticals. Medical products and services were said to be poised to skyrocket as well. In fact, profits for the medical community as a whole were in the toilet thanks to Cannastar. Rxon's profits in the east were down thirty percent alone.

One of the most popular hosts on cable news was the gorgeous Monica Williams. Her success in treating her own ovarian cancer with Cannastar was nothing short of a miracle because it was gone, totally and completely disappeared. It was her first day back at work after being off for a month with her near-fatal illness, and the long-legged blond was once again the picture of health. She made Cannastar her lead story and opened with the following announcement:

"Unsubstantiated rumors are circulating that a number of deaths have been attributed to the use of this Cannastar that's been appearing on the streets. While these rumors are still unverified, the American people should be aware that a potentially dangerous drug has been unleashed and is being sold as a magic cure-all for cancer and heaven knows what else." She pushed her amazing hair away from her amazing face with a slender finger and tucked it neatly behind her adorable ear.

"Does that make any sense, because to me it makes no sense at all. Personally, I wouldn't touch it with a ten-foot pole."

The media picked up on Monica's sound bite that Cannastar was a deadly drug and repeated it so often that, for many, it became the only truth they knew. As wanted criminals, there was little Cyd and Alex could do about it. Clarence, of course, countered the claim via the internet, but the propaganda took on a life of its own to the point that it too became an incurable cancer.

"Rumors of Cannastar deaths run rampant," claimed Joel Potts, the blustering, swaggering, talk show host who followed Williams. Tears welled in his eyes for the victims.

The late-night news was fraught with concern. "Reports of widespread Cannastar deaths are growing every day," the anxious newscaster said. "The numbers are yet to be verified, but this is clearly becoming an epidemic." The crawl at the bottom of the screen, meanwhile, read, *Reports of widespread Cannastar deaths!*

As proof of the growing menace, they played a taped interview with Leonard Shope. Mourning the death of his late wife, he was convinced that Cannastar had killed her.

Popular radio talk show host Quinton Lewis was apoplectic over the possibility that Cannastar was a terrorist plot to take over America. "Who are these people who are trying to shove this Cannastar crap down our throats?" he demanded. "Hippies turned terrorists, that's who! The Green Panthers of the twenty-first century hell-bent on turning you and your children into drug addicts. These criminals are using fear tactics to tell us that we're going to die if we don't start using their so-called miracle. Well, I don't know about you, but when somebody tries to shove something down my throat, it makes me mad!" He took a drink of water because the prescription painkillers he was taking were giving him cotton mouth—probably because he was taking twice the recommended dosage. "Let me ask you something. Are you willing to stand by and let this happen because I . . . *am* . . . *not*! I hope you have a gun at home, and I hope it's loaded because let me tell you something friends, these people are coming, and they're coming for you!"

The US government ordered a scientific study to determine the extent of the danger posed by Cannastar. Subsequent laboratory testing confirmed that the genetic makeup of the alien herb contained not only of marijuana, but another illegal plant as well called the Death Star. Their worst fears were confirmed when a Death Star was located in China and flown to the United States where they began overdosing hundreds of rats with injections drawn directly from the center of its spiked red ball. The final report stated that one hundred percent of the rodents had died immediately, proving conclusively that Cannastar was a deadly drug.

Senator Sam Seeley appeared on national television to assure a concerned nation that Congress was doing everything in its power to deal with the problem. "Americans have a right to know the truth, and the truth is disturbing," the senator intoned with the grave authority and comforting demeanor of a benevolent grandfather. "Recent scientific studies confirm that we have a national emergency on our hands. To deal with this crisis, the DEA has today declared Cannastar a Schedule I drug. Given that no accepted medical uses exist for this highly addictive poison, persons caught possessing or growing it in any amount will face prosecution to the full extent of the law. The criminals responsible for the proliferation of this noxious weed are going to go to jail for a very, very long time, I assure you."

Not all the news was negative. A black comedian covered in tattoos with ropes of gold chain around his twenty-inch neck looked into the television camera like he wanted to kill it. "Telling people that Cannastar is dangerous is bullshit, yo. The government is turning into a police state in defense of the drug companies. Come to my hood and I'll give you the name of a dealer who'll hook you up."

Fred of *The Fred Show* said, "You want to know what you get from taking Cannastar? You get well! You get better! Is that wrong? I don't think it's wrong. If these treasonous anarchists get their way with their nutcase lies, they are going to succeed where the destroyers of 9/11 failed!"

City councils across the country issued alerts for residents to watch their neighbor's backyards for telltale signs of people planting these "seeds of revolt."

Meanwhile, thousands of wildly enthusiastic posts were crisscrossing cyberspace with people espousing the successes they were having with Cannastar. Quality of life was being improved; lives were being saved. Friends and families of the terminally ill were ecstatic and people everywhere were clamoring for the drug. Censors at the social media platforms dutifully labeled these posts "inflammatory" and "misleading" and immediately took them down.

Berkeley Conrad, a balding former economic advisor to a dead president, was the best dressed host on television. Despite persistent evidence to the contrary, in his mind the erudite academic was never wrong about anything. The topic under discussion on his show this afternoon was the efficacy of genetically engineered plants as related to Cannastar.

One of his panelists, Horace Lake, was an expert in plant biotechnology from the University of Iowa. The soft-spoken young researcher with the shaved head was trying to make a point: "Your typical modern farmer has vastly increased his crop yields with the use of transgenics. He gets better weed control and better yield with lower costs. There is no evidence of any negative effects . . ."

His fellow panelists vehemently shouted him down. Berkeley Conrad asked another question: "What if we created another plant that could kill this Cannastar?"

"You're talking about the terminator gene," Horace Lake responded with unaccustomed fervor. "Creating more technology to get rid of a bad technology is a little like hiring a bobcat to get rid of the feral cats in the neighborhood. It creates unintended consequences. Bobcats, for example, like to eat small dogs, too."

The other panelists rose up against him arguing that a terminator gene was in fact a fine idea. Berkeley Conrad went to commercial and when he came back, Horace Lake had been replaced by a congressperson who supported the panel's position.

In response to the panel discussion a popular female comedian posted a comment that read, "Now that people are starting to take Cannastar, the AMA is recommending that doctors start holding bake sales to help cover their overhead."

A young musician promoting her new album tweeted, "People who drink Cannastar tea are coming down with life-threatening cases of joy and happiness. Sing along, America!"

A retired comedian with a large collection of antique cars claimed he put Cannastar in one of them. "Didn't help the gas mileage, but the old heap definitely stopped smoking. Been trying to get it to quit for years."

Flatscreens from coast to coast were once again adorned with the lovely face of cancer survivor Monica Williams. "Next up," she announced, "a report on the Cannastar plague that is sweeping our nation and how it could lead to a national lockdown. But first these words from our sponsor, the Rxon Corporation."

***

Don Bueno's jet touched down at Washington Dulles and taxied to the Executive Terminal where Cyd and Alex disembarked, then watched as the plane throttled back up and taxied away for takeoff. Alex rented a car, and he and Cyd drove to the RV park outside of Arlington where Otis was staying.

Eloise had just popped her famous homemade lasagna into the oven when a knock came at the door of their motor home. She looked out and, with squeal of delight, threw her arms around the necks of her visitors. Otis joined in the group hug, and Elton shook hands with the guests in a very adult manner.

Seated side by side on the sofa in the RV's living room, Otis and Eloise listened in awe to the stories Cyd and Alex told them of the children of the jungle and the Mexican Disneyland on the plateau above *Cola de Diablo*. They then heard how they were now in partnership with a one-eyed homicidal maniac with a soft spot for children who was perhaps the biggest drug dealer in the world.

"Cool," Otis exclaimed at hearing the news.

"Totally," Eloise agreed after a moment's reflection.

"You don't see a problem here?" Alex cried. "Like how do we keep Don Bueno from hunting us down and having us killed if, by some off chance, we can't grow enough Cannastar to supply the world?"

"Let me show you something," Otis grinned, bouncing off the sofa with amazing agility and leading them outside where he opened one of the cargo bays under his bus. Inside, the storage area crammed with burlap bags. "A little trick I learned from Maury," he boasted. "Paranoid hording of Cannastar seeds!"

Cyd whistled softly. "There must be a ton of seed in here."

Otis scratched the back of his neck. "Half a ton, I'm guessing. Now all we need is the dirt to plant them in."

"No problem," Alex replied. "A few thousand acres where nobody is going to notice what we're doing. Shouldn't be all that difficult."

Cyd took his hand and kissed his cheek. "Isn't he cute when he's cynical?"

Otis looked on, nodding in approval. "I thought you two would never get together."

"We made up for lost time," Cyd smiled knowingly.

"What's in the other cargo hold?" Alex asked. "More seed?"

Otis pulled up the door to the second storage compartment. The bay was stuffed with thirty-gallon garbage bags. "Dried Cannastar leaves," he proclaimed proudly. "For our free health clinic."

Cyd was surprised. "Free health clinic?"

"The one Eloise and I started in D.C. while you were away."

Off and on, they had discussed the idea of free clinics to dispense Cannastar, but the economics of such a venture had stopped them. Charity was expensive, and up until recently they hadn't been able to afford it. In addition, Otis was worried about the illegality of it. Eloise argued that the authorities wouldn't dare risk the bad publicity of actually raiding a free clinic and arresting people for the crime of wanting to cure their cancer. In the end, he was no match for her naïve passion for the project, insisting instead they at least call it a free health clinic and not a Cannastar dispensary. Word of mouth had taken care of the rest. Everyone in nation's capital knew this was where they could go to get free Cannastar.

Eloise called from inside the RV that dinner was ready. Crowded around the small table, they enjoyed a happy feast of lasagna, bread and salad. During the meal, Otis explained that Eloise was really the one who made the clinic happen. Her idea was to train people at this clinic so they could open up others. "You wouldn't believe what a big hit our first one is," she enthused. "I can barely keep it supplied."

"I'm the poster boy," Elton announced. "Everybody that comes there wants to be like me."

His mother gave him a proud hug. "And they will." Then looking up at her friends, "My problem at the moment is tomorrow, I don't know how I'm going to be in two places at once. If I don't drop off more Cannastar to the clinic, they're going to run out, but I need to be at Elton's school to talk to his counselor about putting him in an advanced math class, and after that I have to take him to his soccer game."

"I'd be happy to go," Cyd offered. "I'd like to see the clinic anyway."

Eloise smiled in relief. "Would you mind? I'd really appreciate it."

Cyd turned to Alex. "Want to come? Keep me company?"

"I'd like to, but I need to spend some time with Annie so she really understands the part she played in saving all those kid's lives down in Mexico."

Otis frowned. "Don't tell her about the deal you cut with this Don Bueno dude. You'll just overwhelm her and make her feel guilty because she can't grow all the Cannastar we need."

Cyd wasn't concerned. "I don't mind going alone."

Eloise made a bed for her guests on the RV's pullout couch, and they spent a rather cramped but restful night. The next morning Otis loaded a bag of Cannastar into the trunk of their rental car for Cyd to drive to the clinic.

"One bag?" she asked, getting behind the wheel.

"Altruism only goes so far," Otis sighed. "We found out the hard way that if you don't control the supply, they'll just start selling it out the back door."

Alex waved goodbye as Cyd drove off and got in beside Otis in his new pickup. Annie had bought him the truck so he could haul the farming supplies he was always buying, and he was quite proud of it. Eloise, getting ready to drive Elton to school in her Honda, called to them from the motor home door. "Don't anybody be late for dinner tonight because I'm making pot roast."

The pot roast would go uneaten.

Chapter Thirty

Garden of Miracles

Cyd slowed her rental car and looked out at the desolation and ruin that surrounded her, wondering how could a neighborhood this close to the nation's capital look so much like the end of the world.

She didn't need an address to spot the clinic she was looking for. Up ahead, hundreds of people were crowded around the door to an old brick warehouse with a crudely painted sign that read "Free Health Clinic". A long, disorganized line stretched around the block that spilled into the dreary street blocking traffic.

Cyd was forced to park a block away. Pulling over to the curb, she marveled at the hope and faith she saw in the faces of the chronically and terminally ill who stood waiting so patiently for their twice-daily measure of Cannastar. The idea that all of these people could miraculously be returned to life was thrilling. It brought back everything she had been through—the suffering, the fear, the struggle and the pain—and made it all worthwhile.

Smiling, she got out of her car and went around to the back where she opened the trunk and pulled out the over-stuffed garbage bag of Cannastar that Otis had put there. Her hand was on the trunk lid to slam it closed when she looked up and saw a police car pull in front of the clinic. Moments later the area was swarming with armored black vans and police cars, all with their sirens blaring. Squads of SWAT teams in bulletproof vests jumped out with clubs and riot shields and began dispersing the crowd. The line of cancer patients was pushed and shoved until it broke into an angry, milling mob. A black bus with barred windows appeared to haul away the volunteers working inside the clinic and was immediately swallowed up by protesters who began rocking its sides to try and push it over.

Vivid memories of the horrid raid on Otis's attic flashed through her mind as she stood watching, the bag of Cannastar forgotten in her hand. People around the clinic continued to resist, meekly at first, then more forcefully as the policemen's clubs came out and shouts and rocks began to fly.

A bullhorn blared above the din: "By order of the police commissioner, this is an unlawful assembly for the purpose of engaging in the distribution and use of illegal drugs. You are hereby ordered to disperse immediately or face arrest and incarceration."

"Incarcerate this!" shouted a young black man, throwing a rock. The kid had a major league arm and the rock struck a helmeted policeman, knocking him to the ground. The teargas came out, and instantly the whole scene was engulfed in billowing clouds of dirty white smoke that was burning and stinging the skin and eyes of the protestors. Then windows began to break, and the looting began.

Absorbed in the horror, Cyd did not see the squad car that had pulled up alongside her. The siren made a growling moan, and she jumped a foot.

"Move along, please," the car's loudspeaker commanded. "This is a crime scene, move along."

Cyd remained frozen, too traumatized to think. An officer got out of the car with his hand on his gun, and the image of Jesse Long Bow in a murdered tribal policeman's uniform flashed through her mind.

She struggled to collect herself. "What's going on, officer?"

"Ma'am, I need you to show me the contents of your bag."

Cyd looked down and realized what she had in her hand. "This? Some old clothes I was taking to the clinic is all."

"The clinic is an illegal drug operation, not the Goodwill, as I'm sure you're aware. Open the bag, please."

Cyd hesitated . . . just as shots were fired from somewhere in the boiling crowd. The officer, responding to the gunfire, jumped back in his squad car and sped off in a noisy fury of lights, siren and smoking rubber, only to be swallowed up by the escalating riot.

Cyd tossed the bag of Cannastar back in her trunk, slammed the lid and hurriedly got behind the wheel. Tears were streaming down her cheeks, and not just from the drifting clouds of teargas. People—the sick and dying along with the volunteer workers—were being hauled out of the warehouse in handcuffs and prodded aboard the police bus with nightsticks.

Crying uncontrollably, Cyd fumbled with the ignition, started the engine and made a screeching U-turn.

***

Later that same day, Ty Seeley showed up at his parent's house in Virginia for a surprise visit and recognized the big fat guy working down at his mother's greenhouse.

Cyd had arrived earlier that morning grief stricken from her experience in Washington and was inside the greenhouse being consoled by Annie and Alex. Otis had gone outside to try and get over his upset. He was going to have to tell Eloise that the clinic was gone, and he knew she would take it hard.

Sitting on a bench and rubbing his temples, he looked up and saw a round figure in ostrich-skin cowboy boots walking toward him down the great slope of lawn from the main house. The little doughboy with the tiny mouth looked vaguely familiar. Their eyes met and Otis knew in an instant that he'd been recognized.

Cyd was acutely aware that Ty, directly or indirectly, was behind Maury's death and everything else that had happened to threaten their lives. She couldn't prove it, now that Jesse Long Bow had been murder, any more than she could prove that her uncle the Senator was pulling the strings, but she knew it was true. What she didn't know was that Ty, from the very beginning, had spent hours sitting outside of Otis's funeral home to try and figure out who Maury was spending so much time with and why. Thanks to his spying efforts, he was intimately familiar with what Otis looked like.

Alex, Annie and Cyd were startled when Otis came rushing into the greenhouse shouting for them to hide!

But it was too late.

Ty entered the glass-domed conservatory and stopped, mouth ajar, gaping at the canopy of illegal Cannastar pushing up toward the light. Then he saw the three people standing with his mother and a sardonic smile lit his face.

"Well, well, would you look at this," he marveled. "Would you god-damn look at *this*! My own mother! Unbelievable! So, you're the ones after all. You're the criminals who've been growing this shit. I got you now, by God, I got you good."

Annie's soft voice rose to a scream. "Leave here this instant! Get out!"

Ty giggled. "When Dad finds out, he is going to level this place to the ground and you along with it . . . mommy dearest."

"Get out, get out, get . . . out!"

Otis and Alex picked up shovels and threatened to bury him. Despite his bravado, Ty began backing away. They made a grab and missed. Ty turned, bolted from the greenhouse and ran for the house.

Annie stood staring after her son in sudden horror. "What have I done," she sobbed. "What have I done?"

They gathered her in their arms and held her, rocking her as she cried.

Up at the main house, Ty flew through the front door looking back over his shoulder, rushed to the den and fished his cell phone out of his pocket.

Sam Seeley answered his son's call and listened impassively. "Just sit still," he hissed when Ty was done relating the news. Anyone over-hearing the Senator's tone would have feared for their lives. "Don't move! Don't even scratch your ass until I get there."

"They're going to pay big time," Ty gushed, anxious for his father's praise. Surely, Sam would acknowledge his clever son now. "I'm call-ing the cops!"

"You do," Sam replied, "and I'll cut off your nuts and feed them to the dog."

***

Annie didn't know where Ty was. Somewhere in another part of the house, she supposed, waiting for his father to come home. She didn't care.

Since being unmasked in her own greenhouse by her own son, she had come up to the house and taken a long, hot bath to calm herself. Dressed now in a flowered summer frock that accented her still-attrac-tive figure, she stood at the window of her drawing room staring out serenely at her colorful gardens.

Sam Seeley burst into the room shouting and cursing and waving his arms like the house was on fire. Which, in a manner of speaking, it was. "What have you done to me?" he cried. "Have you lost your friggin' mind? Are you trying to destroy me?"

"Mind your blood pressure, Sam."

"I'll mind it after you're fitted for a straight jacket and locked up in the loony bin!"

"I was only trying to help, you see. So many people are relying on me now."

"Tell it to the judge."

"Excuse me?"

"You heard what I said."

She smoothed the front of her already-perfect dress. "Very well, if you insist. I'll tell the judge that every bit of Cannastar that's been sold from Maine to Florida was grown in your backyard. Try and deny it. I'll tell him I was afraid for my life, that you threatened to kill me if I didn't use my new greenhouse for your criminal enterprise. I might still have to go to jail, who knows, but what about you? With the new laws you've managed to get passed, and with all the hate and hysteria you've generated over Cannastar, you'll be lucky if you get out of jail in time for your hundredth birthday."

Sam Seeley's face turned heart-attack red. "I'll deny it," he sputtered, spittle flying from his mouth. "I . . . I'll say it's a lie, all of it!"

"You do that," she advised. "Everybody knows you're a greedy hypocritical bastard. By the time I'm done with you, they'll see how greedy and hypocritical you really are." The idea suddenly amused her and she laughed. It sounded like tiny bells.

"Laugh if you want," he cried. "It doesn't change what you did."

"Imagine," she went on blissfully. "The Senator who's been protecting the American people from this deadly Cannastar menace has all along been the one growing it and selling it. I can't wait to see the headlines."

He was cornered and he knew it. "I'll tell you one thing," he shouted, snatching up one of her crystal vases full of flowers. "Your little garden party is over, and you and your playmates are going to jail!" The vase smashed to the floor, shattering in a hundred pieces.

Annie's smile remained frozen on her face. Outwardly, she was calm; inwardly, she was terrified. "Get out and don't come back! You come near me again, and you'll be explaining to the whole country why your wife is divorcing you for forcing her to be a part of your heinous crimes."

He reached for another vase, but she beat him to it, snatching the heavy crystal off the shelf and weighing it in her hand. She was small, but constant gardening had toned her muscles and made her strong. The vase flew past his head and exploded against the wall. He stumbled back and she picked up a small bronze statue, feeling now that she had better aim. "And while you're at it, take that mealy-mouthed, murdering son of ours with you! I never want to see either of you again! Where I come from, people like you and Ty, we don't arrest them, we stake them out for the coyotes and cougars to eat."

Sam stormed from the room, slamming the door behind him so hard it rattled the walls. Annie stared after him . . . and burst into tears. She was no longer a grower of miracles. Her garden of miracles was over and done. And so was her marriage.

***

"Cannastar epidemic stopped in its tracks!" raved an overjoyed media. As a matter of national security, the exact location of the illegal growing operation could not be revealed, but unnamed sources reported that it was both a Cannastar farm *and* a meth lab that had exploded during a raid leaving nothing but a pile of ashes. Little else was known; officials were not at liberty to discuss the crime as it was an ongoing investigation.

Senator Sam Seeley wasted little time in distancing himself from the scandal by leaking the information the media was currently celebrating. Appearing on national television, he assured a worried nation that the persons responsible for trying to turn America into a narco state and its people into a country of drug addicts had been identified, and that a nationwide manhunt was underway for their capture.

Pictures of Cyd, Alex and Otis appeared on every television screen and the front pages of every newspaper from New York to L.A. A salacious tabloid, famous for often getting a story right when others were still lying about it, had all three of their images on the cover with a headline that read: "Health Drug Heroes on The Run!"

In other news, it was widely reported that Dick Tremble, the CEO of Rxon Corporation, had made a multi-million-dollar contribution to cancer research in the name of the victims who had lost their lives to Cannastar.

***

They fled.

Cyd and Alex led the way in Eloise's blue Honda with Otis, Eloise and Elton in Otis's lumbering RV following a safe distance behind. Hidden in the belly of RV was the thousand pounds of Cannastar seed that Otis had secreted away. It was Cyd and Alex's job to protect the seed at any cost by running block, meaning they were to act as decoy by racing ahead and drawing attention away from the RV should the police appear unexpectedly. Things had been a bit tense while they were still on the interstate, but now that they were headed west and keeping to the back roads, they could breathe a little easier.

Chapter Thirty-One

Shelter from The Storm

The fugitives escaped across state lines and into the Midwest, the heartland, the breadbasket of America where their farming efforts almost resulted in Iowa itself becoming a narco-state. This is how it happened . . .

The dawn was at their backs and still hours away when they crossed the Mississippi River at Dubuque and entered Iowa on Highway 20. A hundred miles further on, they watched the lights of Waterloo come and go. They were running . . . with nowhere to run.

Up ahead, Otis could see the taillights of his wife's Honda leading him through the dark. He couldn't tell if it was Cyd or Alex that was driving. Behind him in his RV, he could hear his family sleeping softly. He didn't mind driving at night; he rather enjoyed it, in fact. He liked knowing the world around him was busting with new growth, liked imagining seeds bursting from the soil, eager for the light. He rolled down his window and inhaled the sweet-smelling earth. It filled him with energy, and he was no longer sleepy. He didn't need food; he could live off this air forever.

Sunrise comes early in Iowa because the curve of the earth is the only place it has to hide. The road in front of the onrushing RV turned from black to gray and, in the growing light, Otis saw fields of checkerboard green laid out all around him in perfect squares as far as he could see. His cellphone rang, startling him out of his reverie. Fumbling to answer it, he heard Cyd's voice complaining that if she didn't get coffee and breakfast soon, she was going to get very, very grouchy.

"You nearly gave me a heart attack!"

"Coffee and breakfast," she insisted.

A roadside sign caught his eye and he read it out loud. "Fort Dodge, 20 miles."

"Lucky thing. I was about to start eating the upholstery."

***

If you showed up at The Early Bird Café in Fort Dodge, Iowa in anything but a pickup, you probably weren't from here. If you showed up midmorning and ordered anything but pie and coffee, you definitely weren't from here. An RV and a blue Honda pulled into the café's parking lot and five road-weary travelers got out. Alex stopped them as they were headed inside and told them to hand over their phones.

They looked at him in confusion.

"Cellphones, please. Cough 'em up,"

Bleary-eyed and road-weary, they did as he asked, then watched in horror as he broke their phones in half and tossed them in a dumpster.

"What the hell?" Cyd protested.

Alex took his own phone out of pocket, broke it apart and tossed it in the same dumpster. "Disposable phones only from now on, okay? Throwaways can't be traced."

"Cyd and I just talked on the phone," Otis worried.

"One call won't matter . . . I hope."

The café was packed and noisy. A group of farmers at a round table were just getting up to leave. The owner, Mable Nash, stuffed the money they left for the check and the tip in the pocket of her apron, cleared their dishes and wiped the table before seating the newcomers. Mabel looked too old to still be working but seemed to have boundless energy. She gave the visitors a motherly smile, dumped menus on their table and filled their coffee cups without asking before rushing off to tend to her other customers. Young Elton immediately adored her because his cup got coffee too.

A wall-mounted TV was broadcasting the news, but no one was interested. Early Bird regulars tended to favor the food, the conversation and the Fort Dodge Messenger over blow-dried pundits and self-serving politicians telling them who to hate and what to fear. Residents of this commercial farming hub, bisected by the beautiful Des Moines River and surrounded by some of the most fertile farm land anywhere, already knew the world was changing and were mad as hell about it.

The hungry fugitives ordered ham, bacon, sausage, eggs, potatoes, toast and hot cakes and ate like field hands, wolfing it all down in silence and chasing it with more coffee. Cyd was wiping her mouth when she looked up and saw their names and faces flash across the television screen. The sound was off, but the crawl under their pictures read, "Reward Offered for Capture and Conviction".

Cyd held her napkin over her mouth. "We need to leave," she rasped. "Now."

Alex kept eating. "Not finished yet."

"Yes. You are." She moved his fork away from his mouth and motioned with her head to the TV.

Alex saw himself on the screen and quickly looked around. No one in the restaurant was looking at the TV or at them. It was almost as if they were deliberately averting their eyes.

Cyd felt it too. She gulped the last of her coffee and started to stand just as a large woman with large breasts and tightly permed hair came up to their table and stood nervously looking down.

"Excuse me," she said. "You're them, aren't you?"

"Them who?" Cyd asked innocently.

Otis grinned and extended his hand. "Otis Appleseed."

The woman shook his meaty paw as if he were a movie star. "Oh, my gracious," she stammered. "Oh, my gracious." Turning to look over her shoulder while still holding Otis's hand, she announced to the room, "Look who's come to town, y'all."

Dead silence. Then a clap, a single sound like a gunshot, followed by another and another, gaining in volume and tempo until the whole restaurant was on their feet applauding.

Cyd was dumbstruck. Alex looked amazed. Otis was thrilled and Eloise clapped in along with them.

"Why are they all doing that?" Elton asked.

Alex tousled his hair. "I think they're trying to say welcome to Iowa, son."

"Does that mean we're not being arrested?" Cyd asked incredulously.

Alex acknowledged the applause with a smile. "Not at the moment, at least."

A work-hardened farmer, tall, quiet and stoop-shouldered with the saddest eyes Cyd had ever seen, came over to their table, introduced himself as Abe Robinson and asked if he could join them. Otis graciously offered him a chair, the man sat stiffly, and suddenly the rest of the room was eagerly crowding around their table all talking at once and peppering the bewildered travelers with questions.

Mabel Nash quietly went to the front door, locked it and put out the closed sign.

Alex, amused at the outpouring of affection and very much enjoying the show, couldn't help admiring how sociable Cyd was being and how interested everyone seemed to be in her. Otis was more or less the center of attention and Eloise politely deferred all questions to him. Elton, meanwhile, had his own audience. With the skill of a natural storyteller, the boy entertained his rapt audience with a rather long-winded version of how he had cured himself of cancer, complete with graphic detail and dramatic pauses.

When asked about his part in of all of this, Alex smiled his boyish smile. "Me, I'm just an itinerate doctor trying to keep the lady he loves from getting tarred, feathered and run out of town for selling snake oil."

After thirty minutes of questions and answers about how Cannastar worked and how the rugged weed was grown, a growing chorus of voices was asking where they could get their hands on this miracle plant.

Abe leaned over and whispered something in Alex's ear. Alex relayed the message to Cyd who passed it on to Otis who nodded and smiled.

Abe stood and cleared his throat. "Everyone, please. Could I have your attention?"

The room fell silent.

Abe liked everyone just as they were and, as a consequence, was loved just as he was. Patient and proud, he liked to say he wasn't that smart because he'd never gone to college. Anyone who knew him disagreed. He was fiercely religious, tenacious as a corn stalk, and did not blame anyone, not even God, for the recent death of his wife. "What do you say we give these young folks a break before we talk them dry?" he went on. "It's a dangerous situation they're in, and I don't think any of us want to see them arrested."

Cyd mouthed, "Thank you."

"Maybe I'm the only one worried about this, but what do you think is going to happen if you go out and tell every person you meet who you met here today?"

"They go to jail," responded the large lady with the perm.

Widespread murmurs of agreement seconded her remark.

"Most likely, that's probably right. And me along with them because they need to get off the road for a while, and I'm taking them home with me."

Otis returned Eloise's surprised look with a wide grin.

"I don't know the legal word for it," the tall, bent farmer added. "Accessory, I think it's called. Any way you slice it, they get busted and I go to jail.

Shocked murmurs of protest.

"My question then is this: How do we protect them and me at the same time?"

A big-bellied, red-faced farmer spoke up in a gravelly voice. "What you're telling us is to keep our mouths shut, is that it, Abe?" Scattered laughter met his remark. "I guess there's a first time for everything." Hearty laughter followed and suddenly five complete strangers were part of a community of neighbors who had known each other all of their lives. It was a covenant, a conspiracy, an agreement to keep something of paramount importance safe from the world, and everyone was excited about it.

"Good Lord willing," Abe concluded, "we stick together, we'll all get through this."

A chorus of amens echoed his small prayer.

An unctuous redheaded scarecrow of a bookkeeper who lived with his mother and worked for the grain elevator in town owned by Farmacopia got off his counter stool and came over to shake Otis's hand, pumping it like he was drawing water from a well.

"I think I speak for everyone when I say welcome, welcome, welcome," the scarecrow gushed. "We're so happy to have you in Fort Dodge, yes indeed. If there's anything I can do, please don't hesitate to call." He took a little metal box from his pocket, opened it, delicately selected one of his business cards and handed it to Otis. "Wilfred Baines is the name, grain's my game."

Cyd shivered the man was so repulsive.

***

Simon Bolivar, the European-educated, democratically inspired Venezuelan aristocrat who united most of Latin America under his presidency before dying in disillusionment, was reported to have said, "All who served the Revolution have plowed the sea." Revolutions would be a lot more fun if so many people didn't have to get plowed under in the process.

In a state with over ninety thousand farms, Abe Robinson's farm was bigger than most since he had borrowed against his three hundred twenty acres to buy three hundred twenty more. He wanted a full six-hundred-forty-acre section so he could grow more feed corn for the government-subsidized ethanol program, but with his purchase of the additional land, his mortgage was eating him alive. If he couldn't generate additional income in the next six months, he would be facing foreclosure. How he could work hard his whole life and end up homeless, he didn't know.

Abe led the Honda and the RV along a rural dirt road that divided his acreage from his neighbor's land, turned in at a battered mailbox with a yellow tube under it for the Fort Dodge Messenger and continued on in a cloud of dust down a rutted drive toward a huge white weather-beaten farmhouse with paint peeling from the siding that sat in the middle of a plowed field. The house was built by Abe's deceased wife's grandparents who had raised twelve children under its roof.

They passed the house and stopped in front of an enormous ramshackle barn with red paint peeling off the sides. Abe got out and pushed open a heavy barn door. The Honda and RV rolled inside, and Abe closed the door behind them. The cavernous interior of the barn was cool and dark and smelled of hay. Otis coasted to a stop behind Cyd and Alex, switched off his engine and let out a sigh of relief.

Elton trailed behind the others as Abe led the way up to the house. "Sweet," he remarked, looking around at the vast expanses of rich, fertile farmland that flowed away from the house in every direction. He'd come a long way from being the dying boy trapped in the boiling humidity of an ugly city. Birds and insects made the only sounds.

They entered the house through the torn screen door to a service porch piled with junk that led to the kitchen. Apart from the puce-colored walls and a fifty-year-old stove and refrigerator, the worn-out linoleum-floored kitchen was the same as it had been before the farm got electricity. Off to one side was a long rectangular table covered in a flowered oilcloth where four generations of hungry farmers had been fed.

Abe led them through to the living room and up the stairs. It was a sad house, cold and lifeless despite the brightly painted walls. The living room was a shocking shade of yellowish orange furnished in brightly colored swivel chairs that sat in a big circle. The chairs had been purchased back in 1950 at a terrific discount when the supercenter was built and put the local dime store out of business. The interior paint was purchased at different times throughout the early '50s, also at great savings, during a time when the stores didn't have paint mixers and had to guess at what color the customers might like, and then sell the rejects at a loss. Abe's deceased wife Brenda knew a bargain when she saw one and considered herself lucky to have been able to buy such pretty colors on sale for less than a dollar a gallon. Decorating was her hobby.

Otis and Eloise were given their own bedroom, Cyd and Alex another and Elton a third, each with a warm soft bed and a fifty-mile view of absolutely nothing. Cyd stood staring at the chartreuse walls of their room as Alex unpacked.

He saw her expression and laughed. "I have a car in L.A. that's almost this same color. Her name is Slime."

"How lovely."

That evening Eloise made supper. Cyd helped, but since she wasn't much of a cook, it was mostly Eloise's doing. In the year since Brenda Robinson's death, it was the first time anyone but her husband had used the kitchen. Abe looked around the table at his guests laughing and talking as they ate, and his eyes grew moist.

Eloise saw that their host wasn't participating in the conversation. "Thanks for having us here, Mr. Robinson. It's a real treat."

The farmer smiled absently. "Please call me Abe, and I'm glad for the company. Have some more lemonade." He filled Eloise's glass from a big pitcher. "Wife made lemonade in this pitcher for forty years before she passed." He looked away and his eyes fell on the purplish-brown walls. "She was sixty-two. The cancer got her."

"I'm so sorry," Cyd said.

"You know," the farmer added bitterly, "I served my country in Vietnam and when my wife got sick, there was nobody to help her. No insurance, no government, no nothing. If your Cannastar had been around last year, maybe . . ." His voice trailed off as the small television set on the table that was always on caught his attention. He reached over and turned up the volume. The same pictures of Cyd, Alex and Otis that had been TV at the café were on the screen. The announcer was saying how the Federal government had stepped up its efforts to apprehend the fugitives. The picture cut away to a soundbite from an impromptu speech by Sam Seeley that the Senator had given earlier in the day on the Capitol steps. In grave, stentorian tones he proclaimed, "These criminals who have harmed so many innocent Americans with their poisonous drug must and will be captured and punished."

Abe switched off the TV. "I've been thinking. This hybrid plant of yours. Where does it grow?"

"Anywhere it wants, pretty much," Otis replied. "It's not overly sensitive to temperature. All you need is sun, water and someplace to plant it."

"I got six hundred and forty acres of arable land," Abe offered. "Not that it's of any good without seed."

Otis smiled slowly. "I might be able to help you with that."

Alex was skeptical. "You can't just plant a square mile of Cannastar out in the open where everyone can see it. The minute it comes out of the ground . . ."

"Not a problem," Abe insisted.

Alex waited. "I'm all ears."

"Exactly," Abe responded. "Ears of corn. Rows of it—dense as fog and twice as thick."

"And in between the corn you plant Cannastar!" Otis cried excitedly.

"Couldn't spot it from a hundred feet up in a crop duster," Abe confirmed.

Cyd sat up listening intently.

"Can you make any money with this Cannastar?" Abe asked as an afterthought.

"Boatloads," Cyd assured him.

Abe nodded. "Then we should all get to bed. Farmers need to get up early."

Cyd went upstairs, brushed her teeth and climbed between the covers with Alex. Instead of closing her eyes, she stared at the ceiling.

Alex grew concerned when she continued to stare without blinking. "What's wrong?" he asked at last.

"Too excited to sleep."

Chapter Thirty-Two

Something from Nothing

Abe's corn should have been in the ground by now. Instead, his fields lay fallow. Devastated by the loss of his wife and the impending loss of his farm, he had lost heart. But sometimes, like fields in winter, the sleeping heart is only waiting for the spring.

Otis wandered out among the furrows trying to calculate how much space to give the Cannastar so it would remain hidden while at the same time not get crowded out by the corn. He stooped, picked up a handful of earth and put it to his nose, inhaling deeply. The smell filled him with hope.

A month later, the former mortician stood in the same spot, looking out over a green carpet of tiny green corn and Cannastar sprouts poking up through the ground. Cyd and Alex were nearby, tanned and freckled from working in the fields. "There was nothing . . . and now there's something," Otis marveled to himself. "It always amazes me."

Everyone they met that first morning at the Early Bird was deeply invested in the project. They kept dropping by Abe's farm to see how the secret experiment was coming along and offer endless advice. Sometimes Abe's driveway was lined with pickups clear back to the road. He had to stay on his tractor and keep well away from the house to keep from getting his ears talked off.

For obvious reasons, Cyd, Alex and Otis could not leave the farm, but Eloise and Elton were able to come and go as they pleased. Eloise did all the cooking and shopping and scrubbed and cleaned until the house looked like a home again. Eager voices, tired and hungry from the field, filled the kitchen every night. Elton would start school in the fall, but for now his new best friend was Abe, and he spent every spare moment riding with him on the tractor. At dinner one night, he announced that when he grew up, he wanted to be a farmer.

"All I can say," Abe advised, "is don't borrow any money if you can help it."

"Won't have to," the boy grinned confidently. "I'm going to be rich from growing Cannastar."

After dinner that night, Alex and Otis went into the living room together. Otis was saying how thrilled he was to see the Cannastar thriving in a natural environment even though he didn't think it was going to be quite as potent as the plants they grew hydroponically. Out of the corner of his eye he spied a row of dog-eared Burpee seed catalogues on a bookshelf. Squeezing himself between two of the colorful swivel chairs, he took down a few of the catalogues and was thumbing through them when Cyd came in talking on one of the throw-away cell phones that Eloise had bought for them in town.

"I called Annie so she wouldn't worry," Cyd told them, holding the phone out to Otis. "She wants to talk to you."

Otis moved to the other side of the room and turned his back for privacy. "Annie!" he cried. "Oh my God, how are you?" He listened a moment. "No, no, we're fine, don't worry. We're back in business, can you believe it?" He took the phone away from his ear to keep Annie's excited squeal from bursting his eardrum.

She asked where they were.

"Iowa," he answered, reminding himself that Annie's phone was not a security risk since nobody was looking for her, so he needn't worry.

"I miss you all so much," she lamented. "Since you left, I've been so bored and lonely in this big house all by myself. I suppose you have all the help you need out there."

"Annie," Otis protested, "don't even think about it."

"Don't think about what, darling?"

"Coming out here. What we're doing, growing Cannastar right out in the open, this is risky business."

"You can't scare me. I'm too old to be frightened of anything. And growing Cannastar is as much my business as it is yours."

"That's not the point . . ."

"The point is, I have my own airplane now. I made Sam sign over the Citation to me along with the house, some investments and a number of rather large bank accounts."

"How on earth did you manage that?"

"Hush money, darling. It's how you get divorced from a scoundrel like Sam Seeley without getting divorced. All the ranch land and natural resources he owns, he'll hardly miss it anyway."

"I'm happy for you, but . . ."

"I'm calling the pilot as soon as I hang up. Be there in a jiffy. Have you got someplace for me to stay?"

Secretly thrilled, he smiled broadly. "We got more bedrooms than a Holiday Inn."

***

Eloise watched from the small private aviation office at the Fort Dodge Airport as a Citation CJ4 appear out of the sun, touch down with barely a whisper and taxied toward her. Annie deplaned and told the pilot to go home, but to stay close to the phone. Eloise loaded Annie's pile of Gucci luggage into the trunk and back seat of her Honda explaining that they thought it best if the others waited for her back at the farm.

The greeting committee heard the Honda coming down the driveway, came out of the house and were standing in the gravel drive waiting when Annie and Eloise pulled up. They were still hugging and kissing when Abe drove up in his tractor. He got down and he and Annie met for the first time. Their friends watched in amazement as the two farmers, one tall and quiet, the other small and animated, started talking and didn't stop. It was almost as if they had stepped on a scale and for the first time in their lives, it balanced. Annie took Abe's arm and together they walked out into the fields chatting like old friends, he explaining the flourishing Cannastar farm and she enthusiastically understanding his every word and offering input.

By suppertime they still were talking. Abe picked up a platter of pork chops and offered it to his new friend. "Annabelle, would you like another?"

She smiled and shook her head.

"How about some more potatoes then?"

"Abraham dear, I'm fine. You wouldn't want me to spoil my figure."

Is he blushing? Cyd thought. I actually think he's blushing.

"I didn't mean to imply . . ."

"Of course you didn't, darling. Would you care to take the air with me after supper? It's such a lovely evening, and I would so enjoy a walk."

Cyd cleared the table as Abe fumbled to help Annie on with her sweater, and they went out the door. He was explaining how the maize they were growing to hide the Cannastar was really a transgenic plant as well, genetically engineered from a virus-resistant strain of corn from the highlands of northern Mexico.

"Part of the genome from the Mexican Maize that coded for resisting against the virus was incorporated into the existing strain of our commercial corn," he added. "The result was corn that's resistant to a virus that used to absolutely devastate crops here in the US."

Annie smiling up at him, not so much listening to what he was saying—she already knew about transgenic corn—as emotionally experiencing what he was saying. He was a good and decent man. Lonely like herself and a born lover of all things that came from the earth. They had so much in common.

Over the summer and into the fall, Annie's joy in the farm energized them all. Laboring right alongside of them, she was as happy as if she had been working in her own greenhouse. Elton became withdrawn and wouldn't tell his mother why he was sulking. Annie realized it was because Abe was spending so much time with her now and ignoring the boy. She started including him in their conversations and walks and before long he had two loving grandparents instead of one. As for Abe, Annie had done what the others couldn't do; she had brought the widower back to life. Going about his chores now, he looked and acted twenty years younger. Certainly, he and Annie had their memories of the past—memories never die—but as each day passed, more and more of the old feelings connected to them seemed to disappear.

***

One morning in late November as the sun was just coming up, Otis woke beside Eloise, slipped carefully out of bed and went to his second story window to look out and admire their field of Cannastar in the early light. He had watched with some concern during the Fall as the green, leafy cornfield hiding the Cannastar slowly withered and died. Now it was brittle and brown with limp, wilted leaves, and he saw to his horror that the Cannastar crop was fully exposed. One square mile of spike-leafed, jade-colored bushes, nine feet tall and hung with brightly colored seeds, was basking in the Iowa sun for all to see!

Otis threw on his clothes and ran downstairs in a panic. Abe was in the kitchen having his second cup of coffee and getting ready for the day when his oversized guest rushed in.

"Abe, the crop is out in the open!" Otis cried. "The whole thing. We need to get it in. Harvest it! Right now! Today!"

The farmer regarded him placidly. "Six hundred and forty acres all in one day?"

"It doesn't take a genius to see it's not corn we're growing out there. The Feds get wind of it, and we could lose everything!"

Abe nodded and quietly reached for the phone.

An hour later Alex and Cyd heard the sound of engines and came out on the front porch to see a convoy of pickup trucks honking and rumbling down Abe's driveway. They watched in wonder as their friends from the Early Bird piled out·and started unloading their farm equipment and tools. It was harvest time Iowa style with enough volunteers to put an Amish barn raising to shame. The women had all brought baskets of food, and Eloise helped them get it into the kitchen so they could start getting ready. It was going to be a hungry day.

The eager army of harvesters descended on Abe's fields, shouldering their way through the dead corn stalks to begin digging up and chopping down the Cannastar. Before long, grain carts laden with bulky green bushes were being hauled to the barn. Abe's combine was of little use since most of the work had to be done by hand.

Inside the farm's colossal barn, Otis directed the stacking of the plants, piling them up like Christmas trees in one corner and working his way out. His fear of discovery had not abated. Dark rings spread out under his arms as he stripped the leaves of their seeds, loaded them into flower sacks and tossed them hurriedly into the cargo bays of his RV. Something told him they were coming—the cops, the DEA, whoever, it was just a matter of time. He had to get the seeds away from there as quickly as possible. It was lunchtime when he looked out of the barn, saw they had cleared only a small portion of the land and realized with a sinking heart that this was going to take more than a day. They'd be lucky to finish in three or four.

Alex, out in the field, paused while digging up a Cannastar plant, took off his hat and drew his sleeve across his forehead. A wrinkled face looked out from behind the bush next to him. "Once a farm girl always a farm girl," Mable Nash grinned, leaning on her shovel. Perspiration soaked the red headband she wore under her straw hat. Before he could respond another voice spoke up.

"Isn't this exciting?"

Alex turned and saw Annie smiling at him, her face flushed and dirty. He smiled back admiringly. "You look radiant, the both of you."

"Beats waiting tables," Mable admitted.

Annie laughed her tiny bell-like laugh. "Beats sitting at home in Virginia worrying about what trouble you're all in when I can be our here sharing in the fun."

Alex heard the shutter on a cell phone camera click, wheeled around and saw the redheaded scarecrow from the Early Bird taking pictures. Wilfred Baines saw the doctor's angry look, gave him an oily grin and tried to slip his phone back in his pocket. Alex grabbed it out of his hand and deleted the photograph.

"I'm sorry, so sorry if I've offended anyone," the bookkeeper groveled, reaching for his phone and mumbling to himself in the third person. "Wilfred Baines was only making a record of this momentous day. May I have my property back, please?"

Alex pocketed his phone. "You'll get it back when the work is done."

"I don't understand, sir, really I don't! Wilfred Baines was just trying to help."

Alex went back to digging up the plant he was working on. "You want to help, grab a shovel."

Eloise rang the lunch bell. Sweaty pickers emerged from the field to find picnic tables that had not been used in years lined up under a big tree piled with food. The harvesters sat on opposite sides of the tables under a waning fall sky, laughing and talking while consuming vast quantities of meat, potatoes and gravy, salads and white bread for an afternoon of hard labor that would be interrupted again at four o'clock with an afternoon snack of sandwiches, cake and coffee. Men and women, who looked gaunt and tired when the fugitives first met them at the Early Bird, were acting like excited children. They could feel the growing sensation that they were all part of something bigger than themselves now, something that could benefit mankind.

Elton, who had been working in the fields right alongside the adults, had his mouth stuffed with fried chicken and was eyeing a layer cake that was just coming out of the kitchen. "This is the best party ever," he told his mother. It came out, *Thth ith the beth party ever.*

"Don't talk with your mouth full." Eloise saw the condition of her son's hands and grabbed them up. "They're bleeding, son. What did you do?"

"I lost my gloves," Elton replied indifferently, still chewing. *I loth my gloveh.* "Abe said he'd get me another pair after lunch."

Alex looked up the table at Cyd who was sitting with a group of farmers who were all trying to talk to her at once. She caught his eye and smiled. It was a good smile, warm and true.

Eloise realized Otis had not shown up for lunch and took a plate of food out to him in the barn. She found him madly stripping and bagging seeds. The frantic look on his face worried her. "Honey, stop and have something to eat," she urged. "Come inside the RV, sit down and eat your lunch."

He pointed to a pile of flour sacks. "Hand me one of those, will you?"

***

Three days later the crop was in, the barn was overflowing with Cannastar bushes and the RV was overloaded with bulging flower sacks. Otis should have been relieved, but he wasn't. The feeling that something terrible was about to happen wouldn't go away. He didn't know where he was going to park the RV, but he knew he had to move it.

Climbing behind the wheel, he backed out of the barn, drove down the driveway and into town where he cruised around until he spotted the airport sitting all by itself out in the middle of an empty field. You want to hide something, hide it in plain sight, he thought, following the signs with the little airplanes on them that led to the airport parking lot.

There were only two other cars parked in the lot when he got there. Weeds grew up through cracks in the asphalt. He pulled into a space that overlooked the lonely runway and called Eloise to pick him up.

***

The Early Bird crew worked in shifts over the weeks that followed to help Otis dry and clean the Cannastar leaves. A growing pile of plastic garbage bags full of Cannastar ready for use rose to the rafters until the barn was literally bulging at the seams. The roots, stems and branches from the Cannastar plants that they couldn't use were thrown into a pile behind the barn. Otis thought the growing pile was becoming too conspicuous and decided to burn it. He lit the pile and a bonfire erupted sending a great plume of fragrant smoke into the air that could be seen for miles around. Realizing he'd made a mistake, he panicked and began running around trying to put it out.

Abe came along just then and saw Otis desperately throwing buckets of water on the fire. "Around here," the farmer grinned, chewing on a straw, "we want to burn off a field, we like to use kerosene."

Then one day the work was done. Alex called Joe Volkova in New York on one of their "burner" phones to tell him the good news and to ask him to contact Don Bueno for him so he wouldn't have to do it. Joe's beleaguered secretary told him that her boss had been indicted for securities fraud and money laundering and had fled the country. Alex hung up feeling sick to his stomach.

Rousing himself, he swallowed hard and tried calling Don Bueno himself using a special number the drug lord had given him. The phone rang and rang. Just as he was about to give up, a gruff Mexican voice came on the line. "*Hola!*"

"The tea you wanted is in and bagged and ready for shipment."

Don Bueno's shout of glee hurt his ear. "How much you got for me?" the drug lord demanded. "How much?"

"More tea than they got in China. Tons."

An explosive stream of Spanish expletives followed that, loosely translated, meant that *El Jefe de Jefes* was pleased.

The next day a big cargo plane, part of a fleet of surplus military aircraft that Don Bueno owned, arrived at the Fort Dodge airport. Waiting on the deserted tarmac was a fleet of pickup trucks piled high with garbage bags. The trucks came and went from the barn until the plane was full. The day after that Abe Robinson went into the bank and paid off the mortgage on his farm. It was a proud day, a day to remember.

***

On December 22nd Abe threw a Christmas party for his now-permanent house guests and their loyal friends from the Early Bird.

The house rang with good cheer. For the first time since his wife died, all twenty-three chairs in his living room were filled with people eating from paper plates and drinking from plastic cups. Abe beamed at Annie with pride. His home, once again, had a lovely hostess.

Wilfred Baines was the only one of the Cannastar pickers that Abe had not invited to the celebration. Alex had told him about the picture taking incident in the field during the harvest. The bookkeeper didn't come again after that, not that he had been much help to begin with. All he had done that day was stand around bothering people, telling anyone who would listen how Alex had stolen his phone and wouldn't give it back.

When Baines found out he wasn't welcome at the party, he made a call to the Federal Drug Enforcement Agency in St. Louis to see if a certain reward was still being offered.

That night at the party, every harvester received a big plastic bag full of Cannastar leaves for their own use with the promise of more to come in the spring. The recipients couldn't have been happier if they'd been handed bags of gold. They began whispering about how much money Don Bueno must have paid for the Cannastar crop that Abe could pay off his farm, and suddenly every farmer in the room wanted to grow it himself. Cyd and Alex had no objection since Don Bueno had made it clear he wanted all the product he could get his hands on. Agreements were made and sealed with handshakes. Next year would to be the year a significant portion of Webster County went into in the illegal drug business.

Once the company had left, Otis sat down and groaned at the thought of the work involved in setting up multiple Cannastar farms. Then he thought about what was going to happen when farmers in the neighboring counties found out how much money there was in growing Cannastar as opposed to corn. Dark rings once again appeared under his armpits. The risk of exposure would increase almost exponentially with each newly planted field. What was going to happen when everybody in Iowa knew about it?

Cyd crawled into bed with Alex and laid her head contentedly on his shoulder. Her hair was warm and smelled of sun and flowers. "Hows your back?" she asked, nuzzling his neck and kissing his ear.

"Aches a bit. I should probably have a little tea. Cyd . . . how the hell do we get off this farm? If it wasn't for you, I'd be going stir crazy."

"Interesting you would say that. I'm so restless I'm about to come out of my skin."

"What do we do?"

She kissed his chest and moved her hands over his body, slowly working her way down. "I don't know. All I know is, we can't stay here forever."

Forever came the next morning when Abe got a call from Mabel Nash down at the Early Bird. Her restaurant was full of DEA agents up from St. Louis all talking among themselves about the big raid they were going to pull off today.

Chapter Thirty-Three

Window Rock

Chaos, confusion and fear. Everyone running around shouting at once and grabbing up their belongings. Cyd helping Annie with her bags. Outside, Alex was throwing what they brought into the back of Abe's truck as fast as he could.

"Put those things *in* something!" Eloise yelled at Otis who was grunting down the stairs with an armload of clothes. He charged back up to find a suitcase.

Eloise turned to Elton, who had begun to cry. "It's okay, honey. We're just going on a little trip is all."

"I don't want to leave. Why do we have to leave?"

Abe sat slumped at the kitchen table, hands in his lap, staring straight ahead. Annie came in and stood over him anxiously. "Abraham, I've called the pilot. My plane will be here any time. We have to go."

"I can't leave," he murmured. "This is my home."

"I have a home too, and I'll go back to it one day, but right now we need to get out of here or we'll be arrested. You don't want that, do you?"

"You go on. I'll be all right."

Annie sat down beside him. "Then I'm staying too. We'll go to jail together."

He turned to her in alarm. "You can't go to jail. I won't allow it."

Cyd came charging through the kitchen just then, and Annie caught her by the arm. "Darling, would you mind getting my bags back out of the truck? I won't be going with you."

Abe blinked rapidly and shot to his feet. "Annabelle, you're coming with me. Not another word about it. We're getting out of here this instant."

Annie smiled. "Yes, dear."

Alex was already behind the wheel of Abe's truck revving the engine when Cyd slid in beside him. They saw Eloise headed for the barn to get her Honda. Otis called to her, telling her to leave it. She did as he asked, but reluctantly, looking back sadly as she opened the rear door of the truck and got in. Otis squeezed in beside her and put Elton on his lap. The only ones missing were Abe and Annie.

Minutes ticked by. Alex blew the horn and still they didn't come. He opened the truck door to go look for them just as they came out of the kitchen. Annie was holding Abe's arm as he dried his eyes. She gave him an encouraging nod, and they headed for the truck. He had been saying goodbye to his home.

The pickup fishtailed out of the drive, jostling the packed passengers inside. Their jumbled belongings in the bed of the truck bounced around like salvage from a fire.

"Where do we go to wait for the plane?" Alex yelled.

"My RV is out at the airport," Otis shouted. "We can wait inside."

No one spoke on the way to the airfield. It was as if everyone was holding their breath. Alex pulled into the lot and parked next to Otis's motorhome. The runway was as deserted and silent as ever. Everyone got out and scrambled into the RV. Otis closed the motorhome door behind them and locked it, hurried to pull down the window shades and flopped exhausted into his chair.

The wait was excruciating. Huddled together like frightened refugees, they kept imagining strange sounds and peering out through the drawn blinds to see if the Feds had somehow found them.

Alex looked out and this time saw a small, silver-winged jet on approach. It touched down and he announced, "Our Uber is here. Saddle up."

The RV and the pickup rolled out onto the tarmac. The sleepy little airport slumbered in the sun as they frantically transferred the bags of Cannastar seed from the RV to the plane. When they tried to transfer their luggage, the pilot stopped them. The plane was already overloaded, he told them. The only thing else they could put onboard was themselves.

"We'll lose everything!" Eloise moaned.

"Everything?" Otis asked her. "Think about it."

Teary eyed, she nodded and smiled.

Otis and Alex got in their two vehicles and put them back in the parking lot where hopefully they wouldn't be noticed for a while.

Annie, waiting with Abe and Cyd, saw their distress and squeezed their hands. "We can always buy more underwear when we get to where we're going."

"Where's that?" Cyd asked.

Nobody answered.

Alex and Otis returned, walking rapidly. "Everybody on board," Alex shouted. "Go, go, go!"

The pilot pulled up the steps, secured the door and settled himself in the cockpit. The engines whined quickly to life and the jet taxied away. At the end of the runway it paused for a moment, the brakes were released, and the wheels began to roll.

The Citation rotated off the end of the airstrip and thundered into the sky. Otis let out a sigh of relief as they rose steeply and banked in a circle over Fort Dodge. Abe looked out the window, saw his farm in miniature below and pressed his hand to the glass in anguish. His property was black with cars and men who were swarming his home and fields like locusts. He turned away, unable to watch.

Captain Charlie Webber leveled off and set a southwest course before turning in his seat to call back to the main cabin. "No rush, Mrs. Seeley, you got a couple of thousand miles to make up your mind, but do we have a destination yet?" The good-natured, gray-haired, somewhat paunchy pilot, with nearly twenty thousand hours at the controls of jet aircraft both military and civilian, considered himself something of a lady's man. Proof of his claim was his three former wives and six children. Senator Sam Seeley was the only private employer he ever worked for that he didn't like. He couldn't understand how a classy lady like Mrs. Seeley could be married to such an arrogant phony like her husband.

"Patience, Captain Charlie darling," Annie called back. "We'll let you know."

Elton sat in the co-pilot seat next to his new hero. The boy's upset over their rapid exodus from the farm had vanished, replaced by his fascination with the dazzling array of colorful glass screens that flashed before him. Staring at the instruments and feeling the raw power of the jet engines in the seat of his pants, he decided then and there that he didn't want to be a farmer anymore; he wanted to be a pilot.

The six adult fugitives sat in the luxurious, leather-appointed cabin still rattled after their narrow escape.

Cyd hung her head. "We could go on to Don Bueno's in Mexico," she speculated, "but the minute we landed there, he'd own us."

"And I thought the funeral business was depressing," Otis remarked.

Eloise looked like she was going to cry, and Otis put his big arm around her.

"Annie," Alex said suddenly, "does this thing have a telephone?"

"It has several, dear boy. Just open that little door in the cabinet next to your seat."

Alex fished out the phone, dialed a number and waited. It rang twice before a familiar voice answered. "Clarence, its Alex!"

Big Foot heard the stress in Alex's voice and his delight turned to concern. "Where are you?" he asked. "Are you okay?"

"No, we're not okay," Alex replied. "Just listen. We need the biggest, most remote Indian reservation in the country. It has to be completely isolated."

"I take it you're on the run and need to hide."

"That would be an understatement."

Clarence was silent a moment while he thought. "You're talking about the Navajo Nation. I'm afraid I can't help you."

Alex's heart sank.

"But Robert can," he added. "I'll call my son."

***

Two hours later Annie's Citation was on final approach to a seven-thousand-foot runway that stretched like a highway to nowhere along the high desert floor. Elton, back in the cabin now with his mother, looked out the window in excitement at the desolate landscape that was rushing up toward them. "Looks like we're landing on an alien planet!"

"An alien planet is just what we're looking for," Alex agreed.

The jet whistled down, laid two smoking strips of rubber on the concrete and taxied to a tiny terminal. A sign said they had arrived in Window Rock, capital of the twenty-six-thousand-square-mile Navajo Nation. The sandy speck of a town lay like a baked and scaly lizard on the northern Arizona/New Mexico border.

Captain Charlie shut down the engines and opened the door. They came down the steps shielding their eyes from the bright winter sun and were greeted by a handsome, smiling Indian with outstretched arms.

"Robert, what in the hell are you doing here?" Cyd cried, hugging him happily.

"I work here," Robert replied.

"I can't believe it! Doing what?"

"Helping the Navajo develop their natural resources. You wouldn't believe the oil, gas, coal and uranium that's under this desert."

Alex shook hands with the ex-boyfriend he hoped he'd never see again. "Never been so happy to see anyone in my life."

"Pop says you're in trouble."

"When are we not?" Cyd remarked.

"Let's get you into town then," Robert smiled. "See what we can do."

Otis refused to move. "I'm staying with the seeds."

"Don't be silly," Annie assured him. "Captain Charlie will guard the plane until we figure out what to do."

Otis nodded reluctantly. "Or until we have to run again. Tell him to keep the engines running just in case."

***

The Quality Inn in Window Rock was a southwestern-looking motel with large, comfortable rooms and an inviting swimming pool. Cyd and Alex lay side by side in bed that night staring up at the ceiling. Despite having produced a huge crop, Iowa had ultimately been a huge failure. The fact that they were safe at the moment was little consolation.

"What now?" Cyd asked in desolation.

"What now, indeed."

"We tried, we really did. I can't believe it's come to this. It feels like a net is about to drop over our heads."

Alex sat straight up in bed. "What did you say?"

"About feeling trapped?"

"No. The net. What kind of net?"

"I don't know. The kind that dolphins get caught in, I guess."

He kissed her quickly. "You're a genius!"

"I am?"

Alex fumbled for his phone.

"Who are you calling?"

"Clarence."

"It's the middle of the night."

A groggy voice answered. "Hello, Clarence? Sorry to wake you . . . No, Robert met us at the plane. Everything's fine. I need your help with something else . . ."

Clarence switched on his night light rubbing his eyes. "This better be good."

"When I was in Iraq," Alex said in a rush, "we had camouflage nets that we used everywhere. Tan mesh ventilated cloth with fake shrubs on it. If you were flying over or scouting from a mountain top you couldn't tell there was anything down there but desert. A city could be hiding under one of those nets and nobody would know it. I need you to use your military contacts to find out the manufacturer of those nets."

Clarence considered a moment. "Actually, I know these people. I set up a computerized testing program for them. The latest version of their netting is amazing. Did you know, during World War II, the original version of that netting was used to hide aircraft plants in Burbank, California from Japanese war planes?"

"Can you call them for me? We're going to need a lot of it."

"It's expensive."

Alex didn't reply.

"That's what I was afraid of." A smile crept into his voice. "Consider it done."

Alex hung up and dialed again. Cyd looked on, baffled but intrigued. "Who are you calling now?"

"Robert."

"I figured there must be somebody you hadn't woken up yet."

When Robert answered, Alex told him to hold a minute and turned to Cyd. "Get everybody in here. We have a lot to talk about."

Cyd padded down the carpeted hall in her bare feet softly knocking on doors. Alex finished his conversation with Robert, broke his cell phone in half and threw it in the trash.

The next morning Robert contacted his friend Harvey Lawrence. The president of the sovereign Navajo Nation was reluctant at first to meet with the uninvited visitors until Robert told him who they were, what they were running from and why.

"I have heard about this Cannastar," Lawrence replied cautiously. "I would like to know more."

That afternoon, Robert brought Alex, Cyd and Otis into Lawrence's office. The President got up and came around his desk to greet his guests. He was a slender, salt-and-pepper-haired man, intelligent and affable, with high cheekbones and narrow eyes. He wore pleated dress slacks and a Navajo shirt with a bolo tie. Cyd thought he looked like a male fashion model. Books on economics, law and business lined his bookcases and priceless Indian artifacts filled his walls as if to suggest an amalgamation of the best of the old with the best of the new.

They shook hands and the President motioned for his visitors to be seated. Alex sensed that under his gracious exterior, Harvey Lawrence had an iron will. This guy is not going to be an easy sell, he thought.

President Lawrence seemed to be particularly taken with Otis and wouldn't take his eyes off him. It was as if he had seen him before and couldn't think where. Then it came to him and he brightened. "You are the medicine man I saw in a dream. You were standing in the middle of a forest you had grown on land where nothing would grow."

"I'm no medicine man," Otis argued, "but I can grow a garden in a desert, if that's what you mean."

"A man lives many lives in this one life until he becomes the man he is meant to be," the President observed. "Tell me, Medicine Man, how does this garden of yours grow?"

Otis explained his hydroponic method of growing Cannastar on top of barren soil or even on concrete if necessary. "The problems in this environment," he surmised, "are A, evaporation and B, keeping the water supplied with enough nutrients. Otherwise it's pretty straightforward."

"Water is not something we have a lot of here," the President remarked.

"Understood," Otis replied. "That means, to do it on a large scale, we're going to need holding tanks for water that will have to be trucked in and generators to run the pumps."

President Lawrence made a pyramid of his fingers. "This method of yours, how well does it work? How effective is it really?"

"In a southern desert like this?" Otis mused. "You have year-round sun, so I'm guessing we could get three crops a year with good yield. The size of the crop we grew in Iowa would probably require twice the acreage here since we're using a different method, but at least there wouldn't be any soil-borne diseases to contend with—not that anything could kill a Cannastar bush."

"You currently have the U.S. government and all of Western medicine aligned against you," the President submitted. "They will send their airplanes to search. Your healing garden will stick out like Central Park in a sand box."

Alex explained about the camouflage nets and how they worked. "If the Garden of Eden had been under one of these nets," he concluded, "the devil himself couldn't have found it."

The President smiled. "What about the light?"

"Cannastar thrives in any light," Otis replied, "especially indirect light."

"Please understand," Lawrence explained. "I have not agreed to anything. How can I be certain this illegal drug of yours even works?"

Cyd told him about all the people on the East Coast that Cannastar had cured."

"What about firsthand? Do you know anyone personally who has been healed of cancer?"

"I'll answer that one," Otis replied, describing in some detail how Elton and Cyd had been cured, then telling his own amazing story. Alex added how Cannastar had helped him deal with his own pain and addiction.

It was impossible to tell what President Lawrence was thinking. He was the picture of inscrutable. When his guests had finished talking, he was silent for a time before sadly shaking his head. "Impossible," he concluded. "Such a thing could never be distributed on a mass scale."

Cyd knew this was coming and had mentally prepared a speech. As she spoke of Don Bueno, the president's face hardened. Hurrying on, she explained about the children of the jungle and the miraculous cures that had managed to bring about in them.

"This guy Don Bueno runs the biggest drug store in the world," Alex explained. "He's on every street corner from Wasilla, Alaska to Tierra del Fuego. Maybe he's crazy and maybe he's a saint, probably he's both. He's taken on the distribution of Cannastar the same way he took on helping those kids that were terminal. He seems to consider it his moral duty to cure everyone he hasn't killed yet."

The president smiled again. "How about transportation? I can't have trucks constantly leaving the reservation filled with contraband."

"Don Bueno has his own air force," Alex explained. "He can be in and out of Window Rock before you know it." He paused. "Mr. President, we need the use of some of your most remote land. We need help setting up our camo nets. We need water trucks and men to drive them, and lastly, we're going to need a lot of year-round help tending and harvesting the crops. In return, the Navajo Nation will receive ten percent of the net profits."

"You're not asking us to put up any money?" He seemed relieved. "A growing operation like the one you propose would be very expensive."

"My dad is paying for all the nets," Robert said.

"And our friend and partner, Annie Seeley, is putting up the money for the rest," Cyd added.

"The Senator's wife, she is with you?"

"Yes," Cyd answered carefully.

The President turned to face Alex. "Twenty percent."

He's negotiating! Alex thought. We got him! "Fifteen percent."

"Seventeen and a half."

"Done."

Alex reached out his hand to shake on it, but the president did not respond.

"I will meditate on it," Lawrence decided. "And then I must present it for approval to the eighty-eight-member Tribal Council. Our quarterly meeting is in two weeks."

Alex tried to keep his disappointment off his face and out of his voice.

Cyd spoke without thinking. "You couldn't get eighty-eight people to agree on the same movie to watch together."

On the way back to the motel, Robert tried to sound encouraging. "All things considered," he surmised, "I thought the meeting went rather well."

Cyd looked out the window at the blowing desert sand. "I just realized it's Christmas Eve."

Chapter Thirty-Four

The Grow

The Navajo Tribal Council building in Window Rock was a beautiful, ultramodern structure designed to look like an old adobe fort. On a warm day in January the Cannastar petitioners—Alex, Cyd, Otis, Eloise, Elton, Annie, Abe and Robert—entered the building through its tall wooden doors, found the big meeting room and took their seats at the back of the auditorium. Watching anxiously, they waited as the chamber slowly filled with members from all one hundred and ten chapters of the far-flung reservation.

The Navajo had suffered a lot of infighting during many long and confusing years of changing leadership, but according to Robert, had put their tumultuous past behind them and, for the time being at least, were enjoying a period of relative peace and cooperation.

The Speaker, elegantly attired in string tie and turquoise jewelry, was a jowly man with wide-set eyes and a drooping black mustache. He brought the meeting to order and moved the assembly through a tedious agenda of routine business. Finally, it was time for the president to speak. Harvey Lawrence rose to his feet and walked to the podium. He had deliberately leaked word of what he was going to talk about, and the news had spread rapidly. The room was charged with anticipation.

Much to Cyd's surprise, it was an impassioned speech. After patiently explaining what he knew about Cannastar, its healing properties, and the pros and cons of growing it on the reservation, Lawrence proclaimed, "On portions of our reservation, we have found four great natural resources that serve both the white man's nation and our own. Be that as it may, less than 10 percent of our land is good for planting even though the very name Navajo means 'place of large planted fields.' We have been presented with an opportunity to live up to our name by adding a fifth valuable resource, one that can be grown on our otherwise useless land.

"The *Dineh* (the people) understand about natural medicine. In our history, songs, prayers and ceremonies, herbal cures are part of our culture, our way of life. The Holy Ones have now brought us a new Medicine Man with a new medicine. I believe he and his people are here to heal the Navajo Nation. I also believe, in gratitude, it is the duty of the Navajo to help heal an ailing world.

"Our faith in the Great Spirit assures us that our Indian nation will live forever, but that alone is not enough. We must participate in our own survival, and this participation must not be a selfish act. Our people did not make the Long Walk for nothing; they made it to bring us to here. There is a reason we thrive, just as there is a reason we have created this miracle called Cannastar that cures cancer. It is part of the old ways, part of our evolution as a people: something new out of something old. *The Ones Who Can Not Be Seen* have shown us a path—a way to honor our past by growing our future. Mankind has lost its way and is no longer connected to the earth. In helping them find their way back, we are helping ourselves.

"It will not be easy. There are dangers along this trail. White men have tried often to destroy us with laws that serve only themselves. They were not successful then, and they will not be successful now! We are a sovereign nation, and our laws are not their laws." His voice rose to a fevered pitch as he raised his fist and a battle cry rose from the crowd. "I will send a prayer in the four directions for the success and safety of this great enterprise."

Tumultuous applause. Everyone talking at once. Like the Iowa farmers, mainly what the *Dineh* were so excited about was the prospect of an ongoing supply of Cannastar for themselves and their families.

***

Annie put Captain Charlie on permanent standby, and in the Spring, Alex asked him for a ride in the Citation.

Sixty miles north of Window Rock, the jet swooped low over the empty desert. All that could be seen in any direction was sand, rock, sagebrush and cactus. Far to the north, the twenty-seven-million-year-old volcanic silhouette of Shiprock rose eighteen hundred feet out of the sand like a mysterious sphinx guarding the prehistoric lands of the Anasazi.

Alex peered intently out the window as the jet banked in a tight turn over a particular tract of land. To his infinite delight, what he saw below looked as barren, desolate and arid as the rest of the landscape. The jet made a final low pass over the area before heading back to the airport. Otis stepped out from under the new camouflage net and waved. Looking down from the jet, it was as if he appeared out of nowhere.

Underneath the net, an army of Navajo workers were laboring in the Cannastar fields. Many looked up as the jet went over, then returned to their labors. They had built an invisible circus with camouflage tents that were pitched over a four-square-mile area of pancake-flat desert. The netting was supported on long, sturdy poles and anchored with support cables that were attached to stakes driven deep in the ground. The ventilated netting gave protection from the rain, snow and relentless sun without blocking the light.

The breeze blowing through the open sides of the netting felt like air conditioning on Cyd's bare arms. Stretched out before her was row after row of Cannastar bushes growing out of water-filled wooden troughs fed by miles of black poly irrigation pipe. Transportation under the nets was by golf cart and dozens of the little four-wheeled vehicles whirred silently up and down the rows. Separate camouflage nets hid the pumps, water storage tanks, generators and portable toilets, and another net hid five single-wide mobile homes where the seven Cannastar farmers and their pilot were living.

President Harvey Lawrence had little trouble finding volunteers to help set up and work the massive project—it seemed everyone wanted to help. The Navajo regarded Otis as a shaman because of his expertise at growing the Cannastar and treated him with great respect. Otis was embarrassed by all the attention.

Captain Charlie began dating a beautiful Navajo woman named Dawn and would have willingly stayed on in Window Rock even if Annie wasn't paying him. Dawn had a daughter named Feather who was Elton's age and the two of them became best friends. Feather was teaching Elton the way of the *Dineh* and together they roamed the countryside in search of adventure.

The Grow, as it had come to be called, had been successfully launched and Don Bueno's planes would soon be making midnight trips in and out of the Window Rock airport to collect the harvest.

The sound of the jet with Alex aboard faded overhead and Otis went back to helping Annie and Abe supervise the operation. They stood together looking out proudly over a sea of tightly packed Cannastar plants flourishing under the camouflage nets. The Grow was indeed a wonder to behold. It wasn't until later, when Cyd decided she needed a short vacation, that the trouble started.

The Iowa crop of Cannastar had produced enough of the life-saving drug to supply a single region for the time being, but not enough to open up the entire country. Don Bueno decided to start with the West Coast.

The new product created a remarkable phenomenon among the thousands of violent drug dealers and gangs in California, and the illegal drug business was changed forever.

Any good enterprise looks for ways to grow its business and expand its product line, but Cannastar offered more than just a new income stream. It brought new pride and new meaning to the lives of countless streetwise entrepreneurs. It gave them a cause, a purpose, a mission; it provided a dignity that hadn't existed before. As a result, a new morality sprung up that added a tenet to the already rigid code of criminal ethics. Just as child molestation was an unforgivable sin to the most hardened of felons, so now was killing and gouging people over Cannastar. In marketing a cure for fatal and debilitating diseases, the drug dealers were helping to heal their customers, not kill them. It felt good and decent; it felt right.

Cannastar distribution quickly became a unifying cause and the act of dispensing it gained in stature until peddling drugs became almost a noble profession. For the first time since it began, the drug trade had something to believe in that was life affirming and grand. Pushers and perps alike had a reason to do something honorable, get richer than ever in the process and still not have to go out and get a real job. It was a win/win for everyone. Otis, at one point, remarked that it was "capitalism at its best."

And Big Pharma, with all the laws and regulations on their side, they helped too. Rxon's fanatical efforts to stop Cannastar were the very catalyst that fueled the astonishing transformation in the drug culture and its legions of murderous criminals. Thanks to Dick Tremble's efforts to destroy Cannastar, the inexpensively grown organic herb was now healing the world in ways even its supporters never imagined. Instead of being part of the problem, drug dealers were becoming part of the solution.

To be certain, tattooed felons and gangbangers did not become good guys overnight. *Gangstas* were still *gangstas*, bless their black little hearts. But Cannastar brought out the best in them, and even they were changed. The LAPD reported a remarkable drop in violence. Junkies were disappearing off the streets. Celebrities were said to be buying it for their pets. Californians on the whole were going absolutely crazy for the new drug; they couldn't get enough of it.

A pall, meanwhile, settled over the medical community. Doctor's offices and hospitals were starting to look as lonely and deserted as the Arizona/New Mexico desert, the health insurance business was in crisis and Rxon's drug sales were tanking.

Dick Tremble, desperate to reverse the trend, pulled out all the stops. A fatherly-looking spokesman from the drug industry went on national television wearing a white lab coat and claimed, "Research has shown that death is a common side effect of Cannastar. Patients who do not follow their doctor's advice are gambling with their lives. Take only drugs that are prescribed for you by a licensed physician."

The public experience didn't match the media spin; people weren't buying it. In response, the medical community rose with one voice, haranguing their congressmen and lobbyists to "do something and do it now!"

Congressman Berkley Bunkmeister, former mayor of a city ravaged by drugs and violence, appeared on television and announced, "Addiction is a terrible thing, just terrible. Your government is not going stand by and enable these Cannastar pushers. This is America, not Amsterdam!"

Senator Sam Seeley appeared once again on the evening news, denouncing Cannastar as "the seeds of destruction." He peered into the camera like an avenging angel. "This drug is a killer and the people who grow and distribute it pose a threat to national security. The three

terrorists primarily responsible for its proliferation are still at large."
Now-familiar pictures of Cyd, Alex and Otis popped up on the screen
as he read off their names. "Anyone having knowledge of their where-
abouts is urged to contact their local authorities or Drug Enforcement
Agency immediately."

***

The first harvest was in, and The Grow became the best paying job
on the reservation. With an abundance of product on hand, Don Bueno
was able to open up the rest of the country—which triggered a frenzied
escalation in the war on drugs. The storm around Cannastar was reaching hurricane strength.

For Cyd, isolated as she was from the outside world in Window
Rock, the national turmoil over Cannastar wasn't real. All she knew was
that she was bored senseless and needed a break. One night in their
trailer she pleaded with Alex to take her somewhere, anywhere. "I just
need off this reservation."

"How about an all-expense-paid vacation to a federal prison?"

"Alex, I'm serious. I can't take it anymore. Let's drive into Santa Fe
and go to a good restaurant, look at the art galleries, soak up some culture. I've never been, and I've always wanted to go. Please, please,
please, can we?"

"Another time, maybe."

"You know as well as I do that our job is done. Otis, Annie and Abe
are perfectly capable of running things without us. Don Bueno is doing
a better job of distribution than Wal-Mart could ever do. There's nothing
left for us here."

"It's not safe, Cyd."

"What are you saying, that we live out the rest of our lives in a single-wide trailer in the middle of a barren desert? Don't we deserve a little R&R after all we've been through?"

"You've got cabin fever. I get it. So do I . . ."

She stood on tiptoe and whispered in his ear. "What do I have to do to convince you?" He lowered her eagerly down onto to the bed, but she resisted. "Not until I get an answer, mister."

He sighed in desperation. "I'll call Robert in the morning and see if we can borrow his car."

Chapter Thirty-Five

Never and A Day

Early the next morning, Cyd and Alex left Window Rock in Robert's SUV, drove through Gallup and then Albuquerque. Out of Albuquerque they turned north toward Santa Fe. Cyd's enthusiasm was infectious and by the time they arrived Alex was as happy as she was.

A restaurant with a gracious log veranda and a sign advertising an authentic Mexican brunch caught their eye. They parked on a narrow side street, went in and were seated on a Spanish tiled patio overgrown with flowering red vines. It was still early, and they were the first ones there. Surrounded by the adobe charm of the oldest capital city in America, they enjoyed a delicious feast. Cyd felt like she was on a real vacation at last.

In an effort to disguise himself, Alex had grown a ruddy beard. It tickled Cyd's face, but she kind of liked it. Her disguise was dark glasses and a baseball cap that only served to make her look cuter and more mysterious.

Alex grew nervous as the restaurant slowly filled with customers, but Cyd was unconcerned. "Come on Alex, relax," she said gaily. "We're here to have fun."

He managed a smile but couldn't stop looking over his shoulder.

She sighed. "Okay then, answer me this. If something *were* to happen, and you never saw me again, would you still love me?"

"What would be the point?"

She ignored the twinkle in his eye. "The point would be that you love me so much you could never stop."

"Never."

"Yes, never."

"How about you?" he asked suspiciously. "Would you still love me if I disappeared?"

"Never."

"Never love me or never stop?"

All pretense gone, she could no longer resist. "Never and a day, my love."

"That ought to about do it," he smiled. "If not, we can always apply for an extension."

"That's what I was thinking." She paused. "Alex, is it wrong that I should want you so desperately? I don't think it's wrong."

"I don't either."

She sat back contentedly. "More coffee?"

After lunch they wandered hand in hand through the historic downtown plaza peeking in store windows, then turned toward Canyon Road, a narrow street that wound uphill with over a hundred little art galleries and studios that sold some of the most expensive southwestern art money could buy.

Cyd danced delightedly in and out of the galleries until Alex got tired of following her around and sat down to study a group of sculptures that caught his eye.

"I'll be up the street," she called merrily, bouncing out the door.

"Um-hmm," he said, resting his feet as he continued gazing at the convoluted figurines. He had decided that all his worry was for nothing and begun to relax when he realized Cyd had been gone for quite some time. He got up to go find her.

A few doors up the street Cyd was inside another gallery, absorbed in the beautiful art that was on display. The gallery owner, Grace Slyly, came up and began explaining to Cyd something about the painting she was admiring. Grace wore her graying hair in leather-wrapped Indian braids that did a fairly good job of disguising the fact that she was from Cleveland.

Cyd had taken off her dark glasses when she came into the shop because Grace's things were so lovely and she wanted to see them better. She told the shop owner she was just looking, but for some reason Grace decided Cyd was a buyer and went to great lengths to offer information about the works of the various local artists she represented. Cyd was having a wonderful time listening to the monologue and getting an art lesson. What she didn't realize was that Grace had recognized her from the television and newspaper pictures the minute she walked in and had sent her assistant into the back room to call the authorities.

Alex was making his way from gallery to gallery, searching for Cyd, when half a dozen police cars screeched to a halt in front of the Slyly Gallery and several more pulled into the alley behind. Armed men jumped out and surrounded the store while a man with a bullhorn crouched down behind the door of his squad car. "Cyd Seeley!" he blared. "This is the Santa Fe police. You are ordered to come out with your hands up."

Inside, the color ran out of Cyd's face. Out of the corner of her eye, she saw the gallery owner back away, reach in her cash register and pull out a gun. Not knowing what to do or which way to turn, Cyd stood shaking as the voice came again.

"Come out immediately! This is your last warning!"

Cyd made a move to go out the back door and Grace raised her gun, blocking her way. Someone was screaming and Cyd realized it was her.

Down the street, Alex heard the scream and bolted toward the sound, only to be restrained by a police officer who yelled for him to stay clear of the area. Watching from a distance, he saw Cyd appear in the doorway with her hands up, then gasped as she was forced to her knees, handcuffed and shoved into the back of a squad car.

***

Sitting at his desk in his home office, Clarence Big Foot had to ask Alex several times what he was shouting about before he understood that Cyd had been arrested.

"I'm chartering a plane," the big Indian said in a halting voice. "I'll be there in a few hours."

As soon as Otis heard Alex's voice on the phone, he knew something was wrong. He held his cell away from his ear so Annie and Eloise could hear. Eloise started crying the minute she heard what had happened.

"Alex, listen to me," Otis warned. "Do not go near that jail. Get back to the reservation as fast as you can."

"I'm not leaving her. I can't . . ."

"You're not thinking straight, man."

"It's my fault, Otis. I should never have brought her here."

"Never mind about that. You have to get out of there. Now!"

Annie took the phone out of Otis's hand. "Alex, darling, I'm on my way to Santa Fe. I'll try and stay as close to her as I can. Your job is to return here this instant, do you hear me? We don't want to lose you too."

"Tell Robert I talked with his father," Alex replied miserably. "Clarence is flying in. Meet him at the Santa Fe airport. He'll be there shortly."

***

On the flight out aboard the chartered Gulf Stream, Clarence Big Foot was able to reach a friend in Washington who made a few phone calls on his behalf. By the time he landed in Santa Fe, he had already hired Santiago Vazquez, a local defense attorney who specialized in drug cases.

Cyd was booked into the Santa Fe jail, and an hour later DEA agents arrived from Albuquerque to question her. It was a brutal interrogation. She was told that if she gave up her fellow conspirators and revealed where the drugs were being grown, she might receive a lighter sentence.

"Lawyer," she said.

"Come on, sister," snarled one of the agents. "Give it up."

"You can spend the rest of your life in prison or just the next half of it," offered a second agent. "It's up to you."

From the way she was glaring at the agents, it was impossible to tell how terrified she was. "Lawyer," she repeated softly.

That evening Clarence, Robert and Annie met with Vazquez at his Santa Fe office. The attorney wore cowboy boots, a turquoise bracelet and a ponytail that was shorter than Clarence's, but just as black.

He regarded his worried clients gravely. "Given how badly they want her and how hard they've been looking for her, I'd say the chances of her being released on bail are zero, zip, nada."

Cyd spent the next two days in a jail cell. The longer she sat and stared at the concrete walls and iron bars, the more terrified she became. Vasquez came and went several times and tried to be as encouraging as possible. Each time after he left, she cried.

Alex hadn't slept since he got back to Window Rock. Eloise was feeding him, but he didn't eat much. He had never felt more helpless in his life. It was time for Annie's nightly call from Santa Fe. He walked over to Otis's trailer so he could hear her latest update. A full moon shining through the overhead camouflage netting lit his way.

Otis opened his door, Alex entered and Eloise poured him some of the Cannastar tea she had fixed for her husband. At least they didn't have to ration it now.

They sat at the kitchen table while Otis dialed Annie's number on his disposable phone. "Thank goodness Abe is running The Grow," he admitted absently. "I'm totally useless."

Annie picked up on the first ring. Otis put his phone on speaker, and they all leaned in so they could hear.

"How you holding up?" Annie asked.

"We're not," Otis replied. "Tell us something good."

"All right, I will then," Annie said brightly. "I think I have a plan."

"She thinks she has a plan," Otis repeated.

Alex and Eloise held their breath.

"Don't get your hopes up just yet," Annie went on. "Cyd's arraignment is set for tomorrow morning, and I won't know until then if my little scheme has worked or not. Call me at ten and every hour after that until I pick up."

An hour later Sam Seeley returned his wife's call. Annie listened to him gloat over Cyd's capture approximately one minute before cutting him off.

"Sam, I need to say something, and you need to listen." She waited quietly for him to stop fuming. "I want the charges against Cydney dropped."

His laugh was more of a shout. "Too late for that," he gloated. "Couldn't make it happen if I wanted to."

"Then I'm going to the tabloids," she advised evenly. "I'm going to tell them how you enslaved me and turned me into a criminal. How you forced a helpless old woman to help you grow your illegal drugs. I'll say you thought you were above the law and could get away with growing it in your own greenhouse because that's the last place anyone would think to look."

The Senator exploded. "What the hell did I give you all that money for?" he bellowed. "You promised to keep your mouth shut! You said it would be the end of it all if I paid you off!"

"I lied," she admitted calmly. "I'll ruin you, Sam. I swear."

"I can't make this go away," he whined. "It's too big now. It's out of my control."

Annie hesitated. "Then I want her out on bail. I want Cyd out of jail this instant, I don't care how you do it!"

A long silence. "Let me see what I can do."

***

Alex sat miserably on the edge of the bed he shared with Cyd in their trailer. His pain and longing were unbearable. Faced with the horrors of her arrest, an agonizing collage of unwelcomed pictures swirled through his mind:

Cyd in her truck picking him up at the airport the first time . . . Maury's body . . . Otis . . . Cyd's ranch . . . the fire . . . the Cannastar bust in the mortuary attic . . . Betty Little Horn . . . Cyd on horseback in the Montana wilderness . . . Finding the Cannastar seeds Maury buried and digging them up . . . being attacked and their escape . . . the night in the cave and their desperate treck over the mountains . . . Clarence Big Foot and his preposterous house . . . Throwing away the pain pills . . . Cyd and Mary and Tiffany kidnapped . . . the rescue and the Great Swimming Pool Massacre and dancing at the Snake Snot Saloon . . . Alicia's suicide . . . the sadness that led to his recovery . . . his journey east to find Cyd . . . her courage, her tenacity . . . Joe Volkova and Mexico . . . Oh God, Mexico! he thought. The river, the jungle, the bungalow . . .

their marathon love making. He buried his face in her pillow and inhaled deeply, her smell conjuring more images . . . Don Bueno and his insane amusement park for all those sad and beautiful children . . . Annie, wonderful Annie and her brave greenhouse . . . Running down the midnight roads to Iowa and Abe and the faithful farmers of Fort Dodge . . . their desperate flight to Window Rock and The Grow, the glorious Grow and . . . Santa Fe . . . "Don't let me lose her!" he wept aloud. "Not now. Not after all this."

***

The U.S. courthouse in Santa Fe was made of stone, and even in the warm morning light looked cold and indifferent.

Cyd sat with her attorney, Mr. Vazquez, at the defense table. Behind her in the courtroom she could feel the anxious eyes of Annie, Clarence and Robert on her neck. U.S. Attorney Orville Fisk sat at the other table with two ambitious junior prosecutors.

The bailiff stood. "All rise! U.S. District Court is now in session, Chief U.S. District Judge David Young presiding!"

A judge in a black robe that covered his substantial belly came in and took his seat, awkwardly adjusting the donut he sat on. The fringe of gray hair that circled his bald head made him look like a Franciscan monk. Judge Young's principal virtue was a monumental ego that supplanted his less-than-monumental intelligence. Politics preempted his limited knowledge of the law in most of his decisions. He listened impassively as the charges were read and the attorneys argued over bail.

Mr. Vasquez stated plainly, "If it pleases the court, my client has absolutely no criminal record. She's never even gotten a speeding ticket. Ms. Seeley is a botanist and an outstanding researcher who, for some reason, has been singled out for persecution in a corporate and political witch hunt that bears no relationship to anything concrete or factual. Not a single shred of evidence exists to link the accused to this or any other crime. We move that she be released on her own recognizance."

Orville Fisk rose and ceremoniously buttoned his suit coat. "Your honor . . ." The words stuck in his throat, and he paused to take a drink of water. "Ms. Seeley is responsible for unleashing on the American public a ghastly drug more dangerous than nerve gas. Her heartless greed has killed thousands already, and the death toll is rising as we speak. This is a national epidemic, and she holds the key to identifying her fellow conspirators and locating the source of this poison. A runaway train is less of a flight risk than she is." He confidently took his seat.

The judge banged his gavel. "Bail is set at a hundred thousand dollars."

Annie, who had been holding her breath, exhaled loudly.

Fisk bounded to his feet. "Your honor, surely you'll want to reconsider . . ."

"Sit down, Mr. Fisk. I've made my ruling."

"But the government . . ."

"One more word," the judge threatened, "and I'll hold you in contempt!"

It was done. Fisk's mouth worked open and closed, but nothing came out. Annie threw her arms around Robert's neck crying. They waved triumphantly to the accused who was led back to jail until Clarence could post her bond, which he left to do immediately. Cyd smiled back at her friends as she went out, weak with relief

***

The night before Cyd's arraignment, Judge David Young received a phone call from the distinguished Senator Sam Seeley, whose coveted endorsement he had yet to receive in his bid for New Mexico's vacant seat in the U.S. Senate. The judge would give his first born to win the election, but his budget was much smaller than his opponent and the polls showed he was losing. He was both puzzled and delighted that the senator would be calling him so late at night.

Sam didn't waste any time getting to the point. "Judge Young, you ready to play Let's Make A Deal?"

"Go on," the judge replied cautiously.

"It's simple. I want that Seeley woman out on bail."

"I thought . . ."

"Never mind what you thought. The guy running against you for Senate is kicking your ass. You don't stand a chance in hell."

"I'm fully aware . . ."

"Then be aware of this. Cyd Seeley needs to get out on bond. See that she does, and you'll get unlimited funding for your Senate run. You'll also get my unqualified endorsement, which trust me, will put you in the winner's circle. The broad stays in jail and you go back to being a small-town judge, simple as that. So, we got a deal, or what?"

The honorable Judge David Young smiled broadly. "See you in Washington, Senator Seeley."

"Yes, you will, Senator Young."

Chapter Thirty-Six

Tea Under The Bridge

Captain Charlie lined up on the Window Rock runway and brought the Citation in smooth and quick.

Alex, Otis, Eloise and Abe, accompanied by Robert who had driven his car back from Santa Fe, waited eagerly on the tarmac as the jet taxied up. They had decided that the safest way to bring Cyd home was to fly her back. At least this way, she couldn't be followed.

The engines shut down, the door opened . . . and Cyd appeared, rushing down the steps and into Alex's arms. They hugged desperately, covering each other in kisses until she had to tell him she couldn't breathe he was holding her so tightly. Annie and Clarence emerged from the plane and they all embraced. Captain Charlie, witnessing the reunion, swiped quickly at his own eyes mumbling something about the dust.

Clarence put his arm around Cyd and she looked up at him gratefully. "I can never repay you for what you did," she smiled, "but I can pay you back for my bail. In fact, I have almost enough saved from our profits from The Grow to buy back my mortgage from you . . ."

"Keep it," Clarence interrupted. "You'll need it where you're going."

"Going?"

"We'll talk about it tomorrow. Right now, you need to go home and get some rest."

They arrived back at The Grow and Alex followed her into their trailer. She went directly to the bedroom, fell onto the bed fully clothed and curled into the fetal position. He stood over her seeing the pain she was in and carefully laid down beside her.

Cyd stared at the wall, her eyes red and forlorn, her dark hair dirty and matted from her ordeal. Alex folded her gently in his arms and she began to weep, softly at first, then harder and harder as wave after wave of the trauma washed over her. Sometime in the night he realized she had finally fallen asleep.

The next morning she got out of bed first, entered the bathroom, took a long hot shower and, when she came out, Alex saw a fixed smile on her face. He asked her how she was feeling.

"What's for breakfast?" she replied. "I'm positively starved."

It was the last time they talked about it.

Clarence was waiting for them in the lobby of the Quality Inn when they picked him up. He was anxious to see The Grow, and they were anxious to show it to him.

The big Indian, wearing his trademark shorts and loud Hawaiian shirt, ducked under the camo net and walked down one of the rows between the flourishing Cannastar bushes. Cyd and Alex trailed behind as he smiled at the workers who looked up and smiled back at the impressive visitor. He came to a bench and sat down shaking his head. Cyd and Alex stood by waiting for him to say something.

He looked up in amazement. "I couldn't be more impressed, you two, if it was the streets of heaven you were showing me."

Cyd, pleased at his response, sat down beside him. "Credit where credit is due, Otis, Annie and Abe did most of the hard work. And let's not forget who paid for it."

"According to the Navajo," Alex added, "the Great Spirit had a hand in it."

Big Foot nodded wisely. "They would know."

Cyd sighed and leaned against their benefactor's shoulder. "Clarence, why does everything have to be so hard when all we're trying to do is help people get well and stay that way?"

Big Foot stroked the back of her hair. "The trouble with miracles, Cydney, is they are always met with suspicion and they always threaten the powers that be. It makes doing good difficult, if not impossible sometimes." He turned her to face him. "And now it's time you were gone."

She looked at him sharply.

"It's over, Cyd. You and Alex need to get as far away from here as you can and as quickly as possible."

"How?" she asked, visibly upset. "I don't see any way . . ."

"He's right, Cyd. I've been thinking the same thing. We need to go."

Clarence stood and helped her to her feet. "They're talking about putting you on the list of known terrorists. You show up for trial after that happens, and the Feds will take you into custody as an enemy combatant. No habeas corpus, no court of appeal, no liberties, no democracy and no America. You'll be tortured until you tell them everything. You think you won't talk, but you will. They'll find out about this place, everybody involved will be arrested, the Cannastar will be lost and everything you've done will have been for nothing. Is that what you want?"

She shook her head as her eyes filled with tears.

"Then run. Now. While you still can."

"But where . . .?"

"Out of the country."

"What about passports?" Alex asked.

"Working on it," Clarence replied.

***

That afternoon, Cyd went to Annie and told her she and Alex were leaving.

The blue eyed, gray haired lady smiled sadly. "Good. I'm glad."

Cyd hugged her. "I'll miss you like crazy."

Annie kissed her cheek. "You'll always be my daughter wherever you go." Cyd waited as a shy smile lit her face. "I have a confession to make. I hope you won't think too badly of me. Abe and I have moved into the same trailer together."

Cyd laughed and hugged her again. "You go, girl. What's it like?"

Annie grinned. "Like riding a bicycle."

***

That evening, Abe and Annie stood talking in their trailer. The Iowa farmer was a foot taller than his new love, but somehow, they fit together nicely.

"With Alex and Cyd leaving," he mused, "maybe I'll go on back to the farm for a while."

Annie took one of his calloused hands and held it between her slender palms. "I think it's still too dangerous, dear. This is your crop now, these rows of Cannastar. You, me and Otis, we have a job to do."

"Aren't you homesick, Annabelle? I know I am."

She smiled brightly. "I have an idea. How about we take a little vacation?"

"Where on earth would we go?"

"I'd love to show you my place in Virginia. It's only a hop, skip and a jump by plane."

"Is it fancy? You know I don't like fancy places."

"It's just a big farm with a big house, darling. Not as big as your farm, of course, but please let me show it to you. You won't believe my greenhouses and everything I can grow there. You'll love it, wait and see."

***

The next day, shortly before leaving the reservation for the last time, Cyd and Alex met Otis and Eloise out at the building site of their new house in Window Rock.

Otis listened to the news with a heartbroken smile. "I understand," was all he said.

"You know you can never go off the reservation now," Alex warned. "Not after what happened to Cyd."

Otis smiled at his wife. "We're happy right where we are, isn't that right sweetcakes?"

"I can't believe it," Eloise gushed. "I've always wanted to build a Santa Fe-style house and now I'm actually getting to do it."

Cyd inwardly shuddered at the mention of Santa Fe.

"I'll hold your Grow money for you as it comes in," Otis told them. "You get to a place where you need it, let me know and I'll wire it to you."

"Thanks," Alex nodded. "I'm thinking I'd like to start a clinic in the tropics somewhere."

Otis took them both in his big arms. "Be safe."

Just then Elton and Feather, flushed and dirty from their latest adventures, bounded up onto the wood subfloor where the others were standing. When Elton was told that Cyd and Alex were going away, he ran anxiously into Alex's arms.

"When will I ever see you again?" he asked.

Alex hoisted him playfully into the air. "I don't know, sport."

"Probably when Cannastar gets legalized," Otis guessed.

"When will that be?" the boy asked.

"Someday," Cyd assured him.

"Someday soon?'

Eloise smiled. "Someday."

***

The following afternoon Cyd and Alex met with Clarence in his suite at the Quality Inn. Big Foot ripped open a manilla envelope that UPS had just delivered, inspected its contents and handed Cyd and Alex their new passports.

Alex looked his over closely. "This is good work."

"Ought to be," Clarence replied. "The guy that made them for me is the guy that makes them for the CIA."

"How did you get our pictures?" Cyd asked.

"My wife still had digital shots of you on her camera from when you and Alex visited us last year." He reached in a drawer and handed them two more packages.

Cyd tore the brown wrapping off of hers and took out a blond wig. "Okay . . ." she said slowly. Alex opened his package and removed a long-haired wig that looked like it was straight out of the sixties.

Clarence motioned for them to try the disguises on. "Stop stalling. Think of them as hair hats."

They went to the mirror, settled their wigs on their heads and Cyd giggled. "He looks like a pimp and I look like his hooker."

"As opposed to America's Most Wanted," Clarence cautioned. "When are you leaving?"

Alex grimaced at his image in the mirror. "Captain Charlie is flying us out to the West Coast first thing tomorrow."

Clarence extended his arms. "Then I'll say goodbye now. I hate men who cry in public, don't you?"

Cyd cried for them both as he hugged her.

***

The morning sun heated a breeze that sanded the airstrip with tiny swirling tornados.

Clarence stood apart from the others as Otis, Eloise, Elton, Annie, Abe and Robert bid Cyd and Alex goodbye. So much had happened and there was so much to say that they said very little. Otis bit his lip and Annie waved bravely as they boarded her Citation and it taxied for take-off. Minutes later the plane made a thundering run down the runway, left the ground and disappeared into the western sky.

Clarence shielded his eyes from the sun. "God speed," he whispered.

***

Pharmaceutical industry profits were down roughly fifty percent due to the rampant spread of Cannastar and the miraculous results people were experiencing. Rxon's profits were down seventy-one percent as a result of their heavy reliance on drugs to treat cancer and other viruses like flu and sexually transmitted disease that were rapidly becoming a thing of the past. Big Pharma, sensitive to the seismic shift in customer demand, was on fire with new discoveries in curative medicine. Rxon hadn't kept up. Rather than investing in research and development, they put every penny of profit into stock buybacks and high dividends to keep their stock price up. Their inability to keep pace with the rapid evolution in medical technology had cut their financial jugular vein. Rxon was hemorrhaging money faster than a gunshot wound to the femoral artery.

Dick Tremble never dreamed that Cannastar would work as well as it had. From the very beginning, he doubted the efficacy of the drug. If he'd known then what he knew now, he would never have destroyed Maury Bernstein's research. Without the documentation, there was no way to claim ownership of the drug or even prove that the hybrid plant had ever been invented. As far as anyone knew, it grew itself.

Tremble buried his head in his hands. What a fool! He could have patented the damn thing and sold it for a thousand dollars a cup. Tea under the bridge, he thought bitterly, tea under the bridge.

A year from now Rxon's campus would be overgrown with weeds, the windows broken out, the buildings deserted. Around the base of the corporate tower, legions of vines would be sprouting from the ground and creeping up the sides of the monolith, leading the way for others to follow in a determined effort to do what vines have always done to empires after they fall.

And alone in his ruined tower, Dick Tremble would sit at his desk staring at a pharmacy-size bottle of sleeping pills. Slowly, methodically, he would fill a water glass with vodka, then unscrew the cap from the bottle and shake out a handful of pills.

***

Cyd fell in love with Alex's sailboat the minute she saw it. The cutter's long lines and low profile made the boat look fast and strong and safe even sitting in the slip. She went below deck to see where she would be living. Looking around at the bottom of the ladder, she scanned the interior. It looked like home and smelled of adventure.

Slime, Alex's wreck of a sedan, was parked in the marina parking lot. He opened the door and Cyd got in so they could go to the store for groceries.

"Nice car," she remarked.

He smiled proudly. "I was hoping you'd like it."

One of the first things Cyd did after moving aboard was change the name of the boat from Pequod back to the one it had been christened with when it was launched twenty-five years earlier. She and Alex stood on the dock admiring the new gold leaf lettering on the stern that spelled out "Volunteer". It was almost as if the boat had renamed herself now that she knew her purpose.

Every day they spent on land they risked discovery and they hurried to be gone. Dozens of repairs had to be made to almost every part of the boat before they could leave. Alex marveled at how handy Cyd was, especially with a paintbrush.

They had fun running around buying everything they would need to spend months at sea. Every time Cyd looked at Alex in his silly wig, she had to turn away to keep from laughing. Alex thought Cyd actually looked pretty good as a blond but was always glad at night when they went below and she could go back to being a brunette.

Cyd was in a grocery store buying last minute supplies when some dust or pollen got in her eyes and made her sneeze. A harried housewife with three children in tow came up to her thinking she had a cold and whispered, "I know where you can get some Cannastar if you need it."

"That's okay," Cyd whispered back. "I think I have a source."

After much hard work, the day finally came. The Volunteer was as ready for the open ocean as they could make her. Cyd cast off the dock lines in the early dawn, and Alex backed out of the slip for the last time. A low-hanging fog hung over the water as the lone sailboat motored slowly out of the harbor past rows of docks filled with boats rocking silently in their wake. They cleared the breakwater, the sun came out, the fog burned off and they joyfully threw their wigs overboard.

Alex raised the sails, and the boat shuddered as she came alive. The ocean rippled with the first sign of wind and they ghosted in the direction of Catalina Island. Not wanting to alarm Cyd, he kept a close watch for any last-minute assault by an overzealous Coast Guard boat that might be coming after them.

Deep in the hold and sealed in waterproof bags, she had secreted away a year's supply of dried Cannastar for her personal use, plus hundreds of pounds of seed. Their intention was to plant the Cannastar wherever they went so that it could be spread around the world. He hoped to build his clinic for indigenous people in some remote place and she planned to study the exotic flora that grew in the faraway places they were headed.

Off the west end of Catalina, they turned southwest toward the southern latitudes. The sails rustled and flapped, then filled and began to draw as the wind freshened and backed into the north. The Volunteer heeled as she picked up speed, her bow plunging into the whitecapped waves, the ocean hissing by under her lee rail.

The sea quickened their blood. Cyd stood at the helm and the wind blew back her hair. Alex put his arm around her and together they looked out at the horizon. They were in the wind, they were on the wind, reaching for a distant shore, for a place unseen, unknown and yet to come.

Coming Soon!

STEPHEN STEELE'S
THE TROUBLE WITH MIRACLES
BOOK TWO
THE ORGAN GRINDER FACTOR

A 3-D printer that replaces human organs
without removing the old ones first.
What could go wrong?

In desperate search of a safe place to grow their Cannastar where they won't get arrested, Alex and Cyd are drawn into the dangerous world of drug trafficking and child slavery in Africa, and then into the horror of the Israeli-Palestinian conflict in Israel. The Palestinian bomb that leaves Cyd's life hanging by a thread is real. The medical miracle that is her only chance of survival is fiction—at least, for now.

The Organ Grinder Factor, Book Two, of The Trouble with Miracles series, is part adventure, part mystery and part love story; a timely thriller, based on true events, that ranges from Africa to Israel.

For more information
visit: www.SpeakingVolumes.us

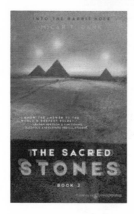

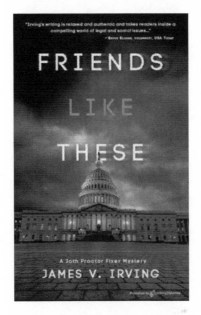

Made in the USA
Middletown, DE
05 April 2021